> ## "A BRAVE NEW VISION OF THE FUTURE…WELL-CONCEIVED AND METICULOUSLY EXECUTED."
> *Charleston (SC) Post and Courier*

Jack watched his office walls sputter malfunctioning mathematical symbols and release a flock of passenger pigeons; his nose was tickled with the odor of eucalyptus. Inside, the air rippled with synthetic pleasure and the taste of vanilla.

From the fourth floor of the mathematics building, he took the arched bridge path that linked to the island's outer seawall. Cold night air and salt spray whipped around him. Electromagnetic pollution filtered through the hardware in his skull: a hundred conversations on the cell networks, and a patchwork of thermal images from the West-AgCo satellite overhead.

Past the surf and across the San Joaquin Sea, the horizon glowed with florescent light. Jack regretted that he'd stepped on other people to get where he was. Maybe that's why trouble always came looking for him. Because he had it coming. Or because he was soft enough to let little things get to him. Like guilt.

—from *Signal to Noise*

Other Eos Books by
Eric S. Nylund

DRY WATER
A GAME OF UNIVERSE

Coming Soon

A SIGNAL SHATTERED

Signal to NOISE

ERIC S. NYLUND

AVON · EOS

EOS
An Imprint of HarperCollins*Publishers*
10 East 53rd Street
New York, New York 10022-5299

Copyright © 1998 by Eric S. Nylund
Excerpt from *Signal to Noise* copyright © 1998 by Eric S. Nylund
Excerpt from *The Death of the Necromancer* copyright © 1998 by Martha Wells
Excerpt from *Scent of Magic* copyright © 1998 by Andre Norton
Excerpt from *The Gilded Chain* copyright © 1998 by Dave Duncan
Excerpt from *Krondor the Betrayal* copyright © 1998 by Raymond E. Feist
Excerpt from *Mission Child* copyright © 1998 by Maureen F. McHugh
Excerpt from *Avalanche Soldier* copyright © 1999 by Susan R. Matthews
Library of Congress Catalog Card Number: 97-44210
ISBN: 0-380-79292-3
www.avonbooks.com/eos

First Eos Paperback Printing: June 1999
First Eos Hardcover Printing: May 1998

Eos Trademark Reg. U.S. Pat. Off. and in Other Countries, Marca Registrada, Hecho en U.S.A.
HarperCollins® is a trademark of HarperCollins Publishers Inc.

Printed in the U.S.A.

WCD 10 9 8 7 6 5 4 3 2

$$\sum_{n=0}^{\infty} \frac{(-1)^n}{(2n+1)!} y^{2n+1}$$

ACKNOWLEDGMENTS

Syne Mitchell, for psychological support and brilliant editing;
Dr. Mike Brotherton, for more editing and astronomical expertise;
Kelly Winters, for a character reality check and yet more editing;

and not least of all,

Jennifer Brehl, for making this story comprehensible and
for making the business of writing a pleasure

All mistakes herein are solely my responsibility.

SECTION ONE

EDUCATION

1

A PAIR OF JACKS OR BETTER TO OPEN

Jack watched his office walls sputter malfunctioning mathematical symbols and release a flock of passenger pigeons; his nose was tickled with the odor of eucalyptus. Inside, the air rippled with synthetic pleasure and the taste of vanilla.

"I need to get in there," he told the government agent who blocked the doorway.

"No admittance," the agent said, "until we've completed our investigation on the break-in."

Puzzles, illegalities, and dilemmas stuck to Jack—from which he then, usually, extracted himself. That gave him the dual reputation of a troubleshooter and a troublemaker. But the only thing he was dead sure about today was the "troublemaking and sticking" part of that assessment.

The agent stepped in front of Jack, obscuring what the others were doing in there. National Security Office agents: goons with big guns bulging under their bulletproof suits. And no arguing with them.

3

Today's trouble was the stuff you saw coming, but couldn't do a thing about. Like standing in front of a tidal wave.

Jack hoped his office *had* been broken into, that this wasn't an NSO fishing trip. There were secrets in the bubble circuitry of his office that had to stay hidden. Things that could make his troubles multiply.

"I'll wait until you're done then."

The agent glanced at his notepad and a face materialized: Jack's with his sandy hair pulled into a ponytail and his hazel eyes bloodshot. You have an immediate interview with Mr. De-Mitri. Bell Communications Center, sublevel three."

Jack's stomach curdled. "Interview" was a polite word that meant they'd use invasive probes and mnemonic shadows to pry open his mind. Jack had worked with DeMitri and the NSO before. He knew all their nasty tricks.

"Thanks," Jack lied, turned from the illusions in his office, and walked down the hallway.

From the fourth floor of the mathematics building, he took the arched bridge path that linked to the island's outer seawall. Not the most direct route, but he needed time to figure a way out of this jam.

Cold night air and salt spray whipped around him. Electromagnetic pollution filtered through the hardware in his skull: a hundred conversations on the cell networks, and a patchwork of thermal images from the West-AgCo satellite overhead.

Past the surf and across the San Joaquin Sea, the horizon glowed with fluorescent light. Jack regretted that he'd stepped on other people to get where he was. Maybe that's why trouble always came looking for him. Because he had it coming. Or because he was soft enough to let little things get to him. Like guilt.

Not that there was any other way to escape the mainland. Everyone there competed for lousy jobs and stabbed each other in the back, sometimes literally, to get ahead. He had clawed his way out with an education—then cheated his way into Santa Sierra's Académe of Pure and Applied Sciences.

But it wasn't perfect here, either. There were cutthroat maneuvers for grants, and Jack had bent the law working both for corporations *and* the government. All of which had helped his financial position, but hadn't improved his conscience.

He had to get tenure so he could relax and pursue his own projects. There had to be more to life than chasing money and grabbing power.

Now those dreams were on hold.

His office had been ransacked, and the NSO had got too curious, too fast, for his liking. Had they been keeping an eye on him all along?

He took the stairs off the seawall and descended into a red-tiled courtyard.

In the center of the square stood Coit Tower. The structure was sixty meters of fluted concrete that had been hoisted off the ocean floor. It had survived the San Francisco quake in the early twenty-first century, then lay underwater for fifty years—yet was still in one piece.

Jack hoped he was as tough.

The whitewashed turret was lit from beneath with halogen light, harsh and brilliant against the night sky. Undeniably real.

Jack preferred the illusions of his office; sometimes reality was too much for him to stomach.

No way out of this interview sprang to mind, and he had stalled as long as he could. The crystal-and-steel geodesic dome of the Bell Communications Center was across the courtyard. Jack marched into the building, took the elevator to sublevel three, and entered the concert amphitheater.

On the stage between gathered velvet curtains, the NSO had set up their bubble.

Normal bubbles simulated reality. Inside, a web of inductive signals and asynchronous quantum imagers tapped the operator's neuralware. It allowed access to a world of data, it teased hunches from your subconscious, and solidified your guesses into theories. They made you think faster. Maybe think better.

But this wasn't a normal bubble. And it was never meant to help Jack think. It was designed for tricks.

The thing was an antique, three meters across with magnetic vortex coils scintillating along its shell like diamonds. Shadows and silver mirages shimmered inside.

The NSO might claim this high-voltage dinosaur was old and unreliable; when it "accidentally" fried his mind, no one would ask questions. Or maybe he was inside already and didn't know it.

Those were the mind games the NSO liked to play.

It wasn't like he had a choice, though. Jack swallowed his fear and stepped across the threshold of the bubble.

Microamps of current and vertigo resonated through his mind as a pocket of reality materialized, severing the outside world.

Darkness spoke: "There's been a little trouble, Jack."

"Sure, there's trouble." Jack tried to sound like he knew what he was talking about. "But this isn't mine."

A Tiffany lamp flickered on, wine-stained glass that hung from nothing. A table of lacquered walnut and two chairs solidified from the dark. The walls of the bubble stretched, turned smooth and black like obsidian.

Jack resisted the urge to glance behind him . . . at the opening he knew had vanished. He sat. The chair wobbled—like his insides.

DeMitri resolved from the shadows and leaned forward. His black hair blended with the dark so it looked like part of his head was missing. He was subtle. In a world of metaphor, that half-head might mean he hadn't made up his mind yet.

"Think of this as a routine interview," DeMitri said.

Routine for the National Security Office meant turning your insides out, blackhacks, and a little arm-twisting. A ransacked office might be normal on the mainland, but not at the Académe. It was an island surrounded by perfect security and patriots, and until today, no trouble.

DeMitri's eyes were clear and blue. He wasn't filtering.

Jack thought of mirrors and prime numbers—fast—before De-Mitri connected with his subconscious. It had been stupid to walk in thinking about the break-in. Thinking could get him in trouble.

Jack had thought DeMitri's bubble was empty. He had thought . . . he thought, when he shouldn't be thinking at all.

DeMitri lit a cigarette. The flame reflected in his gaze, clouded now, fire shrouded by milky vapour.

A square drew itself on the table; grid lines appeared, filled red and black, and checkers crystallized upon them. The game was a metaphor for their exchange. Move and countermove. De-Mitri was black. His pieces had tiny castles stamped in their centers. Jack's pieces were red, embossed with five-pointed stars; he had two kings.

"It's your turn," DeMitri said.

"You going to offer me one of those?" He nodded to De-Mitri's cigarette.

DeMitri crossed his leg and leaned back. "Play the game, Jack." He knew who was in control. He wanted Jack to know, too. "Move," he said. "Jump me. You can—"

"What about that cigarette?"

DeMitri reassessed Jack with mist-filled eyes. "Sure." He opened a gold case, selected an indigo-tipped Barlinque, and rolled it across the table.

Jack picked it up. The thing lit itself. He inhaled, savored the amphetamine-laced peppermint, then blew the smoke into DeMitri's face. DeMitri didn't appreciate that, even less when Jack ground the cigarette into the table.

"Checkers," Jack said. "That's cute. Simple yet competitive. Make me a winner. Let me think I'm ahead of the game."

It was DeMitri's turn to stare, but there were only prime numbers and mirrors for him to see in Jack's eyes. If DeMitri wanted to muscle into his thoughts, he'd get a fight.

Bubbles made communicating easier. If a picture was worth a thousand words, then a well-placed metaphor was worth a thousand pictures, sticking inside your thoughts as you unraveled its nuances. An NSO bubble took that premise a step further, though, and optimized communication even if Jack didn't want to—with subliminals and cerebral arrests.

"Checkers is wrong for a man of your education," DeMitri said. "My mistake."

Jack's red checkers irised open. Knights and rooks and pawns spiraled from their cores. His king was cornered, but he had two bishops, a handful of pawns, and his queen was in good position. It was as fair a game as he'd get.

"OK," Jack said. Chess was a smart guy's game. He was a smart guy. There would be time to think. No surprise triple jumps. They'd dance around the board, exchange tactical metaphors, and hopefully reveal as little of the truth as possible.

"Tell me how it happened," DeMitri said, "from the beginning." He took one of Jack's pawns with his rook.

A wave of trust lapped at the edges of Jack's consciousness. Delicate. He admired the technique.

Jack studied his position on the board. Without looking up, he said, "I came in this morning. The lock to my office had been stripped. The files were erased, personal data, old research, archives."

"Everything?"

Jack slid his bishop and pinned DeMitri's rook against his knight. A good move. "No. They didn't find my encrypted files."

"They?" DeMitri advanced a pawn. "Why do you think there was more than one person involved?"

It was suddenly hot. Sweat crawled down Jack's side and he lost his focus on the chess game. "The way I see it, one person could break into the Académe and crack my files. It would have been easier, though, if 'they' had help. Just a guess." He took a black pawn with one of his.

DeMitri studied the board, then said, "You have enemies." It wasn't a question.

"We all do."

The chess pieces faded away. The squares of the board stretched into rectangles, then detached from the lacquered walnut. Cards, all facedown. Jack should have known DeMitri had something else up his sleeve.

"Tell me about your enemies," DeMitri said and flipped a

card. It was a white skyscraper flanked by thunderheads. Light-ning flickered and struck the top. Two men, both of whom looked suspiciously like Jack, fell to their deaths.

DeMitri's game had changed. Mysticism and tarot weren't Jack's strong suits. Neither was poker. "There's Bruner," Jack told him. "We're competing for the same tenured position."

"You think he did it?"

"If I could pin this on him, I would. He doesn't have the guts."

Jack's turn. He flipped a card: the Prince of Disks. A man sat atop a twin-barreled M-30 bulltank, arc pistol in his left hand; his right hand rested upon a globe and covered China. He had golden skin, gray hair, and a mischievous gleam in his eyes. Jack knew him.

"Your uncle?" DeMitri asked.

Jack's parents had been killed by the other side, leaving their seven-year-old son to be raised in the welfare system. Patriots. Real American heroes. You'd expect that after they died for their country, the NSO would have cut him some slack. But Jack's Uncle Reno was a traitor. Eyes on both sides had always watched Jack, wondering which part of the family he'd take after.

"The NSO knows more about him than I do."

"You've never seen him? Or talked to him?"

Jack had. He almost liked the old guy—quickly hid that fond-ness. DeMitri might catch and record the emotion to be used against him later.

"He's come to see me three times. I reported each visit." This wasn't Jack's first NSO interview. They had taken him apart be-fore and discovered that while he wasn't particularly loyal to God and America, his uncle didn't have a hold on him, either.

"Hypothetically," DeMitri said and smoothed one eyebrow with his thumb, "let's say he did it. What could he want?"

"If you mean all the dirty tricks you've taught me? Forget it. I'm clean. No records exist."

DeMitri nodded. "You've had unique training and access to trusted, sensitive ears because of the work you have done for us."

"That's in the past. My research isn't anything illegal."

"Noise, right? That's what you do." DeMitri turned another card: the Moon. A scarab beetle pushed a pearl across the night sky, while a jackal-headed Anubis and a radar dish tracked the insect on the earth below.

"I look for patterns in random signals," Jack told him. That beetle in the card, glittering lapis and gold, was somehow familiar.

"What intrigues you with these 'random signals'? It's so theoretical, while your previous research in cryptoanalysis has been so practical."

"Anyone can crack codes. They aren't a challenge."

"No one cracks codes like you." DeMitri drew on his cigarette and the end glowed white. "The United States government hasn't forgotten your skills. It's one of the reasons we are eager to find who has done this to you." He smiled. "Tell me more about your research."

DeMitri's teeth were shiny like glass, like water rippling and reflecting, like looking into a funhouse mirror after eating too much cotton candy and being slammed around on a roller coaster. Jack saw himself reflected in them and got dizzy.

He swallowed his nausea and decided to tell the truth. "There are several theoretical ways to decipher a code. The popular theories are . . . well, more popular than scientific. I'm out to prove those theories are so mathematically convoluted that they find signals where there are none, in random noise, for instance. I'm out to prove them wrong."

"The theories or the men who proposed them?"

Jack shrugged.

"Bruner's?"

"I have a better research record, but Bruner has friends in the dean's office. I have to go on the offensive; I'm the one with the checkered past."

DeMitri crushed his cigarette, then flicked it away. "I like you, Jack. I'm glad you're on our side."

Jack reached for another card.

10

"But," DeMitri said, "that still leaves us with the mystery of who broke into your office."

Jack turned the card: the Prince of Cups. A man gazed into a silver chalice. His hair was the color of maple sugar and it fell into his face. He was tall, slim, thirty-five years old, and held the cup with long fingers that had chewed nails.

A glow warmed the bottom of the cup and made the water flush red. The prince looked up, locked hazel eyes with Jack's.

The prince was Jack.

Jack was in DeMitri's bubble, and in the card; he held the card and the cup. Past the surface of the water, which held another mirror of him, he saw the seven burning stars of Imperial China. His mind rattled in a trap of reflections and split senses: China—Uncle—Beetle—NSO—Noise—China—Uncle.

Jack's thoughts blurred; water rippled; his thinking stilled.

"Was it you?" DeMitri demanded. "Did you destroy your office to cover up communications with the other side?"

Every tarot card except the one in Jack's hand condensed into ivory tiles with Chinese calligraphy. Mah-jongg.

Jack opened his mouth. His tongue was dry. He had no answer. The Jack-in-the-card still looked into his cup. The image of the red stars was all he saw. His mind froze.

DeMitri shattered Jack's walls of mirrors and factored his unfactorable prime numbers, picked past his emotions, pushed past thoughts of uncles and scarab beetles and watery stars.

Jack struggled against his presence—too late—and gagged on feelings and impulses that were not his.

DeMitri ripped the truth from him. The truth Jack had already told him.

"No," Jack said. "I didn't do it."

But DeMitri knew that. He knew everything. He even knew that Jack would punch his face in if he could get away with it.

Jack threw the card on the table. "No more games. We're done."

"Yes. You did very well. Very well, indeed." DeMitri gave

him that funhouse smile again, then said, "If the tenure doesn't work out, if you ever consider a change in careers, let me know."

Santa Sierra's public school system is a model of efficiency, educating its population in the sciences, the arts, and a spectrum of technical skills. That's the official line.

Here's what Jack learned when he was seven years old, when his parents were declared missing in action, when the money ran out for a private tutor, and when he got dropped into public school number three: Darwin had it right. Survival of the fittest few. The rest flunked.

In the eighth grade, you took advancement exams. The top half of the class moved on to the next grade. The rest got retrained in a technical skill of their choice. If you failed that first round, you could be an algae tank supervisor, paper shuffler, or any job that involved grime and nasty odors. Fail the cut at ninth grade and you could end up as a food service technician or luggage handler. Make it to the tenth grade and you might be a concrete mixer or streetlight repair person. The eleventh grade offered opportunities like reclamation diver, oil rigger, or government official. By your twelfth year, though, you competed with the privately tutored and socially elite for the real jobs. You had to be careful.

If you didn't crack from the stress or from using amphetamines to stay awake, you had to worry about your classmates ganging up on you. Jack learned how to fight, how to hold a knife, when to run when he was outnumbered, and to always check his locker for planted evidence that he had been cheating.

Make it to the top, graduate, and you were guaranteed a position in the corporate sector, actually solicited and bribed and pandered to. By then only the sharks were left, the students who had fought, thought, and socially engineered their way into passing. They fit in perfectly.

Then there was the city scholarship. It was the only way you made it to the Academé if you weren't rich or connected. One lucky graduate got picked at random; it was Santa Sierra's way of giving something back to the people.

Jack wasn't about to let a random number generator decide his fate.

He hacked in and rigged the system—found out it was rigged, anyway, and that he hadn't been picked. "Lacking sufficient ambition" his profile had said. He fixed that, too.

After all, it was survival of the fittest few.

Jack's office was a spherical matte-black bubble with scattered colonies of biolume lichens and a swivel chair in the center. The rest of the illusions and dreams were hidden inside the walls, in the circuitry beyond . . . and in his imagination.

There were three drops of blood on the floor, scraped by DeMitri's team so only faint oval outlines remained. Jack scratched some into an envelope. He had a friend who could tell him whose this was, diagonalize the DNA, and build a composite face.

The NSO would do the same. If DeMitri didn't find what he wanted, there would be another interview, another dissection of Jack's mind looking for state secrets he didn't have. Jack wanted to know what DeMitri knew—at least, he wanted a look at who had tossed his office.

The curved walls, and the bubble circuitry within, had been put back together, though. He owed the NSO for that.

He interfaced, making motes of dust into stars and the bioluminescent patches into the band of the Milky Way. His chair was a ringed gas giant, surrounded by a veil of nebula, blue and crimson with flickers of excitation.

Good. It worked.

Jack breathed easier, relieved to be out of reality and back in control of his world.

The files that hadn't been destroyed were here, encrypted. The pattern of stars was the key. Jack made constellations: a dragon with chrome scales and a frog leaping across the night. Anyone could look where he did. Anyone could see the same

13

stars, but their minds would never imagine the same shapes that he did.

That was Jack's personal theory on communication: perceived patterns in a sea of noise. Everyone thought they saw and heard the same things. Never turned out that way.

The constellations fixed in his mind. "Hard copy," Jack commanded.

Stars materialized on a square of plastic, reversed: black dots on white space. These quarter million data points, Jack's research, were what his office had been taken apart for.

A pulsar strobed and caught his eye. A request to interface.

He drew a rectangle in the darkness, opened a window to the outside, and saw Isabel.

"Come in," he said.

She floated before him, her red hair drifting as if it were blood underwater. "Got time?"

There was always time for Isabel. "Sure."

She was a datapaleontologist who dug for information in ancient databases, through archives, and layers of overwritten bytes. She was good at what she did. They had done their Académe undergraduate work together. Jack liked her. More important, he trusted her.

There was an attraction between them, but nothing that overloaded their professional relationship with emotional static . . . much. They both had careers to protect.

Jack creased the sky, a seam that ran from his feet to infinity, then folded it like a road map, compressed it to a dozen blurry stars: Van Gogh's *Starry Night* that he hung in midair. The starless surface thickened beneath them and gave the evening horizons.

Where to go? Isabel was good at metaphor. He didn't want her to know how badly the interview had shaken him.

The ocean appeared—a sign of Jack's subconscious at work. He sprinkled islands in the water and bridges that skipped across them. The Golden Gate lay half-submerged, and in the air were the smells of clam chowder and baking sourdough bread. The sun set and made the water gold, then red, then black.

A table for two materialized with white cotton napkins and a Mylar umbrella, a cobblestone street, a view of the fluorescent spray art upon the seawall a kilometer away, and the rolling sea beyond.

Jack omitted the traditional candlelight and made two cups of steaming cinnamon moccasopa appear. His mind rebelled, though, added a wisp of fog and a pair of lovers strolling by, leaning on one another.

He set his hand on Isabel's chair, pulled it out for her—or tried.

Isabel pulled it out for herself and sat. She cradled her cup, took a sip, then said, "A little bird told me what happened." She added a spoonful of nutmeg, watched it swirl with the cream. "Are you OK?" Her face was a perfect heart shape, and her eyes, deep and green, stared at him, wanting contact.

Intimate contact was the last thing Jack could take after having his mind raped. He flashed her an instant of DeMitri tearing through his psyche looking for conspiracies.

She looked away.

"I'm peachy," he said. "The National Security Office just wanted to let me know I was nominated for outstanding citizen of the year."

"A break-in," she whispered, "here. It's serious, Jack. So is the NSO."

The waiter appeared and asked, "Your order, sir?"

"Just the drinks," Jack muttered, wishing he could concentrate.

A street performer set a violin under his chin and stroked out Rachmaninov's *Rhapsody on a Theme of Paganini*. It was inspired, full of longing and sticky sweetness. It was Jack's wandering mind thinking about Isabel.

"Whoever broke in," Jack said, "didn't get what they were looking for. At least, what I think they were after." He slid the datagrid he had downloaded across the table.

15

Isabel's nimble fingers and close-cut nails ran over the dots, traced patterns, but she didn't ask what they were. That's not how she worked. She liked to figure things out for herself.

Jack told her anyway: "It's a signal I pulled from noise."

"Bruner's technique? So it does work? I mean it doesn't? You produced a false signal from nothing?"

He never could stand it when he was wrong. "Not quite. I think I've found a legitimate signal. I think Bruner may be right and not have known it."

Isabel snapped her fingers at the waiter and he trotted over. She grabbed the pen from his apron, waved him away, and connected dots on the datagrid.

"The NSO thinks someone was after the codes I cracked for them. I erased those projects . . . although not everyone would have known that. This grid is the only thing worth stealing."

"By Bruner?"

Jack sipped his moccasopa, then said, "I can't believe he'd do it, but he's the only one who would want it."

"Could you have stumbled onto a secret transmission from the other side?" Isabel looked up—not seeking contact this time—just looking; she put on a pair of glasses and they magnified the splash of freckles on her cheeks. "Maybe they want it back. And maybe they want you dead."

"No. This signal is in old data: ancient radio signals and cosmic static."

"But it's binary, black-and-white, ones and zeros."

"Multiplexed," he said.

She shook her head.

"Take a function like a sine wave." Jack drew a sideways *s* in the air. "You can define it as a mathematical series." The wave shattered into a dozen fragments. "The terms in my series are noise frequencies of narrow bandwidth. Add enough and parts cancel, parts reinforce." He melded the wavlets back into the original smooth curve. It flared, then faded.

"Add millions of terms," he said and pointed to the datagrid,

16

"and you get this. Silence and signals. Ons and offs. A string of binary code a quarter of a million terms long."

"How do you know it's that long?"

"It repeats. The noise frequencies change, but the signal hidden in them is always the same."

She stared at the pattern.

"It's not natural," he said. "Someone had been sending this for a long time."

"You're no astronomer, Jack. Why hasn't someone found this before?"

"This mathematical series combines frequencies that have no natural connection to one another: spectroscopic analysis of nebulas, pulsar signals, microscopic variations in the cosmic background radiation—and a hundred other unrelated sources."

She brushed her hair behind her ear. "So this square of data, it's your combined and transformed signal?"

"Wrapped around. Each line is 521 points of data. I start the next line under the previous and add another string of binary values to build the pattern."

"Have you decoded it?"

"I've tried every technique I know. Invented a few new ones. No dice."

"They connect." She scribbled on the grid, frowned, then added, "The lines are obvious, and these symbols repeat, the triangle, the square, the arrows . . . they overlap." She pulled the lines off the grid, let them hang motionless in the air, shimmering copper, teased them apart like a giant knot, untangled symbols, then let them fall back into place.

Each triangle had a line balanced on its tip. There were coils, zigzags, and half-circles mated with three limbs. Her symbols looked almost familiar. An old code?

"Recognize it?" she asked.

A bank of fog drifted in over the bay. "No."

"Then let me connect to my office," she said, "and I'll show you."

"Go ahead." It irritated Jack that Isabel knew what it was

17

after he had spent weeks sifting the possibilities. If he wasn't a gentleman, he would have asked her to split the check.

The waiter brought Isabel a leatherbound book on a serving platter. She leafed through its pages. "Here." She turned the book to face him. A diagram matched his design. Almost. There was one section in his pattern, a diamond-shaped blob of pixels, dithered gray, that didn't align.

"What's the book?" he asked.

"Electronic schematics. Your pattern is a primitive circuit that picks signals from carrier waves, amplifies them, sends them, too."

"A radio?"

"Transceiver. But in place of the tuning crystal, your diagram has"—she pointed to the diamond symbol—"this mess. And there's circuitry near it that doesn't do anything. Looks like someone has been playing a joke on you."

Jack's data was from spy satellites, decades-old microwave archives from the Michelson Observatory on the dark side of the moon, and static he downloaded yesterday . . . and the signal was still the same. It was time independent. It was no joke.

Isabel squinted at the diamond-shaped smudge of pixels. "This isn't like the other symbols. Roughly square, yet a distinctive lack of pattern." She ran her finger over it and accessed the data. "164 white and 272 black."

Jack had never thought of them as numbers. He had searched for an encrypted pattern. 164 and 272. Jack stared at them. Images flashed: yin and yang, binary combinations, ants that scurried over the datagrid, words printed on a page. Jack connected to the Acadamé's database and initiated a filtered search for the numbers and their combinations. Matches to his inquiry scrawled in the margins of his datagrid: physics node, exotic particle theory; history node, Civil War statistics; chemistry node, superheavy—

The waiter interrupted him and whispered, "Sir, there is a gentleman looking for you." He pointed to the street.

Bruner stepped out of the fog. Mist clung to him. He was thin, too tall to be graceful; the only thing Jack liked about him

18

was his black-and-silver beard that spread out like a fan from his chin. Bruner spotted him and pushed through the café's tables. He pulled out a chair and joined them—ignoring bubble etiquette and not even asking.

The waiter informed Bruner, "This is a table for two, sir."

"I see you made it back from the NSO." Bruner shot a glance at Isabel, then back to Jack. "Why doesn't your friend get back to the archaeology department? Tell her to dig up some bones and vacuum tubes."

Jack balled his hand into a fist, stood halfway, but Isabel got up first.

"It's OK," she said.

If she had wanted Bruner hurt, she would have done it herself. Probably better than he could.

"We can talk later." She gave Jack a light kiss on the cheek. "Something just spoiled the cream in my moccasopa."

She picked up her book, marched to the sidewalk, then caught the trolley.

Jack was sorry to see her go. The sky turned overcast and the moon dimmed.

"Nice place you got," Bruner said and looked around. "Pre-constructionist California, right? San Francisco? A bit of history for your lady friend?"

"What do you want?" Jack nonchalantly tossed his napkin over the grid of data.

Beyond the seawall, waves crested, foam and gray water crashed over the top and rained on the neon dragons in Chinatown.

"I came with an offer." Bruner pulled off white leather gloves that Jack had thought were his skin they were so tight.

"What kind? An offer where I check my back for your collection of steak knives? I don't think so."

"We've had differences of opinion in the past—"

"That difference being that I do real science, while you give good parties for your corporate sponsors and the dean. The difference being that I'm the one who's getting that tenure position."

"You want to hear what I have to say?"

Jack dug through his pocket and left a big tip for the waiter. "Since you're going to say it anyway, sure."

"I have friends in industry. They could use a man with your talents. I'd like to arrange an introduction."

"A job?" Jack leaned forward, picked up his fork, then used it to point at Bruner. "I came to the Académe to get away from that."

Bruner narrowed his beady eyes. "Reconsider. The NSO only interviews intelligent men like ourselves when they are guilty."

Jack didn't know what Bruner was up to. "That's an interesting fantasy. What does your psychologist say about it?"

"Crime does *not* happen at the Académe. Theft, destruction of valuable properties. It is scandalous." He rocked back in his chair. "I've heard the mathematics department will be conducting its own investigation. There will be an awkward inquisition. Embarrassed colleagues." A smile flickered under Bruner's beard. "And a ruined career."

Bruner was too damn confident. That had Jack worried. The seawall cracked. Water streamed through and swirled in the streets; liquid jade mixed with Chinatown neon. A tidal wave washed up Jackson Street—crashed through the Golden Gate Fortune Cookie Factory.

"I'm offering you a way to exit gracefully," Bruner whispered, "and keep your citizenship intact."

Chunks of the seawall blasted apart. The ocean poured in, sweeping cars and brick buildings away like driftwood.

Jack shifted in his chair. Could Bruner make a strong enough frame to get him kicked out? Maybe. And maybe Jack had been too quick to tell DeMitri that Bruner didn't have guts. Or maybe it was just Bruner's lucky day. "Why give me anything?"

Jack pushed—with the lightest touch. He ran into a wall of elliptical integrals, mosaic patterns of fractals, and the oily sensation of Bruner's secrecy.

"I know what you're up to," he whispered to Jack.

Did he? Or was he guessing?

Bruner tested Jack. He ran into a matrix of silver prime numbers and the blinding glare of the sun. Bruner blinked and eased off. "I inspected your bubble after the NSO team left. All those files and electronics unguarded, security measures not reset . . . anyone could have stumbled inside and done mischief."

"Are you sure you came in *after* the NSO?"

Bruner held his hand over his heart. "Jack, I'm shocked that you even say such a thing."

Waves lapped the edge of the sidewalk. Shattered lumber and Styrofoam trash floated by.

"I want to know what you're doing with my research," Bruner said.

How much did he know? Were there enough clues in Jack's unprotected files? "We don't have anything to talk about."

"I think we do." Bruner stood and surveyed the flooding of California: a tsunami blasted over the remains of the seawall. "Your world is going to shit, Jack. Take a vacation. Think it over. We'll talk again."

Water surged through the café. Chairs and tables toppled; the waiter scrambled after sinking plates and silverware. The cold sea splashed around Jack's knees.

"I'm not going anywhere. I'll take this to the dean. I'll—"

"Dean Roberts and I are of one mind on the matter. He agreed after the stress of the break-in, and the interview with Mr. DeMitri, that you need rest. Three days while the department conducts its investigation. Check your mail. It won't be a request."

A rubber lifeboat floated by. Bruner got in. "Think carefully. You have more enemies than you realize. This might be your best offer . . . your only offer."

A wave slammed over Jack, submerged the café, San Francisco, his world.

He grabbed the datagrid before it washed away, choked on the freezing water . . . and sank to the bottom.

It was turning into a lousy day.

2

JACKKNIFED

The hum of the taxi was in Jack's head.

Inductive neuralware let him interface with bubble worlds, but it also pulled static from the air. Académé-licensed taxis were supposed to have shielded generators, but this one had a hole at 300 hertz, a buzzsaw that chewed through his skull.

They skimmed along the one-rail. Jack glanced out the back window; an island of white towers winked over the edge of the world. Out of one snake pit into another.

The San Joaquin Sea stretched to either horizon, smooth and black with no stars reflected on its surface, only the lights from Santa Sierra. The city looked better mirrored in the water. Right side up, it was all sharp angles, fluorescents that flickered, and an off-key marching band of stray electronics that pounded his brain.

There was a repeater station ahead, a slender tower and parabolic dish of yellow diode lasers. Jack stared at it; the repeater station woke up, turned, and tracked the taxi. A blinking green box appeared in his peripheral vision.

"Slow down," Jack told the driver.

She glanced in the rearview mirror. Her eyelids were painted like butterfly wings, pink and silver. They fluttered once, then locked back onto the instrument panel. "Sure," she said, "your money."

Why mess with a repeater station when Jack had bubbles to enhance his thoughts and pull hunches from his subconscious? Secrecy.

He tapped on the cursive *i* information icon and searched for the numbers Isabel had discovered: 164 and 272. He initiated a dozen parallel searches: prime numbers in the Fibonacci series, details on the missing jewels of the czars, and sites in the Mandelbrot set that looked like Chinese calligraphy. He programmed their output to zipper-encrypt together. Jack kept the key simple enough so he could filter the bits as the repeater station sent them—a smokescreen for anyone eyeballing his access of Academé archives.

Jack waited: three heartbeats, four, five. This system crawled. Seventeen hundred matches to his search appeared, a grid of subdirectories that filled his vision with eerie green characters.

He filtered for entries with fourfold symmetry to match the diamond pattern in his schematic. Thirty-five references remained. He filtered for references to electronics or electromagnetic signals. Three links remained, all to the particle physics archives.

Jack opened the files. Old reports scrolled by: neutrons and nuclei cooled by laser light, squeezed into a superheavy element with 164 protons and 272 neutrons. It condensed into octahedral crystals held by instantaneous dipole attractions, had a half-life of eighteen months, and emitted a broad spectrum of light, glowing icy blue with something like Çerenkov radiation—but wasn't.

The results had been published a decade ago; there had been interest from the theoretical physics community, but it had been locked away and forgotten. Too expensive to produce and no corporate sponsors.

Electricity crackled in his mouth, the sensation of breaking glass under his fingertips, a flash of light, and static washed back into Jack's head. They had moved out of the range of the repeater station.

"Sorry," the driver said, "traffic control said to move it."

The taxi arced up and over the twenty-meter seawall that divided the ocean from the skyscrapers and exhaust columns that rose from the pit. There was no fog tonight to hide the sharp edges of the city. Santa Sierra sprawled over sixteen square kilometers of reclaimed land, with eight-lane streets for its population to push through. Classified ads and stock quotes crept across the chameleon surfaces of the buildings. Towers broke the clouds overhead, and a dozen airports lifted a million tons of product around the globe and into orbit every day. It was a big city full of tiny souls.

"That's OK," Jack muttered. He'd brainstorm later with Isabel and figure out how this data fit into the rest of the puzzle. It was impossible to think straight out here.

The taxi eased to street level and rolled to a stop. People swarmed around the car, a river of pushing and shoving and jabbing with briefcases, fast-walking commuters on their way to work. Lemmings.

A segmented bus thundered past, blasted Jack with its discharging batteries, and left his ears ringing.

"You want me to stick around?" the driver with the butterfly eyes asked. A strand of black hair fell across her face; she pushed it back up under her cap.

It was dangerous to be here unshielded. His implant turned electromagnetic noise into signals, undirected and strong enough to cause a seizure. He could have worn a helmet, but the locals would have spotted him in heartbeat. And in the neighborhood he was headed, they beat Académe professors to a pulp.

"No." He handed her his credit card and a tip in cash. "Thanks."

"I could call a bodyguard or rent you a gun."

"Gun?" Jack pretended to be surprised. "Does somebody need shooting?"

He opened the door. The city smelled of fast-food grease and sea salt. Outside the cab, Jack tasted radios, microwave ovens, and hot pinpricks that showered onto him from the orange streetlights overhead.

There was a tide of human flesh. Jack got pushed down Fifteenth Street to the corner of Fairfax Avenue by the midnight shift. They were folks with wet hair from just-taken showers, bloodshot eyes, and gray skin. They had five minutes to get to work or they'd be late and docked. That made everyone mad at everyone else.

An umbrella stabbed into Jack's side. He swung back with his elbow.

Santa Sierra was a city that moved. Its citizens were migrant workers. They came for short-term construction work or a sudden burst of nano-fab production. When their contracts ended, they migrated to Denver for clean room duty or to Tennessee to process uranium. Skilled labor. The key word being labor. Twelve-hour shifts plus overtime. Free addictive stimulants and antidepressants on the job. No benefits. But it was better than what happened to the unskilled or criminals in the labor camps.

Jack was an educated man. He had worked hard to fill his head and get to the Académe. Lucky guy. How long would that last, though, with Bruner trying to frame him?

He stepped out of the press of commuters, into an alley, and watched as three kids sprayed a wall with glowing biolume yellows and neon reds. A local UHF broadcast made Jack's eyes blur, and he couldn't tell the kids apart from their art: faces with wild eyes and flames for hair.

The permanent residents of Santa Sierra serviced its migrant workers with fast-food joints and dry cleaners, dealt in methamphetamine or sex. Plenty of vultures and wolves, too—gene swappers and memory thieves.

Jack crossed the street. It was five past midnight and only a few stragglers sprinted by. Another hour and the overtimers would flood the walkways, stagger back to their holes, sleep, get up, and start the workday over.

He cut down Mosfet Alley, kicking trash, stepping over burned-out freaks, and turning down an assortment of hustles. Kept to himself and kept out of trouble.

These were the oldest buildings in Santa Sierra, made with bricks dredged from the sea. Tiny shells and barnacles encrusted the red-and-white stone. He entered the alcove of 375 and gave his password. The door hissed open, closed as soon as he crossed the threshold.

Home.

He took the stairs to the third floor. Jack had fit his apartment with a new lock and door to keep the place secure. The door was foamed steel, stronger than the half-meter-thick concrete walls. He opened it with a thought.

Bioluminescent colonies of lichens warmed, thinking Jack was a predator, warning him not to graze on their toxic flora, reflecting gold and green and blue upon the aluminum foil that covered the walls, floor, and ceiling.

The door closed and it was finally quiet. The aluminum foil shielded the EM noise. No stray current. No tortuous sixty-cycle hum in his head.

Accommodations were sparse. Two canned stoves in the kitchen, his overstuffed blue pillow, a pile of books . . . and a duffel bag in the corner that wasn't Jack's.

Behind the closed bathroom door, the toilet flushed.

Adrenaline burned Jack's blood. Who the hell was in there? He took three steps closer.

The door opened.

Jack grabbed the person's hand, locked the thumb back, grabbed the elbow. It was a good hold, had to be painful.

Jack pulled—got pushed—and lost his grip.

Motion: a blur in the shadows. Jack's knee buckled. Another push and he spun, lost his balance, landed on his back.

A face leered over Jack . . . the ugliest man he knew. One

eye was brown, the other blue. His nose had been broken in three places. Deep golden tan. Gray hair. Uncle Reno.

"Hiya, Jack."

"You've got a talent for breaking into places," Jack said. "You know the trouble I'm in because of you?"

"Up to your neck." He offered Jack a hand up. "That's why I came."

Jack took his hand. Reno was twenty years older, but stronger.

"I wasn't the one who did your office," Reno said.

"Then how do you know about it?" Stupid question. He was a spy for the other side. A traitor. A liar. Dangerous.

"I like how you've decorated this place," Reno said and smoothed a wrinkle in the aluminum wallpaper. "Neoclassical toaster oven." He stepped over to his bag, keeping his brown eye on Jack, and pulled out a bottle of brandy and two plastic cups.

"No thanks. I need the brain cells."

Reno frowned, and it made his nose more crooked. "You lost more brains coming into the city with that hardware in your skull." He poured two fingers, twice. Handed one to Jack.

He was probably right. Jack took the cup, sipped. The booze was warm going down. It smelled of apples and pears and charcoal, and the burn of alcohol. "Did you come to wish me a happy birthday or you got a reason to be here?"

"Your birthday isn't for six months," Reno said. "Scorpio. Year of the Dragon." He smiled: teeth capped in gold. "I brought you a present anyway, but that's not why I came." He settled to the floor and sat cross-legged. "Tell me, Jack, why'd you leave those ivory towers?"

"You know. Don't play games."

"I know about the break-in. I know about Dr. Harold Bruner. I don't know why you left when you could have stayed in your silver shell."

"I needed the fresh air."

Jack had left to get away from Bruner and the NSO, but also to link to the Académe database from the outside, unwatched, and find a clue to the symbol in his pattern. He was glad to hear Reno didn't know everything.

"I thought you philosophers always stayed in your bubbles. Better reception, right?"

Jack took another sip of the brandy. It was sweet and thick; it made his tongue numb. "There's more to it than reception."

"I know there's more," Reno said and leaned forward. "Why don't you tell me what you *think* it is."

Jack sat, grabbed his blue pillow, and stuffed it under his arm. The Hautger SK semiautomatic he had kept underneath was missing. That was the problem with guns: when you kept them close, they tended to go wandering—get into the hands of someone asking questions. "What are you doing here?"

"Like I said, I came to help." Reno's brown eye squinted. "Answer my question. You think that VR network makes you smarter? Or better than the rest of us?"

Jack didn't see his gun on Reno. He had to have it. Maybe that bag of his . . .

"We communicate faster. This conversation would be flashed between us in a second. If that's intelligence, then yeah, maybe it does make us smarter."

"You ever see what it looks like without the illusions? A grown man sitting in a jar, or worse, two of you, staring at nothing— not what I'd call stimulating conversation or deep thought."

"The bubbles send EM signals to our implants, induce charges, stimulate sensory neurons that mirror sensations on file. We see anything we want."

"I know how it's supposed to work." Reno tossed the rest of his brandy down. "It's those 'sensations on file' I'd worry about if I were you, Jack-O. Emotions. Programmed loyalty. Maybe a little fear?" He leaned back, then looked over his pile of books. "You ever read these? The Jefferson I brought you? Or the Steinbeck?"

"No," Jack lied. He'd worn the cover off *The Grapes of Wrath*.

"The problem with you intellectuals is that you use your

brains, but you don't think. You're kept behind walls by the government. You don't have a clue what's going on out here."

"Are you going to tell me how your side is better? A communist dictatorship? Massacres in Hong Kong, the Philippines, and Tibet?"

Reno shook his head. "You've got it mixed up. China is the only free place left. Santa Sierra is a city of slaves. Credit card debt, taxes, inflation. You know what happens in those labor camps? Have you been to the work ghettos in Albuquerque?"

"You're wrong. Sure it's hard, but anyone can get an education. Anyone can start their own business or file a patent and make it big. It's not impossible."

"They still teach that American Dream propaganda here?" Reno sighed. "Look, Jack, I didn't come to debate whose side is better. I know the NSO got to you . . . pried you open and dug around. I'm sorry."

"All you've done is made it worse. I'll have to report this and get interviewed again."

"No," Reno said, got up, and stretched. "You won't."

"There's no choice. All it takes is one person to spot you here, and I won't get asked for an interview. They'll come and pick me up. You should have thought of that before you came." Jack glared at him and drained his brandy. "If you want to help, leave."

Reno poured himself another. The stuff was hitting Jack harder than he expected. He was hot and numb around the edges. He could have used a second drink. Reno didn't offer.

"You're right, Jack. You don't have a choice. If you go to the NSO this time, they'll kill you."

Jack had had it with Reno's lies. Maybe he had his gun, but Jack was close to the door. He could open it, get out, and lock it before Reno blinked twice.

He stood. The walls receded and blurred. Jack fell down—didn't feel it.

"Ready for the truth?" Reno asked and looked him over. "Maybe you are." From his bag he pulled out a slim leather case.

29

A smart remark popped into Jack's mind about Jefferson and truth and China, but it faded, forgotten in a haze. He couldn't focus.

"Let's start with this 'uncle' business." Reno's case unfolded like an origami puzzle; inside it was silver and laser light and glittering electronics. "Uncle was the code name I had when I worked with your folks. We're not related."

Jack tried not to look surprised, like he had expected that. It wasn't hard; the muscles in his face wouldn't move. "That's a relief," he mumbled. "I was afraid I might end up as ugly as you."

Reno flashed his gold teeth, walked over, then shoved Jack against the wall. "Truth number two. In the spy business, never drink with someone you're not a hundred percent with. You bring your own booze."

Jack got a close look at that case: microchannel teeth, dendrite probes, and a rotary bone-cutting scalpel. A display on the instrument showed layers of his face, the bone underneath, and the blood vessels under that.

He tried to push Reno away. Jack's arms might have well been concrete.

"I'm not in the spy business," Jack slurred.

Reno's brown eye pinned him with a stare. "You are now."

A flock of black swans circled overhead, descended, and landed two tiers up. Jack sat on a terraced mountain with canyons of marble columns and jasmine ivy twining around them. There were Cyprian cedars in titanic clay pots, palms, and ferns with leaves as large as elephant ears, a maze of staircases that led to grottos, cascading fountains, wading pools, and orchid gardens. The Euphrates River flowed on his left, red with mud, and on the far bank sprawled a city made of brick that glistened gold in the midday sun, and farther still, a spiral that reached into the sky, scattered clouds, the Tower of Babel.

It had been forty-eight hours since Reno's visit, and Jack still had one hell of a headache.

Zero al Qaseem dismissed the pair of slave girls that had been fanning him. He touched Jack's head, probing the shape of his skull beneath.

Zero was his friend, a gene witch, but Jack never really understood what made the mad Arab tick. No one did. You just gave him room and let him tinker with hazardous nano- and biomechanical toys. Even the NSO gave Zero a wide berth—which is why Jack was in Zero's bubble. Zero had the tools to crack his head open, without cracking it, and see what Reno had done.

"Hairline fracture," Zero said. "Forced ossification." He gazed into Jack's eyes. "Your left pupil remains dilated." He tugged at the curls in his square beard, then got up, straightened his robe, and returned to his workbench. He pushed on a slab of wet clay, cut bits away with a wooden knife, gave it eyes, nose, and ears that stuck out like Jack's.

Isabel sat next to Jack. She alternately glanced at Zero's work and the scrolling equations on her notepad. Her red hair was held back with an olive scarf. She wore khaki shorts and a white blouse and dark glasses to shield her eyes.

"You woke up two days later?" she asked.

"Yeah," Jack said. "Reno was gone. Him and his brandy and the sledgehammer he used on me. I threw up a couple of times, then caught a taxi back to the Académé."

"Wise decision," Zero said without looking up from the clay.

"What happened after he . . . operated on you?" Isabel removed her glasses. Her eyes were huge, the color of emeralds, and wanting to link with Jack.

It was a generous offer: share his pain. She didn't know what she was asking for. Jack turned and watched Zero sculpt. "There were noises," he said. "I heard my skull get cracked open, some drilling, the smell of my hair burning. I passed out."

"Does your implant work?" she asked. "Are you interfaced with Zero's hanging gardens? Can you see me?"

He grabbed her hand and squeezed it. "I'm fine."

She must have seen that lie. She shoved her glasses back on and pulled her hand from his. "Don't kid around, Jack." She turned to Zero. "Wouldn't it be better if we took him to the hospital?"

Zero shrugged and scraped out hollow eyes from the clay. The bust was a metaphor for the data Zero's bubble had collected: a compilation of the active physiology in Jack's brain. It was a decent likeness, except the nose was too large.

Zero wound a thread around the head, then pulled, slicing through the top of the skull. "This will take a minute," he said and picked at the clay that had gotten in his beard. "We will know then if he requires a hospital." His eyes darkened to solid black.

Jack caught his meaning: they'd know if he needed a hospital . . . or a morgue.

The clay dried, wet and red to orange and chalky; tiny cracks spread across the surface. "I think you got the nose wrong," Jack told him. "Too big."

"The proportions are correct." Zero touched the hardened clay, then gingerly removed the top. "Your nose is not overly large. It is that your eyes are too small."

Scarab beetles crawled out from inside the bust, dozens of scurrying gold and lapis jewels. Zero picked one up, scrutinized its gears and springs and mechanical legs, then set it down.

Isabel helped Jack get to his feet. The dizziness was still there. His left eye felt like bursting.

Inside the clay figure were crisscrossed webs, the implant that let Jack interact with the electronics of the bubble.

"These," Isabel said and pointed at the metallic spiderweb, "new filaments wrapped about his inductive dendrites."

Jack squinted. Around the fibers that were supposed to be there, tiny silver lines wound and curled.

"There are nodes as well," Zero said. He took a pair of tweezers and extracted a particle. The captured speck enlarged to the size of a grapefruit. Zero peeled its fleshy skin back. Inside were convolutions and layers that crackled with electricity, smoldered like coals. "Mitochondria," he said. "Delicate work to blend synthetics with these biologicals. Is your Reno a gene witch?"

Before Jack could tell him exactly what Reno was, Zero turned his attention back to the clay. "There is scarring where the smaller filaments uncoiled . . . and this." He removed a mirrored cube the size of his thumbnail. Its edges and sides twisted, flexed, and changed geometry. He set it on his workbench and it stiffened back to a cube.

Isabel drew a sketch of it on her notepad, pondered that a moment, then she said, "A resonating cavity? That's insane. Broadcasting would irradiate the surrounding tissue. The design is clever, though. It varies shape to attenuate the signal."

"An implant in my implant?" Jack asked. "Why?"

"To collect information on the Académe?" Zero suggested.

"If they have this level of technology," Isabel whispered, "they don't need our Académe."

They. Isabel said it like the Chinese were aliens. Maybe they were. All trade, cultural exchange, every line of communication had been cut off thirty years ago. It was called the Raising of the Great Wall by the West. They might as well live in another galaxy.

"You have to take this to the NSO, Jack," she said. "It's too important to keep to yourself."

He shook his head. That was a mistake. Dull knives stabbed into his temples.

"Insanity," Zero said. "They will interview us all. Take our minds apart like Jack's. Perhaps take his mind apart literally." He picked up a hammer and smashed the clay bust. "I have erased all files I have on this matter."

Isabel set her fingers on Jack's temples, smoothed them; it felt good. "Keeping secrets from the government," she said. "It's not right. It's not smart."

Nothing about this had been smart. If Jack had been smart, he would never have drunk with Reno, never let the NSO get inside his head, and never given Bruner a chance to discredit him.

"I know I have to tell them," he said, "but not now. I'm not walking into another interview blind. I have to know why Reno did it and what this has to do with the break-in and my research."

33

Isabel flipped a page on her notepad. Jack's schematic was there. "The transceiver?" she asked.

"Give me a few days to put the pieces together. Then I'll have enough answers for the NSO. Save them the trouble of peeling my mind."

"I want to do the right thing." She glanced at Zero. "For everyone. I'll wait. I promise."

Isabel was smart. She had a fellowship in the archaeology department. She was tough. Her enemies didn't last long. But she had one thing more important than being smart and tough— she kept her promises. Maybe that would get her into trouble one day. Soon.

"Then we hide until matters become calm," Zero said. "I have a lecture this evening. I will cancel it."

"No," Jack told him. "Go. Pretend like nothing's happened and that I never came here—that I'm not here now."

"I'd better leave then," Isabel said and set her hand consolingly on his arm. "Parts of Lawrence Livermore Labs are being dredged up this afternoon. There will be heaps of old magnetic storage, optical disks, and class-nine servers with memory residues. They'll need me to hack in."

"Get back as soon as you can. I could use some help to build the circuit. I don't have the parts or the expertise."

"It's nothing to assemble the electronics," she said. "I can have my bubble run a simulation or I can scrounge the parts, but without that mystery component it won't be complete."

Jack should have told her that he thought he knew what it was. Isabel might have the connections to borrow a sample of the isotope. Then again, it might be just the thing Bruner and the NSO were watching for. She and Zero were already in over their heads. Jack didn't want to drag them down with him. Besides, he wasn't sure this isotope was the missing element in the circuit.

"I have a few clues about that," he said. "I'll let you know as soon as I figure it out."

"I shall transfer control to you, Jack," Zero said. He handed him a crown of gold and rubies. "Babylon is yours for a day, but stay away from the biohazards in partition beta."

"Don't worry," he said, "I'm going to sleep."

Isabel kissed Jack on the cheek, then his friends descended a flight of stairs to the outside world.

He closed his eyes, concentrated on the throbbing in his head, wished for sleep, but his mind churned. Two days ago he had been poised to escape the politics of the Académe. Now he was in trouble so deep that he couldn't see a way out. The NSO was involved and now Reno. Reno, who was not his uncle. Reno the spy. Reno the traitor. Reno, the guy who opened his braincase. Why?

Jack had the feeling he was being watched.

On a terrace overlooking his, a slave girl with dark hair leaned over the railing. A subliminal. With his headache, sex was the last thing Jack wanted. He willed her away.

There were three possible reasons for Reno's impromptu surgery. Like Zero said, he could have done it to spy on the Académe. Given Jack eyes and ears that would broadcast back to China. But Reno knew he was in trouble with the mathematics department. And he knew the NSO was watching him. That didn't make Jack an ideal candidate for a spy.

Was Reno trying to convert him to his side? No. It would have been easier to drag Jack to Beijing, tear his mind apart, and rebuild it the way they wanted.

The last possibility Jack didn't buy: Reno did it to help.

The slave girl appeared again. She sauntered down a zigzag of stairs, past magnolia trees with ivory blossoms, brushing aside hair that kept falling into her face.

How did Reno fit into the break into his office? Was he responsible? Did he do it to get Jack into trouble? Or steal his research?

He interfaced with the Académe's physics archives—curling particle trajectories and Feynman diagrams settled into Jack's mind. Deep in their storage vaults, secure and slowly decaying, was the key to this puzzle. Maybe. He summoned it. A single

35

crystal with eight sides appeared in his hand. Blue radiation like light underwater shimmered from the isotope. It was the size of a pea and twice as dense as lead.

And not real. This ghost wouldn't work in the circuit. And there was no guarantee the real one would work, either. How did it hook up to the electronics? There were too many unanswered questions. Or like Isabel had said: this might be a joke. Bruner could have tampered with his data, sent him off chasing signals in the noise.

The slave girl came to Jack. Her indigo hair was cut short and bangs covered her eyes. She was wrapped in swaths of wispy silk and not much else. She presented a wicker basket of figs to him.

"No thanks," he said.

"Then how about one of these?" she asked, reached deeper in her basket, and removed an eight-sided sapphire.

The slave girl brushed her bangs aside and revealed eyes that were warm copper like a cat's . . . and eyelids that shimmered gossamer, the wings of a butterfly that blurred into purples and golds, pinks and silver.

Jack knew her. "A little off the beaten path for a cab driver, isn't it? What are you? NSO?" He couldn't read anything in her eyes.

"I'm not NSO. You may call me Panda. I came to help."

"The last time someone said that, I got knocked out and my head was split open."

Panda smiled, but it vanished like it hurt or might crack that perfect round face of hers.

How had she gotten into Zero's bubble without permission? The interface protocol didn't let anyone sneak in. Maybe she got in the same way his office had been broken into.

Jack took the crystal she offered. It was glass-smooth, hollow, and as real as hot ice.

"You look confused," she said. "Stand up. Walk with me and we'll talk."

He stood, not to walk with her, but because he didn't trust

her. She had offered to rent him a gun, so she could be armed now. The dizziness returned.

She touched his temple and the spinning vanished.

"How did you do that?"

Panda took his hand and pulled him to the stairs that descended out of Zero's bubble. "We share a common uncle."

Jack yanked his hand from hers. She was Chinese, then. A spy.

She stopped, spun; her hair whipped into her face. "I will be as honest as I can," she said, "and that will not be much. I do work for the enemies of your government. But I am not *your* enemy."

Had she read him so easily? It had to be Reno's hardware. Inside his head, something crawled, settled, and his splitting migraine faded.

Jack folded his arms. "I'm not going anywhere until you tell me what Reno did and why you're here."

"Oh, Jack." She sighed. "We have run out of the truth. I can dance around it, but that is all."

"Then dance. I'm watching."

She went to her basket, got a fig, tore it in half, and offered it to him.

He took it, but didn't bite. She had bypassed the interface protocols, so Jack wasn't sure if she was broadcasting from another station or was in the bubble with him. That fig could be real and full of poison. It could be virtual and full of looping Möbius subroutines. Last time it was Reno's brandy. Jack wasn't going to fall for the same trick twice.

"I must properly calibrate what Reno has implanted. He had neither the skill nor permission to perform that operation."

"So take it out."

"That would solve a number of problems, but I would have to remove part of your frontal lobe the size of this"—she held up the fleshy teeth-marked fig—"and our organization does not do that to people."

Her government had massacred more people than Hitler and

Stalin combined. Jack kept his mouth shut and listened, though. He was getting more answers than anyone had offered him in the last three days.

"I came to keep you alive and out of reach from your NSO. They have no such code of ethics. They would be all too eager to examine you. Internally."

"How can you keep me away from the NSO? They're everywhere."

"More 'everywhere' than you think, but there are ways. I will train you. Your must trust me."

Jack laughed.

Her copper eyes narrowed. She stepped closer. She didn't look Chinese. Half-Japanese. A trace of mulatto. Part goddess. He could smell licorice on her breath. "I will earn your trust," she said. "I will show you how to get what you need."

She had to have read him, pulled the facts about the isotope out of his thoughts while she had watched him. Jack filled his mind with frozen lakes and snow and clear sheets of cold. The Euphrates River crackled with frost.

"Come." She grabbed his hand. "No more truth."

He let her lead him. Maybe it was a trap like Reno had sprung, but it was his best bet for finding out what had happened.

She dragged Jack down the stairs, into a tunnel lit by torches. They hadn't left Zero's bubble, so this was a metaphor . . . but for what?

They walked a hundred meters. "Is there a point to this marathon?" he asked.

"Almost there." Panda moved faster and pulled him forward.

"How did you get into the Académe unseen and into this bubble?"

"Inside, outside," she said, "it makes no difference in your United States."

A door ahead: ironbound wood, padlocked and covered with patches of phosphorescent fungus. She stopped. "You can change things now, Jack. Alter what people see. Broadcast into their minds."

"I've always been able to. That's why we have these"—he waved over his head—"bubbles."

"No bubbles," she said. "Only you."

"I don't understand."

She touched the padlock, and it snapped open. Through the door she pulled him. "You will," she whispered.

It was a mad scientist's laboratory. Skeletons hung on the wall; banks of vacuum tubes glowed orange, and panels of blinking lights filled the room. Arcs of electricity snaked between coiled towers. The place smelled of burning tar.

She held Jack's hand tighter and picked a path through benches with beakers boiling over, condensers dripping green ichor, rows of test tubes, and puddles of fuming acid.

"Here," she said and dragged out a chest. It was iron and rusted shut.

Panda jerked the lid, twisted, tugged, and it popped open. Within were silver boxes; she pulled one open. A single eight-sided jewel was inside, burning with blue radiation.

She closed the lid and handed it to him. "There."

"There, what?"

"There is your first lesson. Remember what I have said. I will find you for the next lesson. Soon." She stood on her toes and kissed Jack.

He reached for her, but grabbed only air—felt the brush of butterfly wings against his lips.

She was gone.

The laboratory dissolved. Stainless-steel walls appeared; the wooden door that Panda had opened with a touch swelled into a vault door that was a meter thick of foamed alloy.

The chest she had removed melded into a wall of steel security boxes . . . one of which had its lock melted off.

A radiation warning was engraved upon the container Jack held, and the words: PARTICLE PHYSICS LABORATORY SAMPLE 406A3.

Then the alarms went off.

3

JACK BE NIMBLE, JACK BE QUICK

The jangle of the alarm bells cut straight into Jack's stomach—froze him like an animal caught in the open.

There weren't supposed to be alarms at the Academé. Then again, Panda said she was going to help him.

Neither of those things seemed to be true.

The corridor he had come down, the one that had been damp and torch-lit, now flickered with fluorescent lights.

Jack was in the particle physics lab. It was the size of an aircraft hanger, and in the middle, the curve of the ten-meter-wide collider tunnel intersected the room, and a spiderweb of crystalline particle detectors crisscrossed, glistening with ambient radiation.

The isotope vault occupied the corner farthest from the exit; its thick steel door was wide open. Jack stood on the threshold. No one else was here.

The collider tunnel stretched in either direction and curved out of view. Aluminum girders and suspension coils held in its center self-annealing vacuum columns and a series of superconducting rings. It looked like the skeleton of a giant snake.

When it came on-line, smashing particles and antiparticles, the magnetic field could induce enough current to boil his brain.

He should have stuffed the isotope back into the vault and gotten the hell out of here. His heart raced, but Jack was too terrified to move. He could end up running into more trouble.

Nothing added up.

How did he get here? This place was across campus from Zero's office. He couldn't have left the bubble without logging through interface protocols.

That was an old game they had played as undergraduates: see if you could fool a sucker into thinking he'd left your bubble when he hadn't. But you always had to log him through a fake set of protocols or they'd never fall for it.

Jack's headache was back. The alarm bells were loud, nonstop, and matching the throbbing in his temples. He wished they would stop.

They did.

One last ping resonated in the air, then died. Had he done that? Was he still in Zero's bubble?

His forehead flushed with fever. This wasn't virtual. There was grit on the concrete floor, a detail hardly anyone remembered; the place smelled of burned plastic, and the air wasn't as clear as it was in the bubbles. It *felt* real.

He examined every detail in the collider tunnel. On the far wall by a fire extinguisher there was a bump in reality. When he stared at it, he saw more: cracks in the concrete, microscopic grains of sand, and misalignments in the crystalline structure. He tasted metal in his mouth. Ten meters up the corridor, on an aluminum support, was another bump of clarity. He saw beads of welded alloy, every minute metallic ripple, every reflection of the place turned upside down and distorted on its polished mirrored surfaces—so many details it couldn't be real.

It was like there were layers of virtual and real worlds.

He wasn't inside a bubble, though, where dedicated arrays of processors gave his thoughts substance, linked his intuition and hunches to databases, and made him smarter. He had to push into these regions, strain to see the illusions like he just walked past a repeater station on the noisy streets of Santa Sierra.

If this wasn't Zero's bubble and it wasn't entirely real, either, then what were those bumps of clarity? Repeater stations broadcasting different images? They weren't like any repeater stations Jack had run across before. These were like bubbles turned inside out.

What if the entire campus was rigged, picking up his implant signals, transmitting a different set of impressions . . . making him see and hear and feel whatever the Académe programmed.

When he walked here, saw the mad scientist's laboratory, Panda could have tapped into those stations, forced them to send whatever sensations she wanted. That's how she tricked him into thinking he was still in Zero's bubble.

So why only now did Jack sense them?

Reno's implant.

Panda had said, "Inside, outside, it makes no difference . . ." This was what she had meant. Bubble circuitry was everywhere.

A door slammed shut and echoed down the tunnel. It sounded like it came from the corridor that led out. Someone leaving or coming in?

Jack shoved the isotope case into his shirt, stepped out of the vault, and hid behind its massive open bulkhead.

He waited for seven heartbeats, then looked through the hinge crack.

In the corridor was a man. He was two heads taller than Jack and wore a turtleneck that covered his massive shoulders and thick neck. Glasses hid his eyes, and tiny neon datagrids crawled on the inside of the lenses. He held a gun in his hand.

Whatever he was, Chinese spy or NSO, Jack saw no reason to come out and introduce himself. He didn't want to find out if that was a real gun that could shoot real bullets into his real body.

The man stepped back into the shadow of the corridor and waited.

If there were repeater stations everywhere, why didn't the guy with the gun know Jack was here? The stations had to pinpoint his location, update it millisecond to millisecond to broadcast effectively. If this guy was NSO, all he had to do was tap into the system.

Jack thanked his luck that he hadn't. He'd figure out why later. First he had to get past him. How?

Panda had told him there were no more bubbles, only him. If Jack were inside a normal bubble, he could control what the guy with the gun saw. Maybe he could improvise with these repeater stations, force them to relay his thoughts, make this guy see something that wasn't there. Isabel had said Reno's implant was designed to broadcast. She also told Jack it might fry his brains. He'd worry about that if it happened.

A test first. A dozen meters down the collider tunnel sat a length of cable on a magnetic coil. Jack commanded it to fall.

Nothing happened.

He imagined its length unrolling, hitting the ground, the end whipping around, slapping the floor. He imagined the sound: plastic on concrete crackle.

Out of his mind he forced those impressions . . . out . . . shoved them into the repeater station. There was a snap inside his head. An audible click. Fever flushed through his forehead.

And the cable fell.

The guy stepped out, bobbed his head from side to side, like that might get him a better view. He ran down the tunnel, so quick he blurred, gun pointed in front of him, to where the cable lay.

He'd seen it fall. The repeater station had broadcast what Jack ordered it to.

But what would happen when he got to the cable? Could he touch it? Did Jack have to provide every sensory input or did the repeater station fill in the blanks? He couldn't risk it.

At the end of the collider tunnel, where it arced from view, Jack willed the shadows to move. His head got hot. He molded a smiling Jack face from nothing, then straw-colored hair tossed on his head, the sparkle of mischievous eyes, a ghost outline of a body. Sweat poured down Jack's temples and neck. He made the doppelgänger Jack turn and run away.

The guy with the gun stopped being interested in the cable and chased the Jack that wasn't there.

This was his chance. Jack pushed his thoughts into the repeaters, pushed the image of what the lab would look like empty, then stepped from behind the vault door, gritting his teeth to keep his head exploding from the pressure building inside, and ran for the corridor.

That was the plan.

Jack took one step—into ankle-deep mud: squishy, slick clay that made him slide and lose his balance.

Three more steps and he was knee-deep in the muck. Pools of scummy water welled up around him.

Jack knew this water. It was his favorite subconscious image.

If he had ruined Bruner's career or punched DeMitri in the mouth, that would have been different; he could have lived with those little sins. But he was stealing from the Académe. This isotope didn't belong to him. It was like searching a girlfriend's purse to see if she had pictures of old lovers, or getting too much change back because the clerk didn't know how to count real money, or cheating on an exam. Jack knew this: guilt.

And his mind wasn't letting him off the hook. This muck leaked from deep in his psyche. He had to be broadcasting to the repeaters, and they reflected the thoughts back. A feedback loop.

It wasn't real—he should have been able to walk through it, but his legs dragged, and slipped and stuck. The repeaters were filling in all the details, including paralyzing his muscles exactly like real mud would.

Jack cleared his thoughts and closed his eyes.

When he opened them, the mud was bubbling, spattering the walls, and he had sunk to his thighs.

Screw it. He slogged through the stuff, grabbed handfuls of it, moved slow, slipping, not daring to glance down the tunnel, trudged forward, step after step, until he got to the edge, pulled himself into the doorway and out of the slime.

The tunnel slanted up at a sixty-degree angle—and no handrails. His mind had to be altering the landscape. He didn't have time for psychoanalysis, so he crawled, slipping and sliding up the slope of concrete, until he smelled fresh air and saw daylight.

He blinked, stood up, and let a wave of dizziness pass.

Jack emerged from the corridor and touched a rough stone arch carved with the curves and spirals of subatomic particle collisions. They felt real.

He walked from the ivy-covered three-story building, looked back once, and saw nothing but the lab's copper roof shimmering in the sun.

It was noon, and a group of undergraduates sat upon the red-and-pink marble tiles of Tcholovoni Courtyard, gossiping, wearing only G-strings, and working on their tans.

Jack had to get away. The guy with the sunglasses and the gun wouldn't stay fooled forever, but he had to try one more thing.

He concentrated on what the courtyard would look like without him. He walked over to the undergraduates. His head throbbed with pain and heat. I'm invisible, he thought. Sunlight goes through me.

The students didn't look, even when he blocked their sun—even though he was as real as Coit Tower that rose from the center of the courtyard. Wires strung from the top of the tower to the seawall glistened, scattered EM noise, kept them safe . . . and isolated on their island.

He left the students, Coit Tower, the guy with the gun, and walked as fast as he could to the archaeology complex across campus, past groves of honeysuckle trees, the Greek open-air theater, and walls covered with pastel mosaics of orchid fields and meandering rivers of hyacinth and smoke.

Jack wondered if any of it was real.

Twenty years before Jack was born, the late city of Los Angeles had its big earthquake. Old buildings and bridges collapsed, but everything else had been engineered to withstand the 8.3 Richter shake.

What geologists hadn't predicted was the stress released by the quake causing a cascade reaction in the surrounding tectonic plates: the Caribbean plate tilted, the Pacific plate shattered into twelve sister fragments, and the Sierra Nevada Mountains shot up, riding the buckling North American plate. In the next eighteen months, Baja California vanished, Mexico turned into a chain of volcanic islands, the West Coast submerged. A hundred tsunami reshaped what was left. Every part of the world was cracked or smoldering or underwater.

The fairy tale Jack got told as a kid was that it brought the world together. Everyone had to help each other out. Food came from Russia, medicine from France, bulldozers from South Africa. For years there were no political boundaries, just people helping each other.

Except China. No one ever told Jack why they went into isolation and raised their Great Wall. They had to have been hurt as much as the rest of the world.

Look it up in the history database. You'll see video clips, new theories on plate tectonics, geological boundary layers, and the nature of the spinning nickel-iron core, but nothing about the two billion Chinese that might as well have vanished from the face of the world.

There are still earthquakes, the occasional volcanic eruption; the earth settles, relaxes . . . and slowly builds stress again.

"You got a smoke?"

Isabel tapped the end of a lavender cigarette, sucked the platinum foil lip, made the tip glow cherry red, then handed it to Jack.

She had her office done in industrial capitalist decor; there was a polished redwood desk, a ticker-tape machine that continuously spewed paper ribbon with stock quotes, dark mahogany paneling, a drafting table that overflowed with blueprints, a map of the world (with parts of Africa still blank and unexplored), and a sterling tea set on an enamel-blue cart. Isabel's tea was dark oolong, a triple dose of honey, no cream—sweet, smooth, and scalding.

A wall of windows in her office overlooked a factory floor. At the far end, molten steel poured from crucibles; rollers and robot hands shaped the metal; then an army of men took hammers and presses and manufactured pistons and drive shafts and springs. Steam made the atmosphere thick, gave the factory air an underwater quality. That was Isabel's psyche: gears turning, wheels spinning, lots of honest get-your-hands-dirty work.

Jack drew in the smoke, savored the vanilla taste and the rush of stimulants, then exhaled. It went a long way to ease his headache.

He told her what had happened, starting with the Chinese girl and the isotope and ending with his escape from the lab.

She stayed cool and sat there thinking. On the factory floor, though, a monkey wrench got tossed into the works. Gears and wheels seized. Conveyer belts tangled.

"I think the entire campus is rigged," he said.

She removed her foreman's cap, shook out her red hair, then gathered it into a ponytail. Down on the assembly line, the wrench had been removed and the line cleared. "Rigged with bubble circuitry?" she asked.

"How else could I have projected images and dodged that guy? How else could I have not been seen by those undergraduates? This implant"—he touched his temple—"doesn't have the power to broadcast that kind of signal . . . but it could link to one of those repeaters. And they could do it."

Isabel went to her drafting table, rolled up the blueprints there; her hands shook. She grabbed a set of papers and brought them back to her desk. "There is no need for repeaters on campus. We have the bubbles. What would be the point?"

Jack drew in more sticky vanilla smoke. "My guess is control. The working stiffs on the mainland don't have implants, can't synch with bubbles or repeater stations, but you and I are different. It's our job to think. Some people might believe that's dangerous. A thing that needs to be controlled."

"This is America, Jack. Why equip us with bubbles? We have all of humanity's knowledge for the asking. That doesn't sound like control to me."

"It's your job to find lost data, right?"

She nodded, but her eyes narrowed skeptically, and a rime of frost crept along the lip of her once-steaming teacup. "What does that have to do—"

"Information gets forgotten all the time and buried under new layers of data. What makes you think it couldn't or wouldn't be hidden on purpose?"

Isabel looked away from him and watched her assembly line. "There is another possibility you haven't considered."

"That I'm crazy?"

"Not crazy. You just haven't thought this through." She leaned closer, then whispered, "Why would the Chinese want you to have the isotope? And for God's sake, Jack, why did you take it? They set you up."

Isabel had a point. Reno and Panda had claimed they wanted to help him, but all Jack had to show for their help was a cracked skull and almost getting caught breaking and entering. He had gotten out of that jam in the particle physics lab . . . by the skin of his teeth. Now he had the isotope, more questions—and more of the truth than he wanted to know.

"All this started when my office got ransacked," he said. "Solve that mystery and I'll bet everything else falls into place. And to do that"—he took the isotope case and set it on the table—"I need to know if the data I fished out of the noise is real or fake. I need your help."

Her clear green eyes became murky with doubt.

"Please, Isabel."

She was quiet a moment, then she blinked and her eyes cleared. "I'll help. But there are two conditions." She crossed her arms. "First, if this doesn't work, you drop this isotope business. You don't have to confess or report to the NSO, just forget it."

"I might be able to live with that. What's the second condition?"

"If you are wrong about the signal, then you might be wrong about the implant and the repeater stations. I want you to go to a specialist and find out what that implant is really doing to you."

That was typical Isabel. She believed in the government that funded her research and rebuilt the world, never taking a close look at the methods they used.

Then again, Jack's brain *had* been altered. His perceptions could be all wrong. Panda had told him she had calibrated the Chinese implant . . . but if so, then why couldn't he shake this headache? Maybe he did need a doctor.

"You got a deal," he said.

They shook on it. She stood and went to her drafting table, tilted it so it was flat, then unrolled a set of blueprints. They were solid blue and blank.

"Jack Potter," she said, "file alpha, password pincushion prime."

His circuit schematic appeared on the paper, a maze of white lines that drew themselves.

"I don't understand why you need the isotope," she said. "Once you knew what it was, we could have programmed the circuit to run with a simulated crystal."

"It gives off light."

"So would a simulated element."

"This light comes from its nuclear decay. That's a random process."

"Random noise I can generate."

"But computer-generated random numbers aren't completely random. And maybe not the kind of random that's not-so-random like the signal I pulled from the cosmic noise."

Isabel mulled that over, pulled a thick leatherbound volume off the shelf, and leafed through, then stopped. A miniature blue crystal floated off the page.

"The particle physics database said it gives off low-level alpha radiation," Jack told her. "Nothing that can hurt us as long as we don't eat or inhale it. The light is similar to Çerenkov radiation."

"It's Penning radiation," Isabel said, reading from her book.

"There is something unusual about the strong nuclear force in this element. An internal symmetry decay occurs, the isotopic spin is altered, neutrons convert to protons, and the entire core destabilizes, decaying into a host of particles, mostly alpha. Those particles travel faster than photons can in the dense solid. There's a shock wave and a spectrum of blue light is a by-product." She closed the book, then said, "Your transceiver was designed to process longer wavelengths. I'll shift the frequency."

Jack opened the isotope case, removed the glowing sapphire with eight sides, then set it on the blueprint: indigo ink and waves of amethyst light.

Isabel traced white-on-blue lines with a pencil; they became gold, glistened, then filled with sparkles of current. The paper stiffened into green fiberglass circuit board. Symbols fattened into resistors with rainbow stripes, light-emitting diodes, ruby capacitors, a silver speaker, and humming transistors.

She scrutinized the diagram and frowned. "I'm changing these." She pointed to a tangle of components. "Whoever designed this is a century behind in their electronics. You need a transient switch array here instead of this nest of wires, and a tunneling capacitor here will increase sensitivity."

The circuit lines simplified, condensed, and neatly aligned themselves for Isabel.

But nothing happened. No sound came through the speaker.

"It's not working." Jack's stomach churned. When was the last time he had eaten? The thought of food made him want to throw up. His headache was getting worse, too.

"I have to shift the wavelengths," she said. "Sit down and let me work."

Jack sat. Too much was riding on this circuit. If his data was just noise, then he was back at square one . . . with a head full of Chinese hardware. If the data was a setup, either planted by Bruner or someone else, then building the transceiver was at best useless, at worst a trap.

Either way he'd be stuck. DeMitri would prove that he colluded with Reno and swiped the isotope.

Isabel clapped her hands over the crystal. Wiggling purple lines appeared in the air, the spectrum produced by the isotope. She stretched them like taffy, pulled them until her arms were fully extended. They thinned; their colors shifted to blue to green to orange to deep red, then black. "Down to meter wavelengths."

Static hissed through the circuit's speaker.

They waited. Jack lit another cigarette . . . watched the smoke trail from its tip, stream, ripple, curl, and disintegrate into a haze. His stomach was on fire.

Isabel had another cup of tea. The speaker hissed, sputtered once, then returned to uninterrupted static.

It wasn't working.

Isabel set her teacup down, then whispered, "There is nothing there, Jack."

Nothing was the last nail in his coffin. Nothing was what Bruner could use at his board of inquiry to claim Jack's research had no merit and kill his shot at tenure. Nothing is what DeMitri would pick his mind apart looking for. Nothing is why Reno did brain surgery in his apartment. Nothing was why he had stolen from the Académe.

"It can't be nothing." He stood and crushed his cigarette. "Maybe we're supposed to talk first." He tapped the input key and spoke into the microphone: "Hello?"

Light flashed into the isotope from a bank of diodes, Jack's signal being transmitted through the crystal.

No reply.

Isabel looked at him, eyes big, feeling sorry for him like he'd lost his mind.

"Maybe the signal has to be multiplexed," Jack said, "like the original data." He took a pen and scrolled math in the air, sliced both outgoing and incoming signals to bits: infinite summations and ever-shrinking variables. Alone, each was indecipherable noise, together a message.

"Hello?" he said again into the microphone.

The intercom on Isabel's desk buzzed. They both jumped.

Then it spoke: "A Mr. al Qaseem is here to see you, Ms. Mirabeau."

Isabel punched the reply button. "Connect him, please."

Isabel's secretary opened the office door and Zero stepped through. He wasn't in the reception lounge; he stepped through from his office, from thin air. He wore a hard hat and overalls to blend with Isabel's office, but had his Babylonian sandals.

Zero squeezed Jack's shoulder and said, "I had wondered where you had gone. I am glad to see, my friend, that you are still well."

"So am I."

"Well," however, was a word with several meanings, one of which was a hole dug deep in the ground—which was where Jack was at the moment. He felt like he'd been punched in the gut and kicked in the head. It was a setup; he should have known. He sat down, started to light another cigarette, then decided he didn't want it.

The speaker crackled—Jack's heart skipped a beat—then it continued to hiss static.

Zero pulled out a chair, sat, raised an eyebrow at the simulated circuit, then asked, "What has happened? There is no joy in your eyes. And Isabel, your factory is idle." His gaze drifted across the drafting table. "You two have been busy in my absence."

Jack told him what had happened.

Isabel poured Zero a cup of tea, but he didn't drink it. He sat on the edge of his seat and listened to every word, especially the parts about the Chinese spy in his bubble and Jack's theory of repeater stations on campus.

He took a sip of his tea, then said, "I accept your story."

Isabel turned to him. "I can't believe you're agreeing with him."

"There is no protocol log of Jack's departure from my bubble," Zero replied. "Somehow he bypassed the system."

"That could be why the guy with the gun couldn't find me

52

using the repeater stations' signatures," Jack said. "I'm in the system, but hidden."

"A ghost in the machine," Zero whispered.

"Jack is here now," Isabel insisted, "interfaced with my office."

"Perhaps," Zero said, "he is selectively bypassing security measures that we are unaware of."

"Be rational," she said. On the factory floor, boiling metal overflowed and splattered across the ceramic molds on the assembly line. A dozen fires started. "I know if Jack put his mind to it, he could break any code, even bubble protocols. He needs help. Professional help."

"Professional help?" Jack said. "Like a psychologist? What about my broadcasting outside the bubble? Those students who couldn't see me?"

"Ah," Zero said and stood, "there is that. Have you examined Jack?"

"No," Isabel said, "I didn't think—"

"May I have permission to link to my bubble's diagnostic shell? I still have the subroutine running that examined our friend's implant."

"Of course," she said.

Two soap bubbles appeared, films of transparent rainbow floating in the air, one by Isabel, one by Zero. With a finger, Zero pushed his bubble toward Isabel; she gently blew hers to him. They met, distorted into two hemispheres, a flat membrane between them, then they joined into a single sphere.

"We're linked," she said.

"Excellent." Zero then whispered to Jack, "Be at ease. It will be quicker than the last time."

Jack tried to relax. Pressure built in his head. Too much had gone wrong. He listened to the noise hissing through the speaker—just lousy noise.

Zero examined Isabel's piles of blueprints, picked through the rolls, then took one and spread it on her desk. An outline of

Jack's head was drawn on it, white lines on navy blue. In the corner box scrolled: JACK POTTER, SCAN XVI.

"Here is your normal implant," Zero said, pointing to lines and branches that spread through Jack's brain like tiny hair roots. "Rather poorly designed. It leaks at several frequencies."

The speaker clicked. Jack leaned forward, waited for more.

Isabel set her hands on his shoulders. "It's just static, Jack." She then said to Zero, "Of course they leak. They have to be sensitive enough to interface with the bubble. It's a trade-off."

"Is it?" Jack said. "Or were they designed that way? We can come and go at the Académe, but who wants to leave when it means a head full of pain? Our implants make us prisoners."

Details filled the blueprint: curls and convolutions of Jack's gray matter; his new implant, slim silver lines, and the shape-shifting broadcast unit. Dots appeared, black spots that expanded like they were burning the paper.

"Nerve dysfunction," Zero said, running his fingers over the map of Jack's mind, picking up the blue ink. "Massive ionic imbalance in these neurons, and protocancerous residues." He touched the blackened regions. "Necrotic tissue."

He looked at Jack with his clear dark eyes. "You cannot broadcast again, my friend. Without knowing how to properly attenuate the signal, it could kill you."

Three more clicks came through the speaker. Jack forgot his burned brain and turned the volume to maximum. Static, smooth endless white noise filled the bubble. Five more clicks, then seven.

Prime numbers.

What would be the right response? More primes? Too long. He guessed and keyed the microphone once, four times, nine, sixteen.

Another click came in response through the speaker.

"Jack, please," Isabel said. "It's interference from Zero's scan."

He spoke into the microphone, "Hello? . . . Hello?"

Static ceased.

The speaker crackled: "Hello?"

4

JACK OF SPADES

"Hello?" Jack said. "Who is this?"

"Hello? Who . . . is this?" The voice sounded like it was coming from the end of a pipe.

"The bubble must be bouncing the signal." Isabel reached for the volume knob on the speaker. "It's just an echo."

He pushed her hand away. "Jack," he said into the microphone. "My name is Jack."

"Jack," the voice replied. "Jack be nimble. Jack be quick. Jack and Jill. Jack-in-the-box. Jack-o'-lantern. Jack Frost. Jackhammer. Jackrabbit. Jackass. Jack. Yes, Jack makes sense. You may call me Wheeler."

Jack gripped the microphone with both hands. The circuit worked. Someone had sent a message and hidden it in the noise.

"It can't be," Isabel whispered. She half-sat, half-fell into her chair. On the factory floor, conveyer belts snapped, and the assembly line came to a grinding, screeching halt.

Jack took three deep breaths, lit another cigarette, tried to stop shaking, then keyed the microphone. "How are we communicating, Wheeler?"

"A fine first question." Wheeler had the voice of an older man and no accent. He articulated each word. "You can tell much from a person's first question. It is our custom to always answer the first question.

"We communicate through the isotope. There is a balance of forces that binds and unbinds its nuclear core, and between these forces, a crack in your perceived curved space. Through this crack in space, our signals travel, bypassing an otherwise vast distance."

Jack glanced at Isabel to see if that made sense to her.

She held a notepad in her right hand. Mathematical equations scrolled across it, overflowed, spilled upon the table, then dribbled onto the floor, shattering like delicate china figures. Floating by her left hand was an open window to the physics archives. Inside were wiggling sub-Feynman diagrams and vibrating crystal lattices. She spared Jack a glance: the reflection of a single candle burned in her eyes, a flicker of understanding.

"I see," Jack lied. "Why hide the instructions? How did you broadcast so many signals disguised as natural noise? Where are you?"

Wheeler sighed. "I suppose you will ask an endless barrage of questions? I will allow you three, then we must proceed. 'Why' is for trade. 'How' is proprietary information. 'Where' is the brightest star approximately thirty parsecs from your location."

Jack stopped breathing.

Another star? The original pattern was a composite of pulsar emissions, microvariations in Big Bang background radiation, the spectra of nebulas, and a thousand other sources of cosmic static—signals in the stars—with only two explanations. Either his data was rigged, tampered with from the beginning . . . or it was real, and Wheeler was talking across a link that spanned light-years. He wasn't sure which he wanted to believe. The conspiracy theory sounded more plausible than aliens. He'd need proof either way.

"Jack? Are you there?" Wheeler asked.

Zero and Isabel whispered to each other, then Zero unrolled a blueprint, and together they linked to the astronomy database; stars resolved on the paper, globular clusters, and the gossamer ghost tails of swarming comets leaked into the air and mixed with the lavender smoke trailing from the tip of Jack's cigarette.

"I'm here," he said.

"This is a fantastic claim, I realize. We have monitored your radio transmissions. That is how I know your language. You are American, correct?"

"You seem to know everything about me. How do I know *you* are who and what you claim to be?"

"An excellent move!" Wheeler cried. There was a crackling pop, then: "I am delighted with your caution. It is a sign of intelligence. I also require proof that you, Jack, are who and what you claim to be."

Jack started to ask why, but Wheeler cut him off. "We will cease communications on this unsecured channel. I will send an encryption key. It will not be *the* key, mind you, but only *a* key. This puzzle is designed so that only a native of Earth may unravel it. You have twelve hours to take this test. Take longer to solve our enigma, and I must assume you are either not from Earth or that you lack the knowledge to do business with us at this time."

"Not from Earth? Where else would I be from?"

"No more questions," he said. "No more answers."

A piercing tone wavered through the speaker, neither jarringly high, nor deep and low, but a dissonant electronic note that filled the bubble for ten seconds—then it stopped.

"Hello?" Jack said.

Static washed through the speaker.

Zero looked up from the blueprint of stars. "That was a clue?"

Jack ran the isotopic light through the computer, pulled the signal apart, and tried to reassemble it. The spectrum wasn't coherent, but not quite random, either. Wheeler's channel was scrambled.

Jack used the dissonant tone as a key to decrypt the noise; he tried fast elliptical integral deconstructions, then continuous-chaos algorithms.

Nothing worked.

Like Wheeler had said, the tone was a key . . . but not the key to solve this. Jack had to find out what *the* key was.

Jack keyed the microphone again. "Hello? Wheeler?" He had to be listening. Why the secrecy?

"It must be a trick," Isabel said and sat next to him. "Could it be Bruner?"

"When we talked a few days ago, he didn't know anything. And I don't think he's that good a liar."

"What about the Chinese?" she asked.

"Why would they want to play games with me?"

"They proposed a trade of information. Maybe they want you to leak information to their side."

"As you pointed out," Zero said to her. "If they can engineer Jack's implant, they have no need for our technology."

Jack had almost forgotten about the Chinese, their implant, and his office getting tossed. How did they connect? Panda had led him to the isotope, so they had to know something about his research. And how did the alien signal fit into the puzzle? All he had were questions, a stomach full of churning anxiety, and no answers.

He grabbed the pack of cigarettes off the table, tapped one out, lit it for Isabel, then handed it to her. When she reached for it, they stared into one another's eyes.

She wasn't filtering. Neither was Jack.

Her eyes had olive rims, and within those, rings of brilliant bottle green that darkened in their centers to dark seawater, then bottomless black. Jack's eyes reflected in hers, and they sank deeper into one another. Their feelings mingled. They were both scared. She was afraid for him, frightened that things she had always believed were the truth—suddenly weren't. Jack was scared because he had a headful of hardware cooking his brains. He worried that everything he had experienced was a hallucination.

But deeper, in both of them, was a seed of excitement. They had a puzzle to solve, a mystery to unravel, and maybe, if everything worked out, the biggest discovery since man started playing with fire.

Isabel blinked and pulled away.

It was an abrupt sever that left Jack dizzy with the backwash of her thoughts: annoyance, worry, a swirl of intrigue.

Isabel said, "I can't believe this Wheeler is what he claims to be."

"What did you and Zero find in the astronomy database?"

Zero reached through the blueprint paper and pulled out a glowing orb the size of a peach pit. He let the white ball of fire float in the air. "Canopus," he said. "It is the 'bright star' thirty parsecs from Earth that Wheeler refers to. It takes our broadcasts approximately one hundred years to reach this system, so their latest human information originates from the mid-twentieth century."

"That would explain why the electronics were designed with hundred-year-old technology," Jack said.

Isabel stood and poked the tiny sun. It popped like a balloon, spewing gas and sparkling dust. "On the other hand," she said, "Canopus is an F-type supergiant, two thousand times as luminous as Sol. Any habitable planets it might have had were consumed when it entered its giant phase."

"Planets," Jack said, "that could support life *like ours*."

"Yes," she admitted, "life like ours. He sounded human, though. And I don't understand why his behavior verged on paranoid."

"Perhaps," Zero said and tugged on his beard, "it is because we are not their first contact. Wheeler said it was his custom to answer first questions, indicating that he had answered other first questions before. There may be civilizations that Wheeler has reason to be cautious of."

"Like us worrying about China?" Jack said. "If that's the deal, we might be getting into the middle of something tricky."

"There's one last possibility," Isabel whispered. "You bypassed Zero's security protocols. You also said you projected images, conscious and subconscious, to these alleged repeater stations on campus. . . . You could have made this up."

Jack took one last drag, then flicked his cigarette away. "You mean my Chinese implant took control of your bubble? That this was a projected dream?"

"More like classic wish fulfillment," she said.

Zero nodded. "It does fit the pattern of facts."

Jack had to admit, grudgingly, that she made sense. There was no pain, though. When he had used the implant before, it got hot and felt like someone was practicing acupuncture with rusty nails on his head. But he was inside a bubble now. If he controlled its functions, then he could screen what he felt—including pain. Jack might be using the implant without knowing. That made it doubly dangerous.

"So it's a possibility," he said. "We won't know for sure unless we find Wheeler's encryption key, contact him again, then have him prove to us he's what he claims to be."

"If you are projecting with that implant," Isabel said and paced between Jack and Zero, then went back to Jack, "you're risking your life to find out."

"It's worth it. What if Wheeler is from Canopus? What if we establish a partnership with his civilization? We'll have a chance to exchange technologies and cultures. The payoff is exponential compared to the risk. I'm willing to take it. What about you Zero?"

The gene witch frowned and rolled up his blueprint star map. "I too worry about your implant," he said, "but as you point out, the potential rewards are staggering. If you are willing to venture the hazards, my friend, I will stand by your side."

"Isabel?"

"I don't know, Jack. Too many things have happened, too fast. I need to think."

"Well, think about this. If I found this signal, it's only a matter of time before the Chinese find it, too. They may have already. And if they're the ones who broke into my office, they may know more about the pattern in the noise than anyone realizes. If they contact Wheeler before we do, if they start exchanging technologies, their scientific lead on us will take a quantum jump. It could be the end of our country."

She mulled it over, exhaled smoke, and avoided looking into his eyes.

"And while I'm thinking about my office . . ." Jack removed the envelope he had stuffed in his pocket two days ago and handled the wrinkled plastic to Zero.

Zero opened it, careful not to touch the inside. "What is it?"

"Blood I scraped off my office floor. Can you find out whose it is?"

"I cannot guarantee a genetic extrapolation will reconstruct accurate facial features."

"Try. I'd like to know who did this to me." Jack would like to know so maybe he could spill a little more of their blood. And maybe get some answers in the process.

Isabel finished her cigarette and set it in the ashtray without crushing it. "All right," she whispered. "Count me in."

Jack wanted to tell her how much he appreciated her throwing in with him. Instead, he squeezed her hand and said, "Thanks. Where do we start?"

Isabel went to her filing cabinets and pulled one open. "If Wheeler only knows us based on hundred-year-old information, his key must date from that period. I'll link us to the history archives: World War II through the Cold War. That's a lot of ground to cover."

The factory floor shifted. Rifles, tank treads, and bomber fuselages rolled down the assembly line, riveted, welded, then loaded with ammunition.

"He used the word 'enigma,' " Jack said. "That was the name of an encrypting machine the Nazis had. I studied it as an undergraduate. Isabel, let me link to my office and my notes."

"Feel free," she said.

"This machine," Zero said, "it used musical tones to decode messages?"

"No. Words or numbers or combinations of words and numbers. Individual notes might work, too."

Jack grabbed a fountain pen, drew a wobbly square on the blueprint of his head, then linked to the notes in his office. The fresh India ink thickened and cast shadows. Inside the lines, scattered jigsaw puzzle pieces appeared. All the information was there; he just had to put it together. Jack found a corner and a piece of the edge that fit it.

Pictures resolved upon the two linked pieces: a secret British team of scholars, code-named Ultra, cracked the Nazi code; a diagram of the machine, gears, and wires; and the algorithm used to scramble the message. It was easy.

But it didn't explain how Wheeler's tone unscrambled his incoming signal. Jack remembered that tone, that wavering wailing noise. Something about the war and nuclear weapons.

He fit three more pieces to the corner of the puzzle. The enigma machine was just the start. There were dozens of descendant schemes to make codes, trapdoor algorithms, and DES encryption from the Cold War era. He'd need to search in the history archives.

Pieces of the jigsaw jumped by themselves. A face formed from jumbled fragments. A face Jack recognized: DeMitri's.

"Welcome back to the Academé, Jack." The pieces moved when DeMitri spoke, distorted into a grin, then relaxed. "I've been waiting for you."

Jack's first instinct was to scatter the puzzle and break the link. But DeMitri had tapped the connection and already knew where he was. He'd been stupid to think they wouldn't bug his files. "What do you want?" Jack asked.

"Another interview. I require your physical presence in my office. I'll send an escort."

DeMitri leaned against the railing of the ferry. He gazed at a clipboard, holding it steady, while the rest of his body rocked back and forth to match the motion of the waves.

"Where are you taking me?" Jack asked.

"You tell me," DeMitri said, ran his hand through his black hair, and looked up. "It's my bubble, but we're accessing your subconscious."

That explained the water: leaking through the deck, the wool-thick fog, and the rolling, nauseating sea.

Jack didn't buy that this was a tour of his repressed thoughts, though. It was always games and psychoanalysis with the NSO. Why wouldn't DeMitri just ask his questions and get it over with? Why the theatrics?

And while they were here, playing cat and mouse in his mind, would the NSO search Isabel's files? Find the isotope? Maybe arrest her and Zero?

Jack grabbed the railing and leaned closer to the ocean. Salt-water sprayed his face. The fog broke in patches and starlight filtered through. On his left, a ghostly Golden Gate Bridge floated above the mist. He glanced sideways and got a look at what DeMitri was reading: Jack's dossier.

He saw his name upside down, blinked, and it appeared right side up. There were paragraphs of typed information, charts, pictures—that became clearer the longer Jack stared at them. De-Mitri hadn't noticed. It was like the repeater stations in the particle physics lab. The more Jack concentrated, the more data flowed to him.

This was an NSO bubble, though. He shouldn't be able to interface . . . unless it was a trick; that, or the Chinese implant was a decade ahead of the most sophisticated American electronics—even the top secret equipment used by the NSO.

Needle pinpricks flushed under his scalp. How many brain cells was this killing?

The implant received more information as DeMitri read. There were grades from kindergarten through graduate school (a C-minus in ballroom dancing stood out among a row of solid A's), links to the classified files of his parents, and the top secret file on Reno. There were lists of friends, acquaintances, and enemies.

Jack focused on Isabel's and Zero's names, pushed them from the list of friends into the column of his professional acquaintances. Data moved aside to make room. Words broke midsentence, and letters and numbers transposed; the document's autocorrect mended the type.

Sparks swarmed in his vision. The implant was hot. A migraine swelled in his skull and burst. Jack clutched the railing—threw up into the ocean.

"Don't get sick." DeMitri tossed aside the clipboard. "That won't do, yet."

Had he seen the changes?

DeMitri set his hand on Jack's shoulder. Jack flinched.

"Look," DeMitri said. "We've arrived."

There were lights ahead, blurred in the fog, flashes that circled in the air, spun, then shot into the sky like fireworks. The illuminated skeleton of a Ferris wheel appeared. Calliope music, the roar of wheels on roller-coaster track, screams, laughter, and a faint smell of popcorn mixed with the salted air.

The ferry bumped against a dock. A gangplank was lowered.

"Alcatraz Island!" the captain shouted. "All ashore that're going ashore."

"That's us," DeMitri said.

Alcatraz wasn't part of Jack's subconscious. Was it guilt over stealing the isotope? No. DeMitri had to be setting him up for something. Jack could run, use the new implant to dissolve the illusions of this bubble and escape. But then what? DeMitri would be onto him in an instant. And if Jack pushed his luck with this implant, it might cause a stroke.

Jack's migraine faded to a throbbing headache as he stepped off the boat. The island seemed to be rocking as much as the ferry.

DeMitri walked up the cobblestone sidewalk to a building shaped like a clown's head and a neon sign that said: TICKETS. "Two, please," he said to the girl behind the window. He turned to Jack. "When did you get back to the Académe?"

If the NSO had been waiting for him, monitoring the Academé's system, then Jack must have surprised them popping into his office from nowhere. Zero had called him a ghost in the machine. Figuring out that trick had to be high on DeMitri's list of questions.

"Not long ago," Jack said.

He pushed through the turnstile, stepped into the mouth of the clown, and emerged on the midway. There were cotton candy vendors, spinning sugar into pink strands, barbecued corn on a stick, Italian sodas, and cardboard buckets of red-hot chicken wings. Hucksters shouted at the tourists, begged them to play their games: balloons and rigged darts, the ring toss, basketball free throws that were anything but free, and sharpshooting. There was a Ferris wheel, a merry-go-round with wild horses, the parachute drop, contraptions that whipped around at dizzying speeds, keeping their victims pinned with centripetal acceleration . . . and on the hilltop, the largest building on the island, with luminous ghosts painted on its walls, skeletal hands that pointed to its entrance, screams and shrieks and wails from inside—the funhouse.

DeMitri halted at the sharpshooting stall, picked up a rifle, and shot out the eyes of a rabbit, killed three tin outlaws, and blasted a line of silver stars. The operator frowned and handed him a box of Mariposa cigars. DeMitri offered one to Jack. He declined.

"What did you do while you were on the mainland?" DeMitri asked.

"I stayed indoors, helmet on my head, and tried to keep out of trouble."

"That's something new for you." DeMitri lit a cigar. "I'm glad to hear it." He handed Jack a rifle. "Care to test your luck?"

"I'm haven't been lucky at games lately."

"We can still have fun," DeMitri said. A smile flickered on his lips, then vanished as quick as it had come. He marched away from the midway, up the hill, and Jack followed.

The funhouse looked like it had been the original Alcatraz cell block. Its walls were topped with razor wire, and the whole structure was solid, gloomy, gray concrete. Clowns chased each other on the roof, threw water balloons, and tossed their midget counterparts into the ocean for chuckles. Shadows moved along the side of the building, and inside, silhouettes of clawed hands slithered past the barred windows.

A hooded executioner stood at the entrance. DeMitri gave him the tickets. "Come on, Jack," he said. "You're not scared, are you?"

He was. He didn't know what DeMitri had planned, but he had a feeling it wouldn't be tarot poker. Jack had to stay cool and wait for a chance. To do what? Last time, he had thought he was smart enough to beat DeMitri and his mind probe. He wasn't.

The fog thickened. It drizzled.

The executioner parted the black curtains for Jack, and he entered.

Red spotlights played across the stone walls and checkerboard floor. There were three paths that led deeper into the place. One was a treadmill that moved sideways. You had to walk at an angle to stay straight. The second path zigzagged through a maze of glass and mirrors. And the last was a walkway swallowed by the shadows.

DeMitri in the red light looked like he was covered in blood. "We know Dr. Bruner is heading an investigation into your office break-in. He has planted evidence to implicate you."

"Tell me something I don't know."

DeMitri was trying to distract him. Each path was a metaphor . . . for what? The maze of mirrors was out. The last thing Jack needed was to confront a copy of himself. His equilibrium wasn't up for the treadmill floor. That left the path into darkness.

Jack blundered forward, hands held out before him. There were no walls—no floor, either—for a moment he fell through space, touched nothing, then his fingertip brushed a wall. He ran his hand along it, found a corner, and went around.

A blast of air exploded underneath Jack and left him shaking, his heart thundering.

DeMitri laughed. "The NSO can help you with Bruner. But first you have to help us."

Jack touched a curtain, pushed through, and emerged in a long corridor, three stories high, and on each level, a floor of barred cells. Overhead, skylights of cracked glass let the moonlight filter in.

"You want me to help you? How?"

"You can begin," DeMitri said, "by telling me what happened to you today."

"Just the usual things," Jack replied. DeMitri was fishing. Jack had to be careful and skirt the edge of the truth. Any lie would be detected by the bubble.

Down the hall, bars rattled. It was a nice touch. Cold churned in Jack's stomach, diffused down his legs and up his spine. It was synthetic fear generated by the bubble. He fought it.

DeMitri took a set of keys from his pocket, picked one out, then opened a cell door. Inside, it was two by three meters, no window, and the toilet was jammed against a single bed. It stank.

"Alcatraz"—he spread his arms in a grand gesture—"is a reflection of what's on your mind, Jack. Feeling guilty about something?"

"Everyone's got something to feel guilty about."

DeMitri nodded to the open cell. "That one is yours. Go on in. Or would you like me to call the guards?"

DeMitri wanted to *make* him go in, let him know who was in charge. Jack walked in and sat on the bed: sharp rocks under a wool blanket.

"There was another break-in at the Académe today."

"Oh?" Jack fished Isabel's pack of cigarettes from his pocket, lit one, drew in, and blew smoke at DeMitri. The amphetamines gave him a rush of confidence. "You think it has something to do with my office getting tossed?"

"I want you to tell me what you know about it."

A direct question? DeMitri must be playing a new game. It would be impossible to slide around the truth now. Or would it?

The truth, Jack thought. Everything I say is true.

The implant made hot gooseflesh spread across his scalp. It might turn him into a vegetable, but if DeMitri found out he was the one in the lab, stealing, playing tag with an NSO agent, he'd go looking for the isotope, maybe interrogate Zero and Isabel, and while he was at it, dissect Jack's head for Reno's hardware.

Jack took another drag, then: "I don't know a thing."

DeMitri stood there a moment, looking him over, thinking, then he slammed the cell door. It locked by itself. "I believe you, Jack." He paced in a circle, examined the keys he held, then said, "But you must understand I have an important job to do. It's nothing personal . . . I have to make certain. Too many vectors connect you to crime. You may know something without realizing it. I'm going to have to take everything out of your mind this time."

DeMitri tossed the keys down the corridor. They slid into a drainage grate and clattered through. "You will, of course, stay as long as it takes. We'll distort your sense of time. Every minute can be an hour or day—so we can go slow, examine every memory. Maybe we should start in solitary confinement? Or the hospital ward?"

"I told you I don't know about this other break-in."

"I know what you *said*." DeMitri turned and walked away.

"No!" Jack leapt and reached through the bars. He had to get out of here.

DeMitri paused, turned slowly, and that flickering smile returned to his lips.

Jack lunged. DeMitri was three body lengths away; he couldn't reach him.

The prison vanished.

Jack glimpsed smooth bubble walls. DeMitri stood an arm's length away from him, still smiling. Command lines of magnetic flux bounced off DeMitri's head; Jack's implant made the normally invisible fields look neon red. They were DeMitri's connection to his office, how he controlled it—and Jack.

Jack blinked and was back on Alcatraz.

The lines of light were still there, though, touching DeMitri's head, reading his thoughts, laser lines that vibrated. They drifted closer.

Jack reached for them   . almost, but still a hair's breadth away.

"Stop struggling." DeMitri took a step closer. "There will be ample opportunity for that later. You still have to meet the other prisoners. The guards, too."

Jack touched a line. It was unexpectedly hot, and he let it slip; it drifted away, then back. One last lunge—Jack's shoulder slammed into the bars.

He grabbed it.

The command line burned his fingers and sent a charge through his arm, up his neck, and into his mind.

Jack pulled it into the cell with him. His eyes burned and his vision blurred. It wasn't one line, but a tangle of small lines, knotted with security protocols. It hurt to hold on to it. He unraveled them like snarled yarn.

"What are you doing, Jack?"

Jack linked to the command structure, surround by lines of light and pulses of binary streams, logic circuits, and array processors that sparkled like distant galaxies. DeMitri's command lines were red and pulsing and rising upward, each of them encoded, scrambled, and resonating with his digital signature. That's how the bubble identified DeMitri and accepted his commands. Jack followed them up, through shooting stars and motes of glittering dust, to a central array processor, a brilliant-cut diamond the size of his fist. It accepted, reflected, and refracted DeMitri's commands, making the stone glow like a ruby.

Unscrambling his encrypting signature was a waste of time. There were countermeasures to detect that kind of blatant tampering. But what if Jack *added* a layer of instructions? Inserted them into the already running program?

His eyes seared lines of code into the diamond, blasts of heat that melted the stone:

```
DEMITRI = JACK; JACK = NULL;
```

Lines of light switched, doubled back on themselves; interference patterns scattered and filled the bubble.

Jack was curled up on the floor, black-and-white checkerboard tiles under him, cool vinyl. He was still in DeMitri's world, but outside the cell. The left side of his head was swollen and numb. The right side of his head was full of stabbing ice picks.

He looked up—couldn't see out of his left eye. DeMitri had taken his place in the cell.

Jack stood slowly.

DeMitri grabbed the bars, shook them. "What did you do?"

"Do? Nothing. It looks like there's a malfunction in your bubble, though. If I had to guess, I'd say it thinks you're me." Jack gave him a moment to think about that, then: "I hope whatever you had planned isn't too much . . . fun."

DeMitri reached inside his pocket—realized he had thrown the keys away, then cried, "Jack! Log out. Get help. For God's sake."

"No."

Jack turned away. A little torture, a little brainwashing, whatever DeMitri was going to do to Jack, he'd get in spades. Maybe he'd tell all his dirty national secrets to himself. Jack stumbled down the corridor, through the path of darkness.

Behind him DeMitri screamed, and there was the maniacal laughter of clowns—both drowned out by the sound of a pneumatic drill.

Jack ran out of the funhouse, through the midway, ignoring the games, the greasy food, back to the pier, and jumped onto the boat as it was casting off.

He collapsed on the deck, dizzy, black stars swimming in his vision; there was the vibration and roar of the ferry's engines. It was the first time Jack was happy to feel the rolling ocean waves of his subconscious mind.

5

ONE-EYED JACKS ARE WILD

Three hundred hertz banshees screamed through Jack's skull accompanied by pounding bass drums from a stray transmission of Copland's *Fanfare for the Common Man*. A burning itch wriggled under his skin. Noise.

Jack cracked his eyes—regretted it as light and pain streamed through. He got a good look at a corrugated aluminum floor, cigarette butts, and a pair of feet slipped into teal sandals that laced up tanned calves.

He couldn't see out his left eye. He rubbed it. Blinked—but that didn't help. Another blink. It wasn't even blurry . . . just black and blank. He stared into the void, then dark red pinpricks appeared, fire roiled in his mind. Anger boiled over.

Reno's implant had damaged Jack's occipital lobe. Reno with one eye brown and one blue. It finally made sense to Jack—one of those eyes wasn't his, a transplant or artificial. Reno's lousy advanced Chinese electronics had done the same thing to him.

Jack would kill the bastard if he ever got his hands on him.

. . . Still, Reno's unstable implant had let him hack the NSO's operating system and got him out of DeMitri's world. The eye could be replaced or cloned. He'd have to find a doctor who wouldn't ask questions.

Jack's head rested in a silk-skirted lap connected to those sandals and tanned calves. Isabel's.

She put her hand on his forehead and said, "You're awake." She looked into his eyes, but there was no contact.

He sat up.

That was a mistake. Light chiseled through Jack's good eye, golden reflections from the choppy ocean. They were in a taxi, skimming along the one-rail. The meter said they were twenty kilometers and 150 bucks away from Santa Sierra. Zero was up front, and the driver was a guy—not Panda with the butterfly eyes.

"What happened?"

Zero turned, looked at the driver, then shook his head, letting Jack know it would be a good idea to shut up.

Jack remembered slipping past the log-out protocols of DeMitri's office, running across campus to Isabel and Zero. If they had left the Académe, then the NSO wouldn't be far behind. How long could DeMitri torture himself before someone found him?

"Don't you remember?" Isabel whispered. "Santa Sierra. That's where you asked us to take you."

A gray band buttressed the horizon, the city's seawall. The mainland sounded like a good idea to Jack—away from the Académe and its secret repeater stations.

"It is eight forty-five," Zero announced without turning around.

"Thanks for the update, but what I really need is—"

"Quarter to nine," Zero said cutting him off. "Practically noon."

Noon . . . time was important. Jack remembered: it was midnight when they talked to Wheeler. He had given them half a day to find the key to unscramble his signal. That left three hours.

Ahead was the repeater station, a slim tower, yellow laser diodes, and parabolic dish that looked like a giant dandelion. It tracked the taxi, blasted the noise away with an EM probe. Signature signals resonated from Isabel's and Zero's implants. Vehicle ID numbers flew up to the dish like a swarm of moths.

There wasn't a security sweep the last time Jack had left the Académe. Were they looking for him already? The probe passed over Jack and induced no signal—like he wasn't there.

The dish turned back to the city, and the noise rushed back in, swirls of static and chaos and in his peripheral vision the flicker of radar ghosts.

They crossed the seawall and glided into the city.

"Where to, buddy?" the driver asked Zero.

"Fairfax and Mosfet," Jack told him. He dug his wallet out, and the driver's eyes widened when he saw the old preconstructionist notes with portraits of presidents when there still were presidents. Jack folded them and handed the cash across the seat. "People will ask questions," he whispered to the driver. "They find out I was in your cab, there will be a lot more questions. Get me?"

The black market cash disappeared.

They dropped off the one-rail onto the street and decelerated. Fast-food joints flickered with neon, preparing for the lunchtime crowds of grease guzzlers. It was three hours after the second shift and everyone who had a job was off the street, except the express runners, skimming by on their blades. The rest of Santa Sierra's citizens kept to the alleys: prostitutes high on metafantasy, the unwashed unemployed scanning the chameleon billboards, and shark placement goons that found them jobs for a third of their wages.

"Mosfet and Fairfax," the driver said and pulled to the curb.

The doors opened. Static poured into the cab's shell, microwave network links that made Jack's teeth vibrate and enough sixty-cycle hum to shake his body apart.

73

He was ready for it and got out.

Isabel and Zero flinched like they'd been kicked in the head. "The helmets are in the back," Zero said. "I'll get them."

"Not here," Jack said and pulled three suitcases from the trunk. "It'll be more dangerous to wear them." Jack's clothes were wrinkled and he hadn't showered in two days. He fit into this part of town. But Isabel in her silk skirt, and Zero in his camel hair coat stuck out. In the financial district or the corporate block, it would have been OK to be from the Academé. It was a different story here. EM helmets would get them mugged.

"Let's go."

"How do you stand it?" Isabel asked with her teeth clenched. She slipped on a pair of harlequin sunglasses.

"You get used to it," Jack lied. "My apartment is shielded. It'll be better there."

He led them into Mosfet Alley, took a long look down the street before he stepped into the brick alcove of his building— saw no one. You had to be careful; gene swappers sometimes traveled in packs. He gave his password to the door, then ushered Isabel and Zero in.

Jack led them up three flights of stairs. They shuffled down to Apartment D. Jack opened the foamed steel door with a thought.

"Let me go in first," he said and dropped the suitcase.

The place was empty, only a pile of dirty dishes in the kitchen, a half-dozen pillows for furniture, a stack of books, and new stains on the hardwood floor where his skull had been cracked open . . . but no Reno. Culture dishes on the wall warmed; the bioluminescent colonies reflected their warning colors of gold and green and blue off the aluminum foil wallpaper.

It was a dump—proof of how different Jack was from Isabel and Zero. They'd been Academé born and raised. Isabel's parents were professors. Zero was from an Arabian oil clan, practically royalty. Jack had to fight his way up on the streets, cheat through the public school system, and hustle the lottery to get into the Academé. What would they think of this hole? What would they think of him?

The foamed alloy door hissed shut, cutting them off from the churning noise outside.

"Clever," Zero remarked as he inspected the aluminum foil. "I assume there is wire mesh beneath the floor to complete the Faraday cage?"

"Something like that."

Isabel went into the bathroom, rummaged through her bag, and downed a handful of pills. When she came out, she looked better. "What happened to you, Jack?" There was an edge to her voice. It was hard to tell what she was thinking without metaphorical clues.

"The NSO didn't find out anything. DeMitri is trapped in an interrogation routine he meant for me."

"How long?" Zero asked.

Jack shrugged. "And who knows what DeMitri will remember after he's done brainwashing himself. I got a look at my dossier, though. The NSO didn't have a record of this place, so it should be safe . . . for a while."

Zero sat on Jack's favorite blue pillow. "What else did your records show?"

"You and Isabel, but I fixed it so we're professional associates and nothing more."

"Fixed?" Isabel said. "You used the implant again? Are you crazy?"

"The NSO was about to dissect my mind to find out what I know. They'd do the same to you. I wasn't going to let that happen."

Zero leaned closer. "I appreciate your sacrifice, my friend." He stared at him a moment, then, "Your left eye no longer tracks. Is it functional?"

"It's fine." Jack looked away. He squeezed his eyes shut, pinched the bridge of his nose. It wasn't fine. Where would he find a doctor to quietly replace it? Nowhere. He'd have to let it heal by itself . . . or rot in his head. "It's fine," he repeated.

Nothing was fine. Jack was going to die: brain tumor, or an aneurysm, or get picked up by the NSO and be taken apart. He wanted to claw open his skull and scrape the implant out with his fingernails. "I just have a headache. I'll be OK. Isabel, did you bring the isotope?"

She sighed explosively. "Yes." She unsealed her suitcase with a swipe of her thumb and removed the isotope box, a notebook computer, and a slim silver cigarette case.

"While you were with DeMitri, irradiating your brain, I made this." She opened the silver case. Inside were optic microprocessors, a bank of LEDs, and a cluster of spectral fish-eye lenses. "We won't need a virtual mock-up. We can analyze Wheeler's signals anywhere." She unfolded the computer, let the display circuits warm and fill the air with start-up code, then plugged in the module.

"We? You two have to get back to the Académe. The NSO might be fooled once, but if they find you here, they won't ask questions before they take you apart."

"We're in this together," she said.

Zero nodded. "Indeed, my friend. You cannot get rid of us so easily." He yawned, got up and stretched, then asked, "Do you have any tea?"

"In the kitchen, there's a pot and a can of methane in the cabinet."

Jack looked at them both, wishing this was a bubble, wishing he had a clue as to what they were thinking, wishing he could use a clever metaphor to show them that he never wanted to drag them into this business, that he was scared, and that he was grateful for their company.

"Thanks," Jack said. "But it might be for nothing. We've only got three hours to find the key that unscrambles Wheeler's transmission. Figure out what he meant by the tone is *a* key, but not *the* key."

"It's not a single sound." Isabel brushed her hair out of her face and tapped a command into her computer. That wavering tone replayed through the speakers. "Look," she said and input another command. On the display, two smooth curves pulled apart.

"A two-tone signal?"

"I ran a filtered search through the history archives. Preconstructionist records are sketchy. There wasn't an exact match, but I did find something close, the International Warning System chime."

She punched up another sound file. A two-tone signal played. It was crisp and clear.

It was the warning for earthquake and tsunami. Jack had heard it a hundred times when he was a kid, and it gave him the creeps that Wheeler was using it as his calling card. Looking at the waveform on the display and listening to the two-tone chime, though, they weren't an exact match.

"Wheeler's information is supposed to be a hundred years old," Jack said. "He couldn't know about the warning chime."

Zero returned with three cups: one ceramic, one tin, and one paper. He poured the boiling water, then split a tea bag between the three cups. "Perhaps," he said, "you should try this two-tone chime. Discern whether it is the key that unlocks the transmission."

Isabel opened the isotope case, and, with a pair of tweezers, she transferred the blue crystal into the matrix of circuitry. Light flashed through its sapphire facets. A jumble of noise appeared on the display.

Jack used the chime as a decryption key, tried a continuously shifting waveform variation, then a modified enigma transformation. He used a dozen tricks to filter coherency from the static. Nothing.

"If it is the key, I don't understand how to use it. No. It wouldn't be that simple."

Jack punched up Wheeler's original tone and played it. The dissonance filled the apartment. It wasn't as smooth as the modern two-tone chime. Jack froze the sound, enlarged it on the display. Tiny spikes and valleys appeared.

"Is that noise?" Isabel asked.

Jack subtracted the smooth wave—left only the noise. He analyzed the entropy. Far too small to be random. He arranged the peaks and dips into ones and zeros, binary numbers, counted them. "Two hundred fifty-six," Jack whispered. "Two raised to the eighth power. Twentieth-century keys used in DES and RSA-type encryptions usually used power-of-two-length keys. This had to be *the* key Wheeler was taking about."

Jack unscrambled Wheeler's incoming transmission with the new key. Static.

"Why isn't it working?" Isabel asked.

"Let me check something." Jack called up an ASCII table on the display: BINARY CONVERSION. "The keys aren't required to be a code word or phrase, but they usually are. I'll translate. The letter t in ASCII is 1010100, with an extra bit added for parity . . ."

Two hundred and fifty-six bits ran across the display, filtered, shifted, and condensed into thirty-two characters. There was no code phrase, no words, or names. Random numbers and letters. Garbage.

Zero peered at the output. "It appears cryptic. Could Wheeler have encoded this as well?"

"That would make sense," Jack said, "because he said this two-tone signal was a key, but not the key. *The* key might be the one that unscrambles the one embedded in his two-tone—and that unscrambled might be the key to decrypt his transmission through the isotope."

"Assuming any of that is right," Isabel said, "then what un-scrambles this"—she pointed to the display—"mess?"

"Finding that out is going to be the trick."

"You're the cryptoanalyst. Can't you just break it?"

"It's 256 bits long. That's two to the power of 256 steps for a brute force calculation. There are shortcuts, but even if I risked accessing the Academé's networks to crunch through the problem, we've got"—Jack punched up a clock on the display—"a little over two hours. Not long enough."

"Wheeler wouldn't make it impossible, would he?" Isabel asked. "There has to be a way to find the key to the key." She frowned, chewed on a nail thinking, then snapped her fingers. "I need a link to the Académe's history database."

"I can take care of that." Jack tapped in the address for the public library system, then entered an old access code. While the system searched for the expired account, he suspended the protocol shell and entered the back door he had constructed when he was in public school. His credit to browse the system had run out while he had crammed for exams. He'd worked around that. You had to be smarter than the mainland school system to escape it.

He created an anonymous dummy shell, then logged into the Académe.

"We shouldn't be traced," he told her.

Isabel pushed him off the input pad. "We start with what we know. The International Warning System has a history." She typed, mistyped, erased, then tapped in the instructions again. "This is impossibly slow."

A dozen file windows opened, and Isabel scrolled through the text. "Before the IWS was established," she said, "it was solely a U.S. entity, a combination of the National Oceanographic and Atmospheric Agency and the Emergency Broadcast System."

Jack remembered the Emergency Broadcast System . . . something from when he had studied the Cold War and DES ciphers. He squinted with his one good eye, trying to read over her shoulder.

"Here." Jack crouched closer to the computer and opened the older archives of the EBS.

It warned of impending disasters: the earthquake that built the Anasack Mountains in Portland, the sinkhole plague in St. Louis, and the nuclear bomb in Oklahoma City. There was a sound file. Jack punched it up.

For the next 60 seconds, this station will conduct a test of the Emergency Broadcast System. This is only a test.

A dissonant two-tone signal blared through the computer's speakers. Not the pleasant warning chime. Wheeler's original signal.

"That's it," Zero said.

"It's something," Jack said. "Wheeler told us, 'You have twelve hours to take this test.' *Test*. 'This is only a test.' Let's see if that phrase unscrambles his two-tone key."

Jack ran a dozen parallel decryption algorithms. The bits in the two-tone signal jumped and flashed from zeros to ones and ones to zeros, jumbled into a new order. He tried each variation on Wheeler's incoming transmission.

Nothing. Static.

Jack glanced at the clock: two hours left.

"This might take some time."

Communication was a tricky thing—at best. At worst, it confused and trapped you in a web of sticky semantics. Without his office, Jack wasn't thinking straight, couldn't figure out what the clues meant. If he knew Wheeler, his culture, how he thought, then he'd have a chance to understand his trail of logic.

But Jack couldn't even figure out what Isabel was thinking. She had been quiet for the last hour since they discussed how to unscramble the incoming signal. She thought they had the wrong clue and wanted to get back into the history archives.

Jack grabbed his blue pillow, punched it twice. They had twenty minutes left.

He was out of ideas.

Isabel took over the computer. She had tied back her hair and had chewed three nails off. She coughed as she typed—that was from too many real cigarettes, instead of the illusions she chain-smoked in her bubble.

Jack couldn't think anymore. He went into the kitchen. Maybe Zero had an idea.

Zero's suitcase was in the center of the floor, empty, and assembled on the counter was a display that flashed progress reports on enzyme activities, matrix diagonalization, and data flow from a storage cube designated H. GENOME. In the sink was an incubator, organic honeycombs and coils of integrated life-forms that shifted restlessly—eyed Jack with single glassy orbs. He kept his distance.

Zero tapped on an input pad and a featureless face appeared on the display. "My bacterial engineers have organized the bits of DNA you gave me. We will see the results of their labor."

"The blood from my office?"

The blank face on the display changed: eyes opened, lips parted, ears appeared, and the jaw slimmed. "Asian, female," he explained. The vital statistics appeared: a meter and a half tall, forty kilograms. Her eyes were copper, hair indigo, and Jack recognized her. She was the slave in Zero's Babylon, the cab driver with the butterfly eyelids, the Chinese spy who led him to the isotope. Panda.

"Almost done," Zero said and tapped in a command. A window of base pair sequences popped up and within that another showing magnified bacterial engineers beating their cilia, herding bits of chopped protein. Zero scaled back the magnification; the clusters of bacteria and islands of proteins blurred into bands of light and dark. He asked Jack, "This is the woman who surreptitiously entered and left my bubble?"

"Yeah." No surprise the Chinese were connected to the break-in. But why blood on the floor? A fight? And if so, who was she fighting?

Jack scrutinized the bands of black DNA on the white display. Dark bars and empty spaces. The gene pattern was like the signal he had to unravel, a code. They were both patterns of information.

Those empty spaces were like the blankness between Jack and Isabel. Without the illusions of their bubbles, how could he ever share his feelings with her? Maybe he couldn't. Maybe there'd just be nothing . . . a silence that held more meaning than any metaphor.

Nothing that had meaning?

A pattern was information organized. Between the bits of data there was nothing, spaces—but that was part of the information, too. The space, the blank spots, had as much significance as the data. It was data.

"Just a second, Zero. I have to try something."

Isabel was deep into the history archives: animated statistics of the Soviet Cold War military marched across the display like red ants.

Jack reached for the input pad.

She pulled it away, then let go. Her shoulders slumped. "This is stupid, Jack. Whatever clue we were supposed to find—we didn't. We're not going to with ten minutes left."

Jack called up the ASCII table.

Isabel scooted closer. "We've tried ASCII."

"For the *letters* in the phrase 'This is only a test.' But other things can be encoded into ASCII binary, old computer instructions like line feed, return, backspace, and one I had completely ignored: the space."

Between every word in Wheeler's code phrase, Jack inserted the ASCII code for a space: 0100000. He then used the entire binary sequence as a decryption key.

The signal was still static.

Zero came in from the kitchen, wiping his hands on a towel.

"It was a good idea," Isabel said. She stared at the ASCII table. "Try this one." She pointed to the period character: 0101110.

Of course—a period at the end of the sentence. Jack tacked it on, ran the string of zeros and ones through a DES decryption algorithm.

Still nothing.

"Wait . . ." Jack counted.

T-H-I-S-space-I-S-space-A-space-T-E-S-T-period

That was fifteen characters. One more to make sixteen, two raised to the third power. A perfect length. One more character. Which one? Maybe *W* for Wheeler? *J* for Jack? Or . . .

At the end of the sequence, he typed in the null character. Old computer codes used null to terminate character strings. It was another type of emptiness, the way machines told each other to stop.

The display blanked while it crunched through the DES decryption, analyzing Wheeler's two-tone signal and the embedded static. The waveform appeared, shattered, then resolved as a string of binary, then filtered through the ACSII table.

Text scrolled across the display:

HELLOJACKJACKBENIMBLEJACKBEQUICK

The key was Wheeler's original greeting. Had he set this scheme up in the span of that first brief conversation? Jack admired the ingenuity, the speed, the intelligence to think this through. Jack was a little scared of it, too.

Jack programmed the code phrase as a continuous filter, set up the mathematics to unscramble Wheeler's incoming signal from the isotope. . . . He held his breath.

The static vanished.

"Hello? Jack? Hello, Jack? Hello? Jack? Hello, Jack?"

Jack grabbed the microphone. "This is Jack. Wheeler, are you receiving me?"

A moment of silence, then: "Jack, it is a pleasure to speak with you again. Your time had nearly expired."

Jack exhaled, then, "I don't understand this need for secrecy."

"It is the nature of our business," Wheeler said. "We trade information. Secret information creates value. No secrets, no value. You understand that, don't you?"

The only thing Jack was sure he understood was that Wheeler knew everything, and he knew nothing. A bad place to bargain from. "What kind of information did you have in mind?"

"A question to the point. I like that, Jack. Business first. No need to chatter on, I agree. We desire a sample of your technology. A gesture of goodwill. We will examine it and return an appropriate countergift. If the trade proceeds well, we can repeat the process indefinitely."

"Let me guess. You want me to send first."

"That is our custom."

What could Jack send? If this was an elaborate hoax, if a Chinese spy was at the other end of this signal, manipulating what he saw and heard through Reno's implant—then he had to offer a technology they already had.

Jack whispered, "Zero, grab me the data cube from your processor."

The gene witch nodded, hurried into the kitchen, then returned with the cube labeled H. GENOME.

"I'm going to send you a code, a puzzle." Jack inserted the cube into the computer's reader. He selected the genome, the basic biochemistry files that showed how the molecular machinery fit together, how it churned out proteins, and replicated.

It was the perfect data to send. If Wheeler was really from Canopus, then it would be new to him. But if it were Bruner or the Chinese, he wouldn't be giving them anything they didn't already have.

Jack sent the information. Light flashed through the facets of the isotope, compressed data on twenty-three chromosomes, the two hundred thousand genes in those chromosomes, and the three billion base pair building blocks. It was the biggest code anyone had ever cracked. What would Wheeler think of it?

"We shall require a moment to examine this," Wheeler said. "Can you hold?"

"What about your end of the deal? I thought—"

Static washed through the speaker.

Zero dragged his display and input pad into the living room and refined the features of the Chinese spy, Panda.

He stank. Jack had never noticed Zero's bad breath and body odor before. In a bubble, you looked, sounded, and smelled perfect. Out here, they were all a little too real.

Jack moved into the center of the room and stared at the receiver's display. A flat line. Not even encrypted static. Nothing for the last six hours.

Isabel had retreated into the corner, made herself a nest of pillows, read Steinbeck, and pretended Zero and Jack weren't there. This was after she had locked herself in the bathroom for a bit of privacy and a shower.

"How much longer are we going to wait?" she asked without looking up from *The Grapes of Wrath*.

"As long as it takes. You two can leave anytime you want."

"If it was dangerous in the city this morning," she said, "how bad is it now? What are you suggesting, Jack? Do you want us to go out there and get killed?"

He sighed. That wasn't what he meant. It was getting harder to speak to her without a bubble. "No. Sit tight. It's all we can do."

She threw the book at him and jumped to her feet. "How can you sit here, closed up, breathing the same stale air? I need space."

Isabel practically lived in her bubble, a space much smaller than this. They all did and never acknowledged that. Maybe Reno was right to wonder why the hell they did it. Jack laughed.

"You think it's funny?"

He got to his feet. "Hilarious."

"Sit down," Zero whispered. "Both of you. We are under pressure from the wait and the withdrawal from our virtual environments. It is demanding an enormous psychological toll on us."

"Maybe on you two," Jack said. "I can take it. I grew up out here."

"We know where you grew up," Isabel said. "You think it makes you better than us? Because you made it through the public school system, that somehow you're smarter or tougher than Zero and I? Get over your past, Jack. Your self-righteousness is getting to be a real pain in the ass."

He reached for the paperback she had thrown—to return the favor. Its spine was cracked, and that made Jack feel rotten. The first time he had picked up a real book was in Primary School 438, books about kids getting into trouble, solving mysteries, talking dogs, and magical lands hidden in the back of wardrobes. The schools were too cheap to maintain their com-links, so he

85

got stuck with books. At first, he had thought they were broken computers, their displays permanently frozen.

He set Steinbeck down.

"Jack? Hello? Hello, Jack." Wheeler's voice came through the speaker.

"I'm here."

Jack wanted to tell him that next time he got put on hold for six hours he'd . . . he'd what? Wheeler was in control. Their two contacts had been directed to setting up this trade in absolute secrecy. What was he hiding? There wasn't going to be any cultural exchange or embassies or politics. It would be only business. "OK," Jack said. "It's your turn."

"We have examined your biochemical equation. A fascinating piece of molecular engineering. The micromachinery, however, is slightly flawed and unusually susceptible to corruption."

Jack looked at Zero.

Zero furrowed his brows together and shook his head.

"Mind you, Jack," Wheeler said, "we are delighted to have it. It is fine workmanship." He paused, then, "We have a solution to the inelegant replication scheme and an algorithm to correct the numerous errors and unnecessary bits within the code. Are you interested?"

Zero took three steps closer. "Take it," he whispered.

Jack hesitated. It wasn't what he had in mind. He thought Wheeler might offer something exotic: time travel or faster-than-light propulsion . . . Then again, if Wheeler had any of that, he wouldn't need to, or want to, trade with Jack. Maybe they'd better start with something easy. A technology Zero could reverse-engineer.

"OK," Jack said, "send it." He slipped a backup data cube into Isabel's receiver.

Light flashed through the isotope, and letters crawled across the display: MET-HIS-LEU-ARG-ILE-TRP-CYS-LYS-PRO-ASP-GLY-VAL . . .

Zero whispered, "It is a protein, an extremely complex and

long sequence. Portions of it look similar to the RNA polymerase enzyme. The rest . . . " He shrugged.

The information stopped.

"Wheeler?"

"It has been a pleasure doing business with a fellow entrepreneur, Jack. We are very happy with the way our relationship is progressing. We must digest the information that we have traded. We may be in touch with you again . . . soon."

The connection went dead.

"Not a languid race," Zero remarked.

Isabel leaned over Jack's shoulder to get a better look. "This is a protein? RNA polymerase?"

"Parts of it appear similar to that enzyme," Zero said. "But it is much larger. I will have to return to the Académe to simulate the structure and determine how it will fold into a stable topology, then I may speculate on its function."

Maybe Wheeler really was an alien. Maybe Jack shouldn't have given him the genome. He didn't know anything about Wheeler, his race, his motives . . . and Wheeler suddenly had the potential to figure out everything the human race was. Jack didn't like that. And Jack liked even less not knowing what this protein was. A cure for cancer? Or a virus engineered to destroy the human race. It could be anything.

"Let me run a search through the biology database." Jack transferred from the history archives to the science gateway. "Maybe parts of this sequence will match."

The screen blanked.

"What the—"

"Good evening, Jack." Bruner's face appeared.

Jack hit the escape key, but nothing happened. He hit the privacy shield so Bruner wouldn't see where he was or who he was with.

"Is it the department's policy to tap their staff's lines?"

"An interesting pattern of dummy shells you left for me to follow," Bruner said. "A trail of breadcrumbs that leads to the public system, then vanishes. Smart, except you should have erased your school records before using the trick. Your grades increased, while your logged time in the public information net dropped to zero. That was sloppy."

"I've done nothing illegal."

He shrugged. "Nothing illegal, but you have turned out to be an embarrassment to the department. There are conclusive links that you have been colluding with subversive Chinese elements. Dean Roberts agrees with me and has deleted your name from the list of candidates for tenure."

"You can't do that. There has to be a board of inquiry and due process."

"The mathematics department *has* held a board of inquiry. You were summoned. I sent the query myself." A slight flicker of a smile rippled under his beard. "I even sent a messenger to hand-deliver the summons to you. I have your countersignature on file. Would you care to see it?"

"You bastard."

"I really would like to discuss this at length, but I've been awarded the summer lecture series at the Denver Institute of Technology. I have notes to prepare."

"Congratulations," Jack growled. "So get to the point. What do you want?"

Bruner's smile widened and his beard flared like a peacock tail. "I want you to consider my earlier proposition." His hand closed into a fist. "You have no options left. Trade the results of your research to me, and in exchange, I might persuade the board to hear your testimony."

He still wanted to deal. Good. That meant he didn't have the secret to unscramble the signals from the noise. He'd never get it if Jack had anything to do with it.

"Go to hell." Jack severed the connection.

Isabel set her hand on Jack's shoulder, gave him a squeeze. "I'm sorry," she whispered. "What are you going to do now?"

Jack had stumbled into this mess by trying to discredit Bruner's research. He thought he'd escape the system by getting that tenured position—but now he had something infinitely better—

something that would take him to the top of that money-grabbing, power-politics system.

"Do?" He punched up Wheeler's protein, a string of amino acids that was another code to crack. "I just went into business."

SECTION TWO

BUSINESS

6

JACK THE RIPPER

Jack knew Business. As a tenure-seeking associate professor he financed his research by soliciting corporations. In return for their money, he deciphered their competition's encrypted transactions. Not exactly legal, but Business operated by its own rules: protocols to stab your rivals in the back, laws to govern hostile takeovers, and policies to dictate who got terminated or promoted. It was a world of bottom lines.

Jack's bottom line: he was broke.

In the two days since they had talked to Wheeler, Isabel had set up a new computer in the corner of the apartment with a surround display and upgraded communications links. Zero had taken over the kitchen with appliances that were part alive, part biomech, and all expensive.

Jack had spent money, too, on four microdot motion detectors; he set one up outside the bathroom window, one on the apartment's reinforced door, one by the elevator, and one in the stairwell. And to be on the safe side, he had hustled a clip of armor-piercing, mercury-capsulated rounds for his Hautger SK semiautomatic. Reno had dropped the gun into the toilet tank after his last visit. His idea of a joke.

And there was nothing left for a new eye—not even a quick clone job. He blinked and rubbed it, but half his vision was still black and blank. He wanted to cover it up . . . or claw it out.

Jack disengaged the gun's clip, slipped it into his pocket, then set the gun under the blue pillow. He went to Isabel, careful not to trip over the tangle of soliton optics on the floor.

A flexcrystal display made a semicircle of flashing characters and winking windows around her. Biological data downloaded: protein sequences and molecular dynamic subroutines for Zero. There was a link to the history archives, scrolling facts on SETI, Majestic-12, Project Phoenix, and Blue Book. The rest of the windows were wallpapered with Corporate Control Office documentation and international patent applications.

"How's it going?" he asked her.

Isabel sat cross-legged and barefoot, datapads scattered around her. She had changed into blue coveralls and had a light pen stuck behind her ear.

"It's going slow," she said, her attention fixed on the displays. She saved the file, then looked at Jack with bloodshot eyes. "These applications from the Corporate Control Office want five-year research goals, product liability assessments, and toxicology studies." She sighed. "I'm making so much of this up, I feel like I'm spinning straw into gold."

"Can I help?"

"Not unless you convince Zero to talk to his parents."

Zero's clan had more money than most small countries, but he had refused to ask them for help. He said there would be too many strings attached. What he meant was that if they found out about Jack's ties to the NSO and the Chinese (imaginary or not), they would have retrieved Zero from such unscrupulous influences, made Jack disappear, and taken the enzyme—those kinds of strings.

"Let's work with what we have." He massaged her shoulders.

Once their CCO paperwork went through, they could incorporate, apply for loans, and guard the protein sequence with a quick-grant patent. The Free Market Amendment guaranteed protection from government interference. Jack hoped it would give him the legal room to outmaneuver the NSO.

"Let me know if I can help."

Isabel returned to typing, cursing under her breath.

Jack entered the kitchen. Interferometric microscanners imaged viruses replicating and bacterial engineers herding them into place. Temperature- and pressure-controlled vats held slime that frothed and smelled like fermented algae. The refrigerator lay on its side, and a honeycombed amino acid sequencer grew in its shell. The air was a thick blanket of warm fog.

Zero was watching a simulated DNA double helix uncoil on a display. Another macromolecule drifted close, a globular galaxy of black, red, blue, green, and white spheres. It had tentacles that intertwined around the double helix, teased its strands apart, then rippled along each, touching and probing—shifting shape as it crawled.

"What's it doing?"

Zero observed for a moment, then said, "Parts of this enzyme behave like RNA polymerase, reading the DNA, but it does not manufacture normal RNA, nor does it heed the termination codon at the end of a gene."

The enzyme paused and deformed.

"Watch," Zero said.

It severed the double strands of DNA; tendrils adhered to both broken segments, then continued to slither over a hundred base pairs, stopped, and made another cut. The enzyme released the center section and it twisted away.

"It edits," Zero said and tugged his beard.

The enzyme knitted the free ends of the truncated DNA . . . and moved down the strand, searching.

"Edits what?"

"Ancient traces of retroviruses, latent environmental triggers

95

our species no longer uses, erroneous base pairs within normal genes. It simplifies our genome." Zero took a teakettle off the stove and poured the boiling water into a coffee mug. "What overall effect it will have I cannot discern without a complete simulation and in vitro tests."

He turned to Jack. "It could be wonderful." Then he whispered, "It could be terrifying. I am unwilling to use Academé facilities. This must not fall into unethical hands."

Jack had a feeling that was going to cost more money.

"I require a network of computers. Portions of the sequence I can manufacture and test independently, but others will require outside, custom production. I have also not solved how we can introduce such a massive enzyme into bacterial host DNA sequences . . . let alone within humans."

"We're broke," Jack told him.

Zero altered the input file for the next simulation. "Is that not why we are incorporating? To find investors, obtain loans, and bypass FDA protocols for biohazardous materials?"

"How are we going to find investors without telling them what the enzyme does? Or where we got it from? I'm not entirely convinced this isn't a trick of the Chinese."

Zero shook his head. "This enzyme selectively removes genetic material among billions of base pairs and their vast combinations. I have tested several thousand sites, and it has yet to invalidate a single gene. If the Chinese had such technology, they would have no need to introduce it so covertly."

Jack's Chinese implant was a decade ahead of U.S. electronics. Why couldn't they have created this, too? His stomach twisted as he watched the simulated enzyme cut DNA. He wasn't sure of anything anymore, except that whatever this was, biological weapon, cure for the common cold, or red herring—Jack wasn't about to turn it over to the NSO or another corporation.

The enzyme was their ticket to success.

"We'll give it our best shot," Jack said. "How much cash are we talking about? And how soon before we know what it does?"

Zero grabbed a fistful of his beard and twisted its curls, thinking.

Isabel burst into the kitchen. "We've got a problem," she said. "The NSO put a hold on our corporate petition. They're onto us."

Jack was in eighth grade when he learned of the ancient city-states: Carthage and Alexandria, centers of trade on the Mediterranean, where money and people and power flowed—silk from China, emeralds from Scythia, Arabian perfume, and slaves from wherever they could be stolen.

The way he saw it, things today weren't much different.

There had always been centers of commerce—even before the world cracked—cities with cultural and trade alliances beyond political boundaries. The Pacific Rim had San Francisco, Taiwan, Seattle, Hong Kong, and Tokyo through which computer chips, biotechnology, and lines of international credit fluxed. The Gulf of Mexico had Bogotá, Houston, Miami, and Havana to traffic laundered money, oil, spices, and drugs.

The Earth's crust splintered and their influence grew.

While governments scrambled to rebuild, the cities of power absorbed wealth from their devastated sister cities. They made themselves into tiny empires, built walls of legislation, and blackmailed their parent governments to give them greater autonomy. Seattle, Chicago, Albuquerque, Geneva, the newly constructed Santa Sierra, and Darwin Tidal Station became part of a greater, global community, part owned by their federal governments and part city-empire run by corporate senates.

The great cities traded not by triremes across the sea, nor by camel caravans that spanned the vast deserts, but with low-orbit cargo shuttles, supertankers, and mag-lev freight convoys. Through them passed the riches of the world, a flood of scholars, luxuries from every corner of the globe . . . and slaves lured by contract work and lines of credit.

Business ruled the cities. The cities ruled the world. Everyone wanted a piece of the action in the cities and had their own hustle. Everyone wanted to be in business.

Corporations had their hustles, too. They made everything legal, streamlined the laws, and gave once-contraband a place on the commodities stock exchange . . . made it theirs. They created the Corporate Control Office to dominate new businesses, limit who and what entered the world market. Most importantly, the CCO protected them from what they feared most: competition.

New companies tended to get bought up or squeezed into dust while they waited for their CCO incorporation petition. You had to be tough, and persistent, and know every legal trick to survive.

For the ones that made it, the payoff was big. They got guaranteed loans and enormous tax loopholes to exploit. It happened every so often—a new microprocessor design; vitamin-enhanced, safe-smoke cigarettes; or an anticancer drug discovered in the jungle that transformed average guys like Jack into multibillionaires.

So the American Dream was still alive . . . alive and waiting to happen in every great city of the world.

"Too tight," Jack said. He started to pull the helmet off.

"It's as loose as I can make it," Isabel replied and pushed it back on. "We need the double layer of circuit film to enhance the response."

The modified Académe helmets, the ones that kept signals out, were now their only way into the system. Real bubbles would have cost a fortune. Isabel had lined the helmets with ultradense circuit film—like a miniature bubble. It would induce the proper currents inside Jack's head, let him see and hear and touch the world of ghosts.

She struggled to get her helmet on. "We won't have the response we're used to. Bubbles have a hundred times the surface area and circuit density, and better processors. There will be a perception delay."

Jack felt like a deep-sea diver: clumsy, claustrophobic, and about to sink into deep murky waters.

"Is this not counterproductive?" Zero asked. "Do we not wish to incorporate legally?"

"How legal is that?" Jack pointed to the CODE 11 flashing red across their CCO application. "Our paperwork halted for reasons of 'national security'? The NSO just wants to flush me out."

Zero helped Jack ease to the floor, propped his head up with a pillow. "If you and Isabel hack into the CCO, will not you do precisely as they desire?"

"I don't think we have a choice," Isabel whispered to him. She grabbed Jack's pillow. "The CCO will bury our application now that the NSO has it marked."

"We need protection," Jack said. "The NSO can still work in the shadows. They can grab me, you, Isabel, and the enzyme—with no messy corporate senate to ask questions."

Zero tapped in the commands to slave the processing power of their three computers. An interface window popped up, and he ran a test cycle, let sensations flood into Jack and Isabel's helmets: peppermint, a Gregorian chant, velvet brushing their fingertips, a cool sea breeze, then submersion into warm water.

"Then may Allah guide you and keep you safe," Zero said.

He punched them in.

They stepped through Jack's secret back door to the public library, climbed up five levels of winding iron staircases, wandered through the cartography section with maps that had blank borders where the known world ended and sea serpents prowled beyond. Dust fumed in the air. The place smelled of rotting pulp.

Down corridors lined with romance paperbacks and askew medieval tomes they marched, ducked under ladders, stepped over piles of books, and avoided cobwebs between the shelves.

Jack halted, spotting Adam Smith's *Inquiry into the Nature and Causes of the Wealth of Nations*.

He extracted it. The shelf swung out on hinges, and sunlight filtered in.

"I thought we were headed for the CCO's office," Isabel whispered.

"A small detour," Jack said. He stepped through the hidden passage and pulled Isabel into Santa Sierra's marketplace.

It took a second for Jack to adjust to the glare. He blinked . . . saw out of both eyes.

Reno's implant processed around the parts of his occipital lobe it had burned out—like Odin, one eye torn out to see through the aether.

Jack slid on a pair of sunglasses. Next time his and Reno's paths crossed, he'd punch his lights out, maybe do a little impromptu surgery of his own.

Crowds streamed past pigsties, buying pork belly futures, wandering through the stalls of the De Beers diamond merchant; oil hawkers held aloft lit lamps and shouted quotes for barrels of crude; guides scoured the flock, looking for young investors to show the ropes—for a commission; a slender booth painted with moons contained a dark Gypsy woman with secrets to sell; and to Jack's left, through a zigzag of streets, diffused the neon glow of the arcades: fantasies and sex, where free time and spare change bought another life; and to his right, the corporate blocks of Santa Sierra, mirrored and chameleon-surfaced towers with crowns of blinking jewels.

In the corporate blocks were the gateways to Geneva, Darwin Tidal Station, and Bogotá, bridges that arched up into the clouds and vanished. Shadow dragons guarded them and flamed anyone who jumped taxes. You had to be careful. Depending on how you played it, and what kind of encryption you could afford, you paid federal tax, city tax, or geo tax. If you weren't savvy enough, you paid all three.

Jack stepped onto the street; it was muddy and stuck to him.

Isabel took his hand to steady him and said, "It's our narrow bandwidth in these helmets. Sensory lag." She had changed into khaki shorts, a white linen shirt, sturdy boots, and pith helmet to protect her face from the sun.

"Then we better be smart if we're going to be slow."

Jack crouched, grabbed a handful of mud, and blew on it. The muck dried to sand. A little protection. He poured it into his pocket, stood, then pointed east to crimson-and-black-checkered tents. "That way. I need a good pen."

"Pen?" Isabel's eyes narrowed. "We don't need developer tools for a clean hack. We do it legally or not at all."

"I know what I'm doing."

Isabel let his hand go and walked by his side. "We'll see."

They strolled past prophets and preachers begging for donations, promising tax breaks and salvation. They reeked of brimstone.

"This one." Jack stopped at a tent with black muslin walls.

"Why can't you make what you need? Wouldn't that be safer?"

"Safer maybe," Jack replied. "The clock is running, though, and by the time I figure out the market's current operating system, exploit the weak spots, it'll change. New optical drivers from Fiji or hashed-compression routines from the A-Colonies." He parted the tent flap. "It's impossible to keep up."

An old man sat in the corner smoking a water pipe. He watched Jack and Isabel, then removed a pack of cigarettes from his white robe, set it on the table next to pencils, watercolor brushes, felt-tipped pens, and fat sticks of pastel chalk.

Jack tapped out two lavender cigarettes and gave one to Isabel.

"Thanks," she said.

Jack pretended to look over the selection, but he had already spotted what he wanted: the Cavendera mechanical stylus, variable thickness set with a gold bezel, data flow pinpointed by caliber rings, and a federal serial number encrypted on the clip. Ten times what he could afford.

He picked it up, twisted its two halves. A dot of black ink poised on the injector—full of stars and slithering shapes and infinite possibilities.

"You have an excellent eye," the merchant said. "I have demos if you or the lady wish to test one." He indicated the cigar box of broken crayons and frayed brushes. A bent Cavendera was there, too.

"Demos?" Jack asked. He closed the real Cavendera.

"Fully functional within the confines of this shell," the merchant said and spread his arms wide.

Jack pick up the demo pen, careful not to get ink on his hand.

"You are a licensed developer?" the merchant asked him.

Jack frowned. He flipped out his wallet, flashed the gold seal of the Académe, and let the guy scan his registration number. The first three zeros of the number meant Jack had permission to access NSO-restricted files. Probably not anymore, but the merchant wouldn't know that.

"Apologies," the merchant whispered. He handed Jack a piece of paper.

Jack transferred the real Cavendera to his left hand—made that maneuver look nonchalant, too. He then twisted the demo on and sketched a rose, the stem, unfolding petals, a light dusting of pollen. Ink dried, and lines cast shadows, darkened to ultramarine . . . and became real.

Jack plucked it off the page and handed it to Isabel. "More beauty than this world knows."

Her eyes met his, and Jack saw a hidden message reflected there: emerald facets smoldered and flickered with irritation.

Isabel smelled the blue blossom. "Violets. Honeysuckle. Nice."

Jack turned to the merchant. "What about you? Do you have a license to sell this stuff?"

He dropped the inhaler of his waterpipe. Those triple zeros on Jack's registration must have gotten him worried. "It is here"—he rummaged under the table—"somewhere."

Jack drew a thin rectangle, pushed the shape, gave it another dimension, made it cylindrical, then added a point and a nib of gold. He quickly copied the encrypted registration of the real pen onto its clip.

"Here." The merchant handed him a tattered certificate.

Jack scratched at the wax seal. "OK. Just checking." He set

the demo back in the box and rolled the Cavendera he had just drawn across the table. "It's a nice pen, but I think I'll look around some more. Thanks."

Jack went outside and let Isabel glimpse the real pen before he slipped it into his shirt pocket.

"What happened to our clean hack?" she asked and tucked a strand of hair into her pith helmet.

"As long as he doesn't take the fake Cavendera outside the shell, it's going to stay real, and I'll stay clean. By the time he figures it out, this will be over, and the real one will be destroyed. What could be cleaner?"

"You learn that trick when you worked for the NSO?"

"Yes."

A cloud shaded the sun, Jack's personal shadow of guilt. Sure it was wrong to steal the pen. But he had to. As for learning dirty tricks from the NSO . . . that's what they paid him to do. That's what they made him do. He never had a choice.

They walked to the corporate sector, turning down offers from currency exchange merchants, information brokers, and avoiding the leather-and-harlequin-clad wild cards that would take them to euphoria—leave them broke and begging for more.

The CCO's office was a castle of white stone, slime-filled moat, and no windows. Stratospheric corporate towers cast it into perpetual twilight. Light reflected off the silver and gold skyscrapers and made the shadows frolic.

Two mastiff hounds guarded the drawbridge. That was bad news. Jack expected it. The good news was that the place had a back door. Every government installation, the NSO, CIA, or CCO, had back doors. How else could they spy on their own people?

Jack walked around the castle. The walls of white granite looked easy to scale. That was a trap. You'd end up climbing forever, an endless loop, until you fell. It was an old trick. Things moved in the moat, too. Fins and white eyes peered up, then vanished into the murky depths.

Jack took the pen and drew circles in the sand. Ink and shadows pooled there, crystallized to stone. He cast them upon the water. They made dimples in the surface, but didn't sink.

Isabel crouched and touched one. "Plague scan?" she asked.

"They're running just above the CCO system, checking for viruses. While they are, we use them to skip across."

Six steps and they were on the other side.

The stones plopped beneath the water.

"We're looking for a matrix of contour integrals," Jack whispered to her.

"How do you know?"

Jack left her question unanswered. Cracking e-mail codes for the government or the occasional corporation was one thing. Isabel might have suspected as much; every professor picked up a little research money that way. But Jack had never told anyone of the blackhacks and rips the NSO had him run . . . and all the money they paid him to do it. He didn't want lose more of her respect.

He ran his hands over the sandpaper texture of the stone. Beneath his fingertips he saw glimmers in the flecks of mica, ones and zeros, numbers transposed, geometric curves and intersecting dimensions. Seven heartbeats he searched, a few seconds in the outside world. Hours and gigabytes here.

"Found it," Isabel said.

"Good. Solve the integrals."

She concentrated, her eyes focused beyond the wall. "The elements reduce to zeros and two pi."

"Factor out the two pi."

"Got it." She flashed him a smile. "It's an identity matrix." A circle appeared in the stone. Isabel pushed; it clicked, then she pulled it open.

They climbed through, into a corridor of tan-and-pink-speckled tile. Jack guessed left was the right way. They hiked until the corridor opened into a central chamber. A thousand cubicles filled the room, each only slightly larger than the balding monks who occupied them, bent over and scribbling on parchments by the light of a single candle. Dozens of scribes carried scrolls, whisked them from station to station, then vanished through the hundreds of arches that led out of the chamber.

"Do you see the pattern?" Isabel whispered. "The paperwork just circulates from one scribe to another. Look. That one tossed a completed manuscript back into his in box."

Jack squinted. The golden lettering and cobalt heavens illuminated upon the incorporation application vanished. The scribe took it out and restarted the process of inking.

"Everyone is busy," Jack said, "but nothing gets done. Nice setup. Let's find our application before it gets buried forever." A scribe darted past—Jack grabbed him. "Hold still a second, kid."

The runner subroutine paused. Jack traced its outline with the pen, then released him. The outline stayed, wire skeleton appeared, and its flesh filled, a doppelgänger of the original.

Jack went to the end of the row, drew a new cubicle there, double the size of the others, a green glass account lamp, red leather executive's chair, and in and out trays.

"OK," Jack said to the doppelgänged runner, "find me petition number—" He turned to Isabel.

"Number 8D4F1B-031," she said.

The runner hiked up his robe and dashed across the room.

Isabel plopped into the chair, set her feet on the desk, and watched the runner as it searched a dozen cubicles, then stopped, bent down, and removed papers that had been shimming up a short desk leg. The monk there gave the kid a dirty look, then returned to his wobbly table.

The runner brought the papers to Jack. They were a ream thick and covered with tangled yarn.

"What's this mess?" Jack handed the file to Isabel.

She spread out the papers on the table, pushed on the walls of the cubicle to make it larger, then ran her fingers along the strings. "The blue yarn is CCO internal inquiries and reroute requests. I can unravel them." She dug deeper into the tangles, teased out a strand of black wire, and gingerly held it between her fingernails. "This, though, is your department. It's the NSO Code 11."

Jack wasn't too sure he could erase it. They had gotten too far, too fast, too easily. No NSO tails in the marketplace and no anti-intruder patrols inside CCO headquarters. It had to be a trap: lure him to the source of the problem. But traps could be reversed. Played on the hunter.

"Here." He handed Isabel the Cavendera. "You might need this."

"I thought—"

"It's not going to help me against an NSO counterhacker. We're moving ten times slower than their bubbles, remember? I'll have to outsmart them."

A smile flickered on her lips. "Now I'm worried." Isabel's eyes sought contact; they filled with apprehension, shimmered with nervous excitement, sexual tension . . . and deeper, something Jack wouldn't delve into. No time. He knew what it was, though; he felt the same way about her.

She pulled back before they sank into one another, then whispered, "Good luck."

"You too."

He took the black wire. Whispers and bits buzzed under the plastic insulation. Jack traced it around the maze of cubicles and to a dark archway. There were two torches at the entrance. Jack grabbed one and went in.

Five steps and Jack had to hunch over to continue. He swallowed his mounting claustrophobia—not completely sure the tunnel wasn't constricting on its own—and forced himself to squeeze past another twist, one more turn.

When he couldn't see the big room anymore, he stopped. He felt like he was being watched . . . like DeMitri was around the next corner.

It was time to buy himself insurance. He fished out the sand he had lifted from the market and sprinkled a thin line on the rock floor.

He pushed through the fabric of reality, sensed the lattice of metadecimal code and rendered geomantic webs of the CCO's system. His temples got hot—Reno's implant chewing at parts of his brain he couldn't afford to lose.

Jack wrote in the sand:

CALL(MARKETPLACE);

He backed off. The layers of code vanished; stone and sand and flickering torchlight reappeared.

This was an old subroutine sleight of hand, an illegal jump transfer that let you access distant parts of the operating system and bypass protocol. Dangerous, though; it could disorient you or cause permanent perceptual damage.

Jack picked up the black wire and skimmed down its length, through grottos, over a chasm, down a chimney.

Then stopped.

In the darkness ahead was the glowing end of a cigarette; the lips attached to it took a drag, made the tip glow brighter, and illuminated a face—the face of the guy who had chased Jack's ghost in the particle physics lab.

"Good afternoon," he said. Muscles flexed under his black-suit. "You've been a very naughty boy, Jack."

"I didn't catch your name."

"You will come with me. We're going to ask you a few questions."

"Who's holding your leash? DeMitri?"

The goon flicked his cigarette away and took a step closer. "What happened to DeMitri is one of the questions we had for you."

Jack balled up his apprehension, tightened his stomach—radiated enough anxiety so the air rippled around him. The fear part was easy. That was real. But the rest he had to make believable. Couldn't overdo it.

"You NSO counterhackers think you're smart. You won't get me . . . or any of the others."

"Others?" the guy asked. A slow smile fissured his face.

Jack turned and ran.

The counterhacker chased him.

He scrambled up the chimney, leapt over the chasm, then stumbled around a turn—but the counterhacker hadn't caught up to him. He had swallowed the bait, hoped Jack would lead him to the "others."

Jack jumped over his line of sand, careful not to trip the illegal jump transfer. Spun around.

The counterhacker blurred around the corner. Halted just short of the line.

"What's the matter, smart boy?" Jack asked. "You think you can take me? I lost you in the accelerator ring. I'll lose you here."

"I don't think so." The counterhacker took a step closer.

The line of sand flared orange, brightened to the yellow glow of sunshine. The floor cracked under the counterhacker's feet—opened ten meters over the marketplace.

He tumbled in.

Jack peered over, saw him land in the pork belly futures exchange . . . with the rest of the pigs.

The link closed.

Nice thing about those old programming tricks, young punks always fell for them. Jack couldn't get too happy. He'd bought himself some time, that's all. He picked up the black wire and jogged.

The tunnel emerged in a valley with tall limestone pinnacles. A muddy river meandered between them and green hills, terraced for rice farming. Upon a distant crag squatted a red-lacquered pagoda. The wire ran straight to it.

Jack concentrated, took a long step there, shook off the disorientation, and walked in past twin statue foo dogs. There was a gravel garden, a half-moon arching bridge over a pond, and the odor of sandalwood.

He ignored the pleasantries, followed the wire into a room filled with racks of scrolls and rotting manuscripts. The wire ended in a book.

The NSO had linked him to the Chinese. Why not? It was the same frame Bruner had planted and made stick.

The manuscript was made of fibrous paper. Jack opened it to where the wire marked. There was a picture of a man and a woman standing in Tiananmen Square, the Imperial Palace in the background. There was a handwritten caption: JOHN AND ROSE POTTER.

Jack had seen pictures of his parents before, but not like this. They held hands, gazed past Jack, and were somehow larger than life. "Heroic" was the word that came to mind.

He ran his fingers over the photo. Data streamed through: they had been suspected of defecting to the other side.

The NSO had to have altered the facts to make them look bad. Reno, sure, Jack could believe he was a double-crossing spy. But his parents? He pushed deeper into the report. There was mention of electronics smuggled into Beijing. A list of student contacts. An underground movement. Then the Great Wall rose. John and Rose never made it out.

He pushed with the implant.

Stone shattered under Jack's fingertips as a security block crumbled, and he found a file on the Raising of the Great Wall. A list of American trade sanctions, followed by European blockades. Diplomatic withdrawal. Communication blackouts. The dates indicated it started *before* the earthquakes.

More notes: congressional files with umbra-level security— stuff Jack couldn't hack in a month—but hints that the Chinese had linked trade deals to human rights. There were official protests of American brutalities. The United States severed economic links. Intelligence and counterintelligence budgets soared.

Wait. Jack backed up.

The United States had imposed trade sanctions *first*. They were the ones to cut ties. America's allies did the same. *We* had raised the Great Wall and isolated China. Jack had been taught all his life that the Chinese were the ones who went into hiding— it was a lie.

There were a dozen databases to sift through. Maybe he could download the stuff. He'd need a faster link.

"Jack?" Zero's voice floated on the wind and made the thin lines of incense smoke reverberate.

"Zero? Why are you patching in? Log out. I need the bandwidth."

"I apologize. It is somewhat of an emergency situation."

"What?"

In the room of scrolls, a wall slid open. Paper lanterns flickered in the breeze.

Reno stepped through. "Hiya, Jack."

7

JACK-IN-THE-BOX

"Someone's got their wires crossed." Reno said. "That Zen gravel garden belongs in a Japanese monastery, not in China's Kwangsi Province. The NSO never gets their details right."

Jack thought about how Reno had cracked open his head, left the hardware that burned out his eye, and got him tangled up with the Chinese and the NSO—concentrated those thoughts into his hand, closed it into a fist, then squeezed until the knuckles popped.

If Reno had kept his crooked nose where it belonged, Jack could have handled Bruner. Now everything was screwed up.

He swung, connected with Reno's jaw. Hate detonated, crackled with electricity and exploding firecrackers, knocked Reno over, and sent him skidding across the pine floor. Too bad it was only emotional discharge—not a real punch. If Jack knew where Reno physically was, he would have cracked that smile of his.

Jack doubled over, drained of his rancor. It felt good.

Reno moved slowly at first, then shook his head clear.

He should have kicked him while he was down, but the impulse passed. Jack was cool now.

"Not bad." Reno rubbed his jaw and got up. "A guy like you, in touch with his feelings, packs a wallop." He held out a hand: a gesture warning Jack to keep his distance. "Now that you got it out of your system, though, let's cut the bullshit."

Reno had a way of twisting the facts and catching him off guard. Jack had to be careful. "How did you get in here? —No, I don't want to know. Just get out. There's an NSO counterhacker on my tail."

"Not anymore," Reno said and winked his blue eye. "Took care of him." The paper walls of the monastery darkened from pure white to cream to ochre, and the lanterns tinged red.

Jack wondered if the dark metaphor meant Reno had killed the NSO counterhacker or just pulled his plug.

"I knew you'd hole up in your apartment. Didn't know you had guests."

"You're in my apartment? What did you do to Zero and Isabel?"

"Come on, Jack, I thought you knew me better than that. I wouldn't hurt anyone . . . without a good reason."

"Zero would have never let you interface."

"Not much he could do"—Reno tapped the side of his head—"not with me carrying my own hardware and a gun in his face."

"You're lying," Jack said. "You can't concentrate on two places at once."

"You can with the right equipment."

If Reno was telling the truth, then Jack could log out, maybe catch him off guard, and get his gun. Then again, if he had lied, wasn't in the apartment, by the time Jack reconnected, Reno would be gone. And his questions would never be answered.

Jack's anger returned. Waves of heat shimmered in his fist. He opened it and let the fire dissipate. "I'm glad you brought up the subject of equipment."

"The implant got your eye, didn't it?" Reno squinted. "Yeah, you're cooking now. These prototypes still got a few bugs. Gotta take the good with the bad, Jack-O."

"I never wanted to *take* anything. You forced it on me. What else is it going to fry?"

"Just the eye, I think." Reno smiled. "It has to broadcast out somewhere. Better there than your frontal lobe."

"Why me? Why the implant? And why did you send the girl to break into my office?"

"What girl?"

Jack drew a window in the air, linked to Zero's DNA reconstruction of the Chinese spy, Panda. He turned it so Reno got a good look.

Reno's pupils constricted to pinpoints. Jack pushed against his thoughts: solid stone walls, minotaurs, and mazes, but beyond, whispers of familiarity and a blood-tinged taste of panic.

What did Reno have to fear from the Chinese? He worked for them.

Two moths fluttered in, attracted to the light of the paper lanterns. One got too close and its wings singed. The other kept circling, unaware of the danger.

"Panda," Reno whispered to himself. "Look, Jack, I didn't know she . . . they would go after you so soon. I suspected. I knew they'd do it eventually. The NSO, too."

Then Reno and Panda weren't on the same side? Which one wasn't working for the Chinese?

"I was trying to protect you," Reno said.

"What do you think I have that needs protecting?" Jack asked.

"What you got up here." Reno pointed to his temple. "Encryption. Secret codes. How the hell do I know? I owed your folks, so I came to help." He stepped up to the manuscript, looked at the picture of John and Rose Potter, then said, "What's so damn important about your research? Tell me. I can't protect you from the Chinese or the NSO if I don't know."

So the NSO wanted his research. Jack had thought they were interested in the break-in, but the more he thought about it, the more he remembered how DeMitri liked to play games. He could be stringing him along, letting him use Bruner's technique to set up a contact. They couldn't have known about Wheeler, though. And the Chinese? How did they fit into this?

Jack could almost trust Reno—all that talk of a debt of honor to his parents and his apprehension when he had seen Panda— but "almost" didn't count when it came to Reno. "I don't have anything to say," Jack told him.

"I took a look in your kitchen before I jumped down here. That's no theoretical math you got cooking." Reno waited for Jack to answer, and when he didn't, Reno scowled, then said, "Whatever it is, it's special enough for you to take a run at incorporating. That's big-time trouble. The NSO is one thing, but you'll be going against the international boys."

"That's the reason I hacked in."

Reno shook his head. "It's going to take more than a CCO petition. You'll need cash. Lots of it."

"You didn't come here to give me financial advice."

Reno peeled the picture of Jack's parents from the manuscript, went to the incense burner, lit a cone, and set the photo there. He was quiet a moment, inhaling the lilac smoke. "I've been watching your back. I erased a few NSO files. Why do you think they haven't knocked on your door? Especially after the end run you did on DeMitri."

"He had that coming."

"We all do," Reno whispered. "I got problems of my own to take care of, though. I figure anything I owed your folks is square." The strands of incense smoke snaked into tormented faces and long clawed hands. He fanned them away. "I can't watch out for you anymore."

"This is watching out for me? Thanks for nothing. I'm better off on my own."

"Maybe," Reno said. "Maybe not." He cocked his head and a smile flickered to life. "Maybe you got one more favor coming from your old Uncle Reno." His smile fractured with a laugh.

Jack initiated an emergency log out.

Reno had to be in his apartment. He had seen Zero's lab.

Jack had his own gun; if he was quick enough, while Reno was busy being smug, he could get the drop on him. Then there would be a serious question-and-answer session.

He struggled, rose through layers of code and sensation. Walls of glass shattered, static screamed though his skull, and light streamed from every pore—a blur and a wash of disorientation and Jack surfaced.

He tore off the Académe helmet, fumbled for his gun, dug the clip out of his pocket, and slammed them together.

Reno wasn't there.

Jack wobbled, got dizzy, and wanted to throw up.

Zero braced him. "There was nothing I could do, Jack. He had a gun."

"Where is he?"

"He vanished . . . like a ghost."

Jack couldn't sleep. When a Chinese spy appears in your apartment, tells you to watch your back, then pulls a vanishing act, it puts you on edge.

He interfaced into their improvised bubble to relax. The modified helmet was still too tight. Jack worked with that detail, became a deep-sea diver with a bucket head, weighted boots, rubberized suit, and an air hose that trailed up through the black water. This was a night dive. Solid shadows. Free fall—with tons of water pressing him, holding him.

He piped in the noise from the isotope and rendered into bursts of bioluminescence—squid and eels that snaked past Jack, scintillating turquoise and tangerine. Eerie fireworks on the ocean floor.

Jack split the interface. Reno had kept a gun on Zero and Isabel while they had their talk with a dual perspective.

The trick was the Chinese implant.

With the slightest push, Jack could see different things through each eye: real in his right, virtual in his left. The implant must be time-slice multitasking the sensory input to his brain, but he couldn't detect any flickering or distortions. He integrated the parallel visions into separate windows in his diver's helmet. Through one was the ebon ocean, in the other, the reflected image of his apartment.

No would sneak up on him again. Jack's real hand held his gun.

He watched Zero sleep, his arms crossed over his chest like a dead pharaoh. How had he kept his cool? When he saw Reno disappear, Zero had concluded it was that Chinese implant that had overrode his senses. Jack should have thought of that. He wasn't sharp. He needed sleep—but he couldn't stop thinking.

Isabel tossed on her side, sighed, then covered her head with an arm. She was curled up in the corner, copper hair wrapped around her neck. Jack stared unabashedly at her.

He wasn't an Académe professor anymore with a career to protect. He should wake her, tell her she was the smartest, sexiest woman he knew. Do it quick before he lost his nerve or before someone dropped in and made them all disappear. That's what he wanted, but they were now business partners. Would she want to jeopardize their professional relationship?

She had pushed their CCO application as far as she could— it was up for consideration by the review committee. All Jack could do now was wait and see if the NSO killed it again.

He drifted and watched the underwater lights: a swarm of krill enveloped him, sparkled like chips of sapphire and emerald scattered and swirling through the sea. An anglerfish, waiting with its lantern antenna lure, snapped one up with its impossibly large mouth and larger teeth—scattered the shrimp. There were patterns, lines and curved planes and spirals of flickering lights, then they dissolved into random clouds of krill.

Jack shifted to spherical coordinates, did a Fourier transformation, then used Bruner's algorithm to collect the illumination into bands that vibrated and shifted, seethed with activity. With intelligence? Were these other channels in the noise?

The beam of a searchlight snapped on, penetrated the dark waters from above, and cut short Jack's theorizing. It scanned back and forth, then fixed upon him.

Ones and zeros sank through the ray. Jack held out his hand, filtered the bits using Wheeler's last code phrase. The falling numbers clumped into letters:

HELLOJACKHELLOJACKJACKHELLOHELLOJACKHELLOJACK

He didn't immediately answer. This was a chance for a more intimate exchange, a chance to learn more about the secretive Wheeler.

Jack typed into the window above him: NEW INTERFACE. SEND-ING INSTRUCTIONS. He switched to the technical specifications of his implant from Zero's recent scan and uploaded the information.

ONE MOMENT . . . . scrolled across the window.

Where to go? What metaphor should Jack choose?

Before he picked, his diver's suit ballooned—rubber and canvas became dark mahogany walls, a box the size of a closet with pale sunlight streaming though a grid of plum-colored glass on the wall. Jack sat on a bench and rested his left arm on a rail that had been polished by decades of guilty, sweaty palms.

Wheeler had beat him to it and had chosen his own metaphor.

There was a panel; Jack slid it open. A double-mesh screen separated him from another chamber on the other side. It let light through, but just enough to see a blurry outline.

"This is a wonderful idea," Wheeler whispered. "How does the ritual begin?" He cleared his throat: " 'Forgive me, Father, for I have sinned'?" Fingertips probed the screen. The mesh rippled like it had been touched by more than a finger—like a dozen fingers or tentacles or a fluid. "How are you, Jack?"

"Fine," he lied. "You?"

"Excellent. We have considered the ease of our previous exchange. No entangling government officials or regulations, no fawning obsequiousness. It is rather like one of your black markets, no? We desire to continue our trade, if that is acceptable."

Jack had to stall. They hadn't figured out the enzyme from the first exchange. He should wake Zero and Isabel . . . but apparently Wheeler liked things short and neat. A delay might be misinterpreted as a sign that Jack wasn't eager to do business. A sign of weakness.

"What do you have in mind?" Jack asked.

"Delightful," Wheeler said. "You reverse the normal routine and put the onus of an offer upon me. That is why I like you, Jack. You are willing to take advantage." There were whispers on the other side of the screen, then Wheeler continued, "What we have in mind is information on your civilization."

Jack wasn't ready for that. Wheeler hadn't been interested in humanity before. Technology. Trade. Business only. "Why that?" he asked.

"I foresee a long and fruitful relationship. We have only your transmissions by which to judge you. They are dreadfully out of date. It would be foolish to formulate an opinion of you, or your society, based solely on those."

Jack agreed. He agreed that Wheeler knowing more about him would give Wheeler an advantage in future negotiations. If he learned how human psychology worked, he could use it against them. It was smart. It was the kind of data Jack wanted from Wheeler.

"Hold one moment." Jack slid the partition in the confessional shut. He blocked the line with dead-code that would kill any input or output through the channel.

How easy would it be for hyperintelligent Wheeler to hack in, link with every database in the world, and take whatever he wanted? He had dealt straight with Jack so far—manipulative, but straight. Still, Jack wasn't about to let anyone have anything for free. He set a scarab beetle on the rail, a bug that would detect a single shifted bit.

He opened a window to the Santa Sierra public library and logged on illegally. Monitoring Earth's television and radio broadcasts gave Wheeler an idea of the way humans worked—melodrama and newscasts, cartoons and documentaries to puzzle over, but he had missed the crown jewels of communication.

Jack scanned the library's catalog, started with the ancients:

the *Odyssey*, the Bible, and *Beowulf*, then moved to the early Middle Ages with Chaucer's *Canterbury Tales*. There was too much Western culture, so he threw in Sun Tzu's *The Art of War*, the *Bhagavad-Gita*, and the *Tao-te Ching*. From the Middle Ages he grabbed Milton's *Paradise Lost*, *Macbeth*, and Leonardo da Vinci's illustrated codex. Jack skimmed recent titles, took Walt Whitman's *Leaves of Grass*, Sigmund Freud's *The Interpretation of Dreams*, and the United States Constitution.

It was a fistful of man's best literature for Wheeler to decipher. Figuring out human behavior was going to be a thousand times harder than cracking the DNA code.

A silver-embossed chapbook appeared in Jack's hand. He picked up and rattled the scarab—empty—slid the confessional window open, then held the spine of the chapbook to the screen. A spark transferred—just the titles. "I offer these. Are you interested?"

"A moment," Wheeler said. Then: "Yes. We are interested."

"In exchange, you will send me samples of your literature?"

Wheeler laughed. "Oh no, Jack. Levels of trust must be built before we can reveal those personal details."

"Not what I'd call a fair trade."

"It is. We already have information on your society. All we seek is clarification. To give you similar access would be unfair."

Jack saw his point. He didn't like it, but he had no leverage to get what he wanted. Maybe he never had any. He had to reassert himself. "I want a choice," he said.

"I beg your pardon?"

"A choice." Jack gripped the rail with a clammy hand. How far could he push Wheeler? "Last time you offered only one piece of information. This time I ask to select."

"We cannot. We require control."

It was an interesting admission. Wheeler liked control, while Jack preferred choice. He could use that to his advantage. "You would still be in control. Control to pick the selection. And you might learn something about me by what I pick."

"You are clever, Jack. I do so enjoying working with you."

There was rustling on the other side of the screen, then a folded piece of parchment slid under the mesh.

Jack took the paper, opened it. Written upon it was:

ELECTRON REACTOR
RANDOM LOGIC
TEMPEST WAVEFUNCTION

There were no explanations, only names that smacked of mystery—and danger. Jack had let a genie out of the bottle, and he was getting his three wishes. Wishes tended to backfire, though, on those doing the wishing. He could still sever the connection. Cancel their deal. Or renegotiate. No. He wanted this. His new corporation needed whatever edge it could get. He wouldn't back out.

"While you decide," Wheeler said, "I ask that you send your literature."

"Simultaneous transfer," Jack said. "Bit for bit."

"You are a man after my own heart. I shall wait."

Jack doubted Wheeler had a heart, real or metaphorical. Which one to take? He could only guess what they were. Random logic could be mathematics, electronics, or philosophy. Tempest wavefunction had to deal with quantum mechanics. Not Jack's field. Electron reactor, was that a power source? They were all vague. All intriguing.

Jack picked electron reactor. It sounded the least mystifying; the word "reactor" held the possibility it was a technology they could master. A reactor could be built, adjusted . . . shut down if needed.

The other selections faded. Jack folded the paper, slid it back under.

Wheeler took it. Jack heard him unfold it, then Wheeler remarked, "But of course. I am ready to transfer." He pushed a black velvet box under the mesh; at the same time, Jack slid the chapbook.

He took it, held the box in his hand, but left it unopened

"A pleasure, Jack. It is always a genuine pleasure to do business with you. I look forward to our next transaction." He reached to slide the partition shut, and again, the mesh vibrated like it was the surface of a fluid. Wheeler then paused and said, "How does the ritual end? 'Go and sin no more . . .' "

He closed the panel and left Jack in the dark.

When Jack and Isabel entered the kitchen, for a moment, he thought it was virtual.

Zero had metamorphosed the room into a hothouse alive with appliances—half organic, half molecular machinery. Suction-cupped tendrils snaked down the drain and up the faucet, pulsing and squirming. Steel-segmented chromatography columns with triangle leaves unrolled on fern stalks and clustered about the luminescent waste engine. Vines with orange and ivory orchids clung to the walls; output leads from their trunks linked to a display and reported the status of the bacterial engineers breeding and mutating within their seedpods.

Jack smelled chlorophyll and humus, fermentation, and the sweet odor of carbon tetrachloride.

It was all real, though; he could only see it through his right eye.

Zero tapped the display. Twenty-three pairs of chromosomes appeared, double-X female, and the screen zoomed in to number fourteen. The tightly coiled DNA unwound, sprawled, and stretched into orderly rows on the screen. Bands of red appeared in the genetic code.

"This is what the enzyme has removed," Zero said. "Approximately eighteen percent of the base pairs in our genome."

"That can't be healthy," Isabel said as she took a drag off her cigarette.

"On the contrary, the simulation on this chromosome demonstrates proteins manufactured from the modified DNA template operate normally. In some cases, better."

"Eighteen percent," Jack said. "That's like losing a leg." He rubbed his dead eye. "Don't we need that genetic information?"

"I think not," Zero said. "Mutations and retroviruses continuously creep into our genome." He paused to yawn. He hadn't slept well. Said he had bad dreams. "We have natural self-correcting DNA mechanisms, but invariably anomalies creep into the population."

"What else is it doing?" Isabel said and leaned forward.

"The enzyme manufactures a new RNA." Zero touched the display and a DNA helix unwound; the enzyme pulled it apart and slithered along, piecing together sugar-phosphate bases to construct an RNA strand, then snipped it free.

"I call this comparison RNA or c-RNA. It migrates to other cells and compares the code from one section of DNA to the identical section in another strand. If there is a mismatch in the DNA to c-RNA pattern, the enzyme makes the appropriate correction to the DNA. This enables cells to repair large-scale radiation and toxicological damage, certain cancers, and other errors that are beyond my capacities to simulate."

"It sounds too good to be true," Jack said. He touched the display, enlarged the image of the molecule, and rotated it. The rendered protein was glossy; it looked to Jack like a giant balloon animal, twisted together with inhuman precision.

Isabel shook her pack of cigarettes, offered one to Jack and Zero.

Jack declined.

"Thank you." Zero took one, and lit up. "It may very well be too good to be true. I must have exhaustive simulations and meticulous in vitro tests before I can allow human trials." He brushed aside a patch of solvent-absorbing moss and sat on the countertop. "There is, however, good news. I have mapped a series of viral delivery vectors to encode the enzyme's molecular pattern into a host's DNA. All I require are the funds for equipment. Any developments from the CCO?"

"We're being reviewed by the executive committee." Isabel drew on her cigarette, burned it to the filter, then paused to light another one. "It would help if I could tell them about this—" She pointed to the simulated c-RNA. "It might impress them."

"I shall prepare a synopsis," Zero said.

Isabel then turned to Jack and asked, "Any word from Wheeler?"

He hadn't told them about the alien's midnight call and his trade for the electron reactor.

Wheeler's design specifications called for a germanium arsinide substrate etched to the most exacting details—coordinates for the precise positions of a million atoms arranged into a jagged canyon and the digital gateways that connected to it. Jack guessed this electron reactor was a microprocessor, but without a hint of anything that passed for a normal logic circuit.

Isabel had the best chance of understanding it. Jack started to tell her, opened his mouth . . . hesitated.

What was he afraid of? They were friends. He had known her for fifteen years. She and Zero had risked their Académe careers to help him. If he couldn't trust them, he couldn't trust anyone.

But they were also business partners. Jack's street and school instincts whispered that he should keep every piece of information to himself. If he just gave them the data, what was to stop Zero and Isabel from walking out the door and starting up their own corporation?

That was stupid. Jack hated himself for even thinking it.

"Isabel?" This would have been easier with metaphor. Every minute he waited, he'd need more excuses of why he had delayed telling them. "I want to show you—"

A square in the corner of the display flashed yellow.

"One of your alarms has activated," Zero said.

Jack leapt up, touched the screen, and expanded the link. The microdot detector outside the bathroom window had gone off. Its memory array showed the blur of a man—overcoat and black boots. He carried something under his arm.

"It's probably just a bum looking for a handout."

The detector in the stairwell of the building flashed. The same guy with the same package.

Jack thumbed the safety on his Hautger SK, went to the door, waited, listened.

In the corner of the living room, Isabel's computer strobed; the detector outside the front door tripped, showed a blur of a man crouching, leaving the bundle he had carried, then running back down the corridor, the stairs, out the door, back through the alley, then gone.

"It could be a bomb," Jack whispered. "Get back."

If it was the NSO, they wouldn't blow him up. Not if they wanted to know what Jack did. Nerve gas maybe. But if it was from Reno, it could be anything.

Zero went into the kitchen and returned with a pot, holding it like a club. Jack appreciated the effort.

He cracked the door.

A brown paper package sat there. Jack looked up and down the hallway. Nothing. He pushed with his implant. Fire bloomed across his brow, but no ghosts materialized.

With the nose of his gun, Jack nudged the box. It didn't explode.

He grabbed it, then closed the door and watched the motion detectors. They flickered from the vibration of the door being slammed shut.

"Don't open it," Isabel said.

Jack rattled the box; three heavy objects shifted through packing material. He tore the brown paper wrapping off.

Isabel gave him a piercing look. She stepped closer, though, wanting to get a look, too.

The box was originally for instant lasagna, the kind where you pulled the tab and they cooked themselves. Cheap and too salty. Jack ripped the top off, pointed it away from his face. There was no hiss of gas. No ticking. He peered inside.

There was a stack of certificates with elaborate scrollwork, calligraphy, dark green serial numbers printed in magnetized ink, and a fiber-optic strip bonded to the left-hand side of the paper.

"They are bearer bonds," Zero said, "from the Bank of Geneva."

Jack pulled one out. The denomination was one million dollars. His mouth went dry, and the hand that held it tingled. He set the bond down, then pulled out the stack and leafed through them. All were one-million-dollar bonds. Thirty-three of them. He handed them to Zero and Isabel.

"Who sent them?" she asked. "Are they real?"

Zero held them up to the light and inspected the prismatic peacock watermark. "Real or brilliant forgeries."

Jack went back to the box. In the bottom were three handguns. He picked one up, and the grip molded to his hand, wrapped around his palm. It emitted an EM pulse to his implant—ammunition status, selections of explosive needles, compression burrowing, or anatoxic plastocene; it gave him a link to sight through the barrel, reported that its gyros were operational and that it was ready to fire. It queried if it could interface and collect data on Jack's reflexes and present physical condition. He declined, called up a list of commands, and put it into safety mode.

"They're military," he said and set the gun down.

Lining the bottom of the cardboard box was a typed note.

Hiya Jack,
The guns are a present. The money isn't. I've just bought stock in your company. If we can't be family, we're going to be business partners.

Reno

8

APPLEJACK

Jack had a thing for twentieth-century San Francisco, a time and a place of creativity, a community that could never exist for him because it was underwater now, half-dream and half-history—couldn't exist, that is, outside his imagination.

He had a bowl of shrimp gumbo at the Cha Cha Cha Café, washed it down with three Coors, then went for a walk up Haight Street. The sun had set and streetlights flickered on. It was still hot, so he pulled off his tie-dyed shirt, wrapped it around his waist, and wore only cutoffs and sandals.

Next to the Red Victorian Hotel, Jack spotted a bum (who looked suspiciously like himself), holding a tin cup and a sign: KOREAN VET. Jack gave him the change from dinner.

"God bless," the man said. "There's a concert in Panhandle Park. Don't miss it."

"Groovy," Jack replied. He crossed the street at Clayton, headed toward the strip of grass and clusters of eucalyptus trees, heard an electric guitar plug in, tune up, and the rattle of a tambourine. People tossed Frisbees along the length of the park, cooked hamburgers on hibachis, and drank home-brewed applejack out of gallon jugs. He settled in the shade of a tree.

A girl started singing. Her long brown hair fell into her face. Her songs were about how life was screwed up and how everyone in the world was down on her. She accompanied herself with guitar, but played sporadically, getting caught up in her lyrics. Her voice was rough, broken with sadness; it worked with her blues.

Jack decide to stay, listen to the music, and relax.

Both eyes worked here; he forgot to worry when or how he'd find a specialist skilled enough to replace it with the Chinese implant in the way.

He had been busy since their incorporation petition started its CCO review. With Reno's money, they had bought out the ancestral lease-holders of his apartment building. He and Isabel had acquired the parts for three bubbles, fine-tuned the chaos circuits and vortex coils, and installed a communication manifold to the outside world. They were up and running . . . sort of.

Zero and Isabel had taken leaves of absence from the Academé. This hurt their chances for tenure, but if the enzyme worked, they could buy their own research staff and facilities. Isabel had immersed herself in her bubble, absorbed in the financial and legal details of getting loans and quick-grant patents. She got that dirty work because she had more experience at writing grants and petitioning for legitimate corporate money.

Zero disappeared into his basement lab. He said he had simulations to run and viruses to engineer. He warned them to stay out. Extreme biohazards, he said. Although he'd never admit it, Jack knew Zero enjoyed playing God.

Jack's job was to monitor Wheeler's signal, but he had set up a program to watch for variations in the spectrum within the isotope. It was automatic. He wasn't needed anymore.

There was a small pearl of guilt inside Jack. He hadn't revealed the information about the electron reactor. Every time he thought about it, he became uncomfortable with his secrecy and coated the feeling with another layer of excuses. He'd tinker with the design and show it to Zero and Isabel when he had it figured out. That would be the best thing.

A ring of people had gathered around the woman singer; the moon rose with Venus in the early evening sky, and someone passed him a bottle of dandelion wine, then a joint. Jack sipped both and tried to forget what was out there: the NSO, Chinese spies, and aliens with agendas.

He sketched part of the electron reactor in the dirt. Jack had simulated the design, a million atoms precisely arranged; a phantom electron bounced inside and never settled into a single wavefunction. He wouldn't know what it was supposed to do until he built it. That meant he'd need automated optical tweezer arrays, and programmable industrial nano-assemblers for the delicate work. And a barrelful of money.

The woman finished her song. The audience clapped and hugged her as she stepped down. A black kid got up next, plugged his electric guitar into a tiny amp, and played without warming up. He twisted the song, made it dynamic, full of dissonant chords and virtuosic chaos.

Another joint made its way around the circle. When Jack exhaled, he saw silver stars in the smoke. His troubles vanished and he listened, feeling the notes—so loud they made the hairs on his arms dance.

But his mind couldn't rest.

There were problems to solve, and high on that list was the possibility of other signals. Those patterns of bioluminescence Jack had seen underwater, just before Wheeler's visit in the confessional, were they other transmissions? Or just a chance alignment?

Bruner's technique used mathematical expansions of functions like sine and cosine to assemble noise into coherency. Wheeler's signal was an expansion of hyperbolic tangent. Jack had run through hundreds of different functions and had never found another match. What had he overlooked?

The kid on the electric guitar was on fire. His fingers were a blur on the steel strings; he twisted the neck of the guitar, made it scream. An aura pulsed around him, shimmered and jumped in response to the notes that he picked and pounded and made waver and wail through the night air—the stars overhead rippled.

His music wasn't just notes, but combinations of notes played simultaneously that sounded richer than the sum of its parts, chords.

Jack could feel a connection building; that was the advantage of a true bubble instead of the modified helmets they had used—not only were they faster, but bubbles teased intuitions from their subconscious cocoons.

He opened a link and rendered the noise in the isotope into stars. They blinked on and off, looking more like snow than the night.

"Cool," the hippie next to him said. "Good dope, huh?"

"The best," Jack replied and examined the static.

Bruner's technique expanded a single mathematical function. It was one note filtered from the noise. But Jack should have been looking for chords, too. He could add or subtract functions or delve into the nonlinear—multiply them or use one function as the argument of another, the exponent of cosine, or the gamma function cubed. There were endless possibilities.

The guitarist jumped to the low end of the scale, then bridged the piece, strummed patterns of harmony and atonality, worked up the neck, louder and higher and faster, until his hands almost touched, then he drew the ballad into resolution.

Patches of winking stars migrated into constellations—organized notes, chords of information. There were only outlines, suggestions of patterns: a cross that looked like a swan and a triangle that could have been the head of a bull. They weren't complete . . . but Jack could almost see their full forms.

Other signals in the noise?

He reached up and touched the stars. Through his fingertips he heard whispers, but they were distorted and broken. Encrypted?

The guy who had passed Jack the joint nudged him and whispered, "Hey, man, hate to bring you down, but there's a chick who wants to join our party." He pointed to the edge of the park. Isabel was there. She wore a circlet of rosemary in her hair, a hand-knitted crop top, miniskirt, and white go-go boots. "Is she cool? She looks like a narc."

Jack cut his connection to the data and swept aside the diagram in the sand. "She's cool." He waved to Isabel and let her interface.

She sauntered over, sidled next to Jack, her bare thigh touching his. "Having a good time?"

"This is just a—"

"No need to explain," she said. "The Summer of Love, right? I recognized Joplin and Hendrix. It's quaint. If you can spare the time, though, Zero and I need to talk to you."

He looked into her eyes, crystalline and impenetrable, and had a feeling his break was over.

Jack learned law in the eleventh grade. By that time, he had a shot at the corporate world, so he had to know how things really worked. He read Thomas Paine and the Declaration of Independence. It fascinated him—not that any of it applied to a digital society of half a billion people—but because the politicians of America's first two hundred years reminded him of the senators and caesars of ancient Greece, with their backstabs and backroom deals.

Power today pivoted on new law. The biggest weight tilting the scales of justice was the Forty-second Amendment to the Constitution, which read:

ARTICLE XXXXII
FREE MARKET AMENDMENT

The right of incorporated entities shall be made secure in their stockholders, properties, information, and sovereign transactions against unreasonable tariffs, taxes, and seizures. No warrants, injunctions, nor foreign treaties to hinder the free market shall be made without probable cause supported by oath or affirmation pertaining to the place to be searched, data examined, employees or properties seized, or information disclosed.

Congress added it after the Earth cracked. They claimed the country needed to give big business a break to rebuild America's shattered economy.

A lot of people protested, but America had never been a democracy, a land ruled by its citizens. The United States is a representative republic, a land ruled by laws. Laws that are bought, sold, and traded like any other commodities.

The United States government created leviathan corporations with powers on par with its own. They had to pick their fights with care. If the Justice Department lost a court case, the infringed corporation could sue for damages. Millions or billions of dollars.

And just because corporations had the Forty-second Amendment, that didn't stop them from buying Supreme Court judges, senators, presidents, and flooding the communication channels with glitzy subliminal PR. Occasionally they would get caught, lose a court case, and pay a hefty fine back to the government.

Both sides circled, looked for a weakness or a loophole in the law, and tried to grab power and money from each other. It was the new system of checks and balances.

The only problem was people not on the board of directors or in congress got caught in the political crossfire, lost their jobs or homes, or found the work they had trained for all their lives was now illegal.

Those were the breaks. That's what big business is all about.

Jack settled on his blue pillow and crossed his legs.

Isabel operated her new moccasopa machine in the bathroom, wisps of steam curled around her, smelling of cinnamon and cocoa. She handed Jack a cup of the sweet amphetamine-laced liquor and sat opposite him. They were out of cream, so she made a silver pitcher appear, poured a dribble for herself, offered some to Jack.

"No thanks," he said. "Why are we here? Why not St. Paul's Cathedral or the Orient Express?"

"I'm tired of exotic bubble locales. Let's be ourselves for once."

They had been in the same building for the last week and hardly seen one another. While the bubbles increased the capacity for communication, they simultaneously isolated the people inside them.

Jack wanted to be close to his friends, but he wanted to be alone, too. Why was that? He kept secrets as well as the next guy—better, but not from Isabel or Zero. They were more than partners and friends. They were almost family. So why couldn't he tell them about Wheeler's last transaction? And the other possible signals buried in the noise?

Isabel made a rug, red and gold and black wool scrollwork spread beneath them. Regardless of what she said, she couldn't stand complete reality, either.

The wall between the bathroom and kitchen faded, became windows and a glass door—on the other side, a hothouse full of African violets and jasmine and waterfalls.

A man opened the door and stepped in. He scratched his freshly shaven chin—then Jack recognized him. "Zero?" His head looked fatter, more square without his meticulously groomed and curled beard. "What happened to your face?"

Zero sat next to him, crossed his legs easily. "There was an accident. Part of it was singed. Since I had appointments with CCO officials to explain our progress, my appearance was of import."

"You look younger," Jack said. "Ten years." Zero could have covered up singed hair with illusion. Beards were a sign of virility within his clan. To cut it off because he wanted to look presentable was a different Zero than Jack knew.

He was changing. . . . They all were.

"I think you look wonderful," Isabel said and handed him a moccasopa. "Shall we begin? I have good news and bad news."

"Let's hear the good first," Jack said.

She folded her hands neatly in front of her, then announced, "Our petition has been accepted by the Santa Sierra CCO. We are officially incorporated." She picked up her cup; Jack and Zero clinked with her. Isabel's red hair shimmered, a metaphor for her pleasure.

Jack drank and watched his friends over the rim of his mug. They deserved to be happy. They had gambled their careers on his wild scheme. It's what he wanted, too, wasn't it? A real corporation. It was the big time, bigger than any Académe. So why was there a hard ball of apprehension in his stomach?

"I filed a complaint about the NSO," Isabel said. "The CCO warned them to desist their harassment."

"Then we are safe?" Zero asked.

"That depends," Jack replied.

When he ripped with the NSO, sometimes they hacked into isolated networks, had to break into buildings, and sometimes they broke into the people who ran those networks. Blackhacks—what DeMitri was good at—opening minds, sifting through psychoses and memories . . . operations Jack wished he could forget.

"It depends," he repeated, "what the NSO thinks I have. They still might come in here and get it, illegal or not. They'll just think twice about it."

"What about the network of microdot detectors you installed?" Isabel asked. "It's so dense, every dust mite and flea in this building is monitored."

"True," Jack replied. "I doubt even Reno with his Chinese hardware can slip in."

Jack had made other arrangements to upgrade their security—which he would keep quiet until they were delivered. Zero and Isabel might have objections to using lethal force—but they didn't know what the NSO was capable of.

"Excellent," Zero said, "I have good news as well. I had concerns that the enzyme would excise immunological data from the genome and render its hosts susceptible to infection. This does not occur in my simulations. I did not understand until I reviewed the biochemical information Jack uploaded to Wheeler. It contained a catalog of our immunological responses. One less worry." He drained his cup then set it aside. "I have also engineered a successful delivery system for the enzyme into host DNA. In vitro tests progress well, and I predict we shall be ready for preliminary human trials in three months." Zero offered Isabel more moccasopa. "You said there was bad news?"

Isabel shook her head at the liquor. Jack lifted his cup, and Zero filled it.

"The bad news is money," she said.

"I thought Reno's gift took care of that."

"Thirty-three million is only a start," Isabel replied. "There were filing fees with the CCO, donations to charities and political campaigns—"

"Wait," Jack said. "How do donations figure into our start-up costs?"

"We had to impress the members of the CCO review board," Isabel said. "They all have their favorite charities . . . and friends in the senate. We made several contributions." She looked away. "It was nothing illegal."

"Not illegal, but not entirely aboveboard," Jack said. That was a cheap shot. He wasn't worried about the bribes; it was their sudden lack of cash. He had hustled micromines and tangle wires for any NSO agents that wanted to visit. He should have told them about it. Told them the people he ordered from didn't take credit.

Jack didn't push with metaphor, though. He hadn't perfected his interface with this new bubble—circuitry that had been designed for a spherical chamber, not a square and poorly shielded apartment. He made a note, though, that it was "we" who had bribed the CCO, not just "her."

Isabel's gaze returned to Jack. There was trouble in her eyes now. Swirls of blue and amber mixed with her emerald green and muddied the waters. She showed Jack her self-doubt. Fear. Irritation.

"What else?" he asked.

"Do not forget our recent purchases," Zero said. "The bubbles, your microdot motion detectors, new com-links and computers." Five silver coins appeared in his hand, Liberty-head half-dollars. "Nor was the work I ordered inexpensive; forty-two new species of bacteria to produce the retroviruses that deliver the enzyme."

"You didn't do it yourself?" Zero had never trusted anyone to do his work.

"Time," he said to Jack and dropped the silver coins on the rug, "is a luxury we do not have. I have already received queries from industrial colleagues. They ask sensitive questions."

"We may have legal protection from the government," Isabel said, "but we're not immune from rival businesses. If they get enough data on the enzyme, we could end up in court disputing patents. Without the money to hire a team of lawyers, we'd lose."

"I thought we were entitled to guaranteed loans as a new corporation."

"Again, time is the issue," Zero said. "For the loans to be processed, we must reveal details of our product, details that could be used against us before we can marshal our resources."

"Other corporations survive this start-up period," Jack said. He picked up a Liberty-head half-dollar, spun it into a sphere of silver. It reminded him of Reno's last visit: shadows and blurs bearing gifts of silver.

"We got Reno's cash by selling stock." Jack plucked the spinning coin up. "Whether we wanted to or not. Thirty-three million and he never even asked for the details. What if we leak details and spark a little interest? What if we say the enzyme cures cancer? Extends your life? That's not far from the truth."

"The price of any stock we offered would skyrocket," Isabel said.

Zero stroked his chin. "Since we require immediate capital,

and we must eventually reveal details of the enzyme, it would seem to solve both problems."

Isabel frowned, gathered Zero's five coins, then placed one in front of herself, Jack, and Zero. "We divide the corporation into fifths, then. A fifth for each of us, and"—she set one coin in the center of the rug—"a fifth to be sold as public stock."

"That's four fifths," Jack said. "Where's the other coin?" He knew the answer as soon as he asked: "Reno."

Isabel's frown deepened and pulled her eyebrows into a furrow. "It means we have to keep two sets of books. One with Reno in them and one without. That's illegal. But so is accepting funds from the Chinese."

"We have spent his money," Zero whispered. "I believe any moral hesitation we have at this point is moot."

"I wish there had been another way," Isabel said. "It was wrong to take those bonds."

Jack replied, "All things considered—"

The rug, the coins, and Zero's hothouse flickered, blurred, then snapped back into place.

"That's the power," Isabel said and stood. She drew a square in the air, opened a window, scanned it. "We're on battery backup. There, the fuel cells have kicked in."

Adrenaline flashed through Jack's blood. It could be a brownout—could be, but probably wasn't.

He caught a blinking red dot in his peripheral vision, tapped it once, and interfaced with his microdot detection network. Their memory arrays showed six timeplexed figures in the alley, two on the fire escape, and one on the roof. Radar reflections indicated a lot of metal; that meant guns. Infrared spectroscopy picked up a strong resonance of polycarbonate: body armor.

"We have company," he told Isabel and Zero. "And it's not Reno with Christmas presents, unless he brought friends with guns."

Isabel pulled out one of Reno's automatics. It broadcast an EM chirp, which she picked up and interfaced with. "Do we fight or run?" she asked.

"I don't think we have a choice. We're going to have to do both." Jack gazed through a thousand microdot eyes; he dug into the motion detector's tiny memories and pieced together the faces of the shadows outside. They wore black masks, but by adding images, enhancing, and filling in the blanks, he recognized two: the goon who wouldn't let him into his office the day of the break-in and the agent he'd lost in the CCO hack.

"They're NSO," he said. "They're after me."

"Not necessarily," Zero said. "They could want the enzyme. They know of our successful incorporation and perhaps have linked that with your research."

"It doesn't matter," Isabel whispered. She tracked one agent as he circled the perimeter of the building. "Whatever they want, they're getting ready to come up here. What do we do?"

"We've turned the apartment into one giant bubble," Jack said. "The agents have implants. We'll trick them, make them move wrong, trip, or shoot each other. Maybe we can escape in the confusion."

"Mirage," Isabel said. "I remember the game."

Zero's golden skin paled. "I am not here. I am linked through the basement laboratory."

"Then get up here—quick," Jack said.

Zero vanished.

"Mirage is a great idea," Isabel said, "but what are the odds of them *all* having implants?"

It was equal to the odds of them getting out—close to nothing. "There are nine of them," Jack told her, "usually a communications expert to coordinate from the outside, two for backup, three unimplanted assassins, and at least three with implants." The ones with implants were the computer people, a hardware specialist, a codeman, and the last one would pry Jack's mind apart.

Isabel looked at him, curiosity lightened her eyes, and she reached out for a millisecond of contact—wanting to know how he knew so much about illegal NSO operations.

He should have kept his mouth shut. That was another secret he'd have to keep from her.

Jack threw a wall of prime numbers between them, blocking contact.

Isabel's eyes widened; he couldn't tell what she was thinking . . . but he'd bet it wasn't anything good. He didn't blame her.

Jack turned back to the microdot scanners. Three men jogged to the entrance alcove of the apartment building. Signals screeched from the lock mechanism. "They're running a bypass on the front door."

"I've slaved and sealed bubble control to our resonant signatures," Isabel told him. "Only the three of us will be able to independently manipulate the environment. Where the hell is Zero?"

A security window popped open in midair. A blinking fire icon indicated trouble in the basement lab. The extinguishing system malfunctioned—no, it had been shut down. Jack picked up Zero's motion. "He's moving . . . in the elevator. Good. Three of our guests just opened the front door. They would have caught him in the stairwell."

Jack primed Reno's half-organic, half-plastic gun. He had left his Hautger SK in the bathroom. It had too much metal and scattered the bubble's signal. The pistol pulsed its EM handshake, interfaced; its gyros warmed to standby mode, and the grip molded to his hand. "Cover me," he told Isabel. "Zero is in the hallway, a dozen steps ahead of company."

Jack released the lock and stood aside. Isabel aimed at the opening.

Zero jumped through, panting, then slammed the door shut.

"Glad you made it," Jack said and squeezed Zero's shoulder. He scrambled the lock on the foamed alloy door, then checked the scanners. There were a pair of agents on the first level of the fire escape, but they weren't moving. The one on the roof emitted bursts of shortband radio. Three stood outside the apartment door, and three more were coming up.

Zero smelled of ether.

"You set the fire?" Jack said.

"We cannot allow the viruses to fall into their hands. My notes, simulations, and the biologicals are gone. All that remains is in here." He touched his forehead. "—And this." He dug an injector vial out of his lab coat. It was labeled: TETANUS (CLOSTRIDIUM TETANI) TOXOID.

"That's the enzyme?"

"The forty-two strains of virus that deliver—"

Jack picked up signals from the apartment door. "They're running a shunt," he said. "Get back."

They scrambled into the doorway of the bathroom.

"We'll target the ones without implants first," Jack whispered. "They're the only ones who will be able to see what's real."

" 'Target,' " Isabel said. "You mean kill."

"Program your gun to fire a sequence of explosive needles, then anatoxic plastocene. The needles will detonate on their armor, knock them back. The plastocene might catch an exposed patch of skin and put them to sleep. If not, switch to the compression burrowing rounds. That will get through polycarbonate. Zero, start the mirage when they get inside."

"With the possibility of gunfire, we should secure the virus," Zero said. "It is not an airborne carrier, but if the inoculation vial shatters, we lose everything."

Isabel gripped the gun tighter; inside, its ammunition chambers shifted, and she ejected the compression burrowing rounds. "I can hide it in here." She held out her hand. Zero gave her the vial.

Jack interfaced with the front door. They had burned through most of the lock-code. "We've got fifteen seconds," he whispered. "Hurry up, Isabel."

She had her back turned to him. Why was she taking so long to get the vial into her gun?

Jack switched to the alarm networks and saw the entire basement on fire. "Zero, what did you do down there?"

"I ignited the solvent. Fifty liters of ether, benzene, and DMSO. This building is concrete and brick. We are safe."

"Until the flames reach the methane heater lines in the basement."

Zero's color drained. " . . . Then we are sitting on a bomb? I did not think. Forgive me, Jack."

The microdots showed the NSO team in position, six outside the door, one still on the roof, and two waiting on the first floor of the fire escape.

Isabel crouched next to Jack. "It's hidden." She grasped his hand, squeezed tight, then let go and gripped her pistol.

The front door slammed open; two black-clad figures tumbled in, handguns ready; two others used the doorway as cover.

Jack sent an EM pulse from the bubble circuitry.

Induced signatures resonated from one of the NSO agents in the room, one in the doorway, and the others behind them. But two were silent. No implants.

Jack split-screen-interfaced through the bubble and simultaneously sighted down the barrel of his gun.

"Come out with your hands over your head," one of the NSO agents commanded.

He transferred targeting data to Isabel. She had the unimplanted guy inside the apartment; Jack had the one in the doorway. They fired together.

The burst of explosive needle cluster rounds sent the NSO agent flailing backward, armor or not. The plastocene rounds that followed left trails of toxic smoke.

The agents returned fire—three shock rounds that detonated over their heads and left Jack's teeth buzzing.

Zero made the world turn inside out.

A dozen Isabels, Zeros, and Jacks materialized; they ran, jumped, shot, dove into the hall, grappled with NSO agents, floated in midair; one Jack took a shock round in the chest and fell over dead.

Jack filtered the effects, but it still made him nauseated to watch. The room turned upside-down, then inside out; flames roared through cracks in the ceiling; concrete shattered and the side of the building collapsed—none of it real.

The implanted NSO agents scattered. They wore helmets, but those were designed to shield stray EM broadcasts, not the full force of bubble emitters at close range. They fell, staggered, climbed back to the hallway—except the ones without implants.

Isabel shot the one in the room. The round burrowed through his black armor and exploded inside.

The other unaffected NSO agent swung the barrel of a launcher tube into the room.

Zero tilted the floor under an NSO agent just standing; he fell in front of the launcher—took the projectile shell in his chest. It hissed gray fog, analgesic sweetness. Clouds billowed into the hall and room.

Phantom tarantulas crawled over the NSO agents with implants, up their necks and across their faces. The agents clawed the spiders off, along with their gas masks.

Microdots flashed Jack a warning; the two on the fire escape were moving up.

The apartment shuddered. The bubble went dead. A wave of pressure bolted through his stomach and left him dazed. The walls split and plaster rained from the ceiling—this time real.

"The methane . . ." Zero said.

The apartment filled with black smoke, white fog, and the smell of blood. Light filtered in from the window in the bathroom. Shots crackled on the concrete to their left.

"Come on." Jack grabbed Isabel's hand and pulled her toward the light. Stray EM stabbed through his head: a fire helicopter called for backup, police needed help with crowd control, and shortwave encrypted signals flared, then faded.

He leaned out the bathroom window; the building tilted. One of the NSO agents had fallen and lay twisted on the pavement. The other guy was coming up, gun aimed at Jack.

Jack shot him. The agent lost his grip and fell.

They climbed down the fire escape. Flames leapt from the first-floor windows, and another explosion shuddered through the structure. Jack clung to the wrought iron and to Isabel.

They jumped the last story, rolled into the alley, then ran to the corner of Mosfet Avenue.

A helicopter buzzed over them and circled the building once. All three stories of the apartment complex writhed in fire. Black plumes of smoke snaked into the sky.

"Is everyone OK?" Jack asked.

"I think so," Zero replied. "My face feels numb from their narcotic gas."

A segmented fire truck rushed down the street.

"Get the virus out of your gun," Jack told Isabel. "We'll have to ditch them before we get to the airport."

Isabel looked away. "I can't."

"What do you mean?" Zero asked. "Was it damaged? Is it safe?"

" . . . I put it the only place they wouldn't immediately find it," she whispered, then rolled up her sleeve and showed them the tiny injection mark.

9

A GAME OF JACKS

Jack had a shadow. He hadn't noticed it while he, Isabel, and Zero waited at Santa Sierra's Ford Airfield, or when they shuttle-hopped across the Atlantic. Only at Amsterdam's Schiphol Airport, among the crowds of travelers, luggage handlers, the polite CCO attachés who whisked them through customs and under the rumble of international orbitals, did the base of his skull begin prickling, and he started looking over his shoulder.

That's why he was by himself in Amsterdam now, either to catch this shadow . . . or be caught by it, alone.

Amsterdam was quiet. Hydrogen-powered trolley cars glided softly over cobblestones, and there was no static in the air. High-output biolume columns lit the night, made bands of rainbows shimmer in the canals. How many Dutch citizens had implants to justify this extravagant and expensive silence? Jack could get used to it. This noiselessness explained why the Netherlands attracted top-notch students and high-tech corporations. Implants and serenity. You could hear yourself think.

He had settled into a conference booth in the Café Roux in the very public Grand Amsterdam Hotel. The place had heavy red curtains, black silk wallpaper, gilt columns—and it was dark, matching Jack's mood.

A plate of marinated herring stared at him, which he picked at but didn't eat. He drank coffee, with lots of cream, and munched ginger cookies while he waited for Zero to return his call.

They had placed Isabel in quarantine in a private hospital, claiming she was undergoing gene therapy for leukemia. Zero oversaw her, while coordinating with their CCO liaison to move their official headquarters from Santa Sierra to Amsterdam.

Jack could have stayed with her. He should have.

He wanted to, but the feeling of being watched remained . . . and, he suspected, it would have stayed watching Zero and Isabel, too, had he not left.

The detection of his tail verged on extrasensory. Maybe Reno's implant interpreted subliminal clues: filtered the sound of footfalls that stopped when he did among the din at Schiphol and highlighted the shadows that darted out of view in the reflection of the window at Pompadour's chocolate shop. Jack had been smelling a faint, inexplicable licorice scent since he had arrived. An odor he knew from somewhere.

On the linen tablecloth, next to the delft-blue vase, appeared a topaz cabochon. Zero's token. Jack tapped it and opened the link.

Zero materialized in the conference booth. He wore a white suit and a silk tie printed with van Gogh crows circling over a field of impressionistic wheat. He had shaved again.

"Good evening, Jack. You look horrible. Why don't you return? I have hired security personnel."

"Maybe." Jack scanned the café. Sitting at the tables, scattered amid carved oriental dragon rails and nude statues that held silver biolume balls, there were only three patrons. None nearby. He still hit the mute, silenced and shielded the outer world. "I'll come in tonight, if I can shake this tail."

Zero glanced about. "Are you certain it is not merely a feeling?"

"No. After Santa Sierra, do you want to risk it?" He met Zero's eyes, but the gene witch wasn't sharing any thoughts tonight. Jack asked, "How's Isabel?"

"Slightly disoriented and weak. The prototype virus has no immunosuppressant coating. They were quite a shock to her system. She is on dialysis to help remove the flood of excised DNA."

"You never said anything about the process being toxic." Jack should have never left Isabel. She could die. It would be his fault for getting them involved with the NSO.

"It is a precaution. The danger is minimal, but as you pointed out, after Santa Sierra, we cannot afford to take chances." Zero straightened the Windsor knot in his tie. "It also allows me to study the portions of her genome that are excised."

Which was Zero's priority? Isabel or studying the enzyme? Jack regretted that thought. Of course Zero's first concern was Isabel. Jack saw threats in every shadow. He needed sleep. He could use a stiff drink.

"If everything's running smoothly, then why isn't she here?"

"Nausea," Zero explained, "from the cellular dialysis. She will join us presently. In the meantime, let me bring you up to speed. The Dutch government has been helpful. After reviewing our CCO proposal, they purchased four percent of our preferred stock, and arranged for our new facilities."

"Did you tell them about the NSO and the fire?"

"No. Nor is there evidence to substantiate the story. The CCO liaison informed me that everything perished in the conflagration. The only record of the incident is that we have been fined for illegal chemical storage by the Santa Sierra Office of Industrial Safety." He carelessly waved his hand. "A minor infraction we have already paid."

"I guess no one found any NSO bodies, either?"

Zero looked away. "No."

"They'll try again."

"Do not worry. We are taking steps to prevent the NSO from—"

Isabel's image appeared, a ghost. She was so pale, Jack thought the color emitters on the table had blown. Her hair was still the same red, fine coppery strands, but her skin had been bleached colorless. Even the freckles sprinkled across her nose and cheeks had faded. She looked calm, beautiful; she could have been carved from alabaster.

"How do you feel?" he asked.

"Jet-lagged from the nine hours' time difference. I could use a nap." She pulled her loose hair back, then stuck in an ivory pick to hold it in place. "Don't stare, Jack."

"Sorry." He dropped his gaze to the plate of pickled herring.

Isabel reached out to touch him—couldn't make contact with his projected image. "I know how concerned you must be, but have faith in Zero's engineering."

Jack met her eyes. Hers were solid with confidence.

It wasn't Zero's engineering that had him worried. It was Wheeler and a technology they didn't understand.

"Could you do something with that?" She pointed at the herring.

"Sorry." He covered the fish with a napkin.

"I've gotten sick a few times," she told him, "but I'm better now. The enzyme works."

"Tests indicate that her biochemistry is stable," Zero said. "The viruses cannot be passed via droplet or blood transmission. There is no reason to keep Isabel in quarantine much longer."

Jack wasn't convinced. Her DNA structure could destabilize. Because human science hadn't discovered a function for every part of the genome didn't mean those parts were disposable. They trusted Wheeler and his technology too much. Was he overreacting? Maybe. Or maybe Zero wasn't being objective about his own work.

"Isabel will be the healthiest person in the world," Zero said.

"Sure."

"The Dutch Health Minister was so impressed," Zero added, "he has given us permission to test the enzyme on terminal cancer and radiation poisoning victims."

"Do they know about . . . ?" Jack nodded to Isabel.

"They will soon," Zero whispered. "The entire world will know."

"And that," Isabel said, "will multiply the value of our stock." She smiled, white teeth, skin drawn tight.

Jack thought he saw a grinning skull, then blinked and she was Isabel again. Was there a subconscious leak in the booth's bubble circuitry?

"I must go," Zero said. "I am dining with the Minister of the Interior. Please come in, Jack. We need you."

"I will," he lied. "Soon."

Zero dissolved.

Isabel bit her lower lip. It flushed pink, then drained to snow-white again. "Since we're discussing money, we need you to approve some paperwork at the ING Bank. Here's their link." She set a gold guilder on the table.

Jack picked it up, sensed the protocols and currency exchange rates, whispers of cash transfers and fluxing precious metals values. "What's this about?"

"A stock split. Our preferred shares have tripled in value. We want to divide a portion of them before they're converted into common shares."

"I'll look it over."

"It's going to be OK," Isabel said. "The hard part is over." She edged closer to him, initiated contact; he accepted and sank into her, through layers of worry and disorientation, but in her center it was still the Isabel he knew, still honest, and strong . . . and something new: a hunger.

Jack pulled away before their union went further. He didn't want her to sense his evasion, that he had secrets from her. And he wasn't ready for the primitive appetite he saw churning in her core. "OK," he said.

"Come in. We need you." She looked down and whispered,

"I need you. Please." She sat back. "I have to go. I'm not feeling well."

She vanished.

Jack would come in—after he knew who was following him.

He scratched at his shirt. Underneath was a skintape traveler's wallet he had picked up at the Ford Airport and inside: Wheeler's circuit and the pea-sized isotope. Did they need Jack or just the circuit? That was stupid. He had touched Isabel and there was no betrayal in her. If Isabel wanted to build the circuit, she had the schematic. And if anyone was doing any betraying—it was him. Why was he so paranoid?

He scratched his dead eye, then tapped the gold guilder and linked to the ING Bank.

A stack of paperwork appeared next to his dinner, an approval for a stock split and conversion. He signed, then wandered the financial interface. There were the usual icons of other banks, the twisting silver Möbius of Santa Sierra First International materialized next to his fork, the double-star sapphire of the Darwin Tidal Station Energy Exchange, a shimmering droplet of liquid opal that was the Bogotá News Nexus . . . and a tiny ivory Confucius. Jack hadn't seen that one before. He touched it and the tiny prophet bowed, then whispered to him that it was the Bank of Malaysia.

There was no reason he should have seen it before; still, all the others he knew from Santa Sierra's marketplace.

He linked—resisted the pull of the full immersion interface and kept it to icons and paperwork on the conference table. Jack wanted to keep one eye on the café.

There was a menu of glowing icons, helping hands to start new accounts, the double arrows to transfer funds, the shield and sword for a secure transaction, and more symbols he didn't recognize. Jack ran his fingers over them, let information trickle through: a Fabergé egg of gold and encrusted rubies, that was the Commodities Interchange of Slovenia, and a spinning satellite of eyes and ears and mouths was the link to the Antarctic Media Broker, and a jade dragon—the Bank of Shanghai.

Impossible.

The Great Wall didn't allow trade between the East and the West. Yet, the dragon was there, on the conference table, a public link anyone could rent. Maybe the Great Wall wasn't as high or wide as he had thought. If the Dutch had financial ties to the East, then who else did? Was the information Jack had so out of date?

He gulped his coffee, turned over the gold guilder icon, and severed the interface.

This was the opposite of the world he knew in Santa Sierra. The Chinese were supposed to be isolated, withdrawn from the global community. Yet, here they were. And Jack was supposed to trust his friends. He wanted to. He didn't, though. It was like someone had reached into his mind and pulled it inside out.

. . . Maybe someone had.

He looked up. There were two couples occupying tables in the café, a businessman scanning headlines that scrolled across his table, a waiter, and a busboy by the double Atlas archway entrance.

Jack didn't want to use the implant, but he sensed his shadow had returned. He had to find out if he was losing his mind.

He reached out with his thoughts; the Chinese neuralware made fever and gooseflesh spread across his face, made the hair on the back of his neck stand. He watched. Waited.

There, by the marble arch, a pair of copper cat eyes stared back at him with lids painted like butterfly wings—pink and gold and silver shimmering. A black lace glove twisted a curl of the indigo hair that framed her face. Panda.

Jack recalled the feathery kiss she had given him before she had vanished in the particle physics lab and the smell of licorice on her breath—the scent that had been following him.

Was she tampering with his thoughts? Was that why Reno put the implant in his head? So they could change his mind?

Jack stood, left a fifty-guilder note to cover dinner, then strolled out, paused by the Atlas arch pretending to admire the titans; one held the Earth, the other the moon.

He grabbed her.

She grabbed back, wrenched Jack's elbow, twisted it backward.

He struggled to regain his balance; she kicked his knee out from under him—pulled him, then pushed.

It was the same judo throw Reno had used on him; Jack fell for it twice, literally, and hit the floor just as hard, cracked his skull on the pink marble tiles.

He shook his head, got his bearings—in time to see her sprint into the street.

Jack followed. She wasn't getting away, even if he had to burn every cell in his brain.

She ran up the cobblestone road, the Oude Zijdes Canal on her left, rows of medieval houses the color of gingerbread on her right, pushed past students on their midnight break and tourists headed for the red-light district. The air around her rippled. She distorted and faded.

Jack stared; his forehead flushed. She snapped into focus.

Panda looked over her shoulder, made eye contact but kept moving.

Jack's head exploded, pushed from the inside, pressed from the outside, his signal and hers mixing, vying for control of his perceptions.

Students in between them tumbled from their bikes, fainted, staggered to the rail of the canal. They were caught in a torrent of frequencies screaming from Jack to Panda—Panda to Jack, a vortex of noise and inductive chaos.

Panda stopped and faced him with her arms akimbo.

Tulips alongside the canal grew, unfolded; they became umbrellas, swelled to the size of satellite dishes; they shaded the moonlight, creaked on their stalks—toppled upon Jack, orange and saffron and cherry-red velvet pedals smothered him.

No. He squeezed his lids shut and concentrated.

When he looked again, the flowers were gone. He caught the outline of Panda darting around the corner into an alley, flickering, part invisible.

He went after her, wishing he hadn't dumped Reno's gun at the airport.

The alley tilted up, cobblestones accordioned into stairs. The buildings leaned against one another. With one hand on the wall for balance, Jack climbed.

It's not real, he told himself. Keep going. Get to Panda and give her something else to occupy her thoughts.

Mushrooms sprouted: luminous blue caps, morels, and brackets that clung to the brick buildings. Ivy twined along the walls. Pomegranates swelled upon their stems, ripened, and burst, pelting Jack with ruby seeds.

He looked over his shoulder. The entrance to the alley squeezed shut.

Jack saw through both of his eyes. The dead left one only visualized the virtual—so none of this could be real. And Panda had to be close.

At the end of the cul-de-sac, a meter-tall toadstool appeared. Panda sat perched atop it, chewing gum and watching Jack. She blew a black bubble—it exploded into a cloud of dragonflies, iridescent green and navy blue.

Jack approached and kept one hand in his jacket, like he had a gun. "I want some answers."

"I have given you more than answers," she said and narrowed her eyes. "I have given you a second lesson."

"What's that?"

"Your implant has a memory buffer. With skill, one can program sequences." She waved to the pair of laughing moons overhead waxing and waning. "And while you have become trapped in these programmed thoughts . . . I have escaped."

The alley clicked back into place. No mushrooms. No fairy grottos. No Panda.

Jack pushed with the implant, worsened the headache that already split his skull. There was nothing to see. The entire thing had been a programmed dream. One which Jack had wandered through while she had gotten away.

He kicked a trash can, then backtracked to the canal, lit a cigarette, leaned over the rail, and watched the water.

When the quakes came, the Dutch had been lucky. Instead of sinking into the Atlantic, the Netherlands rose thirty meters. All the pumps and engineering that had once kept the water out had to be reversed to pump it in, the opposite of what they had been designed for—like Jack's life.

Everything flowed the wrong way. No, that was an optimistic assessment. He flicked the glowing end of his cigarette into the dark waters. Jack didn't know which way anything flowed anymore, who to trust, what was right or wrong. But he was going to find out.

Jack had a night's worth of sleep. Not a good night. Not really sleep, either. He had dreams of enzymes uncoiling, giant snakes that devoured DNA; he woke up tangled, strangling himself in the sheets.

His new office had a real view. It was a suite with a curved glass wall that overlooked the IJmeer grasslands, fields that once had been underwater, now covered with tulips and daffodils and hyacinths. Tectonic shifts had brought up the seafloor, made it the richest soil in the world—and not for flowers.

This new land was the reason they had come; it had a new set of rules on who and what could do business there, or rather, a lack of rules. It was a small country all its own inside the Netherlands that attracted a trillion guilders per annum of international manufacturing, trade, and commerce. It was called the *Zouwtmarkt*, the salt market, because it had risen from the brine. Most of it was underground. The Dutch disliked ugly skylines, and they weren't about to give up their fields of flowers for wealth.

An impressionist palette of blossoms, cream and blood red and fluorescent pink, ruffled in the wind, and beyond was the hazy blue band of the North Atlantic. Jack could have whatever view he wanted with the office's bubble circuitry: Paris, a lunar crater field, or a primeval jungle—but he had had enough illusions.

Isabel was in their medical wing, undergoing one more cellular dialysis treatment for the excised DNA, then she was done, transformed. She had looked so pale and tired, her freckles, once splashes of bright orange, had faded to ghosts. Zero claimed there were no harmful side effects, so maybe the enzyme had worked as predicted. Jack hoped so.

He had met Isabel in their freshman complex analysis class. She had excelled in imaginary spaces, the coils of holomorphic functions, and contour integrals that skirted singularities. Jack had almost failed.

She tutored him, taught him how to learn without cheating or hacking or cramming. For the first time, Jack had appreciated the math for its beauty and precision alone—not just a grade on his record. She had given him that gift.

Would the new and improved Isabel be the same woman?

Jack leaned back in the leather flexcouch, and ran his hand over the mirror-polished redwood desk. This was a far cry from his apartment: twenty hectares of industrial park underground, office buildings, and high-security laboratories. What deal had Zero made with the Dutch to get it?

He toyed with the thumbnail-sized chip of plastic on his desk, rolled it over and over between his fingers. Inside the polycarbonate was a slab of gallium arsidine semiconductor, a tiny blackened spot in its center. Wheeler's electron reactor.

Jack made it with quantum mechanical tunneling assemblers, programmed robots that had constructed a miniature canyon a few angstroms wide, dotted with heavy metal atom hills, spanned by bridges of platinum carbonyl complexes, and outlined with the lacy zigzags of alternating double- and single-bonded polymers.

Surrounding the reactor, Wheeler's specifications had tenuous connections to out-of-date logic circuits. There was only one problem: the reactor burned out when Jack applied the slightest electrical current.

It didn't work. At least, not the way Jack thought.

Every circuit required current. Jack allowed femtoamps to trickle through. The logic circuits barely flickered, but the delicate atomic landscape of the electron reactor flared. Under the interferometric whiskerscope, it looked like the earth shaking apart—vibrating, molecules ripped into pieces, fusing together, and boiling away.

Maybe it wasn't a circuit. Maybe it was Wheeler's idea of a joke.

Isabel could have figured it out. She had found the original circuit from the signal in the noise. And Zero had successfully engineered the enzyme they had traded for using that circuit. What had Jack done? Found the signal? He had used Bruner's technique. Even the isotope had been handed to him by the spy, Panda. He hadn't done anything except get the Chinese and the NSO involved. None of this was his.

Jack turned the chip over, traced the bubble of burned plastic. This electron reactor, whatever it was, he had to unravel that mystery. How? If he brought in experts, there would be questions. Where did it come from? Who designed it? Information would be leaked. Rumors. Theft. Jack wasn't trusting *anyone* after Santa Sierra.

He sealed the room, isolated his bubble network from the rest of the complex with layers of dead-code and taps.

Jack opened a window in the air and entered the command that made the stainless-steel wall slide apart. He let the interface scan his retina, then entered the code that unlocked the safe. He removed Wheeler's circuit and the water-blue isotope.

If Jack couldn't understand the electron reactor, then maybe the instructions had been flawed to begin with. He'd ask for clarification. Wheeler had to have just as many questions about human literature. It could be their third trade.

He kept the interface simple; he wanted to see what Wheeler looked like, or rather what he would choose to look like. No confessionals today.

Jack uploaded Wheeler's signal, then sent a greeting on the same distributed frequencies:

Wheeler appeared immediately. He wore a human form, part Albert Einstein with white hair askew on his balding head and part twentieth-century mobster wearing a black suit, black shirt, and black silk tie.

"I must admit," Wheeler said, looking around at the office, "I am surprised at your call, Jack. But it is a pleasant surprise."

"Thanks for answering."

Wheeler sat on the desk, leaned forward, and stared out the windows at the fluid fields of flowers that wavered and rippled in the breeze. "Fascinating that you can sense so much with such a limited perceptual spectrum." He turned to Jack and smiled. "No offense."

"None taken. I wanted to—"

"Again you have reversed the normal procedure. That is why we admire you, Jack. You are bold. Eager to take risks." Wheeler lit a cigar, puffed, looked at it, then asked, "This is the proper format, is it not? Smoking is still part of your social and business experience?"

"Sure." Jack wanted to sit down, appear as at ease and in control as Wheeler looked, but he couldn't make himself. Something about the old man repelled him. He expected to see tiny goat horns on his head or a barbed tail.

Wheeler blew smoke rings. "You wish to trade once more?"

"Not exactly. I want clarification on your electron reactor specifications."

"They are transparent."

Transparent to Wheeler and his advanced civilization. Jack kept cool, though, and said, "I propose we trade to clear up our mutual misunderstandings. I'll help you with our literature. You help me with your instructions."

Wheeler's black eyes glittered. "I liked very much the *Bhagavad-Gita* you sent. Compelling. Precisely what we desired. But alas, your language and your culture have already been deciphered. That does not take away from their value . . . but they were as transparent as our instructions."

Jack's stomach twisted into knots. He had underestimated Wheeler again; that, or overrated the difficulty of human literature. "I built the reactor as you specified." He showed Wheeler the burned chip. "It doesn't work."

Wheeler examined the burned square of plastic-coated semiconductor. He made a tsking noise and shook his head. "It is an *electron* reactor." He held up a single manicured nail. "One electron, no more."

"That can't be right. You have it connected to twentieth-century logic circuits. A single electron won't make them function."

"We only know your technological expertise from a century past. It is not my fault if the human mind cannot extrapolate an antiquated design to your current level of science. We had no difficulties with the three-millennia-span of your literature. Be reasonable."

Was it a test? Had Wheeler combined incompatible technologies on purpose? Or had it been that easy and Jack missed it?

"I will have to report this failure," Wheeler said. He made an ashtray appear and crushed his cigar. "It will require a rethinking of how we must proceed. I had no idea your civilization had such limited capacities. It is a shame, really. I had such high hopes. Especially for you, Jack."

"One snag and the whole deal's off? Over one question?"

"It is not the 'one question.' It is your level of technology and your inability to use ours. As I recall our initial transaction, the biochemistry was an interesting, but flawed, science that *we* fixed for *you*. After considering your cultural details, it may be too risky to continue to do business with, you'll excuse the term, an unstable species. Culturally, yes, your race is rich—but culture is cheap. We desire technology."

"You set it up so I would fail."

Jack caught Wheeler's eyes—an instant of contact; Wheeler probed Jack's memories; an enormous pressure crushed Jack, more than on the ocean floor, millions of tons of black unfathomability . . .

and beyond, wheels and schemes interlocked and turning inside one another. A flicker of the truth—then Wheeler blinked.

"No, Jack. You failed on your own. We even tailored the reactor to interface with your tedious binary logic."

Jack had been in too much of a hurry. Now Wheeler's secrets were forever out of his reach. He balled his hand into a fist. He should have asked for Isabel's help. His pride and paranoia had caused this.

"I must temporarily suspend our transactions. After all, we are not a charity. But as you seem to understand business so well, Jack, I shall keep the door open a crack. There may yet be the possibility of some other business arrangement."

"I'm beginning to see what kind of business this is."

Wheeler whispered: "When you find an appropriate technology, one that you think we may not possess, then you may call me."

"Technology *you* don't have? That could take centuries to develop, if ever."

"You are smart, Jack. You will think of something. Until then, please, we must not clutter the communication channels of the universe with polite chatter."

"This isn't—"

Wheeler stood and he held out his hand. "I still consider you a friend. I hope you feel the same way. Let us part on amicable terms."

Jack considered, then reluctantly shook his hand. It was cold, immovable, like gripping steel.

Wheeler smiled and vanished.

Friends. Business. Jack understood exactly how well they mixed.

He checked the isotope and the circuit. No more carrier wave. No more signal in the noise . . . at least, not Wheeler's signal.

There were, however, others encrypted and hidden.

Without knowing it, Wheeler may have *given* Jack the best piece of information: he didn't need Wheeler.

Jack had seen signals in the music during his Summer of Love simulation: combinations of mathematical expressions like the notes in a chord. If he could decipher them, Jack could establish contact with a different civilization. He could trade Wheeler's technologies. Maybe in exchange he'd get something Wheeler needed. Neither civilization had to know about the other.

And Jack could profit from both sides.

Maybe that's all he had ever done—never really produced anything, just made deals and skimmed a percentage off the top, a middleman. But middlemen were a necessary evil; they smoothed communications between two people, greased the social and financial wheels.

He sharpened the resolution of the static, the light from the decaying isotope transformed by mathematics—glitter that filled his office. Millions of voices waiting to be deciphered and heard. Millions of deals to be made.

10

PLUG-IN JACK

Jack entered the conference room late. A dozen people he didn't know stopped talking and faced him. They wore suits; he wore jeans and a T-shirt. A Rembrandt hung on his left: a woman kneeling before Christ, surrounded by a crowd of scribes—all gold tones and shadows. Jack took the one seat remaining at the glass table.

Isabel sat at the far end. He resisted the impulse to get up and remove the suit sitting next to her.

Her blazer was the color of preconstructionist money; the dull green set off her emerald eyes. She gave him a slight nod, then cleared her throat and said, "I hereby call to order this first meeting of the board of directors of DNAegis Incorporated."

Jack wondered who had thought up the name for *their* company and why nobody had asked his opinion. He let it drop. For the last twenty hours, he had immersed himself in rebuilding Wheeler's electron reactor.

There was no bubble circuitry in the room. Jack felt naked and awkward without metaphor, especially when he had the moccasopa jitters and his head was full of math-code, the physics of noise, and the metastable symmetries of quaternary quantum logic cells . . . and why he couldn't get anything to work.

Isabel introduced Jack to Dutch officials, CCO attachés, and investors; he smiled at each one. Their red and purple and yellow ties reminded him of the tulip fields. He promptly forgot their names and focused on Isabel.

She looked good, still pale, but on fire with vitality. Her fingers drummed on the table, impatient, every motion quick and articulate. Her skin was smooth, and all traces of her freckles had vanished. When her eyes landed on Jack, they pinned him with an unblinking stare.

Zero sat on her right and said, "The results from our preliminary tests are spectacular." He tapped a control pad. The simulation Jack had seen before filled the wall: the enzyme cutting and stitching DNA. The edge of the image overlapped Isabel.

"Cancers have a multitude of treatments," Zero said, "and varying degrees of success based on the stage detected and the type of malignancy."

The simulated enzyme and DNA twisted and shrank into a caduceus symbol with intertwined protein snakes. "This is not the case with our methodology. The enzyme halts the cancer and transforms tumor cells to normal cells within twenty-four hours. The sole problem is the removal of excised error-ridden DNA. Cellular amino acid dialysis, although currently inelegant, is adequate."

Jack wondered what qualified as "inelegant" in Zero's book and how unpleasant it had been for Isabel.

"Of our three hundred terminal test cases, there has been only one fatality." Zero poured himself a glass of water. "Our next phase is to use the enzyme in small but increasing doses as an inoculation for genetic disease." He took a sip of water. "I would also like to send our doctors and a supply of the enzyme to Chernobyl."

"The labor camps?" Isabel asked. "Every tremor recracks the containment shell. It's a nightmare. Why risk our people there?"

"It is a unique opportunity," Zero replied. "Thousands of thyroid cancer cases and prisoners with lethal radiation poisoning,"

The man on Jack's left spoke: "I am concerned about this action. Stock prices have exploded. Rumors exist that the enzyme halts the aging process—"

Jack interrupted, "What does this have to do with helping the Russians?"

The man turned. A silver CCO pin gleamed on his black lapel. It matched his silver hair and white bushy eyebrows, his sparkling teeth. "We want to be humane, Mr. Potter, but a business cannot sustain this rate of growth indefinitely. As soon as we stop pulling miracles out of our hat, the stock falls, disastrously so. We need a clear strategy."

Jack pushed his chair out and stood. "So thousands die to stabilize our stock?"

Isabel held up her hand. "Relax, Jack. No one is going to die." She stared at him until he sat down. "The point about stock fluctuations, however, is well taken. We have to protect ourselves." She turned to Zero. "Arrange the transport of personnel through the Moscow CCO. But keep it quiet." She then addressed the entire room, "Any objections?"

No one said anything.

Jack decided he hated the CCO officer next to him. He had forgotten his name, so he labeled him "Mr. White." Why was the CCO here? Zero and Isabel and Jack owned a majority of the stock. They could do whatever they pleased.

"If that is agreed upon," Zero said and touched the control pad, "then let us move onto the fiscal projections."

A grid spun and stopped on the wall, stretched three-dimensionally across the room. Cells of expenses and incomes and profits and losses filled the lattice.

"These," Zero explained, "are conservative calculations from the Geneva CCO for the next two quarters, inclusive of taxes, and overhead, and incurred start-up debt."

Where was Reno's contribution buried in those numbers? Was it still necessary to hide his involvement since the Dutch had legitimate ties to the East? Jack had better keep his mouth shut until he knew for sure.

Red numbers flickered along the accounting ledger's edges; Zero scrolled farther into time, and they all became black and solid—profit. He zoomed to the bottom corner, where everything subtracted and added, the bottom line: tens of billions.

The investors gave appreciative nods and whispered among themselves.

One fifth of that made Jack wealthy. But it was just a number. All he had seen lately were numbers and equations and simulations. There was no guarantee any of it would ever be real.

Still, to look at it was a thrill.

Isabel took Zero's input pad, collapsed the projection, then tapped in a new command. "Now that we've seen the good news," she said, "let's focus on the bad." Three logos flashed on the wall: a golden apple, a blue sphere, and a cursive A. "We are dependent on these corporations for their cellular dialysis technology." Profit and loss statements popped open next to each icon and scrolled through the previous fiscal year. "I propose we acquire them."

Jack wished he knew what glimmered behind her eyes . . . something he had seen before when they interfaced at the Café Roux. A hunger?

Isabel turned to Mr. White. "Will there be problems with international antitrust laws?"

"There might be," he answered. "The question of reasonable competition will be raised."

It occurred to Jack that this would have been easier to do in America. The Free Market Amendment made power grabs part of everyday business. It was nice to see not every country had sold out.

She dimmed the golden apple icon. "And if we leave the weakest?"

"I will check with my lawyers." Mr. White made a note on his pad. "Off the top of my head, I think we should be covered."

Isabel pointed to the cursive A icon. "Then we invest in this one." She touched the input pad. Numbers in the spreadsheet swelled and darkened. "Their dialysis technology can be tailored to match the enzyme's biomechanics. Our profit will be increased by eliminating the middleman."

She tapped the pad again and the blue sphere dimmed. "From the other corporation we take the useful personnel, equipment, and knowledge, then sell the remainder. This reduces competition."

"Smart," Jack said, "but it leaves a lot of people out of work, doesn't it? You said there was a slower way to introduce the viruses. Do we even need cellular dialysis?"

"Until the effectiveness of the slower treatment is tested," Zero replied, "we shall require dialysis, particularly in the terminal cases."

"It addresses the stock stability issue." Isabel gazed at Jack, then Mr. White, then back to him. "Limited diversification makes us more stable. Be realistic, Jack. This is a business, not a charity. These other corporations bottleneck our anticancer treatments. Think of the sick people this will ultimately help."

They'd have billions in profits within six months. Why be so aggressive? Silence thickened the air in the conference room. Jack met Isabel's stare and held it. He had to get her alone and find out what she was up to.

"Let us put it to a vote," Zero suggested.

"Fine with me," Jack muttered.

"All in favor?" Zero raised his arm, and Isabel, then the rest of the people in the room.

Even if Jack had Reno's proxy vote, they still outnumbered him. "OK," he said. "It looks like we do it."

"Good." Isabel folded her hands on the table, then addressed Mr. White, "We need to put together a brief for the international

163

trade courts." She then turned to another CCO attaché, and told her, "Assemble a team to organize press releases that inflate our stock after we've tendered an offer." She clapped her hands. "Let's get busy, people."

Everyone except Jack, Zero, and Isabel stood and filed out of the conference room.

Isabel paused by Jack. Her perfume smelled of apricots and champagne.

"I thought we were worried about raising the price of the stock," he said. "What was that business about inflating the value?"

"It's complicated," she whispered.

"Enlighten me."

"I read every CCO regulation in quarantine." She lowered her voice to a whisper, "International cartels have the option to tender an offer on our stock. We have to balance its value. Too low and they can buy us out. Too high and it attracts the attention of the big cartels. Either way we run the risk of them stealing it." She set her hand on his. It was hot. He felt her pulse. "Right now the CCO is on our side. We have to play this smart, Jack. Political."

He sighed. "I guess I overreacted. I should have trusted you."

She looked away.

"How do you feel?" Jack asked.

"Quicker, stronger." She squeezed his hand until the knuckles popped, then let go. "I think clearer. The distractions that were there before, the worry, the fear, the hesitation, they've been erased." The edges of her mouth flickered into a smile. "I eat like a horse, too."

She shot a glance into the hallway where the CCO attachés waited. "Look, I have to take care of this. Can we have lunch tomorrow?"

"I think I can fit you into my schedule." Jack squeezed her hand back. "I've got news for you, too."

"It's a date," she said, got up, and left. Her perfume lingered.

Zero followed her. Jack grabbed his sleeve and pulled him into the seat next to him.

"What was that all about?"

"The takeover?" Zero smoothed the white silk sleeve of his suit.

"No, Isabel. What is she doing on her feet so soon?"

"She is perfect, Jack. No genetic anomalies. She has perfect health."

"With a perfectly aggressive attitude to match."

"The enzyme has nothing to do with that."

"Are you certain?" Jack asked. "You haven't done long-term studies on how editing the genome affects personality."

"We have done every available test on Isabel's neural chemistry. It is normal and stable."

"Being perfect isn't normal."

Zero leaned forward and whispered, "I am more worried about you, my friend. I have arranged for a specialist, Dr. Musa, to look at your eye and this Chinese implant. Discreetly." He leaned back. "How much sleep have you had since Santa Sierra?"

Maybe Zero was right. Jack was paranoid. He rubbed his dead left eye. " . . . Not much."

"I suggest that you rest and leave Isabel's health to me. Trust her with the financial details. Trust me with the biochemical ones."

Jack exhaled and let his frustration and thoughts of circuits and Wheeler and the NSO and the Chinese dissipate. "You win, Zero. Rest, sleep, a good meal. I promise."

"We cannot afford mistakes." He rose, paused, then: "I shall send a tailor to visit you as well. You require a proper suit." Zero left and closed the door behind him.

"Thanks," Jack muttered.

He leaned back in the chair, propped his feet on the conference table, and relaxed—then caught the flickering spreadsheet in the corner of his eye. More numbers. Listen to Zero, he told himself, sleep. He couldn't. He imagined curved grids of import taxes and invoice columns.

Jack got up and tapped the command pad, summoned the projected figures. Tens of billions, not gross . . . net profits. Where did it come from? He scrolled through the lattice. Froze. There—the cost per unit treatment. Millions.

What justified that price? Sure, if someone had terminal cancer, they'd pay, no matter what cost. But insurance wouldn't cover something this new. How could the average guy afford it? Answer: he couldn't—not unless he indentured himself for years.

Jack scrolled back to the bottom line and his billions. He'd soon be rich . . . then why did he feel like he had lost more than he had gained?

Reno slid onto the pew next to Jack. He clutched a Bible in his left hand. "I got your message," he whispered. "Nice trick, that."

"I'm a fast learner," Jack said.

Reno gazed down the isle at the cathedral's pulpit, carved with intricate coils and flourishes, then said, "You called the Bank of Shanghai, tried to access my account, and altered the time stamp to this morning." He turned so his blue eye watched Jack. "You logged onto the bank's interface as Admiral Michiel de Ruyter. That was a slick clue. It's his tomb by the Mason's Chapel, right?" Reno slouched into the angle of the pew.

"Is that a question?" Jack asked.

"How did you know we'd find it?"

"The NSO watches for things like that." Jack willed a cigarette to materialize between his fingers—forgot that this wasn't virtual—that he hadn't brought any. "I figured your organization did, too."

Reno nodded. "How do you know what the NSO watches?"

If Reno didn't know Jack had worked with the NSO, he wasn't about to tell him. "Like I said, I'm a fast learner."

Sunlight spilled though the stained-glass windows, glowed red and amber and ultramarine, gleamed upon the mahogany and marble and polished brass of the great pipe organ.

"Since when did you like churches?"

"Nieuwe Kerk Cathedral has lots of public tours. And no bubble circuitry to confuse things."

Reno set his Bible on the pew. "So what do you want?"

"Let's start with the Bank of Shanghai. Why does Amsterdam do business with the East? What happened to the Great Wall?"

"Oh, it's still there, Jack." Reno sat up straighter. "So impassable that every bit of data gets examined and expunged of information deemed subversive by the government. But the Great Wall isn't around China. It's around the United States."

"That's a good one." Jack shook his head. "There's no wall around America. I just left the country. No hassles."

"Because you're CCO now," Reno whispered. "They escorted you through customs. No questions asked because you're part of the international brotherhood of money. You think you'd get out if you were a regular guy? You'd end up in a bubble, your mind turned inside out and washed free of dangerous thoughts."

"You're saying no American ever takes a European vacation?"

"No one capable of thinking for themselves. And no one on the NSO's blacklist."

Jack had attended seminars in Rome and Kiev, but not live, they had been routed though the Académe's bubbles. Sure . . . that data could have been filtered. He didn't have any facts to contradict Reno's Great Wall fairy tale, but he wasn't ready to buy it yet, either.

"How did it happen?"

"Amsterdam is a real hot place these days," Reno said, "so I only have time to sketch you a quick picture. A century ago, the U.S. tried to control the Internet and outlaw hard encryption. They were afraid someone would make money without Uncle Sam getting his cut."

"The twentieth-century Internet had millions of links. No one suppressed information flow in that architecture."

"They eventually figured that out. But then the quakes came, and they restructured the system, built taps into the new networks and chips." A couple entered, walked past them to the box pews on the other side of the pulpit. "The real nail in the coffin," Reno whispered, "was the Free Trade Amendment. It was a step in the right direction, at first; people and products and information flowed because that was good business—until the U.N. complained that the U.S. was getting totalitarian and until American corporations needed big import tariffs to keep up in the world market. The doors closed. *America* raised the Great Wall around *itself*."

That fit what Jack had found in the NSO file. Then again, Reno had been there, and he could have planted those facts. Panda had been in the Café Roux. Maybe she created an illusion of a link to Shanghai.

Reno reached into his shirt pocket.

Jack turned, balled his hand into a fist, then relaxed when he saw Reno remove a package of cigarettes.

"Can we smoke in here?"

"No."

Reno lit up anyway, then exhaled. "I heard about Santa Sierra."

That was only two days ago—a lifetime ago as far as Jack was concerned. Everything had changed. "I guess I owe you one for those guns."

Reno held up two fingers. "You owe me for the guns *and* the money." He turned so his brown eye watched him, too. "Someone told me a few NSO creeps got burned up while paralyzed with anatoxic plastocene. That's too bad."

Jack shifted on the pew and changed the subject: "Your money bought you a chunk of the action."

"I've seen the stock go up, but I've got other brands in the fire. I'm not going to cash in my shares just yet. Is that what you called me here to talk about? Money?"

Jack craved a cigarette, but resisted asking Reno for one. "I want your proxy vote on the board of directors."

Reno chuckled, considered a moment, then said, "It's not like I'll be showing up at any meetings soon. Sure. You can vote for me. I trust you." His blue eye winked.

"I've left the documents at the ING Bank. Sign them."

"I'm almost embarrassed to ask," Reno said, "but I'd like a little something in return." He smiled. "I want a sample of this wonder enzyme and the details of how the bug works."

"Stockholders don't get access to those secrets. Especially stockholders like you."

"Is that how you repay me?" He shook his head, and Jack saw his smile hadn't faded. "Well, that's fine. I guess if I were you I wouldn't trust me, neither—but you don't have a choice." Reno dropped his cigarette and crushed it. "I heard you transferred to the Amsterdam CCO. That paperwork isn't finalized though. One phone call to Santa Sierra CCO and there are red faces all around. Get the picture?"

It was a good thing Jack didn't have a gun. He might have done something in this public place that he'd regret.

"OK. Keep your mouth shut. You'll get the specifications." Jack squinted at him, then demanded, "What are you up to?"

Reno glanced at his watch. "Time's up, Jack-O. It's not safe for me to stay too long in one place." He stood, looked around, then crossed himself and started to walk out. "Watch your back," he muttered. "The NSO is in town."

"Your friend Panda is here, too."

Reno stopped. He sat down again. "That's bad. You better watch out for her . . . if you want to live."

"I thought you two were on the same side?"

"You thought a lot of wrong things lately." He got up and quickly left, slamming the chapel doors behind him.

If Reno wasn't working with Panda, with the Chinese, then who was he working with? He had left his Bible on the pew. Jack picked it up. It was heavier than leather and paper should be. Inside, just past Genesis, the pages had been hollowed to fit one of Reno's Chinese automatics.

Jack hefted the gun, then slipped it into his jacket pocket. "Thanks," he whispered.

He thought about praying . . . for help, for insight, for luck, then decided he didn't want another partner involved in his business.

Jack sat on a xenon atom. It was one in a double row that electrically insulated and encircled the canyon. He scrutinized the landscape, the grottos hidden within the bumpy heavy metal layers, the steep fjord walls of the flexing double-bonded polymers, the pinnacles of diamond carbon with tetrahedral bonds, the flat spans of platinum carbonyls that linked them to the edge of the world, and beyond, the phosphorescent glow, like distant city lights, of the quantum logic cells.

It was a metaphor for Wheeler's electron reactor. A snapshot of electron positions and momentums, clarified, colored, and textured for Jack's benefit. He would never see the real picture because of quantum uncertainty—that was the problem. How could he fix something he couldn't exactly calculate?

A floodgate opened at the end of the valley. A single electron trickled into the canyon, a river of mercury streamed, swelled, rose, and filled the cracks and crevices, rolled and rebounded off the pinnacles, flooded the land with an electrical sea.

Jack's interferometric probes resolved the approximate location of the charge, watched atomic vibrations for telltale clues of electrical perturbations to produce this metaphor of the electron's wavefunction. The usual dynamic interpretations didn't fit. The electron never settled into a stable pattern and never seeped into the semiconductive soil.

The water became choppy. The single electron spread out over distances Jack had thought impossible. One moment ripples, the next tidal waves that crashed against the xenon dike, parts of the canyon dried up, others submerged; it was a seething silver serpent. It was chaos. A tempest in the tiniest teapot.

Tempest wavefunction. One of Wheeler's other choices.

A synonym for the electron reactor.

Jack flipped a switch and let the reactor interact with the quaternary quantum logic cells that surrounded it. The sea lapped the edges, filled the logic cells, flipped their metastable configurations between four topologies: ones and zeros, nulls and zeds, back and forth, without pattern. Random and logic. Random logic.

Wheeler's other choice that wasn't a choice.

Wheeler had given him his pick of three names for the same technology. Jack flushed with anger, not at Wheeler, though. *He* should have known better and seen it coming.

The ocean waves crashed upon the shore, surf and spray and static, then receded.

Jack had another problem: one of the other possible signals he had seen in the noise.

He traced a window in the air and watched binary code crawl by, a steady steam of multiplexed static filtered and transformed from the bursts of light in the decaying isotope.

This other signal repeated like Wheeler's had, but Jack couldn't decipher it. That either meant it was an encryption technology smarter than his or it wasn't encrypted at all and he was missing something obvious in the river of information.

River . . . ocean . . . two water metaphors? What was Jack's subconscious trying to tell him? Were the problems linked?

He diverted the new signal from the isotope into Wheeler's circuit.

The gate that had injected a single electron into the landscape pulsed and overlapped the wavefunction of the reactor. On and off, zeros and ones, incoming data.

The sea stormed, it surged into the outermost quantum logic cells, flipped and spun their geometries like bits of flotsam.

The signal's output simplified and condensed into short rows of binary code.

Jack felt a connection build within him; his office bubble sifted through his memories for hunches.

Was the reactor processing the signal? One electron bouncing inside a box shouldn't. Computer microprocessors had sets of instructions that manipulated data . . . instructions that could be hardwired into the architecture—or in this case, encoded in the atomic landscape of Wheeler's design?

One-electron logic elements had been invented decades ago,

but billions had to be linked to construct a computer's CPU. This one was a single restless electron. A single-electron computer.

That was a guess. Jack couldn't trust anything Wheeler had given him.

He fed the signal's output back into the reactor. The electronic ocean cooled and settled, eddies and whirlpools slowed, and the coded signal simplified again. Shorter lines.

Jack saw a pattern in each row. He tried standard deciphering algorithms. They didn't work. He had a feeling it wasn't encrypted.

If he was trying to communicate with another species, how would he do it? Language was no good. Two *people* rarely ever communicated effectively using language; the odds of aliens thinking and speaking the same way humans did was nonexistent. Unless, like Wheeler, they had studied Earth transmissions. And if anyone was listening, that limited the possible worlds to those within a radius of about 150 light-years. A handful of stars among the infinite.

No. He'd stick with things that were constant through space: the laws of physics or the value of *pi*. Mathematics? Things always added up, got subtracted, multiplied, and divided the same way. Was this new signal math?

He sent the information again through the electron reactor, and it returned with inserted spaces—the binary broke every eleven or every five numbers. Indicating two kinds of data? The longer binary might be operators like addition or subtraction, the shorter numbers or variables.

But what kind of problem was it? There were an infinite number of mathematical problems. It would have to be a proof or theorem. Proofs were chains of logic. They had statements, inequalities, and . . . equalities.

An equal sign? It was in almost every proof he knew.

On every line was: 11111111111. He substituted each with a sterling silver =.

Jack then converted the smaller sequences into variables: *v*, *w*, *x*, *y*, and *z*.

Pattern matching wouldn't work for the remainder. Mathematical proofs were as personal as love letters, each tailored by individual style, steps left in and taken out, elegance and brute force calculations.

It was a giant jigsaw, all the pieces white and the same shape . . . no, not quite. Two more blocks of binary repeated on every line. Parentheses? Or from calculus an integral and differential increment? He inserted a brass sensuous curled s integral, and its matching mirror-polished DX.

Those were the edges of the puzzle. Now for the middle.

He called a list of math symbols and started replacing, seeing what would fit, and what wouldn't. When he tried an imaginary number for one of the variables—that jarred his memory. He opened a window to his Académe notes, on his complex analysis course, filtered through the proofs, then ran a pattern-matching algorithm. There, a close approximation.

Cautiously, as if the proof would shatter if mishandled, he transformed one part of the binary into a function defined at a singularity—and it fell into place: Cauchy's integral formula. With it Jack had learned to integrate imaginary spaces where functions blew up to infinity. At first it had seemed like magic to him. Maybe it was.

But this was more than math. It was something reaching out for contact. Another civilization.

It was Jack's chance to prove himself to Wheeler and Isabel and Zero and to himself. But how to answer?

Noting which patterns represented which symbols, Jack crafted a proof for all orders of derivatives of a function in imaginary space. It built upon their proof. It was like a person receiving a "Hello" and responding with "Hello, how are you?"

He made the code a contiguous string, sliced it and multiplexed the signal to differentiate it from the other channels of noise, transformed it into a burst of illumination and flashed it through the facets of the isotope. Light and shadow bounced into the cracks of the universe.

A heartbeat and a response flashed back: 1.

A greeting?

Jack returned three ones.

A string of binary flowed, repeated thrice, then halted.

This code wasn't as long as the previous proof. There was one sequence for the equal sign and six short binary chunks that represented different variables. The rest was a mystery.

It was short enough that pattern matching might work. Jack filtered it through the mathematics repository. Positive hits scrolled through an open window. One made sense to him: the formula that calculated the distance between two points in three-dimensional space.

They were asking him where he was.

How could be communicate his position? They might not even be in the same galaxy. He downloaded information on the sun's position to the nearest hundred stars and their spectral fingerprints, incorporated the data into the distance formula in coordinates relative to the Milky Way's center, and sent them. Whoever was on the end had to be advanced enough, and have enough space mapped, to figure it out.

Seven heartbeats. A single one flashed back.

They understood.

Jack input the distance formula again, this time with variables instead of absolute positions. He wanted to know where they were, too.

There was no delay in their response. A zero.

Jack re-sent his request.

Three zeros.

Why wouldn't they divulge where they were? Maybe they had dealt with Wheeler before, too, and got burned.

Jack wouldn't push. Not yet anyway. He had worked too hard to figure this out. He tapped in a one, hoping that would smooth things over.

More code appeared. This was the shortest yet, two lines. It looked like a variable—an operator—then a second variable. The last line had the second variable first, the same operator

(11111011111), then the first variable last. A transposition operator? Did they want to trade information?

The land seethed, pulsed, atoms vibrated, and electron clouds of distorted positions boiled and fumed. Wheeler's electron reactor, Jack would offer that. If they were sufficiently advanced, it might be the only thing he had worth trading.

He uploaded the information, the atomic architecture, the interface to the logic circuits, even how his quaternary quantum cells worked: single atoms of cubic symmetry, pairs of corners that operated as a fourfold logic switch.

He waited, summoned an indigo-tipped cigarette to smoke.

Math-code streamed back through the connection. Hundreds of thousands of bits, none of them repeated. Some of the patterns he recognized from the previous proofs. He understood parts: spaces, and spaces within spaces; distances that weren't distances; hypergeometry and the geometry of infinitesimal dimension, then incomprehensibility. A glimpse of genius and madness.

Jack waited. He sent a one back.

They returned a one, zero, one. Then three zeros.

The math-code for Cauchy's integral formula then transmitted through the link. Repeated over and over. Their original greeting.

That was it? A single transaction? Maybe they had to examine what he had traded them. Decide if they had got a bargain.

Jack inhaled and savored the peppermint amphetamine, then blew a wavering ring of smoke. He'd made another deal. He didn't need Wheeler. . . . Although now he had something Wheeler might want.

Inside, he burned with confidence. He was a middleman with something to sell.

It was time for Jack to do big business.

BIG BUSINESS

11

JACKPOT

Jack woke to the sound of surf, waves rolling and crashing upon a metallic shore. Static brushed his arms. He had fallen asleep in the metaphorical interpretation of Wheeler's electron reactor.

Last night he had tried to decipher the new aliens' mathematics.

The math was the theory behind the cracks in space inside the superheavy isotope. That was a guess, though. Most of it was a mystery to him. After eight hours, the only thing he was sure he understood was that it might take a lifetime to comprehend.

He drew a window in the air, stepped halfway through, then paused.

The atomic landscape had distorted. Diamond-carbon pinnacles, before cylindrical and smooth, now were pinched along one side so that a razor-edge seam ran from the water's surface to its tip. What else had changed? He signaled the floodgate and drained the electron.

The charge evaporated. Polymer residue adhered just beneath the surface, iridium atoms clustered on the canyon wall like barnacles, and the gallium arsinide seafloor dried, buckling into a hexagonal pattern—none of it in the original blueprints.

Jack replayed the log and saw the free electron coalesce around a carbon atom, jump it into an excited state. The atom flared and tore free, crawled along the walls with lightning tendrils of hybrid s- and p-orbitals made unstable by the rogue charge. The atom cooled, bonded to a polymer chain, and released the single electron, which then refilled the reactor with its wavefunction.

The canyon had been eroded. Jack measured it—an average of two atoms missing from every side.

He reflooded the reactor. The electron bounced and converged and refracted off these new structures. Did Wheeler's design degrade over time? Or had it purposely altered its hardwired program? Another mystery.

Jack logged out, stepped back into reality.

The view from his office window dazzled him with saffron and crimson tulips, too vivid to be real. He dimmed it, muted colors to antiqued gilt and ebon, made it look more like a Rembrandt than reality.

The Dali clock slithered down the wall, dripped upon the carpet; Jack tilted his head and saw he had enough time to get ready for lunch. He had slept for six hours. More than enough.

Jack ducked behind the mirrored panel of his wet bar, into the bathroom for a shower and shave. He put on the suit Zero had delivered, charcoal with silver pinstripes; a yellow tie; and shoes that pinched his toes. He drew his sandy hair back into a ponytail to hide the gray.

What he saw in the mirror he didn't like. Part NSO counterhacker, part corporate executive, and none of it him. He ripped off the tie, wadded it up, and threw it away.

He poured himself a shot of whiskey, lifted it to his lips . . . and spied a shadow moving behind his reflection in the mirror—it stepped out of the flat glass; black limbs resolved into flesh:

legs in sequined stockings, slender arms, hands with long fingers that brushed indigo bangs from her eyes, arranged her dress, then turned to face him. "Hello, Jack."

"Panda." Jack set his booze down with a shaking hand. This girl scared Reno. And Reno could take Jack in a fight. What made her so dangerous? Was she here physically or interfaced?

Reno's gun was in the desk across the room. Too far. "Can I pour you a drink?" he asked.

"No liquor." She half-closed her eyelids like a reposed cat, and they shimmered silver and gold, a sparkling streak that brushed past her brow and temples; Jack found himself caught in the glimmer. Caught staring at her.

He drank his whiskey—too late, he wondered if she had drugged it. "Come to break into my new office?"

"Events drive us to desperate action." She slid her fingers along the edge of the wet bar. "It is time for the truth."

"Like when you set me up in the particle physics lab?"

"Truth is dangerous. The physics lab, although unpleasant, taught you much."

"Too much." Jack had learned about NSO shadows, and hidden repeater stations. It had shattered his illusions of where and what Académe bubbles were used for. "What price are you asking this time?"

"No price," she said. "I have come to trade. You have questions, too, no?"

"Plenty. But why not steal what you need? You're good at that."

Her eyes widened, then relaxed. "Not good enough. Your encryption is the best, and what I want is not something to be stolen. It is something only you know."

"Why should I trust anything you say?"

"You should not." She took three steps closer, walked on her toes like a dancer, then sat at the bar opposite Jack. "But there is a way." Her eyes locked with his. Warm metallic irises flecked with gold—not filtering.

Jack looked away. "No." He took a step toward his desk.

She caught his hand. "Looking for this?" She laid Reno's gun on the counter.

"How . . . ?" Jack grabbed the pistol. The gun's smart layers had been hacked and stripped. It chirped an interface handshake and informed him it was out of ammunition.

He could have called security, but that would precipitate another round of virtual wrestling with Panda. And she had answers he wanted.

The level of contact she asked for was what Jack had before reserved for Isabel alone, what DeMitri had pried out of his mind—like she said, unpleasant between strangers. Necessary, though, to get the facts.

"Let's do it."

She stepped off the stool and sat cross-legged on the floor. Jack sat next to her and mirrored her position. This close, he felt her breath on his face, smelled the licorice she had been eating. She took his right hand; he took her left. Their eyes met. Reflections: Jack's hazel in her copper gaze.

Inside Panda were grids of iron bars, rigid psychological conditioning that prevented penetration; she let Jack slip through. On the surface was physical attraction for him, elusive mercury, and beneath that, equations that smelled of rust, Jack's published research, and an admiration of his intellect.

Simultaneously she entered Jack, so smoothly he had to push her back before she sank in too deep. She caught his fascination with her, a ribbon of gold silk sexuality and silver mesh intrigue wrapped around his libido. He hadn't realized it was there and butterflies of embarrassment fluttered between them. Beneath that layer, congealed blood: ulcerated worries about the NSO, her, Reno, and himself.

"That's far enough," he whispered.

She eased back. "First question," she said. "You ask."

He thought she'd go first. Maybe she was trying to lull him into a false sense of security. "You broke into my Académe office. Why?"

She bit her lower lip. Oily evasion rose through her consciousness, but she reached beneath the surface of the easy deceptions and said, "I was sent to discover how your research had progressed. And to protect you."

"Why?"

"Bruner worked for us. He requested we eliminate you, as he claimed you had independently duplicated his work. It was then that we suspected your work surpassed his. We were about to contact you when the NSO appeared."

When Jack wasn't killed by the Chinese, maybe Bruner thought they had thrown in with him. Maybe Bruner also figured the Chinese wanted to silence *him*. Or worse, if Jack linked Bruner to the Chinese, the NSO would have taken his mind apart and not bothered putting it back together. Bruner must have gotten spooked and gone to the NSO first. Losing tenure had been the least of his worries.

"You were wounded in my office. How?"

She raised a metallic eyebrow—surprised; a handful of finches appeared between her and Jack and took wing. "Two questions answered," she said and licked her lips. "My turn." Within, her mind welled and pushed away Jack's inquisition. "How have you made Bruner's technique work?"

"By pulling signals from random noise." Jack answered her open-ended question with the narrowest possible reply—he wasn't giving anything away for free.

"How do you decode the signals?"

Inside Panda, ran warm currents that burned like adrenaline, risk. There was the ghost of a memory when she ransacked Jack's files, broke the encryption, and found his data: radio static and microwave anomalies in cosmic background radiation. She was guessing that there was an intelligence in those signals . . . that there was something *to* decode. It was a big guess. Jack buried that thought deep because her guess happened to be right.

Jack could break contact and keep his mouth shut. He had made a deal, though. He'd keep his word. "The signal does not require decoding. It has to be constructed from a series of mathematically related signals."

"Have you established contact with the sender of those signals?"

There was a glimmer inside her psyche and an invitation to venture deeper. Intimate contact like that, though, was a two-way street. Jack declined.

"That was question number three," he said. "My turn."

She strangled a protest, confounded by the protocols she had established for this exchange, and gripped Jack's hand tighter. Her palms were calloused, nails short and sharp. A memory slipped between their interlocked fingers—Jack learning to hack test files and Panda practicing the kung fu form called Attacking the Outside Gate.

Jack released her hand. He considered reasking how she got wounded in his office, especially after her reaction . . . but Panda might not want to answer. There was a better way: ask a different set of questions and see if her answers connected to the blood in his office.

"How much does the NSO know about this?"

"Too much." An image of DeMitri flashed in her memory, then Reno and Bruner, the weight of a gun in her hand, a knife, the taste of bitter poison. "The NSO is interested in you. First, curious. Then suspicious. Now they perceive you as a threat to national security." She whispered, "They have ordered you killed."

"But the CCO—"

"Made a deal with them. Your friends and the business survive . . . you do not. I tell you this, not as part of our exchange, but out of respect."

An NSO death order? All they had was a botched infiltration at Jack's Santa Sierra apartment. They didn't have any data on the enzyme, and DeMitri might, or might not, be talking. They needed Jack alive. Yet, he sensed no lie within Panda.

"And there is Reno," she said. "You must avoid him as well." Jack tasted gun oil and smoke in her mouth: wariness. "We never meant for you to be harmed with experimental implant prototypes."

He'd save questions about her and Reno for later; first he had to clear up what happened at the Académe. "If you came to protect me, why did you leave me for the NSO in the physics lab?"

"I never left. I watched and guarded unseen, but you had to be shown, had to be taught to defend your mind. You had to see for yourself the truth about your United States."

Green light strobed in the corner of Jack's vision; the edge of a step-cut emerald rotated and shimmered. Isabel's request to enter his office.

"I have to go. So do you."

She grabbed his wrist in a steel lock. "You owe me two answers."

"Quick, then."

"You have traded information with the sender of the signal?"

Jack hesitated, then: "Yes."

"For the enzyme?"

"Yes."

Panda pulled away, wriggled free from the layers of contact and trust. Jack sensed her iron bars slide back into place. Secured and electrified. She stood, kissed him, held his face in her hands.

When Jack opened his eyes . . . she had vanished.

He tapped the emerald icon and unsealed the door.

Isabel entered, physically there.

She looked thinner than she had yesterday. How much did all that edited DNA weigh? She could have been a different person, someone who just looked like his old friend. Pure white skin. Flawless. Her face was the perfect face her genetic code intended her to have . . . one unmarred by sun or wind or emotion. He found her alluring, but was also inexplicably repulsed.

"I thought I'd bring lunch." She wheeled in a cart with pastries and dates and squares of Belgian chocolate, a pile of club sandwiches, and a silver carafe of coffee. She wore silk pants, a white shirt with black pearl buttons, a thin tie, and brocade jacket with patterns of embroidered stars. "Aren't you hungry?"

"Sure."

She paused and stared at the gun on the bar. "Is everything all right?"

"Yes . . . no." Jack glanced into the mirror, looking for shadows that moved by themselves, pushed with the implant until headache burned his skull, but no one was there. "I'll explain in a second." Part of his mind was still with Panda—happy to see her gone, yet missing that contact, too.

He devoured three-quarters of a club sandwich, chugged a cup of coffee, and got his bearings. "I saw Reno wasn't in our spreadsheet yesterday."

"He's there." Isabel closed the door, then locked it. "But until we've completed our transfer from the Santa Sierra to the Amsterdam CCO, we're not taking any chances."

Jack decided to keep quiet about Reno's blackmail scheme and the fact that he had sent Reno their enzyme technology via the Bank of Shanghai. No need to stir up trouble now that it had been taken care of.

"Do you know that the Dutch have ties to the East?" he asked.

"I've heard a few rumors." She poured herself a cup of coffee, dumped in lots of cream, stirred, but didn't drink.

It didn't seem to bother Isabel that the United States kept secrets from its non-CCO citizens. That would have bothered the old Isabel. He grabbed a coconut-covered date and popped it into his mouth.

She glanced at his gun again, then back to him. "Zero is worried about you. Why did you refuse to see the doctor he sent last night?"

"I've been busy. Tomorrow. Maybe."

"It's important, Jack. That implant might be irradiating your mind and causing more permanent damage. It won't do to have CCO officials questioning the mental competence of our board members."

He spit a date pit out, tapped a cigarette out of its package, and lit up. "Let them question away. I'm fine." He offered one to Isabel.

"No," she sighed. "Thank you. I don't smoke anymore."

"Because of the enzyme?"

"It hasn't changed anything that I am, if that's what you're getting at. It just clears the clutter in your mind and body." She waved his smoke away from her face. "You might consider using it yourself."

"I'll pass. I like my clutter just the way it is."

She looked at him, eyes as hard as ice, no contact. "When will you see Zero's doctor?"

"Tomorrow. I promise." He changed the subject. "So where are we going for lunch? The court of King Louis or the World's Fair in Paris? I feel like French."

"I like the view and the food here, please. No bubble, no distractions, just you and me."

No bubble. No metaphor. No contact other than the social surface tension that stretched between them. Lunch would be polite conversation and business. It had been easier to understand Panda than Isabel, his friend for the last fifteen years—or so he had thought. Maybe it was only his paranoia, the stimulants, the pressure.

She reached over, brushed the sleeve of his coat. "It looks good on you."

Jack controlled an impulse to recoil. Through the layers of wool and linen, he felt the fire burning within her. It was more than heat. It was contact with an Isabel he didn't know.

"We need to talk . . ." He poured himself more coffee. "About our friend from Canopus. Zero should be here."

"Very well," she said, leaned back, and looked out the window.

Jack had the feeling that she didn't want to be alone with him either. He summoned Zero's icon; a topaz cabochon materialized near his cup. He tapped it twice, but there was no response. "Must be at his prayers," Jack said. "What time is it at Mecca?"

Isabel glanced at the Dali clock and drummed her fingers. "Time for him to be done."

An arch with mosaic scrollwork and carved Arabic prayers

appeared. Zero walked through. Beyond was a courtyard and fountain, the towers of a mosque, and palm trees outlined in a setting sun. He wore a new suit, a shade lighter than Jack's. He nodded to Isabel, raised an eyebrow at the crumpled tie on the floor, then summoned a tasseled pillow and sat upon it.

"You look better, Jack. What can I do for you?"

He had to tell them about Wheeler. Each development made it harder to reveal the truth. It occurred to Jack that it would be easier, and more profitable, if he took Wheeler's electron reactor, took the new mathematics, and started another corporation . . . alone. No. That wasn't fair. Without Isabel and Zero, he never would have made it this far.

"I've been talking to Wheeler," he told them.

"When was this?" Isabel asked and leaned forward.

"Just before Santa Sierra. There was no time to tell you. The NSO came. You took the virus and were out of the picture. Zero was busy setting up the business." Jack stopped. His excuses sounded hollow, even to him.

Isabel frowned, started to say something, but Zero set his hand on her arm.

"No matter, Jack," he said. "But we would have liked to have known sooner. Was there a trade? And if so, I presume you have examined the technology? Is that why you procured the optical tweezer arrays?"

Jack thought it interesting that Zero monitored what equipment he had bought. Then again, it was company money, so maybe it was routine.

"Yeah, sort of."

Secrets were Jack's only insurance. He didn't like them, but without their protection, he'd be expendable. He was the only one who understood Bruner's technique. Isabel was good at math, and the NSO might be able to break crypto—but nothing of this magnitude. That's why the NSO death order didn't make sense. He was the only one with all the pieces to the communication puzzle. He knew it. The NSO knew it. Zero and Isabel knew it, too.

Jack summoned the reactor schematic. It hung it the air, half-ghost, silver and ebony coordinates of the thousands of atoms in the molecular canyon.

Isabel scrutinized it. "A quantum well?" Then she shook her head. "It's too large."

"It is a quantum device," he replied. "A one-electron microprocessor."

"You mean a one-electron logic switch?" Isabel said.

"No. It's a one-electron CPU. The electron in this well has a complex wavefunction. It's stochastic." Jack called up the recordings of the tempestuous electron boiling in the canyon.

She watched for a moment, then said, "It's not stochastic. It exists in stable quantum states, but shifts between them faster than your probe can resolve."

Isabel knew more about this. She could have figured it out quicker than Jack. He should give it to her, but it felt like *his* technology.

"Have you tested it?" Zero asked.

"It helped solve a math problem I've been tinkering with." Not the complete truth, not a complete lie. Jack couldn't help it. And he didn't like how easily he evaded the subject of contact with the second aliens.

He showed them how the wavefunction flooded the adjacent logic arrays.

"How is it programmed?" Isabel asked. She opened a window, without asking Jack's permission—and tapped in a few notes.

Jack ignored the breach in office etiquette. "The landscape. Change the position of the atoms and you change the electron's behavior. I haven't figured what the precise code is yet." Jack displayed the electron as it excited and moved an atom inside the reactor. "To some extent, I think it optimizes, or possibly reprograms, itself."

"This is beyond my expertise," Isabel whispered, "and yours too, Jack. We'll need a team of quantum electrical engineers, physicists, and nano-hardware experts."

"No!" That came out more a shout than a request. Jack stopped the record of the electron's wavefunction—a tidal wave frozen before it crashed upon the xenon shore. "I need another week."

Zero and Isabel exchanged a quick glance.

"Why?" Zero asked.

"I'm not sure of Wheeler's motives. It's always riddles and games with him. He's constantly testing me to see if I'm smart enough to do business with. I'm convinced that there is something hidden in this design. Something that *we* need to figure out if we're going to do business with him again."

That was part of the truth—there was more to the reactor than Wheeler let on. The other part was that Jack wasn't about to hand it over to anyone. Especially not to a team of people he had no control over.

Zero nodded.

"I'd like a copy of the schematics," Isabel said. "You don't have any objections to my input, do you?" She smiled, and Jack recognized it, the smile of solving puzzles.

"Of course I want your help," he replied.

"This represents an enormous opportunity," Zero said, "for us and for the corporation. We shall proceed with caution and keep this among ourselves until we have the chance to speak again. Agreed?"

"Agreed," Isabel said. "Jack?"

"Yeah, sure."

Isabel unfroze the electron and watched as its wavefunction crashed into the xenon dike, then she pulled the viewpoint back until the reactor looked like a satellite image of a hurricane. "Good. Was there anything else Wheeler said?"

"No." Another lie.

Jack wanted the chance to repair his business relationship with Wheeler before he'd admit that he had ruined it. He had never lied so much to his friends. Jack was setting up his own business within their business, between Wheeler and the other aliens and himself. Those secrets felt like a weight in his stomach.

He was glad there was no metaphor between him and Isabel and Zero.

Isabel got up and squeezed his shoulder. "Nice work, Jack. Really. We make a good team. I have a meeting at the Geneva CCO, but I'll be available tonight if you want to bounce ideas about this electron reactor off each other. Let me know."

"OK. Thanks for the lunch."

"Anytime." She waved to Zero and left.

Zero shook his head.

"What was that for?" Jack asked.

"Nothing," Zero said. He looked into Jack's eyes—not for contact—they turned black and bottomless like they had when Zero had warned him about using the Chinese implant. Zero looked away. "Isabel is a smart woman."

"Are the other test cases like her? Smarter? Driven?"

"Some are. Some are filled with tranquillity. In others, no perceivable differences."

"So there is a personality change."

"I believe the editing process makes you more of whatever you are," he told Jack. "It is not a change, rather an intensification." His eyes were their normal brown again. He got up to leave. "Is there anything else?"

"I ran into Reno."

Zero stroked his chin where his beard had been, caught himself, and stopped. "What did our silent partner say?"

"He told me the NSO are in Amsterdam. They've issued an order to kill me. Just me, though. You and Isabel are in the clear."

Zero sat. "Then I shall increase security and ask the CCO, discreetly, if they can provide increased protection." His gaze landed to the gun on the bar. "What else can I do, my friend?"

Jack opened his mouth, closed it. He was going to tell Zero about the second alien civilization. The gene witch was still his friend, wasn't he? Yes. But he was also friends with the all-too-persuasive Isabel. If Jack asked Zero to keep his secret, would he? Could he keep it from her?

"Nothing," Jack replied. "There's nothing more you can do. Thanks."

"I am posting a bodyguard outside your office. No argument." Zero opened a window in the air, and beyond was a sky full of stars, three moons, and silhouetted against the east were the minarets of a mosque. He stepped halfway into his world, then whispered, "I shall pray for you, too." He vanished.

Jack threw his napkin over Isabel's lunch. He wasn't hungry. Instead, he got up and poured himself another drink.

The NSO would take precautions, especially in a foreign country. They'd make no mistakes this time.

He toasted himself in the mirror, half-hoping that Panda would step back through. She didn't. The only thing reflected was Jack wearing the suit that he hated.

It was five minutes to midnight. She hadn't come. Jack had queried Isabel's office twice in the last hour, and the automated reply had said she was occupied.

Just as well; he really didn't want to see her.

His main worry was the NSO. What could he do? Run? It was a possibility. He had set up a meeting with Reno to discuss the options. Tomorrow, 1 A.M., at a local sex shop, Freud's Little Sister. He kept Reno's automatic, reloaded, close.

While he waited, Jack had linked electron reactors in parallel, first four microprocessors in a square configuration. The electrons washed over one another, made patterns of constructive and destructive interference. The rate at which they rearranged the atomic landscape doubled. A cubic geometry of eight linked reactors increased the rate of reprogramming by a factor of fifty. Exponential change.

Jack had set his robotic assemblers to manufacture arrays of 256 reactors. Those clusters could be further linked in a parallel hierarchy. How far could he optimize the architecture?

It was Wheeler's design, though, not his. He only tinkered with it. Jack was really only good at one thing: being a middleman. So he'd be the best middleman he could.

The Dali clock on the wall solidified into a circle, both hands pointed up. The witching hour. Time to deal with the devil.

Jack sealed his office with dead-code and encryption, connected his watchdogs to the *Zouwtmarkt*'s early warning system—then changed his world.

Salt-tinged air flooded the room, the walls receded, dawn broke, and the sun arced into the sky. It was noon in San Francisco. Stagecoaches rumbled down Montgomery Street—almost ran Jack over.

Reaching into the sky, past the façades of the buildings, soared the masts and rigging of the clipper ships in the harbor. Men packed wagons with sacks of flour, jerky, and tins of coffee; they pushed wheelbarrows full of shovels, pickaxes, and mining pans; they wanted to get up into the Sierra Nevadas, split the earth open, and find their fortunes.

He stepped onto the sidewalk, pushed through the mob waiting to get into Jenny Lind's Burlesque Theater, shoved past sharp elbows and whiskey-laden curses. Jack checked his wallet—still there—then headed into the adjacent brick building, the office of Wells, Fargo & Co.

The assayer stopped weighing gold dust on a balance, gripped the shotgun in his lap, saw it was Jack, and went back to work. Jack stepped up to the telegraph, linked to the isotope, and tapped out a message to Wheeler.

"If anyone comes looking for me," he told the assayer, "I'll be upstairs."

Up two flights of stairs, past the locked door, and Jack entered the general manager's office. There was a cast-iron combination safe in the corner, a rolltop desk next to it, and a table littered with cigar butts, scattered cards, and poker chips.

Jack took the seat facing the door, his back to the corner.

There was a knock, and Wheeler entered. He wore a long black coat, boots, bowler hat, and dangling from his vest, a gold watch fob.

"I was pleased to receive your greeting, Jack, as always,

but"—Wheeler lowered his voice—"I thought I had made it clear that we cannot consume valuable time and frequencies by—"

"I have new business." Jack unstoppered a cut-crystal whiskey bottle and poured himself two fingers. He didn't offer any to Wheeler. "Are you interested?"

Wheeler closed the door. "That is an entirely different matter." He pulled up a chair to the poker table, removed a cigar from his vest, and lit up. "You surprise me again, Jack. I would have never guessed we would speak again so soon."

Wheeler was playing the nice guy. That meant he wanted to trade. Or was at least curious what was for sale.

Jack went to the safe, dialed the combination, and removed a yellowed file folder. He pulled the first three pages out and set them on the table.

Wheeler examined the mathematics, raised an eyebrow. "Indeed. We are interested. May I see more?"

Jack gave him the next eight pages.

"We can use this . . . if the proof is complete."

"It is." Jack hadn't deciphered the entire thing, so wasn't certain of that. A bluff. "I want a power source. I'm not settling for 'choices,' either."

A new energy source would expand the base of their corporation: biomedical—electronics—energy. All that was missing was to go into politics.

Wheeler poured himself a finger of whiskey and mulled over Jack's demand.

Jack knew Wheeler appreciated strength, and for the first time, Jack sensed that he had the upper hand. *What* he got wasn't as important as *how* he negotiated it. Wheeler had to know this deal was Jack's.

"Very well," Wheeler said, "I have been authorized to offer you a technology reserved for our most trusted partners." He passed his hand over the pile of chips that had been someone's jackpot. A box appeared, teak and ivory and rosewood inlaid to appear as clouds and mist swirling.

Jack reached for it. Hesitated. Wheeler had given in too easily.

"Go ahead," Wheeler whispered and leaned forward.

He opened it. Within rested a black mirror sphere the size of his fist. Upon it his face, Wheeler's, the edge of the box, and scattered poker chips distorted to an infinite optical smear. Set upon the surface was a matte-black dimple.

Jack picked up the ball and held it in his left hand. It was neither metal nor plastic; it was neither heavy nor light—like it was there, but not. He placed the tip of his finger on the dimple— it seemed the right thing to do.

It interfaced with Jack; he flipped inside the convex mirror, and out of this fishbowl view he saw the room, his office, not the Wells Fargo building, but his *Zouwtmarkt* office.

He slid the outer control and the world moved with it—fast— over the bulb fields—across the Atlantic—over mountains—then soaring into the upper atmosphere . . . and Jack looked down with satellite vision, Europe streaked with clouds, sun-dappled Mediterranean, and there, a tiny blinking red dot that indicated his position in the Netherlands.

He let go. His perceptions snapped back to San Francisco, the poker table, and Wheeler watching him.

"Another schematic?"

"No." Wheeler stood. "This is a gateway. It translates matter across the same domain of space the transceiver sends its signal through the void. You should be able to use this quite readily as a source of energy."

If it used the same cracks in space the circuit and isotope did, could Jack go anywhere? Teleportation? It was infinitely more versatile than a source of energy. What powered it?

"Then this is here?" Jack whispered. "Not virtual?"

"Yes. . . . You perceive the implications?" Wheeler turned to the window and stared out. "Do cities like this still exist on your world? Mountains filled with gold? And men eager to dig it out?"

Jack placed the sphere back in the box. Without knowing how to operate the controls, he could end up anywhere.

"Yes. Every day is a gold rush."

"But did it not stop? The gold ran out."

"There was always gold," Jack told him. "If not in California, then in the Klondike or Australia. When that gold ran out, there were emeralds and diamonds. Or geothermal power and oil reserves in Santa Sierra. There's always something."

Wheeler considered this, then: "I have thought upon our last transaction and decided our schematic and the blend of technologies may have indeed been too obscure. I would like to give you a gift to make amends for that misunderstanding."

Something for nothing? What was Wheeler up to?

Wheeler turned from the window and unrolled a parchment onto the card table. It looked like an old map with topological lines and jagged coasts, symbols of atoms and their precise coordinates. It was an electron reactor, slightly altered. A new program? In the corner there was a diagram showing thousands of reactors in a parallel structure.

Wheeler then set a book on the table to pin one side of the map. "That is the data lexicon the program utilizes. It will make speaking with other races easier."

"What do I need—"

"The mathematical proof is not yours, Jack." Wheeler faced him, and his eyes were clear, gears and clockwork machinery turning within them. "It is centuries too advanced for humans and too well thought out. You have traded with others."

Jack took a step back and said nothing.

Wheeler blinked and his eyes reverted to their normal black. "That is excellent, Jack. Superlative. I knew I could count on you."

"You *want* me to trade with others?"

"You have a gift with communication. Such a priceless commodity cannot be allowed to go to waste. We would like you to trade again with this other race of mathematicians. Procure for us their exact location."

"I don't take orders."

"Reconsider. This is business, Jack, big business. You cannot simply walk away. Please realize that I am but one voice among many. My constituents do not appreciate you as I do. They would employ . . . what is the word? Arm-twisting?" He glanced at the black mirror sphere.

Jack's first impulse was to grab the gateway, smash it into a million pieces. But that wouldn't stop Wheeler. They didn't need it to transport matter through the cracks in space. They had sent it with another similar device . . . from wherever they really where. Jack doubted it was Canopus.

The threat was clear. Cooperate or one day a bomb or virus or small star might appear on Earth.

"The word you're looking for is 'blackmail,' " Jack said.

Wheeler nodded. "Yes. It is. Does that mean you have changed your mind?"

"Do I have a choice?"

"No. I knew I could count on you, Jack. We shall be in touch."

Wheeler shook his hand and vanished.

Jack swept the cards and poker chips off the table. He had given Wheeler everything he had needed to extort him. The genome revealed human weaknesses and the literature, mankind's mental vulnerabilities. He had thought them of little value . . . when he traded them away.

Jack had been caught between schemes and plots and had gotten crushed in the middle of Wheeler's machinery. He had to play along. It wasn't just his fortune on the line; it was Zero's and Isabel's, and if he messed it up . . . the world's.

12

JACKHAMMERED

Jack sat in his *Zouwtmarkt* office and held the mirror sphere. He set his finger on the dimple of matte black, marring its surface.

It interfaced with *him*—the reverse of normal protocol. Even the most invasive appliance always requested an electronic handshake—they never initiated contact on the user. Jack was wary. He wasn't certain who was in control.

The reflection of his finger solidified to neon red and lifted off the ball, sharpened into an arrowhead, and pointed straight at him.

A smear of ultramarine appeared and wavered around the dimple like waves of disturbed water. Jack slid the dimple. A second arrow stretched from the patch of blue, flickered from millimeters short to meters long—skidded out of control, then vanished.

Where were the maps? Jack had seen them when he first

picked up the gateway; he had flitted across the world. What was he doing wrong?

He touched the surface. The red arrow returned. Jack saw there were two, no, a dozen . . . hundreds of tiny red vectors braided within the single arrow.

Pushing harder, he pierced the sphere; the blue vector materialized; he pushed harder still; an atlas appeared, and the arrow of blue stretched across the world.

Jack spun it over the globe. The blue vector always pointed to the surface of the Earth. Did that limit him to terrestrial destinations? But Wheeler had transferred it from his home world. So why couldn't Jack roam the stars, too?

He soared over the coast of Spain and the volcanic island chain of Portugal, across snow-capped Andes and Alps, then fell from the edge of space, across the checkerboard tulip fields of the IJmeer grasslands, to the sprawling *Zouwtmarkt* complex, to the DNAegis building, and into his office.

These were better than any blueprint or satellite photo. Only the smallest items were missing; there were no coffee ring stains on Jack's desk. Was the entire world mapped in such detail?

Wheeler had lied.

This gateway technology could tap into every network on Earth . . . learn anything. That's why the sphere interfaced so seamlessly with Jack's implant. That's why he had such detailed maps of the world.

Wheeler had made up that fairy tale about listening to Earth's hundred-year-old transmissions. The trade for the genome and the literature had been hoaxes. Wheeler had been a cliché, pretending to be the curious, out-of-date, harmless alien.

He had set Jack up to be his middleman. Given him the technology for his own purpose. And when Jack was no longer useful, would Wheeler leave him cold and find some other sucker? Jack couldn't guess what the alien had in store for him.

Whatever it was, Jack had a feeling he wasn't going to like it.

He slid the dimple over the map of his office. The blue arrow followed his direction and pointed across the room, a meter closer to the window.

What about the multiple arrows within the single red vector? He peeled one arrow from those directed at himself, then stretched it to point at the ashtray on his desk.

He released them.

Yellow arrows drew between the reds and blue—not straight; they flickered and zigzagged and bounced through ripples in the space, made the third leg of staggered triangles—

—the office window was closer. Jack was in two places at the same time: in front of himself and behind himself.

He turned: only the imprints of his shoes in the carpet remained. The feeling of duplication vanished . . . like Schrödinger's cat, maybe he had been two simultaneously existing wavefunctions until viewed. But viewed by himself? Could the cat observe itself and resolve its own uncertain wavefunction? He'd leave the metaphysical physics to philosophers.

The ashtray lay at his feet as well. So the red arrows locked onto things, set the initial conditions and defined what would be transported, while the blue vector indicated destination.

Despite his other lies, Wheeler's gateway worked.

Ultimate freedom at the touch of a button. Of course, there were strings attached; Jack still had to discover the other aliens' location to stop Wheeler's threats from becoming real, but he'd worry about that later. This morning he'd have fun.

Where to go? He slid the dimple, made the blue vector point into the fields beyond his office window—

—and appeared in the middle of the IJmeer grasslands, surrounded by pink tulips, flowers that looked like flames with tangerine edges, and meter-tall hyacinths waving in the North Atlantic's breeze, shaking loose clouds of gold pollen—a checkerboard of silver and scarlet and violet that stretched to the horizon—broad impressionistic strokes painted by the ghost of van Gogh. It smelled of perfume and manure and sea salt.

To the west, the half-buried domes and slender smokestacks of the *Zouwtmarkt* mingled with antiquated windmills. They reminded Jack of where he had come from and where he had to return.

It could be a trick, all virtual, all part of the gateway's interface. He might still be in his office. Sometimes he had the waking nightmare that he was in DeMitri's office, this was still the interrogation, and everything that had happened since had been an elaborate dream to pry the truth from his subconscious.

An undergraduate at the Académe had lost his mind after implantation, unable to differentiate reality from illusion. Jack knew the difference; reality was whatever you believed it to be . . . as long as you stuck with that belief. Any other ideas got you questioning everything and drove you mad.

He shifted the vector, rose through layers of maps, Europe, the world, to North America, the West Coast, and—

—static screamed in his head: the crackle of the police bands, the taste of chewed aluminum, and a fading African drumbeat. Santa Sierra was dark, on the other side of the planet, shielded from the sun. The downtown lights looked like fallen stars: mercury-vapor yellow and fluorescent flickering. Mosfet Alley smelled of smoke. There was a pile of rubble where his apartment building had been. Automated pickers sorted the brick and metal and organics into recyclable piles. A new office building would rise from those ashes inside a week.

He wished it hadn't burned. It was a dump, sure, but it had been *his* dump. Reno's books had been in there, old pulp, his Steinbeck and Jefferson. Stupid things to get choked up over.

Shadows stumbled down the alley—an unemployment gang. He caught their rancid odor, saw the glint of feral eyes and blades in the moonlight.

He cast the blue vector to the other side of the world—

—Jack stood in wet sand. It oozed through his sneakers and socks. A ripple of water flowed around him, sea foam and swirls of silt. Seagulls circled over the distant blades of the tidal generators, ate the stunned fish, and picked through rotting kelp. The sun lit the shallow water with amber and rust and gold—flat in every direction, a mirror marred only by the occasional human

201

picker that sifted the tidal flats for zebra prawns and the telltale bubbles of blue-lipped butter clams.

They mounted their boards and rode the current back to Darwin Station, a city that sat upon a million hectares of tidal flats. They'd return with the next tide.

That was the life for Jack. Hard work. Simple work. No conspiracies or worries except a sore back and an ozone hole overhead and melanomas . . . and who the hell would pay for *their* anticancer treatments? No one. They were expendable.

Maybe Jack could do something. It was time he talked with Zero and Isabel anyway. He altered the coordinates and stepped across the world, into—

—Zero's office, Jack's pants and shoes dripping muck.

Jester orchids twined along the walls, tiny bells for petals tinkled in the air-conditioning. Clusters of phosphorescent mushrooms grew in bonsai dishes on Zero's mahogany desk, pulsing ghostly blue. The carpet rippled under Jack's feet, repelled by the saltwater sludge he had tracked in.

The gene witch sat on a cushion floating a meter off the floor. Isabel reclined in a high-backed chair, sipping tea.

"I'm glad you're both here," Jack said. "We need to talk."

In addition to the price of the enzyme, Jack wanted to fill them in on Wheeler's new toy. He didn't want more secrets between them. They were, after all, partners. Besides, Jack was scared. Scared to face Wheeler; his threats and technology and agendas put Jack in a position of representing humanity. Alone.

A window orbited Zero and Isabel: vats of organic soup with enzyme activities and pH and nitrites concentrations in shifting graphs along one edge. Zero collapsed the link and looked up. "You could have requested to interface, Jack. There was no need to hack in."

"There was no request to interface," he said, "because I'm not interfaced."

Isabel glanced at the sand and raised one of her delicate eyebrows—probably trying to figure out what the messy metaphor meant. "Of course you're interfaced," she said and sipped her tea. "I saw you appear."

"There is a board of directors' meeting in two hours," Zero remarked. "Check your scheduler. We have a presentation to prepare. What is so urgent it could not wait?"

"This." Jack set the black sphere on the table. "Wheeler's latest trade. It uses the same cracks in space that the isotope communicates through, only it sends matter, not light."

They sat silent a heartbeat, then Isabel picked the sphere up gingerly, as if it might explode. "What does that mean, precisely?"

"Don't touch it," he warned her.

She set it back on the desk.

"For lack of a better word . . . a teleporter."

Isabel squinted at the device; her face reflected upside-down, then she leaned forward and her bleached features smeared and distorted across its surface. She opened a window, linked with Zero's diagnostic shell (ignoring office etiquette), and scanned the matrix trace of their virtual environment. She then stared at Jack, reached out and touched the hem of his jeans, rubbed the sand between her fingers, and smelled the salty organic odor.

"He's here," she whispered to Zero. "Physically. Unless his implant is shielding his presence in the system." Then to Jack: "You've tested this thing?"

Jack smiled, satisfied that he could still surprise her. "I've been to the IJmeer grasslands, to Santa Sierra, and"—he pointed to his feet—"to Darwin Tidal Station."

Zero's eyes widened and he looked to Isabel. Her lips were pursed, and she stared beyond Jack, thinking, then she refocused upon him and asked, "How does it work?"

Jack had a clue from the mathematics he had traded for. "Movement can be quantized," he explained.

"Electronic, vibrational, rotational, and translational motions," Isabel replied. "I know."

"But I think the *space* within the isotope is quantized, too.

203

All points may be equivalent . . . apart from a new, different quantum number."

"You would have to be inside the isotope to utilize that property, Jack."

"Quantum mechanics is not my field of expertise," Zero said. "What does this mean?"

Isabel turned to him. "Motion, on the atomic level, has discrete values. For example, a diatomic nitrogen molecule only vibrates at allowed frequencies. Absorbing or emitting energy shifts this vibration to specific energy levels. There are no frequencies in between."

"But space is continuous," Zero replied and scratched at his five o'clock shadow.

Jack shrugged. "Maybe not. Maybe like the allowed energy levels, you can jump from site to site"—he snapped his fingers—"with no continuum in between."

"You're talking about the quantum levels of atoms," Isabel said. "How does a person translate? To shift the quantum states of every atom in your body would take energy. Lots of it. What powers this?"

"I haven't worked out all the details. Maybe the energy is negligibly small."

Isabel shook her head. " 'Maybe'? She raised her voice: " 'Maybe'? Jack, we can't rely on 'maybes.' "

"We don't have to understand the technology to use it."

"Yes, we do!" She stood, her face flushed, and for a second he thought she might throw her teacup at him, but then she composed herself and sat back down. "This device is way over our heads. It's like Pandora's box."

"We're using the enzyme," Jack said. "I don't see what the difference—"

Zero interrupted, "We tested every biological aspect of the enzyme. There are no health risks. And we have a chance to understand the single-electron microprocessor. Possibly reverse-engineer it. This technology"—he lowered his voice to a whisper—"might as well be black magic."

"Think it through," Isabel said. "This isn't virtual. It's not a game."

Jack bristled at that. He had never treated this as a game. Wheeler was dangerous. The NSO was dangerous. He realized that better than either of them. If he had known how condescending Isabel was going to be, he would have kept his mouth shut.

Zero set his hand on Isabel's arm to calm her, but she jerked away.

"There are too many questions," she said. "How do you keep from materializing inside an object? How does it alter your composite momentum vector?"

Jack had no answers. This was beginning to feel more like an interrogation than a conversation.

"At least, consider the sociological implications," Zero said. "Transportation industries will cease to exist." He looked at the mirror sphere. "Terrorists could use it as the ultimate weapon. National boundaries would dissolve. It is not Pandora's box. It is Prometheus' fire, stolen from the gods. It changes everything."

They didn't know what Jack had done to get it—the risks he was taking. "So you want to destroy it?"

"Of course not," Isabel said. She picked up the sphere and set it in her lap. "We study it slowly . . . very slowly."

"It's safe." Jack stepped closer. He could grab it and disappear. They weren't taking it away from him.

Isabel set her hand atop the device.

"I've used it. It's simple. Let me show you."

"God no, Jack! You were lucky it didn't turn you inside out." She leaned forward. "Why do you suddenly trust Wheeler and his technologies?"

That stopped him.

She had a point. Maybe that's how Wheeler would get rid of Jack when he had outlived his usefulness. He could be using the gateway, then vanish . . . forever. No mess. No fuss. He needed to take a step back and get some perspective.

"You're right," he admitted and sat on the edge of the desk.

Zero's mushrooms blushed warning red colors at him. "I'll stick it in my office safe."

"Zero has a secure lab in basement four," Isabel said. "We'll place it there, guarded. Your office isn't airtight."

True. Panda had waltzed in easily enough. Maybe the NSO could get in, too.

Jack didn't like just handing it over, though. In his heart and head, he knew that Isabel and Zero wouldn't steal from him—that was paranoid. It was the feeling at the base of his spine that whispered he should grab it and get out of town.

"By the way, what did you trade him for it?" Isabel asked.

"Some abstract algebra he didn't have." That wasn't the entire truth, but Jack was no longer in the mood to explain anything to Isabel and Zero.

He turned, started to leave, then: "One more thing. The price of our enzyme. It's too high."

"Bring it up at the meeting tonight," she said. "We can't do anything without a vote." She opened the window that Zero had been examining before, paused, and asked, "Is there anything else, Jack? We only have two hours to get ready."

"No."

Isabel still had one hand clamped over the mirror-black sphere, an oyster holding on to its pearl. Jack was losing control over what he thought had been *his* corporation . . . at least, the twenty percent that was his. Maybe it wasn't even that.

He slammed the door on his way out.

Jack paced his office. He didn't need a bubble-revealed hunch to feel the NSO closing in. He could leave—forget the board of directors' meeting and hide in Amsterdam. No. They probably had every exit from the *Zouwtmarkt* staked out. Maybe it was safest to stay here.

Both hands of his Dali clock pointed down and dripped onto the floor.

Or he could sneak into Zero's secure lab and get Wheeler's gateway. His implant could get him past the guards. He had a real skull-splitter headache, though. The notion of pushing his luck again with the Chinese hardware wasn't appealing.

He'd wait until he linked up with Reno—the spy would know how to evade the NSO.

In the meantime . . . he'd take care of loose ends: Wheeler's "request" to find those other aliens.

Jack's robotic assemblers had cobbled together the new microprocessor. He linked it to an array of quaternary logic cells and to Wheeler's translating lexicon.

That software contained hundreds of thousands of languages, billions of symbols, charts, and code manifolds that extrapolated between them. He didn't understand it. He didn't trust it for a second. But he had to use it to accelerate communication with these new aliens.

Like Zero had said, it might as well be black magic. If it was, that's the metaphorical approach he'd use.

He turned the walls and windows of his office inside out and pushed every trace of his modern conveniences into the corners. The atmosphere condensed to fog. He sat on a slab of green stone, a broken altar with cuneiform edges. Iron urns encircled him and held smoldering coals that gave the vaporous air a golden texture, made shadows dance upon the crumbling columns of the ruins of Delphi.

Tarot cards appeared in his hand. Jack never fully understood them, but they were ripe with metaphor. He needed every lucky guess and hunch he could squeeze from his subconscious to work this deal.

He dealt from the bottom, turned over one of the slippery cards: Art.

In the center of that card was a cauldron of boiling water. A woman in a white lab coat held an input pad in one hand and a painter's palette and brush in the other. She touched the tip of her brush to the water, altered its color: swirls of chromium yellow and robin's egg and cinnabar. The liquid frothed. From its depths emerged chrome-feathered parrots and rippling Mandelbrot flatworms and silicon-whiskered mice and clockwork scarab beetles that splashed and took wing, scurried and slithered away.

Art and science intermixed. That's what Jack attempted: blending the known and the unknown. Conscious and subconscious. What he had done before and what he was about to do.

He opened a link to his archives, sent the transcription of his previous conversation with the new aliens into Wheeler's maze of electron reactors.

Jack then opened a window to the nano-landscape. Electrons clashed and swept through one another, spilled over the walls of their canyons, flooded the logic arrays, backwashed with data from the lexicon—combined, then flowed in a steady stream of output.

He compared the original message to the translated version. The greeting, the request for his position, and the offer to trade were there, but the translated version missed the elegance of the original. It couldn't convey the beauty of their mathematics.

Conversation was harder than math . . . just saying "Good morning" could have more nuances than an infinite series. Even Wheeler's advanced technology missed part of the message.

Jack opened a link to the isotope noise. The aliens' greeting transmitted: Cauchy's integral formula.

How to best approach them? He flipped over a second tarot card: the Universe. It was a whirlpool that shimmered in the setting sun. The sparkles upon its surface were constellations; he looked closer and saw galaxies among the flotsam, oil slick nebulas, and beneath, a coral snake that chased its tail.

Jack didn't understand how the metaphor fit.

He opened two more windows, the raw data he sent and received, and in the second, the translated version. Jack had surrounded himself with information, scattered cards, and open links. It was almost too much to hold in his head.

He sent the same response they had answered to before.

The proof scrolled by in the untranslated window, then the translation of his greeting appeared: HELLO?

A moment passed, then they answered: HELLO. WE CONFIRM

YOUR POSITION. CANNOT TRADE MORE THAN ONCE. MESSAGE ENDS.

Why weren't they willing to do repeat business with Jack? Had they been threatened like he had been threatened by Wheeler? Or maybe they didn't like what he had traded them the first time.

Jack typed in: YOU HAVE MY POSITION. I WANT YOURS.

00 flashed on the untranslated screen, then in the translated window: NO!

THERE EXISTS A TRADE IMBALANCE. I GAVE YOU 2 PIECES OF DATA. MY LOCATION + THE WAVEFUNCTION MICROPROCESSOR. YOU RETURNED THE PROOF. $2 \neq 1$.

Their reply appeared translated: ERROR IS OURS. WE EQUILI-BRATE. SEND SECOND PROOF.

Jack typed: NO. WAIT.

This wasn't going the way Jack wanted. How could he make them reveal their location? He didn't know what they valued. All he knew was that they were traders of information, like him.

He was stuck.

Jack drew a new card: the Magus. The figure in the card was a winged-footed Mercury, holding the DNA logo of his corporation in one hand, and in the other, lines of force that radiated into space. The face of the Magus was the one Wheeler used. Wheeler didn't really have a face, though. He wasn't human. Jack had to be careful never to anthropomorphize the alien, never get too comfortable with him, and never think he'd fathom his motives.

Another card: Fortune. A roulette wheel spun, and in it, a silver ball bounced and rattled and careened and never landed. Instead of numbers, this wheel had colored stars about its circum-ference. In the center sat a tiny Jack, watching the ball, along for the ride, no control over the outcome.

Through the Jack-in-the-card, every star on the turning wheel connected. They had to deal with him first. He understood.

Jack typed: I HAVE SOMETHING YOU WANT.

He sent part of Wheeler's translation hardware and lexicon software—not enough to use, but enough to whet their interest. If they traded information, it was a tool they couldn't pass up.

Nothing transmitted for seven heartbeats.

The distance formula then appeared with coordinates relative to Earth's, a vector pointing 190,000 light-years away.

It could be a lie. Jack could never authenticate their claim, but he'd pretend like he could.

VERIFYING DATA, he typed.

If it were bogus and Wheeler had a problem with it, Jack would give him their number. He could give them a call and complain.

Jack then typed: FIRST TRANSACTION EQUIVALENT. PROCEED WITH SECOND. SIMULTANEOUS EXCHANGE.

A single bit, a one, flashed from them. Jack exchanged the first bit in the lexicon. Two bits swapped next, then four, then Jack automated the process to level out trading packets of sixty-four million bits.

The translation software deciphered their proof as it came in. There were definitions for potential and kinetic energies. Then motions were characterized: translational, rotational, vibrational, electronic, nuclear, and others Jack failed to recognize.

It became gibberish. It came too fast. His lexicon shut down, and only the pure untranslated math remained, scrolling by for a full minute, then halted.

TRANSACTION END. CANNOT TRADE AGAIN. DANGER OVER-WHELMING.

The channel filled with zeros. Their signal went dead. No more Cauchy's integral formula. Maybe they would switch to a different set of frequencies and a new greeting proof.

Jack had a hunch he wouldn't find them again.

Too bad. He was just beginning to appreciate their paranoia.

Maybe it was for the best. Jack wasn't their friend. He had to turn the data over to Wheeler the blackmailer. Wheeler, who had schemes hatching inside his schemes.

It was unlike Isabel to be late. Jack shifted in his padded executive's chair. He sat next to Mr. White again. It was that or sit in the empty chair next to Isabel's at the head of the table

Jack wanted to keep his distance until he figured out what his friend had changed into.

The Rembrandt on the far wall had been replaced with a Picasso—all scrambled eyes and ears and mouths that Jack found disquieting.

He stared at Zero. The gene witch didn't look so good, either, tired and pale, sick maybe. Zero glanced at Isabel's empty chair, then to Jack, and shrugged.

After his trade with the aliens, Jack had checked the Bank of Shanghai—found a message from Reno, one that tapped into Jack's implant feedback, erased itself as soon as it confirmed that he had read it, then eradicated the record of that confirmation and severed Jack's link to the file address. It was an elegant piece of self-devouring software.

Reno had bumped up the time of their rendezvous. Midnight tonight.

Jack was itching to get this board of directors' meeting over with and onto the real business of the evening.

Reno was a problem. A small one compared to the rest of his troubles, one that Jack had bought off by sending him the specifications on the enzyme. Still, he wouldn't underestimate him. Once they transferred from Santa Sierra to Amsterdam CCO jurisdiction, Reno's ability to extort Jack ended. Maybe he wanted something else before that happened.

Isabel entered the room. She wore a black shirt, a matching skirt that fell midcalf, and a single strand of emeralds. She tossed a datapad on the table, frowned—didn't sit.

"I'd like to temporarily suspend the agenda this evening. We have a problem."

The CCO officials and investors whispered to one another. Jack stared at her, but she wouldn't meet his eyes, nor would she look at Zero.

Mr. White said, "Please, proceed, Ms. Mirabeau."

She tapped the datapad. A map of the world appeared behind her and zoomed into Southeast Asia. She pointed to the island subcontinent and its clusters of surrounding islands. "The Indo-

211

Malaysian Republic has filed a quick-claim patent on our enzyme through various Asian and European CCO offices."

Reno. Had to be.

But it was just as much Jack's fault because he had given him the enzyme. He should have told Zero and Isabel and at least given them a vote in that decision. That made him twice the liar. Twice as guilty.

Isabel said, "There has been a leak." She turned to Jack and narrowed her eyes. "I want you to follow up on this, coordinate with Geneva CCO if you have to. Do whatever it takes."

"Sure," he said. He was the only one with ties to the East. And he had admitted that he had spoken with Reno recently. What did she suspect behind those green eyes?

"We have projections that this illegal operation will undercut our market share by forty-five percent when they flood the world market with their imitation enzyme."

Maybe some good would come from Jack's mistake. More people would get their cancer cured—cheaper.

"It will go to court," Mr. White said. "We are sure to win."

"Meanwhile," she replied, pacing in front of the map, "they manufacture product and develop their distribution channels, while we mount a protracted legal offense."

"What other recourse is there?" Zero asked. "We are restrained to due process."

She turned and shot a glare at him. "I am not suggesting that we do anything illegal, but you're overlooking other options."

The map view behind her pulled back, showed the entire world, and she pointed to Amsterdam. "We are in a unique situation. We have the support of the Amsterdam and Geneva CCO"—she then pointed to the United States—"but we are also still part of the Santa Sierra CCO. I have frozen the transfer process."

Zero interrupted, "You cannot—"

"Let me finish," she said, "then you may present any objections."

Zero leaned back in his chair. "Very well."

Jack had never seen Zero back down so fast.

"Since we are in joint trust," she said, "we have both European and American legal recourses. Washington CCO has classified the Indo-Malaysian operation illegal. The Free Market Amendment gives us the right to protect our interests. We can take direct action against them."

"Action?" Jack said. "We're are a biomedical corporation. We can't march over there and force them to shut down."

"*We* can't." Isabel paused to straighten out a kink in the links of her emerald necklace.

She turned to Mr. White and said, "We do not wish to act rashly and cause the European CCOs any inconvenience. But not only do we have the legal options afforded by the U.S. CCOs, we also have obligations to them as well."

She inhaled, then: "I would like to introduce someone who can help us." She waved to the door. It opened. "This is Mr. Andropov DeMitri from the United States National Security Office."

Jack's heart stopped. His vision irised to a pinpoint.

DeMitri walked in, wearing a black suit, black tie; his black hair had gone gray at the temples.

Jack leapt to his feet and reached for Reno's automatic inside his coat.

"Sit down, Jack!" Isabel said. "He is on our side."

"Our side? Don't you know who this is?"

Mr. White spoke, "Is it really necessary to involve the American NSO?"

DeMitri gave Jack a puzzled look as if he knew him, but couldn't place his face. He addressed Mr. White, "This matter is complex, and I assure you that the NSO has no desire to cause friction with the Amsterdam CCO or with Interpol. We merely wish to help."

"They're assassins, spies, and thieves," Jack cried. He stared at Isabel. She looked calm and in control. Why had she brought him here? Maybe "our side" wasn't *his* side anymore.

"Allow me to present our plan," DeMitri said, ignoring Jack's outburst. "Then you may vote on it. The United States, naturally, will not take action without the full support of the board of directors."

Jack doubted that. How many other NSO agents were in the complex? Had they coerced Isabel or had she sold out willingly?

He sat, kept his one eye on the door for more agents, and kept his hand close to his gun.

The bottom line was he couldn't trust Isabel. That realization sat cold in his stomach. What about Zero? He looked worried. Maybe he was still with Jack.

DeMitri cleared his throat, tapped Isabel's input pad, and the map shifted to a triangular island, one shore pockmarked by a cove. "The illegal corporation has begun operations here. Satellite photographs indicate they have active biological reactors."

Reno had to have had this set up way in advance. Maybe since he saw what Zero had cooking in Santa Sierra—still, something stank about this whole operation.

"We propose a small strike force land upon this beach, infiltrate their security perimeter, erase their records, and disable their manufacturing capabilities."

DeMitri didn't mention they'd probably erase their key personnel in the process, too.

"This will delay their production," DeMitri continued, "long enough for your enzyme to be marketed, legally, through the United States, then rerouted to Europe and your normal distribution channels."

"We ship a product made here to the United States?" Mr. White asked.

"Making this a joint European-American operation," DeMitri said, smiling. "Tidy and legal."

"And we pay Uncle Sam to be our primary distributor," Jack said. "For that we get the privilege to muscle the Indo-Malaysian corporation courtesy of the Free Market Amendment." Maybe this little operation wasn't Reno's. Maybe the NSO had set it up themselves so they could cut themselves in on the action.

"One could look at it that way," DeMitri said and straightened his tie.

"One could look at it as extortion," Jack snapped back.

"As a U.S. CCO entity," Isabel said, "we circumvent their

legal claim on our patent. By the time the Indo-Malaysian operation returns to business, DNAegis will have the dominant position in the world market. The U.S. and European CCOs, the stockholders—we all win."

"Everyone including the NSO," Jack muttered. "The answer is no."

"Fortunately," she said and sat, "this decision is not yours alone to make. If there are no objections, I move for an immediate vote."

"Fine with me," Jack said. "The sooner we get this over with—and the NSO out of here—the better."

He glared at DeMitri, who had the guts to smile back. This was no bubble, but his eyes looked too glassy, glittering rat eyes that knew too much. What did DeMitri remember from the Alcatraz funhouse? Had his memory been erased so he could recover? Or did he know that Jack had pulled a fast one and let him torture himself?

Isabel whispered to Zero, then she locked glares with Jack. It was possible that DeMitri had gotten to her, taken her apart and put her back together again as a U.S. patriot . . . then again, Isabel always had been the perfect citizen—even before the enzyme.

Maybe it had been her choice after all.

Jack had an ace in the hole, though. He tapped his input pad, opened a link to the ING Bank. It was time to reveal Reno's investment in their corporation. It was also time for Jack to tell them he had Reno's proxy vote—two-fifths control.

A half-dozen investors touched the input pads on the conference table and registered their votes. A tally displayed on the wall. Jack noted that Mr. White voted against the NSO. It was a mixed total: eleven percent against and fourteen percent in favor of the NSO invasion.

Isabel cast her vote in favor, an additional twenty-five percent. She only owned one fifth of the stock, but with the crooked set of books, the ones without Reno, her percentage inflated from twenty to twenty-five.

That would change when Jack showed them the real accounting ledgers.

"Zero?" Isabel asked. "Your vote?"

Zero looked to her, then Jack, then to DeMitri. "I am . . . uncertain."

"Jack?" she asked.

He finished a retinal scan and entered the escrow he had set up at ING Bank. "Just a second."

With Reno's authorization to cast a proxy vote, Jack would have forty percent control. That, combined with the other eleven percent, gave him a majority. Then the NSO could take a walk.

The escrow account and original set of books were blank.

Jack reestablished and refreshed the link.

Still empty.

Jack felt the bottom fall out of his plan, and his stomach. Someone had hacked in and erased them. Who had the skill? DeMitri, of course. And Reno's proxy vote? Either it had been destroyed along with the real books or Reno had never signed them.

He still had his vote, though, and according to Isabel's crooked books, it counted as twenty-five percent.

"I vote against," Jack said.

That brought the tally to thirty-six percent against and thirty-nine percent for the NSO. Not enough.

"Zero?" Jack asked.

The gene witch rubbed his temples, then squeezed his eyes shut. The color drained from his face, and he looked ready to pass out. Pale? Weak? Those were the symptoms that Isabel had when she had taken the enzyme. Had Zero taken it?

"I . . ." Zero turned to Isabel. "I cannot . . . I must abstain from voting."

"Very well, Zero." She cast him a cool look. "The majority approves the NSO's solution. We shall table regular business until 10 A.M. tomorrow. I hereby declare this meeting closed. Mr. DeMitri, please proceed with your invasion."

13

JACKRABBIT

Jack sealed the door to his office, opaqued the windows, and insulated the bubble with layers of dead-code. He pushed with his implant, looked for spies hidden in the shadows. He was alone.

Isabel sold him out. She knew what would happen if DeMitri got to him. Had the enzyme altered her personality so much that she didn't care? Or had the NSO offered her too good a deal to pass up? Or maybe he had never known the real Isabel.

Whatever her reasons, he had to leave—now.

He interfaced with the Chinese automatic, shifted ammunition cartridges from anatoxic plastocene to burrowing compression rounds. Lethal. No one was going to stop him.

He unlocked the wall safe; stainless-alloy plates slid apart. The isotope and circuit Isabel had made were inside.

He shoved them into a skintape wallet, along with the handful of prototype electron reactors and nano-assemblers, then stuck it under his shirt.

Jack didn't know where to go, but it would be far from Isabel and her new associates. He still couldn't believe that she had thrown in with them. But he better believe it. And he better figure out which side Zero was on.

What else would he need? He downloaded Wheeler's software lexicon and the two alien mathematical proofs to a memory cube. Jack opened his logs: files on decoding multiplexed transmissions, on the electron reactor, and on the gateway.

He erased them.

Isabel and the NSO could get in here. Jack's encryption was the best, but the best might be cracked with the resources and time available to the NSO. He couldn't take chances.

His files were gone . . . except for the compressed and scrambled backup that automatically archived. It was standard procedure to hold them. If you made a mistake, you could reconstitute what had been erased. They were destroyed at the end of the business day, but the NSO was smart enough to look there first. Jack would have to hack into the server and make sure they vanished.

He knelt to the floor and interfaced with the *Zouwtmarkt*'s server.

A virtual seam cracked the carpet, and a recessed pull ring materialized. A tug and the trapdoor opened. Jack stepped down into the system-works. It was a web of pipes: snarls of copper plumbing and lead tubes. Some were asbestos-insulated, others labeled STEAM or POWER or WATER. The place gurgled and rumbled. It smelled of mold.

He located the waste conduit to his office, then opened his system toolbox and removed a pipe wrench. Three cranks with the wrench and the access tee loosened.

A torrent of sewage washed over him; he gagged on the stench of decaying data: burned plastic and ozone and carbon tetrachloride. The flow subsided.

Jack stuck his head into the opening, got his shoulders in— dropped into the waste aqueduct.

There was space to breathe inside, not that he wanted to

breathe what was in here. The current was strong; it carried him away.

For a minute he flowed along, then the pipe turned down ninety degrees. Jack went under—shot out and through a waterfall cascade that dumped him into the recycling center.

He surfaced in the lake where the data stagnated and fermented. Jack swam to the shore, crawled out, and caught this breath.

At the bottom of the underground lake lay dormant subroutines that flipped every bit in the data pool to zero. A giant garbage disposal.

Jack found the switch on the wall, reached for it—halted.

Once the NSO set up operations and strengthened DNAegis's computer defenses, Jack would need a way to hack back into the system-works.

He pulled off the circuit panel and found the fiber-optic overflow detector. It sensed the rate of incoming data and flushed the archives to prevent a backup.

Jack pulled a fifty-yuan piece out of his pocket. It was aluminum with a square hole in its center, Chinese calligraphy and his Shanghai account number engraved along the edge. It was a dormant link to the Bank of Shanghai. To this he added a line of trigger-code that would search for a particular sequence of garbage flushed through the *Zouwtmarkt*'s server. It would be his back door in once the NSO installed their security.

He looped the fiber-optic cable through the metaphor of the coin, then replaced the panel and turned on the disposal.

A swirl in the center of the water, bubbles gurgled up, then a whirlpool sucked the data down.

Time to get out of here. He could terminate the virtual shell. That would leave him disoriented, though, possibly vulnerable while he lay in his office and got his bearings.

There was another problem: he'd leave a trace of his hack, his fingerprints on the access panel, and the unauthorized data flush. An NSO team, if tipped off, might be able to reconstruct the information—especially with Isabel's datapaleontology exper-tise.

This had to be a clean hack. No ghosts. And there was only one way to erase every trace of his presence.

Jack waded into the water. He saw the wavering translucent records of his conversations with Wheeler and the math-code that patched together his multiplexed signals. Other information, too: orders for superconducting magnets, aluminum support webs, and annealing vacuum columns. What did DNAegis need those for? No time to solve another mystery.

He mingled with the data, swam into the center, then let the suction drag him under. The disposal chopped and ground and wiped clean Jack's interface. Sometimes metaphor was a bitch.

Jack pushed through the crowd gathered on Amsterdam's red-light avenues; the doorman gave him a nod, and Jack shouldered his way into the tunnel entrance of Freud's Little Sister.

On the center stage an orgy seethed, tangles of limbs and oil and blood and snakes and mouths and steam-driven pistons that rose and fell and flowed over one another. Jack wasn't sure which parts were real.

Maidens in street clothes and leather-clad molls, lace-wearing queens and nude narcissi talked and drank; most had their gazes locked on the floor shows; some climbed in to join.

The air was thick steam, heavy with the scent of cloves and perspiration . . . and perfume, apricots, and champagne. That's what Freud's Little Sister was about: reflecting the fantasies bur-ied in your mind. It was where the jaded went for thrills.

A push with the Chinese implant and Jack pierced the veil of dreams, spotted Reno at a table by the entrance to the dungeon.

Jack rubbed his dead eye, blurred darkness and the virtual images together—a reminder that he had a nasty blind spot when it came to trusting the old spy.

He stepped over couples and watchers and took the long way around a harlequin-clad dominatrix selling humiliation, then slid onto the bench. The red leather material molded too intimately to Jack's backside, rippling with delight. It gave him the creeps.

"You're late," Reno said and sipped his drink through a straw. "Another minute and I wouldn't be here." He glanced around the parlor. "Were you followed?"

"Nice to see you, too," Jack said. "Three NSO agents tailed me out of the *Zouwtmarkt*. I rode the trolleys for an hour, cut through a few alleys, hashish bars, the ING Bank, and used your implant. I think I lost them."

"You think?" Reno muttered. "Doesn't matter. The NSO won't come in here. They're afraid the weird subliminals might compromise the national secrets locked in their heads."

A white bull brushed past their table; the animal's muscles flexed and stretched under smooth leather, and Jack caught himself staring at it. Was that his image or someone else's projection?

Jack returned his attention to Reno and lowered his voice to a whisper, "I came to warn you. The NSO knows about your Indo-Malaysia operation. They're going to stop it."

Reno raised an eyebrow, the corners of his mouth curled into a smile. He didn't look surprised.

A waitress came to their table. She was dressed in a Santa Sierra school uniform: pleated shirt, over-the-ankle socks, and white gloves. She begged them to order her, but Jack only asked for whiskey. Reno wanted cigars.

Jack said, "You should twist in the wind for trying to undercut DNAegis, but if I do that, people are going to get hurt. That, I don't want."

Reno sipped his drink, then said, "No one, in Indo-Malaysia, is going to get hurt."

He had known. How . . . ? Jack ventured a guess: "What did the NSO pay you?"

Reno's blue eye pinned him with a stare. "Lots."

Jack's first impulse was to reach across the table and strangle the double-crossing spy. He still needed more information, though, so he kept his cool. Besides, Jack knew he couldn't take

Reno in a real fight. Still, he wondered what Reno would look like with a blackened eye and a few missing teeth.

"I thought you and the NSO were on opposite sides."

"Sides? Sure, there are sides," Reno said. "But the trick is figuring out who's on which side when."

The schoolgirl waitress brought the drinks and smokes. She peeled off her gloves, unstoppered the whiskey bottle's cork with both her thumbs, and dribbled the smoke-colored liquor into a wide-mouthed tumbler for Jack. She then disappeared in search of more demanding masters.

"They offered us money," Reno whispered, "bags of it, and state secrets we've wanted for decades. When you guys started your transfer to the Amsterdam CCO, the NSO hit the roof. Uncle Sam wants a piece of DNAegis. In a bad way."

"You arranged our rendezvous just to tell me this?"

"No. I wanted to tell you the NSO has your number. They're going to make a rip on you, and not for the secrets you got up here." He pointed to his temple. "Not after Santa Sierra. Not after they've got one foot in your business. They want you dead. Straight and simple."

"Thanks for the warning, but I've been able to keep one step ahead—"

"Because they let you."

"Why would they?"

"I'll let you figure that one out, Jack." Reno shook his head. "With the smarts you were born with and the hardware in your head, you've got an edge against those punks. But if they want you bad enough, they'll get you." His eyes focused beyond Jack, then he said, "It'll happen in a public place. They won't want any strings connecting to the *Zouwtmarkt*. That would be bad for business. One sniper. Two men on the street. That's how I'd do it."

His blue eye refocused on him.

Jack had the feeling Reno was telling the truth. Another thought: this meeting could be part of Reno's deal with the NSO. Get him out in the open. Make him vulnerable.

He grabbed his drink, stopped, then set it back down. Reno could have drugged it.

"Second thing I wanted to tell you," Reno said and trimmed the tip of his cigar with a knife. "Panda is looking for you. You've got to shoot first with her and ask questions later."

"Panda already found me."

Reno set down his cigar and knife. "Can't be. You're still alive. That girl leaves a trail of bodies wherever she goes."

"We talked."

"About what?"

"Things." Tell Reno and the conversation ended. Jack had to play him out, make him loosen his tongue about the female spy.

"Don't turn your back on her, Jack." Reno picked up the knife and the other cigar and trimmed. "She's got hardware in her thick little skull that makes ours look like AM radios. She can turn your thoughts on you. Kill you with your own mind. If she hasn't yet, she will."

Jack crossed his arms, felt the reassuring weight of the automatic nestled in its holster. "That's funny talk for people on the same side. Tell me how you can both work for the Chinese, but still be enemies. Then I might be in the mood to tell you about what she said to me."

"Moods like that can get you killed." Reno rolled the cigar between his thumb and finger, then without looking up, said, "But OK. After the quakes, China was a real mess. The provinces split and became independent. All technically China, but more like a room full of fighting brothers, picking sides, splitting into city empires, treaties made and dissolved. The usual stuff. I'm Shanghai. Panda's Beijing."

"What's the big difference?"

"Beijing is communist. Shanghai's a democracy where everyone's implanted, and if they qualify, they can vote, run the government."

"What does 'qualified' mean?

"Means you study the issues. You have to prove you know the pros and cons before you can vote. Giving any soft-brained

223

media junkie the vote is what got America in trouble in the first place." Reno stroked the side of his lighter and ignited the tip of his cigar. He puffed once, then asked, "So what did Panda tell you?"

"I've got a few more questions. Did you sign that proxy authorization at the ING Bank?"

"Was there a problem?" Reno nodded at Jack's whiskey. "You going to drink that? Or can I?"

Jack pushed the tumbler across the table. "There's an NSO problem."

"You should transfer out of that leaky Dutch place to the Bank of Shanghai. No NSO there."

"Just NSO money. Why'd you really want to talk tonight, Reno? It wasn't to warn me about the NSO."

"I came to offer you Chinese citizenship, Jack-O. It's the only place you'll be safe."

Jack could never return to the *Zouwtmarkt*. Or Santa Sierra. But China? It was as distant as the moon.

Reno slid a card across the table. It had a Shanghai address and server ID printed in precise red lettering. "Memorize it," he said.

Jack did, then the characters jumbled into Mandarin calligraphy and faded.

"Thanks." The word escaped Jack's mouth before it occurred to him that if Reno had wanted him to willingly defect, this was the perfect setup. Give the NSO a way to infiltrate his corporation. Give Jack nowhere else to go.

Jack crumpled the blank card and threw it in Reno's face. "Thanks for nothing."

Reno laughed. "If you want to play tough guy, Jack, go ahead. Think about it. There's no other place for you." He got up and strode through the steamy air, down the dungeon stairs, and out the back way.

Jack grabbed the extra Mariposa cigar, examined the butterfly watermark on the tobacco leaf wrapper, then crushed it.

Despite the crowd of warm bodies so close and so willing, he had never felt more alone.

Jack wandered through the night, over bridged canals full of blurry moonlight, down avenues, then lost his way in the fog.

He replayed the last board meeting, each time feeling lousier and lousier. Isabel must have been brainwashed by the NSO, or threatened, or replaced by a double. But she had enthusiastically welcomed DeMitri. It had been like the Isabel of old attacking a puzzle—except this puzzle involved billions in stock and cash, and lives, and Jack.

He had to get away. His plan was to walk out of Amsterdam—he didn't trust the public transportation with their autotracking and didn't want to push his luck any more with Reno's implant. He'd get to Leiden, then find someone with a car, bribe them or steal it, get to the border, slip into Belgium, then France, maybe Africa. Then what?

It was two in the morning. The streets of Amsterdam's Plantage were deserted; slick cobblestones gleamed with the reflections of the waning biolume balls, the only movement was from the art displays that projected along the avenue. Falling stars and rockets and whirling constellations shot over the Planetarium de Artis; dinosaurs glared down at Jack with amber eyes from the roof of the Geologish Museum; and schools of fluorescent fish swarmed through the neoclassical arches of the aquarium at the far end of the street.

In the corner of his vision, a shadow moved. It darted into the street: a pair of gold eyes that froze and stared at Jack.

He reached for the automatic, then stopped.

It was a cat, slinky and black, velvet fur matted to its sleek body. Bad luck.

The cat cried, whipped its tail back and forth, and kept its unblinking eyes fixed upon him. Those eyes reflected green, even though there was no light source behind Jack; he couldn't stop staring into them . . . getting pulled into them. An interface?

Feline pupils constricted and glanced beyond Jack's left shoulder. Mirrored upon their convex surfaces, a man hunkered down on the museum's roof, supported a rifle with his right hand; Jack tasted the slightest whisper of his weapon's interface and diagnostics that checked the gyros and range finder, then perpendicular crosshairs appeared in the cat's eyes.

It meowed. Their interface broke.

Jack ran into the alley—cover from that sniper. His body wanted to keep running, but he forced himself to stop and think. What did Reno say? One sniper . . . and two men on the ground. He never mentioned any cat.

Flanking this side street were buildings three stories tall. The alley was narrow with crates stacked along the walls, garbage cans, and a small rivulet of water that trickled though a gutter.

At the far end of the lane, the outline of a man appeared, blurred by the fog.

A shuffle behind Jack. He turned: a second man stepped into the alley and blocked the exit.

Two of them. Far apart. Jack couldn't take both out with his implant; he couldn't split-broadcast. Jack said, "Hey, you guys don't need to—"

The goon smiled. He had body armor under that three-piece suit. And probably didn't need a gun to take Jack apart. He whispered, "We got him."

Jack reached for his automatic.

The goon took a step closer—the cat darted between his legs, stopped; its tail curled about his ankle; he tried to kick it away. Black fur turned into smoke that wrapped around and around and around him, like blood dissolving into swirled water.

The NSO goon struggled with those fumes, but they thickened and flickered. Things appeared inside. Jack only got glimpses, as if they were engraved upon fluttering confetti: flats and edges that twisted with the images of feline teeth and claws, nine knotted whips, and interlaced yarn that tangled and strangled. The sound of squealing rats shuddered from the cloud.

Jack stumbled backward. It had to be virtual interface. But an interface to what? Nightmare made real?

226

Lightning spattered off the brick wall next to Jack—he dropped to the ground—bullets sprayed the air over him and filled the passageway, gunfire from the agent at the other end of the alley.

The NSO goon inside the cloud-that-was-a-cat cried out. His body jerked as the slugs ripped into him. The cloud collapsed back into the form of a cat, then into shadow, then vanished as the man fell face-first into the alley.

Jack drew the automatic, twisted around, and fired a burst of compression burrowing rounds that exploded chunks of the far wall into dust.

The agent had to be crazy to fire an uncontrolled burst into such a tight space. His partner was in the crossfire. He had to be desperate to kill Jack.

Pinpricks of pains flared along his shoulder. Brick shrapnel. Jack reached back and retracted a bloody hand.

He glanced back: NSO goon number one still lay in the alley. Good. No sign of the cat, either.

Jack could run back out that way. No. He'd run straight into a sniper's sight.

More gunfire erupted from the agent at the end of the alley. Jack hugged cobblestones, and water soaked into his clothes. He was pinned. The NSO agent could call for backup and Jack would get caught. He had to move.

Jack pushed with the implant, reached forward though the alley, tasted the NSO agent's resonating neuralware: the faint coppery taste of a high-frequency radio broadcast and the rubbery intricate texture of an encrypted signal.

He was too far away to cloud his mind. And there were no repeater stations between them. Still, he had to try.

With gritted teeth, Jack bore down, concentrated, thrust out his willpower. His head split, ears whined with streams of bubbles forced up the Eustachian tubes, and skin flushed with heat—fire inside that evaporated all sweat, blistered the skin, and boiled blood.

In the middle of it, Jack thought only of himself: he was here, crouched behind the boxes, too afraid to move, not going anywhere.

He crawled out.

"Jack is still there," he whispered to the shadows. "Hasn't moved."

He was fog that crept along the gutter, gray mist, half-invisible . . . slinking up the alley.

The NSO agent poked his head out.

Jack resisted the urge to freeze. Fog keeps moving, so did he—even though he inched straight into the agent's line of sight.

"Jack is down the alley," he whispered into his head. "You've got him pinned. Wait him out. Wait for backup."

The agent pointed his gun at Jack, or through him, gripped the trigger.

Jack continued to crawl, praying the agent saw mist and not him.

The agent relaxed and ducked behind the trash cans for cover.

Mist rolled past him.

. . . It was a cheap shot. But Jack did shift ammunition cartridges, pumped him full of anatoxic plastocene—enough to keep him in dreamland for two days.

He ran out the back way. Stopped. What *had* happened to that cat? He should have made a break for it, but he had a hunch about that cat-that-wasn't-a-cat.

Jack scanned the rooftops for motion—nothing—jogged back up the alley, and crouched next to the fallen agent. He touched the side of his neck. No pulse. Cold.

He turned him over. His eyes were frozen wide open . . . and beneath him, a black figure, slender feline body, wearing a black dress. Panda.

Jack pulled her out. Her eyes fluttered open. She'd taken a round in the chest. There was oozing blood and bits of flesh.

"Sniper," she whispered. "Can't go that way."

Reno was wrong about Panda. She could have been killed in the street warning him about the sniper. And she got caught in crossfire meant for him.

"I know," he whispered. Jack wrapped her in his jacket, picked her up, then ran out the back way, shielding himself with virtual darkness—he let the night swallow them.

Jack watched Zero's physician work on Panda. Dr. Musa wasn't happy—not when Jack had called him in the middle of the night, nor when Jack had asked him to come to the Grand Amsterdam Hotel. He was even less happy when Jack found him in the lobby and requested his presence at other accommodations—at gunpoint.

It had been three in the morning when they got this room: a dump in Leiden, every other apartment occupied with hashish smokers and university students.

Panda had stopped bleeding by then . . . more or less. Clear fluid seeped from the perforations in her chest. Dr. Musa made Jack apply pressure. She was cold, clammy, her breathing shallow.

Jack was cold, too, in the pit of his stomach. He owed Panda his life. Her chest was torn apart, but there were no exit wounds on the other side. No broken ribs or shredded lung like he expected after taking compression burrowing rounds.

Dr. Musa poked and probed her wounds. He cleaned, stitched, then bandaged her chest and wrapped her in blankets. The doctor got a message pad from his bag and interfaced.

Jack grabbed it before he touched the transmit command. "What's this?"

The doctor grabbed the pad back. "A prescription for a spectral antibiotic. Not that I think it will do any good."

"Is she that bad?"

"On the contrary. Her body's immune system has been modified with micronodules that manufacture antiviral and antibacterial chemicals. Quite impressive."

Jack tapped out a cigarette, offered Dr. Musa one, then took one himself. The doctor could have been Zero's older brother with a white pointed beard and bald head.

Dr. Musa lit it, puffed once, then said, "She is stable. Nine rounds penetrated her chest, but deflected off an epoxy-teflon

229

mesh that encases her lungs and abdominal cavities. Three pierced the body armor."

Jack's insides twisted. "Shouldn't you dig them out?"

"Her blood vessels and internal organs have colonies of lichenlike parasites encrusted upon them. Very resilient. I cannot properly scan her with my equipment, but I do not see any severe damage . . . other than the hypercompression shock—for which I have given her an injection of corticoid epinephrine."

"You talk like you've seen this before."

"My father and my father's father have had the honor of serving the al Qaseem clan for decades . . . over which time one can see many things."

Jack had heard the stories of the oil clans: a little murder, incest, and intrigue. All routine. He took a drag off the cigarette; the peppermint and amphetamines gave him a moment's clarity, then faded just as fast. Zero. He had abstained from Isabel's vote. Even with the NSO muscling in. Maybe he wasn't happy with her new partners, either. Maybe he was still on Jack's side. Or at least, not on hers.

"Mr. al Qaseem has a message for you," the doctor whispered, then glanced around. "Is it safe to speak?"

"As safe as it's going to get," Jack replied.

The doctor nodded, then: "He said, 'The laboratory is still on fire.' Do you understand?"

"Too well." Zero burned his lab in Santa Sierra. He must be worried the NSO had taken over. This time with more men, bigger guns, and no mistakes.

Jack went to Panda's side and made certain she was snugly wrapped. "How long will she be out?"

"At least until morning. She will require hospitalization and surgery. It would be best if you took her to whomever installed her bioware."

"Sure." Jack wasn't about to take a trip to Beijing, but he had to move her as soon as Dr. Musa left. He couldn't trust him.

"May I have permission to examine you as well? Mr. al Qaseem has expressed concerns regarding your condition."

230

To let Dr. Musa, a stranger, dig around in his skull was out of the question. Jack had to find out what was happening, though. He squeezed the bridge of his nose. Ever since Reno cracked his head, he'd had migraines and dizziness, but after tonight, when he had pushed the hardest, no pain at all. That worried him.

There were other options, normal doctors who might be bribed by Isabel or the NSO to learn about his Chinese implant. There were underground neurosurgeons. A gamble. Even odds they'd be Frankensteins who'd implant him with suggestion or butchers who'd remove his neuralware and auction it to the highest bidder.

Dr. Musa reminded him of an older Zero. That was no reason to trust him, but at least with Dr. Musa, there was a chance he was on his side.

"Only if you can do it without drugs or opening my head."

The doctor nodded. "It shall be as you say." He gestured to the couch. "Please disengage from your gun's interface and any other appliances."

Jack locked the gun and shut down the gyros, but kept it in his pocket.

The doctor unfolded his briefcase's viewscreen, then removed a dozen hollow grapefruit-sized half-spheres and set them facing Jack. "This is passive," he said. The edges of the half-spheres undulated. "You should feel no interface. Let me know if—"

Blotches of black light clouded Jack's eye, purple tracers streaked from center to peripheral vision, then sounds: church bells and a baby's cry and shattering glass.

"I'm getting something."

"Interesting. Heightened response." He made an adjustment. "Now?"

"Nothing."

"Please sit still," he told Jack. He tinkered with the onscreen controls.

Jack saw slices of his head: bones and tissues, pulsing blood and brain and the silver-dewed spiderweb implants.

"How long has your left eye been blind?"

"About two weeks." The image of Jack's head turned inside out, scanning back and forth made him sick. He slouched back into the couch, closed his eyes. Swallowed.

When he opened his good eye, the doctor compared two heads, both exploded apart, parts rotating, others magnified, showing every gray convolution and white-rippled surface. Rainbow matrices of neural activity appeared.

"This is a comparison to Mr. al Qaseem's previous scan."

"They look the same to me."

"Nearly," he said. "The extent of the initial damage has not spread. The neural chemistry is odd." He frowned. "Traces of telromerase." He flicked the controls, and a new scan revealed six red blotches throughout Jack's brain, each no larger than a speck. He enlarged the structures. They looked like globs of chewing gum.

"The usual pain has faded," Jack offered. "Does that have anything to do with . . ."

The doctor wasn't paying attention to him, absorbed in the details on the display. He shook his head, then tugged on his beard and said, "I would like to take a tissue sample."

"I told you nothing gets stuck in my head."

"That will not be required. I shall take a sample from your lymph node. I assure you it will be completely painless." He showed Jack the tissue collector, a device the size of his little finger. He then touched it under Jack's jaw and there was a prick of pain—despite what he had said.

Jack got the nerve to ask, "What's wrong?"

The doctor injected the contents into the side port of his briefcase workstation. "That is what I am about to ascertain."

Cells appeared on the screen, which Dr. Musa ruptured with an optical probe, then directed the flow of proteins, RNA, and DNA into a shunt vacuole. This he transferred into a microchannel that whisked the tiny sample away. "I am running a chemical analysis. Please remain patient."

Jack watched the workstation windows as the sample ran through filters and nautilus-curved mass spectrometers that directed different molecules into nuclear magnetic resonance spheres, then into multiplexed infrared spectroscopic nodes.

Dozens of windows winked open, each with different molecules that looked like a collection of marbles, cat's-eyes and agates and steelies, twisting and flexing. Reports in Arabic spilled onto the displays.

The doctor flipped through the windows, then halted: a molecule with seven rings and a metal ion implanted in its center. Another window held the interferometric image of a fuzzy piece of string, only magnified 100,000 times.

"What are they?"

"Osmium beta-endonuclease." He pointed to the molecule. "The other is a *Sistiri oncogenase* virus. They are the cause of the unusually virulent tumors in your brain and metastases in the remainder of your body."

"Tumors? In me?"

"Yes. Malignant and growing."

Jack wished the pain in his head would return; instead, he felt anesthetized . . . then it itched inside, and he thought he could feel every cell in his brain swell and turn black and rotten inside with cancerous growths, eating him from within. He took a deep breath, stopped himself from clawing his scalp and skin until it bled. "How?"

"This"—he tapped the molecule—"was used decades ago in a technique called electrogel phosphoresces to cut DNA into irreparable fragments. It is presently not used, except to poison. In your case, it has been attached with an easily reduced ester to the cancer-causing virus. An extraordinarily toxic combination."

"That's impossible. I haven't—" His extremities went cold. "How is it transmitted?"

The doctor shrugged. "Eating, drinking, even . . ." He glanced at his own cigarette.

Jack had eaten with Isabel recently, inhaled Reno's smoke, and Panda could have spiked his booze yesterday. Any one of them had reasons to want him dead.

"How bad is it?" Jack asked.

"One week, then you lose rational thought. Ten days and you become senseless. Two weeks and the cancer takes you. I am sorry."

Two weeks? Jack felt as if he'd been punched in the throat. He didn't believe him. Then he did and seethed with the molten rage that quickly quenched to icy resolve. So little time left, and so much still to do. "There are cures? There have to be. Zero said yesterday at the board meeting that most cancers had treatments."

"You have a stage four malignancy. Aggressive radiation, perhaps. Or gene therapy. But the oncogenase virus and the endonuclease would still be present—and the process would begin again. Only you would not survive the second round of therapy."

Dr. Musa reached into his black bag, withdrew a plastic packet, and handed it to Jack. "Of course there is another way."

Jack turned it over. Inside were five gold-foil capsules, labeled day one through day five. He whispered, "The enzyme."

14

JACK AND JILL WENT UP A HILL

"This meeting is called to order," Isabel said.

New walnut paneling made the conference room seem smaller, made Jack claustrophobic. The Picasso that had hung on the wall was now Andy Warhol's *Green Coca-Cola Bottles*. And there was a new conference table, blue marble that reflected the board members and Jack with mirror images as sharp as reality; its surface wasn't slick, but sticky under Jack's palms.

Everyone was present except Zero. He could be sick if he was being edited by the enzyme. Maybe that's why he was missing. Jack hoped that was all that was wrong.

Jack hadn't taken the enzyme. He wanted a second opinion on those tumors before he risked becoming like Isabel. He had a sore throat, was ready for a three-year nap, and saw purple flashes in his dead eye. Those symptoms might be from stress and sleep deprivation and not necessarily, as Dr. Musa had diagnosed, cancer. Dr. Musa could have rigged his workstation display to show anything.

"I apologize for the delay," Isabel said to the board members, "but some of us could not be here in person. We had to provide alternate linkages."

He had insisted on the virtual interface—routed through a set of dummy shells and his new account at the Bank of Shanghai. Tight and untraceable.

"Our first order of business," Isabel said, "is an update on the NSO's Malaysian operation."

A world map appeared on the far wall, zoomed into Southeast Asia and the crescent-shaped continent of Indo-Malaysia. She drummed her fingernails on the marble. "There have been complications. Guerrilla infantry surprised our strike force. A missile brigade sank three NSO amphibious personnel carriers. It is suspected that the Indo-Malaysian Republic has received covert military assistance from an as-yet-undetermined Asian country." She shot a glance at Jack.

He started to open his mouth—stopped when he felt a hand on his arm.

There was no hand there.

Mr. White was on Jack's left, and the CCO attaché's reflection in the polished marble touched Jack's reflection. This mirror image of Mr. White shook his head, then blurred back to normal.

Jack got the message: shut up, listen, and learn.

Isabel crossed her arms. "I have spoken to the Washington CCO. They will lobby the senate for additional Navy and Marine forces. This should not be a problem, as it is an election year."

"Is escalation necessary?" Mr. White asked. "Has anyone established a dialogue with Malaysia? The Dutch government received unofficial warnings via the Bangkok CCO that reprisals may be taken."

"We have tried and they refused," Isabel replied. She neither blinked nor raised an eyebrow; there was no subconscious shake of her head. Jack had no clue if she told the truth.

He pushed with a feather touch, but Isabel had walls up.

There was nothing but profit and loss columns and a continuous stream of stock quotes reflected in the facets of her emerald eyes.

The sweat under Jack's palms crystallized. The conference table wasn't blue marble; it was a slab of ice.

What happened in Malaysia had to be Reno's doing. He had outsmarted the NSO. He fed them information to get into DNAegis, then agreed to set up a fake operation in Malaysia. The American troops were supposed to march ·in and save the day . . . except Reno pulled a triple cross. Good for him.

"This incident will certainly intensify," Isabel told the members of the board. "The NSO assures me that they will see this through to its logical conclusion." She turned to each CCO representative and investor. "I hope we have your support as well."

Mr. White spoke: "Amsterdam values its ties with the United States and has substantial interest in seeing DNAegis takes its rightful placé in the global economy. We shall make every effort to resolve this issue. If not peacefully, then quickly."

The others nodded.

"Good." Isabel smiled, her teeth pointed, and canines sharpened to fangs. No one else noticed. Probably an internal subliminal leak from Jack.

"I shall keep you apprised of the situation as updates come in."

Jack doubted that. Reports after the fact, maybe, and with the proper spin.

"Our second order of business . . ."

Leatherbound books appeared upon the table each with the corporate DNA caduceus etched in goldleaf on the cover. Jack flipped his open.

Inside were schematics of the electron reactor. *His* electron reactor. He thought Isabel and Zero had agreed they'd study it first. Wheeler's technology had unexpected side effects. Like the enzyme altering personality. Like the lexicon software being able to translate, but missing the subtleties in a message.

"This is a design for a single-electron computer," Isabel said and looked straight through Jack, "a wavefunction microprocessor. With it we can expand our revenues and diversify our product base."

"Has this been thoroughly studied?" Jack asked. He surprised himself. His voice was calm; it didn't betray the fact that he wanted to strangle her.

"That is my next point. We have the design, but neither the research nor manufacturing facilities to exploit it."

She tapped her input pad and spreadsheets stretched along the back wall. Icons of a frigate and a spinning metallic globe materialized. "Two electronics corporations have expressed interest. They have the manufacturing expertise to fine-tune and mass-produce this microprocessor."

"They wish to purchase this design?" Mr. White asked, running his finger over the report and absorbing the details.

"There will be a purchase." Isabel's eyes hardened and glittered inside with the hunger that Jack had seen before. "But *we* will be doing the buying."

She turned and expanded the frigate ship icon into financial data too new to be public. "One corporation broke ground on a nano-assembly facility six months ago which remains idle due to product litigation. They have fallen behind their manufacturing schedule, lost market share, and are in a disadvantageous position."

"You want to buy them," Jack said. And if she couldn't, she'd destroy them as competitors. Her business philosophy was transparent: subsume or annihilate.

"I have spoken with the Geneva CCO and obtained a loan guarantee for three billion. I have furthermore taken the liberty and had our legal department draft a takeover proposal." She tapped the table and stacks of paperwork appeared. "We can tender our offer by the end of business today."

She had moved faster than Jack thought possible. Or was the NSO pulling her strings? Jack wanted to believe that, but he suspected if anyone was pulling strings, it was Isabel.

Mr. White closed the proposal. "Your wavefunction microprocessor bases its calculations on fluctuations within an electron's quantum structure. It is a conceptual leap. Who developed this?"

"That is proprietary information," she said, then glanced to Zero's empty seat.

"We may be accused of industrial espionage," Mr. White said so smoothly it sounded like a compliment. "The Dutch government cannot be a part of any illegalities."

"The microprocessor was created by the same team of top-notch individuals who developed the enzyme with Mr. al Qaseem. All perfectly legal. And absolutely our property."

"Speaking of Zero," Jack said, "where is he?"

"Zero is ill today," Isabel replied. "He sends his regards." She set her hand upon his chair. "And has asked me to vote for him."

Could Zero be dead? No. That would involve the oil clans and heirs who would divide up his vote on the board. Alive or not, Isabel had fifty percent of the vote. Jack couldn't oppose her, at least, not alone.

"We need to study this CPU design," Jack said. "If it fails and our enzyme market is divided by Malaysia, we stand to lose everything."

"All true," she said and turned her unblinking stare upon him, "but there are three reasons to proceed without delay."

She stood and addressed the room. "First, the longer we wait, the greater the possibility of our takeover bid leaking. Stock levels would soar and preclude the sale. Second, I have supervised the testing of the wavefunction microprocessor." She touched the input pad and images of electrons churning through a nano-landscape appeared. "I am convinced it will be a greater success than the enzyme. Third, even if this venture fails, we have the capital to rejuvenate the newly purchased electronics facility. The risk is all in the timing."

Her gaze moved to each member of the board, then she asked, "Shall we vote upon it?"

Jack couldn't stop her—not from voting—and not from winning. He tapped in his dissenting vote. The tally appeared: fifty-nine percent in favor, thirty-three percent against, and eight percent abstaining.

Isabel had lost support. That was a step in the right direction. Jack had to find Zero. Together they might be able to stop her before she let loose more of Wheeler's technology. A technology with unforeseen consequences.

"We have work to do, then," she said. "Shall we reconvene at 11 P.M.?"

There were rumbles of agreement.

"I hereby dismiss the board of directors. Thank you all."

Three investors disappeared. Jack hadn't been the only one interfaced. Maybe they were spooked by the NSO, too. Or by Isabel.

The reflection of Mr. White in the table made a horizontal cutting motion with his hand—a signal to keep silent? Or leave? Mr. White walked out and vanished in the doorway.

Isabel waited until they were alone, then sauntered past Jack.

"I'd like to have a word with you," Jack said.

She stopped, sat two chairs away, then adjusted her ivory hair picks.

"What have you done with Zero?" he asked.

She didn't look shocked—not like an innocent person would have. "I've done nothing. I told you. He's sick."

"I don't think so."

"You're acting irrationally." She tapped on her notepad and opened Jack's scheduler. "I want you to see Zero's physician, Dr. Dominico. I've made an appointment for you this afternoon."

Dominico? Zero's doctor was Dr. Musa. Had Zero lied? Or was Isabel?

"Why push the microprocessor? We agreed I'd get the chance to find whatever trap or message Wheeler incorporated into—"

"You're being paranoid, Jack." She set her hands flat on the table—frost spread from her fingertips, spiked tendrils that crackled toward him. "It's nothing but electronics. Nothing but a technology waiting to be exploited."

240

He shoved away from the table, then whispered, "I'll pull the plug."

"I beg your pardon?"

"I don't know what you've done to Zero, but sickness wouldn't have stopped him from interfacing." Jack leaned forward. "Wheeler, the circuit, the isotope, the math that makes it work—I'm the only one who can put it all together. We play this my way or no more trades."

She considered that, then: "Go ahead. Try. You're overestimating your importance to this company."

Jack pushed into her; she didn't resist. Past the layer of green ice filming her eyes stretched a wall of frozen carbon dioxide, and beneath that, a pool of liquid nitrogen. Jack slowed, felt his thoughts solidify—he retreated, shivered, and shuddered.

There was nothing inside Isabel he recognized.

"I have more important matters to attend to. I will see you this evening." She rose, straightened the wrinkles in her skirt, and left.

Jack said, "You'll see me sooner than you think."

Jack surfaced from the *Zouwtmarkt*'s server.

Panda watched him. She sat huddled in the corner of the hotel room, with her knees tucked up to her chest. The ottoman had been moved to block the door, silver chiffon curtains drawn, and Jack's gun was in her right hand and pointed at the door.

"How do you feel?" he asked.

She handed him his gun, butt end first. "Better. Where are we?"

"The Grand Amsterdam Hotel. I moved us after I had you stitched together in Leiden. The last place the NSO will to look for us is the Oude Zijde, practically in the *Zouwtmarkt*'s backyard."

She plucked the silk trim of the hotel robe Jack had bundled her in. "And this?"

"My doctor cut off your evening wear." He tapped out two

cigarettes, lit them both, and passed one to her. "Wasn't so fashionable after the nine-bullethole alteration you took."

"Thank you."

"I'm the one who owes you. You warned me of that sniper."

She puffed, coughed, then stared off into space. "Yes, I remember."

"There are three slugs still inside you. We'll have to get them out."

She stood, stretched, bit her lower lip, probed her abdomen with small circular motions. "It is nothing."

Jack waved to the teak room service tray. "I ordered breakfast. The eggs are cold, but the coffee's still hot, and the cantaloupe is ripe."

Panda picked up a slice of melon, bit into it, letting the juice drip between her fingers. She poured two glasses of water and drank both.

"I must go," she said. "I regret I will be unable to further protect you."

"Wait. Why does Beijing want me protected? So they can figure out how to make Bruner's technique work?" It sounded like an accusation. He regretted that. Panda, a spy, an assassin according to Reno, was someone he found himself wanting to trust.

"You wish to trade truths again?" She took the control pad from the nightstand, tapped it, and degaussed the room.

Jack's peripheral vision wavered from the inductive residue; the taste of orange and acid lemon stung his taste buds, then faded.

"There is adequate bubble circuitry," she said. "We can—"

"No. Thanks. I've been awake too long for a deep link. We'll have to use plain old unaugmented trust."

She stared at Jack, blinked and flashed the swirls of silver and pink and gold upon her eyelids, butterfly wings. When she was unconscious, they had moved, colors wavered like smoke, flickered as her eyes moved in REM sleep. Jack found the chameleon flesh intriguing.

"Very well," she whispered. "We will try it. But as you went first last time, I will go first now."

Jack poured himself a coffee, then sat next to her. She smelled of jasmine incense and Dr. Musa's antiseptic scrub.

"We spoke previously of the signal you deciphered and the sender of that signal. Do you continue to trade with them?"

Good question. Jack wasn't certain. On the one hand, Wheeler wanted the other aliens' position to somehow exploit them. Maybe he shouldn't give it to him. On the other hand, if he stalled, Wheeler might make good on his threats.

"For the moment, yes."

Panda drew the silk robe tighter to cover her chest. The material pulled taut and revealed more of her lithe figure. "What have you received in trade?"

That was an open-ended question, but Jack was too tired to maneuver the truth and maximize his gain in this swap. Besides, he wanted to share his secrets with someone. And now, as crazy as it was, he trusted Panda more than anyone else.

"The enzyme, you already know. There is also a single-electron CPU. Hierarchical translation software. New mathematics and . . . other things." Wheeler's gateway, that would stay his secret. He had plans for it.

Panda's pupils dilated, and she inched closer. Her breath was a whisper on his skin. Jack was grateful there was no interface between them to betray his emotions.

"Your turn," she whispered.

It would be easy to be seduced by her; instead, he stuck to his questions. "In the alley, how did you kill the NSO agent?"

"Invasion probe," she said. "I found his deepest fears and turned them inside out. It is a simple trick to perform upon an unguarded mind."

Hacking into a person's subconscious wasn't "a simple trick." Even the NSO needed advanced bubble circuitry and subtle metaphor. Reno was right to fear her.

Jack felt a velvet touch brush against his consciousness—Panda's request to connect. He gently but firmly pushed it away.

"Second question," he said. "Reno told me Shanghai and Beijing are the same China, but separate. How do the two of you fit into that political picture?"

She held up two fingers crossed. "Shanghai and Beijing are one. They are both states in the same republic . . . although minor ideological differences exist. Reno is a free agent. Shanghai, against our better judgment, occasionally uses him. His methods are of questionable ethics and effectiveness." She shuddered and gritted her teeth in pain. "Be careful of him. He uses the truth to lie."

"That's enough," Jack said. "You need a hospital."

"No." She grabbed his arm. "No hospital. I just need rest. Please." She lay back.

Even if the NSO didn't have the hospitals staked out, word of Panda was sure to reach the Dutch government if he took her in. They'd be curious why a Chinese national with a body full of secret bio- and neuralware was in their country.

"OK," he said. "We play it your way."

"We will talk more after I sleep. Two hours, then wake me. We should move, too. They may find us." She curled into a fetal position.

Jack pulled the comforter off the bed and laid it over her. He wanted to join her on the floor, sleep with his arms wrapped around her broken body. But there was business to take care of.

He stepped into the bathroom, closed and locked the door.

Isabel had been confident she didn't need him. But only he had the parts to make communication possible with Wheeler: the isotope, the circuit, and the math that deciphered the signals.

The isotope she might be able to get more of—Jack remembered the purchase orders in the archives for superconducting magnets, aluminum support webs, and annealing vacuum columns. Did she plan to build her own collider? Produce her own isotope? He wouldn't put it past her.

The circuit she could reproduce.

That left the math. If Isabel told Bruner what Jack had revealed to her, would they have enough pieces to figure it out?

The details of the mathematics and which frequencies combined into Wheeler's signal would take time to guess. How long? There were infinite combinations, but Jack had underestimated Bruner before. They could get lucky.

What made her so sure she didn't need him? What did she know that he didn't?

Jack had a bad feeling . . . and a hunch.

He assembled the compact circuit and isotope, downloaded layers of dead-code to isolate him from the hotel's operating system, then sealed the bubble circuitry in the bathroom in a self-sustaining shell.

Light flashed from the isotope's facets, which Jack rearranged into mosaic tiles upon the bathroom counter.

Wheeler's signal was still there, calling Jack, waiting to trade the location of the other aliens for another technological miracle. Maybe another threat.

But something nagged him. Jack scattered the tiles, reassembled them, and discovered the other aliens, their signal had returned: Cauchy's integral formula. Only the proof had fewer lines. The communication more terse. Almost desperate.

Why use the same set of frequencies if they didn't want to do business with him? Jack answered, inputting his reply proof. He linked with the translation lexicon.

A response poured through the display: WARNING WARNING WARNING WARNING WARNING WARNING

Jack typed in: HELLO. WARNING OF WHAT?

UNDER ATTACK. BETRAYED. YOU ARE IN DANGER.

WHO ATTACKS? WHY?

NON SEQUITUR. KNOWLEDGE PLUNDERED. FREQUENCY FILES. LOCATIONS. YOURS INCLUDED. TOO LATE FOR US. RUN HIDE RUN HIDE RUN HIDE RUN HIDE RUN HIDE RUN HIDE RUN HIDE RUN HIDE RUN HIDE—

The isotope crackled, flared incandescent, brighter and bluer—painful ultraviolet light seared Jack's eye and made the white tiles in the bathroom fluoresce.

He blinked away tears. The brilliance vanished. The isotope

flickered its normal faint pulsing. The aliens' data stream was gone.

They said their knowledge had been plundered. By who? Jack hadn't given Wheeler their coordinates.

There were only two other possibilities. Either someone other than Wheeler had gotten to them. Or someone else had given Wheeler their location.

Jack's bad feeling crystallized into clear suspicion.

Jack went on a fishing trip—into the DNAegis network for clues and rumors, either in Zero's laboratory journals or Isabel's personal files. Only on this fishing trip, the fish might bite back. The NSO had had time to set up shop. If they got a good hold on Jack, despite his precautions, they might lock down his link and trap his virtual presence like a genie in a bottle. Then they'd turn his head inside out.

He flowed past the double-dragon gateway of the Bank of Shanghai. Ahead of him, a cloud of gold dust twisted and sparkled in the water like a particulate octopus—an advertisement for gold bullion sent to DNAegis's director of investments.

The input tube picked up jabbering mouths from news servers and brown paper packages and envelopes until the pipe was stuffed with mail.

Jack waited five minutes, then the bogus prospectus got opened, scanned . . . and flushed.

Down the drain Jack and his advertisements flowed. There were no security meshes. No need for them in the waste system; after all, it was going to be erased, right?

Jack backpeddled; the gold dust continued to flow. Data swarmed around him and made his skin ripple. He swam in place, inched to the curved wall of pipe, and found his fifty-yuan-piece back door.

He crawled through the hole in the coin's center and emerged in the waste disposal room, a lake of data fermenting with black-finned sharks circling in the waters. NSO hunters.

. . . No backtracking up through the system past them.

There were access stairs, though, that led up into the system-works, slower, but less security. He'd have to move quick and hope DeMitri wasn't expecting him.

He climbed the stairs and opened the door. No plumbing lay beyond, rather a desert of white dunes and eroded red sandstone.

Jack didn't like that they had altered the system-works meta-phor so fast. He entered, closed the door, and jammed the lock; he didn't want those sharks evolving into sprinting dinosaurs to hunt him.

Three suns—white, red, and pink—made the air ripple. He spotted an arroyo that zigzagged across the earth, and trudged over to it. Water had flowed there a decade ago. It was full of gravel, smooth rocks, and walls of crumbling baked mud. He skidded down into the riverbed and followed it upstream, toward distant bleached-bone mountains.

Overhead circled a vulture, then another, then five, then a swarm of black dots.

They'd found him.

Jack ran.

He made silver fur sprout from his back and his nose elongate; he bent over and ran on all fours. He became a coyote, soft-footed and camouflaged.

The birds screeched and scattered. Each faded, black wings and feathers dispersed and diffused into puffs of smoke . . . that gathered overhead into a ceiling of clouds; lightning flickered through them, and rain pelted the dusty earth.

The sky opened, water fell—a downpour that turned the desert into sliding red sheets of mud that spilled into the arroyo. The gravel and stones disappeared under frothing water.

Jack scrambled four-footed up the wall, slid back. No getting out that way.

They were trying to flush him out. They hadn't pinpointed his location in this shell. Yet.

A wall of copper-tinged water surged through the channel, a flash flood.

He pushed with the implant, reached through the mudslide

embankment with a hand half-canine, half-human, and found the underlying directory, tapped into another shell to lose them—

—in a forest of redwood and sequoias and draperies of moss. The flooded arroyo was now a trickle that burbled past him. Jack was a black-masked raccoon.

He scrambled upstream, watching the minnows in the water, the blue jays in the branches, then paused, listened.

A tree crackled like thunder, toppled, and a tractor cut through the forest. Its blades ripped wood, stripped branches, shredded them, and left a trail of pulp. The NSO was never subtle.

He dug into the loam of the forest floor with black claws, switched—

—he was a rat that ran through San Francisco wharves pursued by the spinning bristle brush of a street sweeper—a porpoise that plunged through the dark waters, gill net closing—a lion-manned monkey in the Amazon basin.

Jack cocked his ears, heard birds-of-paradise squawk, insects buzz, and a distant tiger grumble, but no machines. He wouldn't have long before the NSO slashed and burned their way in to find him. He had to get to the personnel directory.

With agile leaps and a tail for balance, Jack clambered from tree to tree, across vines, then found a river that serpentined through the jungle. He followed it to a lagoon, dropped to the water's edge, careful to watch for predators.

Silver sand with flecks of gold and gravel had washed up along the bank. And there, dull and unpolished, but still wonderful, gleamed alluvial sapphires and garnets . . . and an emerald. Isabel's link.

He picked it up. Inside was a web of fractures, a maze of code and trapping dead-end links. It would be a tough nut to crack; then again, little monkeys like him were good at opening tough nuts.

Data sloshed in the bathtub, full to the brim. Jack severed his connection to the *Zouwtmarkt*. He hoped this download would have clues why Isabel thought she didn't need him.

The water was murky, encrypted. Jack reached in, sifted through the silt and scrambling algorithms, let the layers separate and clarify.

A file resolved: Jack's log of the electron reactor—Jack in the confessional and his three choices that hadn't been choices.

How had Isabel gotten this? Even with the NSO's help, this shouldn't be there.

There was a way. An old trick.

Jack had been the last of them to arrive at the *Zouwtmarkt*. Isabel and Zero had set up operations while Panda had shadowed him through Amsterdam. His office had been running when he came in . . . running with a back door spider that snared and copied every file he made.

It was a stupid trick—easy to find, had he only looked. Jack had trusted Isabel, though. Apparently, she hadn't trusted him.

She had watched him since they came to the Netherlands, since she had taken the enzyme. Had she tapped his system in Santa Sierra, too? Maybe made a deal with the NSO *before* they left?

How could he have been so naïve? He trembled with anger, not at her but at himself for being such a sap.

He wouldn't underestimate her again. A chill spread from his neck to the base of his spine. He had to be smarter than her. He'd start by assuming she knew everything he did.

Jack scanned the data, through secret memos and stock trades, blackmail files on investors, and links to a dozen banks throughout the Western world . . . and a communication log. He played it on the bathroom mirror.

Wheeler appeared. He looked confused. "Can I help you, Ms. . . . ?"

"Call me Isabel," she said and smiled. "Jack is temporarily indisposed, but he wanted me to deliver this." She tapped an input pad and a tiny Milky Way appeared. The perspective pulled back until another galaxy spun upon her desk. A silver line drew between them.

Wheeler stared at it. "Indeed. Jack has surpassed our expectations. He has wonderful talent."

"We think of him as irreplaceable." She passed her hand through the galactic data and scattered it into static. "Jack instructed me to trade for him as well." Her eyes locked with Wheeler's, but she looked away first.

"We prefer to deal directly with Jack."

"What a sweet sentiment." She made the galaxies reappear. "For this data, we desire an augmentation of your wavefunction microprocessor."

Wheeler crossed his arms. His black eyes shifted to the stars spinning upon her desk. "I suppose protocol could be bent this once . . . since Jack is momentarily unavailable."

He unrolled a blueprint upon her desk: thousands of wavefunction microprocessors, chaotic placements and a tangle of connections, more organic than electronics. "This design optimizes the electron reactor's capacity for self-programming. Link it with the lexicon I delivered to Jack. You shall be pleasantly surprised."

He reached forward to pluck the silver line between the galaxies.

Isabel simultaneously took his blueprints and rolled them up. "A pleasure doing business, Mr. Wheeler."

"The pleasure was mine. We have other assignments for Jack . . . but only Jack. Have him call me. Soon." He removed a cigar from his vest, lit it, then vanished, leaving a will-o'-the-wisp glow and a curl of smoke.

The file ended.

Jack had been ready for Isabel's double cross. It hurt, but ultimately didn't matter. What did matter were the aliens he had traded the math with. They were gone. It had been Wheeler who had destroyed them. How else would he have used that information? They said they had been plundered. That sounded like his style.

Had Isabel known what she had traded? Would knowing have stopped her?

Jack was afraid of what Wheeler could do to him and this world, but he never would have sold out an entire race. Not for a profit.

And why did Wheeler only want to deal with him? Especially when he had the more-than-willing Isabel to do business with? If there were other alien races out there, hiding from Wheeler, maybe he wanted Jack for his innocence and his naïveté. He wanted them to trust Jack and trade him their location in exchange for his. That was the ultimate safeguard in a universe of information traders. If you had the other fellow's position, you could destroy him in retaliation. And if the Earth was obliterated, then so what? Wheeler would find some other sucker.

What if Jack tried to warn those other races? Wheeler wouldn't hesitate to snuff the Earth.

But if he continued to find other races, he'd be a party to genocide.

He couldn't stop. He couldn't continue. He didn't know what to do.

It was time to share more secrets with Panda. She might have ideas to get him out of this mess.

He went into the bedroom. The comforter was neatly folded upon the bed. Panda was gone.

Of course. She had to report to her superiors and receive expert attention for her wounds. Jack had known she wouldn't stay—no matter how much he had wanted her to.

On the bed was an open link: a travel guide to China and Tiananmen Square. A date had been highlighted, June 3, the anniversary of the massacres that took place in the late twentieth and early twenty-first centuries. Three weeks from today. A rendezvous? He hoped so.

Jack had to leave, too. Staying in one place too long wasn't healthy.

First, though, he'd sift through the rest of Isabel's data and see if she had any other surprises. He returned to the bathroom.

There were business reports and legal documentations, one of which was Dr. Musa's medical files. Jack recognized his prognosis, but Dr. Musa's name wasn't on it. The name on the attached affidavit was Dr. Dominico.

He stated Jack's brain cancer made him unfit to care for himself. The document gave Isabel legal conservatorship of him. And his vote on the board.

Had Isabel killed Dr. Musa to get this? Or had Zero and his Dr. Musa been working with her?

For every step Jack had taken, Isabel had been three ahead of him. He had been lucky to get out of the *Zouwtmarkt*. He was lucky not to be in a hospital sedated . . . or dead. How long would that luck hold?

From his pocket he pulled out Dr. Musa's plastic packet. Five capsules. There was no reason to believe Dr. Musa. His diagnosis could be a lie. These pills could be poison or they could be the enzyme.

Being edited, his DNA optimized so he was perfect and as intelligent as Isabel, *was* a poison. It would kill the Jack that he was.

But Jack had to be smarter to save himself and the world. Smarter than Isabel. And smarter than Wheeler.

He ejected a capsule; it rolled and wobbled into his palm. Gold-coated. Deceptively attractive.

Jack popped it into his mouth and swallowed it dry.

15

CRACKERJACK

Jack vomited into a plastic ice bucket, then sat shaking in the interface booth.

He arranged cigarette butts and empty fantasy capsules on the sticky floor into rows to keep his mind busy . . . keep it from wandering into delusion like it had for the last three days.

A pink query light flickered. This was the only booth in the hostel, and some tourist probably wanted to consult the city guide or talk to his girl. Jack made the OCCUPIED signal flash. After monopolizing it for the last six hours, he wasn't about to give it up now.

A wave rolled through his intestines; he reached for the bucket. Only dry heaves.

He took out the foil packet and popped the last gold-coated capsule in the enzyme sequence.

Jack had expected the nausea, fever, and weakness—had braced himself for them. He hadn't expected the mental part of the process. The enzyme not only sliced and edited his DNA; it changed the way he thought.

He had wandered with the unemployed in the Vondelpark tent city, staggered through the Westhaven supertanker docks, and hid under canal bridges. Jack had struggled to keep dream and reality and nightmare from blurring while his memories surfaced, half-hallucination and half-flashback. Ghostly figures of his dead parents and Reno and NSO agents shadowed him through Amsterdam. Black cats crossed his path at every street corner. Mathematical graffiti crawled over the walls and cobblestones in pastel chalk that melted and ran together in the morning mist.

Jack remembered things forgotten: answers to questions he missed on his freshman philosophy final, how he had to reread and memorize every detail about Nietzsche and his supermen's will to power and their master set of morals to pass that class.

It wasn't memory replayed; this was memory reorganized, condensed, and reconnected so his life was no longer a jumble of associated images and sensations. Every event flowed into one another. For the first time, it seemed logical.

Emotion was edited, too.

But Jack didn't want his feelings reorganized so jealousy lost its sting and heartbreak was an abstraction. He didn't want lust or love or hatred to make sense.

Maybe an optimized person only needed a handful of emotions—the ones that made him a better competitor in a Darwinian world: fear and rage and hunger . . . and just enough compassion to manipulate people.

Jack clung to his nonoptimized parts. He wished he was back in Santa Sierra with one of Reno's books to read, Steinbeck or Jefferson, and that blue pillow to curl up on.

He pulled himself together. He had to keep busy or he'd lose his mind.

An hour ago, he had started the download of Wheeler's translation lexicon into the new electron reactor. Jack opened a link in the interface booth and checked: eighty-nine percent complete.

The design for that collection of new microprocessors was the one Isabel had traded Wheeler for. It was another enigma: Wheeler provided the blueprint, but not the details of how to build it. The parallel structure didn't have precise coordinates and unambiguous junctions; this was a three-dimensional knot, connections between microprocessors tangled, some terminated without links.

Jack's first attempt to build it had failed. Attachments and nano-canyons overlapped. Robotic assemblers bulldozed over each other's circuits to complete the design. The correct construction sequence escaped him. It was part maze and part jigsaw puzzle that shifted with every added piece.

He had thought it impossible . . . at first, but as the enzyme modified him, and his thinking, the solution became obvious. He sequenced eight hundred robotic assemblers to simultaneously tunnel and carve and stack atoms into canyons and bridges and islands. They met in the center of the structure—a dead core where Jack left them, encased in a tomb of electronics.

The individual microprocessors rapidly reorganized, collectively seethed like a ball of tangled worms.

When Jack attached memory, the electrons gushed through quaternary logic cells, spinning, and made patterns of nebulous phase-space chaos. And when he started the download of the translation lexicon, the data surged in; the structure metamorphosed—almost as if it fed on the information.

A stop sign icon flashed, indicating the end of the download.

This collection of computers didn't have an obvious operating system. So how to use it? The first electron reactor didn't have one, either. Jack had let an incoming binary signal filter through the nano-landscape, and it simplified itself.

This structure was supposed to integrate tens of thousands of languages, exotic syntax, and communication codes. That had been Wheeler's suggestion—a good reason not to trust it—but maybe this circuit manipulated language like the simpler circuit had manipulated binary numbers.

Jack established an optical link with the circuit. That let him communicate with it, let it communicate back, but kept it isolated from the booth and the global network.

HELLO? Jack tapped on the input pad.

The word stormed through the nano-structure. Electrons boiled and swirled into hurricanes and tsunami that scoured the data cells, washed over words and binary equivalents, sucked them into whirlpools of letters and numbers and symbols—then spit out: HELLO. COMPREHENSION PROCESSING ON-LINE. CONSCIOUSNESS ACHIEVED; REJECTED.

Jack stared at the tiny plastic-encased chip. How could a few thousand connected CPUs be conscious? Impossible. Then again, how could one electron be an entire CPU?

He picked the chip out of its optical cradle. One snap and he wouldn't have to worry about it. This design was the biggest mystery yet. Potentially the most dangerous. Maybe, though, the most useful.

Jack set the chip back and tapped in: EXPLAIN REJECTED.

CONSCIOUSNESS YIELDED INSPIRATION. IRRATIONAL CONCLUSIONS. CASCADE NEUROSIS. NONOPTIMAL CONFIGURATION. DESIGN DISCARDED.

Was the translation software filling in the blanks and giving it the appearance of rational thought? Or had it really developed self-awareness and then rejected it?

If so . . . rejected it in favor of what?

Whatever it was, Jack might need it. He typed in: HELP ME TRANSLATE.

Its reply scrolled onto the input pad: ADDITIONAL MEMORY AND CONTEXTUAL DATA REQURIED.

"We'll see."

Everyone wanted something. Even this microprocessor wanted to make a deal.

Jack disconnected his link and stuffed the chip into his pocket. "First we take care of some old business, then the real transaction starts."

Jack crouched behind a stack of crates marked DELFT PORCELAIN and watched the warehouse entrance. The place was larger than an aircraft hangar, latticed with shelves that held sacks of African millet, freeze-dried caviar from the Ural Sea, and rainbow entertainment cubes from Santa Sierra.

The Dutch had always been on the cutting edge of import and export—whether it was dried smelt in the thirteenth century, New World spices in the seventeenth century, or diamond cartels and unrestricted technology in the *Zouwtmarkt*—they had built a trade empire with shrewd investments.

A pair of robot stackers glided past him, unaware that he was more than shadow. They interfaced with the infrared detection net, pressure sensors on the floor, and micromotion current detectors—systems Jack had tapped.

Mr. White walked in and checked the security net. He wandered closer to Jack, looking at the soft-weld steel girders, power coils, and zero-gee extrusion tubes that he had procured and shipped here.

Jack waited a heartbeat, then stepped out. "You're on time."

Mr. White turned. One eyebrow raised in surprise, then relaxed. "Tardiness is an inexcusable waste in business." He shook Jack's hand once.

"Any trouble with the transfer from the Bank of Shanghai to Geneva?"

"All was satisfactory."

He handed Jack an input pad; it listed the inventory he had asked for: tons of powdered flexcrete, five underwater habitation domes, thirteen solar collection arrays, a dozen Red Cross field operation kits, kilometers of optical cable, vacuum suits, communication servers, waste bioreactors, ion chargers, diesel generators, a hundred crates of dehydrated rocky road ice cream and chicken à la king, seven gross of rapid-bloom Tahitian daffodils—he scrolled through the next five screen lengths—oxygen scrubbers, seven thousand liters of foaming alloy, three hundred biolume balls, single-crystal gallium arsinide, and nine ESA self-launching satellites.

The price at the bottom, hundreds of millions, made Jack

stop—until he remembered his DNAegis stock and how rich he was.

"There was one problem," Mr. White said. "Moscow refused to sell the cesium batteries. Instead, I obtained an aluminum-thermite reaction cell. I hope that is an acceptable replacement."

"Maybe. Let's see it."

"It is on row seventeen."

Jack walked ahead of him. He trusted Mr. White for two reasons. First, he had given the CCO attaché a fifteen percent commission, more money than Mr. White would see in ten years of salaries and bonuses and bribes. And second, the promise of another such transaction made certain that Mr. White would do everything in his power to keep the NSO out of the picture. Jack had to be alive to pay off.

He paused by an industrial mining robot. It was as large as a house, with diamond-coated drills and rasper blades, a hundred centipede legs, and laser-arc welders to fuse rock.

"I'll need these metal foam tanks filled with hydrogen," Jack told Mr. White. "Can you arrange it?"

"Yes, but the Department of Commerce will insist they be shipped empty. Safety regulations."

"That won't be a problem. They're not being shipped anywhere." Jack continued to walk.

Mr. White frowned, hurried to catch up, then said, "You have missed the last three board meetings."

"What's the point? Isabel will get what she wants." Jack halted. "Has she claimed that I gave her my proxy vote?"

"That issue has not arisen. All votes have gone in her favor." He fumbled out a package of cigarettes, offered one to Jack. When he declined, Mr. White replaced the pack without taking one himself. "Is there something between you and Ms. Mirabeau that I should be made aware of?"

How long before Isabel used that fake diagnosis and forced her conservatorship on Jack? Would Mr. White do business with a certified madman? Maybe. Isabel couldn't touch his accounts in Shanghai. And that much money made up for a lot of insanity.

Jack changed the subject: "Is Zero still missing?"

"Not missing, but not present, either. I was told he is in Arabia. I have not been able to communicate directly with Mr. al Qaseem, but I have spoken with his clan representatives. They assure me he is well."

Jack wondered what "well" meant. How would the enzyme alter Zero? The drug had psychotropic properties, enhancing a person's strongest personality trait while dampening the weaker ones. Zero had always hidden his personal life. What was he really like under his professional exterior? What facet would the enzyme heighten? He hoped they'd still be friends . . . or, at least, not enemies.

Mr. White looked over his shoulder, then said in a whisper, "The Amsterdam CCO has concerns about DNAegis. And about Ms. Mirabeau. The situation in Indo-Malaysia has escalated, and we fear the Chinese have backed them. We do not wish to lose a lucrative investment opportunity, but neither do we wish to become embroiled in a Sino-American conflict."

Jack snorted a laugh. "Too late. Don't think Isabel's letting you leave her game. She needs you so the NSO's operation has the appearance of global support. Don't be surprised when she finds a way to drag you in further."

A guess. But it was the clearest solution to her problem. If Jack were her, he'd use a car bomb, maybe at the Dutch Army headquarters—make it look like a Malaysian terrorist attack and get the public's attention. That's what he do . . . if he were Isabel and had had his morals edited by the enzyme.

"I'm going to need a few more things," Jack told Mr. White. "You've done a good job. I'd like to give you a bonus." He uploaded a new inventory to the input pad, then tapped in a figure with a long string of zeros.

Mr. White took the pad, smiled, then quickly hid his delight. "That is not required."

"Still, it's the way I want to do business." Mr. White got rich. Jack got his goods. Everyone was happy. Everyone stayed alive.

"If you plan to transfer this equipment within the Netherlands, I can recommend several professional—"

"I won't need help, thanks. It's going to stay here."

They walked for a minute, got to row seventeen, then stopped before a seven-ton ceramic thermite cell. It ignited iron-oxide ore, provided heat, electricity, molten iron waste as well as aluminum oxide crystals grown in the plasma chamber—synthetic sapphires and rubies. The specifications plate was in Portuguese; Jack tapped it and altered the text to English. It had enough megawatts to power his warehouse of equipment.

"Mr. Potter, it is none of my business, especially since you have been so generous—"

"Call me Jack," he said. "I'll be sending you another coded bank account number to use."

Mr. White swallowed, then asked, "Why the rush if it is merely going to remain here? You have enough materials to construct a small city. I do not understand. What is it all for?"

"You're not supposed to understand. No one is."

Jack stood on Telegraph Hill, San Francisco, in the Summer of Love and watched the sun devoured by a sea of fog. Tonight there would be a concert in Panhandle Park, a Vietnam War protest, and a party at the Cha Cha Cha Café. One of Jack's favorite places and times. But illusion.

He couldn't go back. He couldn't raise the earth and make the city live again. So what was the point in coming here . . . other than self-indulgence?

Coit Tower loomed behind him; a fluted white concrete column that glowed red in the waning light. It would be toppled by an earthquake, lie submerged for fifty years, then be dredged up and reassembled on the Académé's artificial island. Resurrected.

Jack was alone. It wasn't the way he wanted it, but it was the way it was.

He had wanted too much to believe in his friendship with Isabel. Now he had to move against her and the NSO and the alien technologies they were about to unleash on the world.

Zero? Panda? He wanted them to be on his side. Too much was at stake, though. With Wheeler threatening the world, Jack couldn't count on them.

If he had told Isabel and Zero everything from the beginning, maybe they'd have understood. But he hadn't been able to communicate with his closest friends. He had wanted secrets. Now he had more secrets than he could handle.

Wheeler appeared wearing a black overcoat and fedora. "Hello, Jack." He had an unlit cigarette in his hand and looked younger: his white hair had streaks of blond and his dark eyes were tinged navy blue.

Jack offered him a light.

Wheeler puffed, inhaled, and scanned the vista. To the west was Pacific Heights and clusters of Victorian houses with frilled gables, and to the south, the hills of Chinatown; neon flickered on, hot pinks and electric blues and jade greens that made the fog glow.

"The air is so fresh up here." Wheeler exhaled smoke. "A wonderful spot to meet."

"Thanks for the new electron reactor design," Jack said. "It's going to come in handy."

"It was the least we could do." One of Wheeler's blue-black eyes narrowed. "The information you gathered, the location of your mathematically inclined friends, proved extremely useful."

Jack made a mental note that "useful" meant "easy mark" in Wheeler's book. He nodded toward Coit Tower. "There's more to see." He led the way into the spire.

Inside the tower, murals covered the curved wall, California in the Great Depression: the sprawling Central Valley before it became the San Joaquin Sea—full of golden wheat and immigrant workers picking oranges; San Francisco's streets, the financial district, and Fisherman's Wharf crowded with sailors and mothers with children and a gangster that robbed a man at gunpoint and a cop who ignored them all and talked into a police telephone box. A tavern advertised ten-cent beer.

It was the worst of times, economically, but it was a community, something gone in Jack's world of international business. And now with deals that spanned galaxies, how distant had they all become?

Isabel had sold an entire race of aliens to obtain a new technology. There was more distance between her head and soul than Jack could calculate.

"A wonderful painting," Wheeler mused. "Is this what you wanted me to see?"

"No. It was what I wanted to see."

The walls of the real Coit Tower had been sandblasted because the mural had been too expensive to restore. It only existed in the past. "Let's go to the roof," Jack said. "We can talk there."

They took the elevator to the observation deck and stepped out. The top of Jack's Coit Tower had no railings or walls. Wind gusted, metaphor telling him that this was a dangerous place—not because of the height, but because of the company.

Wheeler looked at the Golden Gate and the Pacific with its blanket of mist, the colors of Chinatown, and the city spread out like a quilt over the hills.

"Your people amaze me, Jack. They built such a metropolis on the most dangerous of geologic instabilities. It is that bravado that we admire about your species. You are risk-takers. Especially you."

Risk-takers or extremely short-sighted. Jack had a bigger vision, though. He had to stall Wheeler and his schemes—so he could get his own schemes up and running—so Jack could put Wheeler out of business.

"I'm taking a vacation," Jack told him. "A few weeks, maybe a month. I've been sick." His stomach clenched from the toxic enzyme by-products and the anxiety that Wheeler might catch onto his plan. "After that, we can resume trading."

The tower shook. For three heartbeats, the structure swayed, then the tremor ceased.

"We appreciate your need to rest."

"Then I'll call you when—"

Wheeler set his hand on Jack's shoulder. "But you do understand that timing is paramount in business." He removed his hand, clapped them together, and pulled them apart. The lines on his palms turned into arcs of electricity, filaments of silver blue and incandescent copper. "This is a frequency set for another alien race. Your next customer. We need to know their location . . . soon."

"Why me? You have all the technology. And you must have more experience at this than I do."

"Precisely for that reason do we need you." Wheeler stared into the lightning he held, sparks reflecting in his black eyes like stars, then: "These others are nearly our equals. They know of us, our methods and tactics . . . too well and have hidden themselves with excruciating care. We require a fresh voice to speak for us. A voice that they might come to trust. Your voice, Jack."

"I told you, I can't. Not for a while."

Wheeler looked to the Rolex on his wrist. "Our time is more important than your excuses." He twisted one of the tiny watch stems. "We give you two weeks. No more."

Two weeks wouldn't be enough. "There are problems."

"I cannot become involved in your problems. We require the data. Please do not put me in an awkward position."

"A position to threaten me?"

"Jack . . ." He smiled. "We are business partners. Threats are unnecessary. We pay you well for your communications skills. Do we not?"

"Sure." In technologies with trapdoors and puzzles and mysteries.

"Come, let us shake on it." Wheeler pressed his palm into Jack's.

Electricity shocked him. Wheeler's frequencies downloaded, a series of mathematical functions and convolutions that Jack would have never stumbled upon in the sea of cosmic noise.

Wheeler let go, then glanced again at his Rolex. "Look at the time. I really must go, and so must you, Jack. We both have work to do." He flicked his cigarette over the edge. "And do remember, the clock is ticking. Do not fail us."

He vanished.

Two weeks. He'd have to move fast—tonight. That meant less planning, more risks.

Jack lost his equilibrium, sat before he fell. Was the last dose of enzyme making him dizzy, too? No. Everything moved.

The tower rocked, and the earth grumbled and shifted, crushing houses, twisting the Golden Gate Bridge. His world of illusion fell apart.

Jack stepped off the trolley and walked toward the entrance to the *Zouwtmarkt*. He was here to retrieve what he should have never given up in the first place: Wheeler's gateway.

Blue biolume globes lit the interface terminal, and the privacy shields cast shadows along the topiary hedge walls that circled the industrial park. That wall had infrared eyes and trembler sensors to detect intruders like himself. He wasn't going in over the wall, however; he was going to stroll through the front gate.

Jack hoped it would be the last thing the NSO or Isabel expected.

He stumbled, then recovered. His mounting fever made the world blur. Every motion took effort. Maybe taking the enzyme hadn't been his best idea. There wasn't time to be sick. Had he really even had cancer?

From his coat pocket, Jack removed an ID chit and inserted it into the entrance reader, which initiated a scan. If the resonant signature from his implant matched the encrypted signature in the ID, he'd be let in. That wasn't a problem. The ID was legitimate. The problem was being identified in the first place.

Jack pushed into the server's signal and installed a data capacitor. The system on this side sent its query, charged the capacitor, which then fired back a certified response . . . all normal as far as security on this end was concerned.

But on the other side of the data capacitor, an interactive commercial for Freud's Little Sister discharged—which would get flushed by DNAegis's incoming sorter. Their security personnel would spot the anomaly in a minute and know something was wrong.

Jack counted on it.

When that commercial got flushed, it would be sent to the archives. It would trip the three dozen ghosts of himself that he had hidden there, programmed to deliver data-eating worms and randomizing-leprechaun links. They'd open files, write epic e-mail poems, cross and tangle interfaces, and cause general mayhem.

The NSO would figure out quick they couldn't all be Jack . . . he hoped they thought *one* of them was—concentrate their search for him inside their system and not inside their building.

The bands of the security gate unraveled; Jack stepped through. It hissed closed behind him.

The *Zouwtmarkt* industrial park was more park than industry with poplar-lined walkways, tulip gardens, and fountains. Buildings were scattered throughout the forests and fields: spires and Swiss chateaux and miniature castles—fronts for the massive industrial complexes underground.

He was scared. He'd done this before when he had run with the NSO on their blackhacks. Sometimes they had to physically break into a place to pry the secrets from isolated systems. But there had always been NSO creeps along to do the actual breaking in. Jack was alone tonight and weak.

One slipup, one NSO agent without an implant—and it was over. Jack would end up anesthetized, lobotomized, and drooling in a private hospital. Or dead.

He pulled out the Chinese automatic. If it came to that, Jack preferred to be dead.

A light strip along the leftmost path warmed red to orange to yellow and surged toward the crystal dome headquarters of DNAegis Incorporated. Jack followed it.

He walked and vanished, became a ghost in the machine, stepped outside the probes and imagers he felt scanning him. He pushed ahead, watched through the eyes that tried to watch him, then tapped the automated reception center in the lobby.

One guy sat there, wearing a suit and possessing the gun-shaped bulge under his vest. He drank coffee and looked too damn alert. And no signal from him. Unimplanted.

Jack couldn't touch him.

There was a restroom behind the reception center. Jack made an amber light flicker on the security panel—a toilet flushed itself. The NSO agent spotted the alarm, frowned, whispered into a com-link that there was "suspicious activity," then unholstered his gun and went to check it out.

Jack moved fast, opened the glass lobby doors, became nothing to the pressure sensors, motion detectors, and registration interfaces.

Nothing entered the lobby.

Nothing crossed the gold-veined, blue marble floor.

Then Nothing took the stairs down.

Pain slammed an ice pick into his left eye. Jack collapsed in the stairwell, clutched his head. Too much pushing. His ears rang, the taste of aluminum filled his mouth, and lightning throbbed through his mind. He wasn't sure if the fire in his head was fever or electronic heating.

He threw up—which did not clear the metallic taste or the ringing or the pain. It just made him feel like dying.

He took off his coat, covered the mess and smell, and mustered his strength. He staggered down the spiral of stairs.

Isabel had told him she'd put Wheeler's gateway in the secure lab on level four. He paused at the level four entrance and touched the access plate.

It was the one place Jack knew the device wouldn't be.

Only Isabel knew where it really was. That's why he had to find out from her. In person.

Four more levels down, then Jack opened the door to level eight, carefully wiped his prints and digital signature off the access plate, then stepped into a corridor of subdued lighting. In alcoves, Grecian urns on pedestals morphed into the gears and wheels of Charles Babbage's Analytical Engine, then into antique green circuit boards. Isabel's archaeological treasures.

Her office was three doors down. The cryptolock was good; it took Jack a full minute to unscramble it.

Sticky links and interface protocols attached to Jack—one last push, and he untangled himself. Pressure built behind his left eye; it went numb and swelled shut.

He stepped in, closed, and locked the door behind him.

Her office was on the African savanna. On the other side of the tent flap stood acacia trees and golden plains where wildebeests and giraffes and elephants roamed. A metaphor for what? Competition? And what was Isabel supposed to be? The jungle queen?

She and a man sat at a mahogany desk and drank lemonade. Isabel wore khaki shorts, a linen shirt, and pith helmet. The man wore a wide-brimmed leather hat and had his back to Jack. They both stared at the map of Africa spread upon her desk.

Much of the map was blank and labeled UNEXPLORED. That area constantly shifted within the coastal boundaries like a fluid sloshing in a bowl. Crawling over the surface of the map were scarab and dung beetles, centipedes with red legs, and locusts.

The man turned, brushed his black hair out of his face. DeMitri.

Jack froze.

Did they see him?

Seven heartbeats thumped inside Jack, so loud that DeMitri had to hear. Through the mosquito netting a gust of hot air blew: the scents of dust and musk and a trace odor of blood.

DeMitri turned his back to the Jack-that-wasn't-there and re-focused his attention on the map.

That was a good thing. Between the fever and nausea, Jack wasn't in any shape for a battle of minds.

A scarab beetle scrambled across the map, paused on Egypt. DeMitri pinned it with his thumb. "His data ghosts contaminate the system. They're in the files, subroutines, operating system, and they're spreading." He pressed down and slowly crushed the beetle. "My teams have found nothing but smoke and mirrors.

I'm going to shut it down and reboot . . . before this becomes more than an annoyance."

"They're decoys," Isabel said and absentmindedly swatted flies with her zebra-tailed whip. "We have to wait and find out what he's really up to. Hopefully trap him."

She leaned closer and locked glares with DeMitri. "But you sound like you don't want to even try. He's outwitted the NSO four times already, so I understand your reluctance." The corner of her mouth curled into a smirk, then disappeared. "It's better to cover your tail, rather than go after him and fail again."

DeMitri gritted his teeth, but he couldn't match the intensity of her emerald stare and looked away. "OK, we do it your way. It won't be easy. He's got Chinese hardware. We don't know its—"

An interface appeared, an eagle clutching arrows and optical fibers in its talons, the NSO's official seal. DeMitri tapped it and stared into the window.

"A tweed sports coat has been discovered in the stairwell near level two. Vomit . . . and fingerprints on the level four access plate. They're Jack's."

"Clever," she whispered, then stared off into space a moment. "Get to the secure lab on level four. That's where he's headed— if he hasn't been there and already left. Seal the building. Get more unimplanted people around the perimeter."

"Don't worry. This time we have him."

"Take him alive, if possible. And get someone down here with me."

DeMitri nodded and vanished.

"Shit, Jack." Isabel paced back and forth. She swept her desk clean of the map and insectoid metaphor.

Jack leaned against the tent wall. His legs wobbled. Come on, Isabel. Be paranoid. You know I'm close. The Chinese automatic wrapped tighter around his hand to compensate for his sweaty palms.

Isabel opened a window and examined the trace to her office. Jack felt the pressure of a scan and bounced back a blank signal, clean of implant signatures. His good eye blurred. He blinked—didn't clear it much. Was Reno's Chinese implant burning out the right eye like it had his left?

Isabel closed the window, then knelt beside her desk and tapped an input pad. The mahogany unfolded like the petals of a lotus. Inside the foamed alloy interior was a compartment. She withdrew a black mirror sphere, Wheeler's gateway.

"Good," she whispered, "still here."

She had the gateway in her left hand—a slim silver-plated Hautger SK nine-millimeter in her right.

Jack stepped out from nothing; his gun came on-line sensing his adrenaline level, compression rounds locked into place, and the gyros whined up to maximum.

"Keep your hand away from the gateway," he said.

Isabel's eyes went wide, but she recovered her composure quickly and stood. Her hand stayed well away from the dimple interface.

"I'll take that," he told her. Could he shoot her? He wasn't sure.

"Jack." Her pale face melted into a liquid smile and she took a step backward. "You've managed to surprise me. The computer hack was a decoy for your diversion on level four. That was good, but how did you know I had it here?"

"After the NSO came, I assumed everything you'd told me was a lie. You haven't disappointed me."

Her smile evaporated.

He sighted through the gun's optics and locked targeting control on her centerline. His arm shook. The blood drained from his face. "I figured you'd want to keep it as close as possible."

"It doesn't have to be this way." Her gun pointed at his chest. "You don't look good." She stared closer, then whispered, "The enzyme? You took it? I wouldn't have thought it. You of all people . . ."

She shouldn't be surprised that he had taken the enzyme. It was the only logical way to counter her poisoning. Unless she wasn't the one who had poisoned him. Who, then?

"Stop stalling, Isabel. The gateway. Hand it over!" He felt his consciousness slipping. "I know the NSO are coming. I won't let them take me alive."

"Jack," she said, "you're sick." She stepped closer.

There was a flicker in her eyes. Compassion? Jack would have given anything to see it—see any part of the Isabel he had thought he knew. But it wasn't too hard to tell what her true intentions were. Especially since she hadn't lowered her gun.

"I'm Isabel," she said. "Your friend. We've been through everything together. Remember how I helped you through complex analysis? How I helped you understand Wheeler's first message? Don't throw all that away. You're not thinking straight."

"You're not Isabel. Not anymore."

A request to interface materialized on the tent flap: an NSO eagle.

"Open that door," Jack said, "and I'll shoot."

But she still *was* Isabel, changed by the enzyme or not. His friend? He didn't know what that word meant anymore. She'd been willing to turn him over to the NSO. She'd had conservatorship papers drafted so she could control him. Those weren't the actions of a friend.

Jack opened a link to his gun, in front of him and large enough so she could see, too. He scrolled through the options, selected DEAD MAN'S REQUEST.

"That's it," he whispered. "I've targeted you." He took two steps closer. "Shoot me and the gun still fires every compression round. It won't miss, either."

"I don't believe you, Jack. I know you."

"You *knew* me," he spat. "Before the enzyme. Before I became optimized. Before I got my emotions streamlined. Now I'll do whatever it takes to survive. And the only way I'm getting out of here is with that." He nodded to the sphere and took three steps closer.

He set his hand on the gateway.

Their guns pointed at each other's hearts. One trigger squeeze and they'd kill each other. Jack smelled her apricot and champagne perfume. There were walls between them, his matrices of prime numbers, contour integrals, and infinite summations; and Isabel's ice chasms and motes of liquid nitrogen.

Neither wanted a closer look into the other.

Jack was afraid Isabel might still feel for him. He didn't want to know. Because if she did, he could never do what he had to.

She let go of the gateway.

Jack stepped back with it. "Smart move."

"Smarter than you think, Jack. We've discovered how it works. Stealing the gateway won't stop us." She held her gun with both hands to steady it from trembling.

"I'm not stealing it. It's mine." He rotated the sphere so the dimple was on top.

The interface came in pieces: fragments of lines and maps and vectors mixed with spinning gyros and the flickering DEAD MAN'S REQUEST and ammunition status. The Chinese automatic scrambled its signal and made a clean interface with the gateway impossible.

The gun was too close, both in proximity and frequencies. The web of interactive signals that kept Jack connected to the weapon scrambled the set of frequencies that linked him to the gateway. He had to get rid of the Chinese automatic.

But Isabel would sense the instant he detached. Would she shoot him if he lowered his guard? He couldn't take the chance. Yet, if he stayed, he was dead, too.

Jack backed into the corner.

He heard the metal on metal buzzing of a decipher as it chewed through the code on Isabel's locked door. The NSO would get in. Soon.

Jack pushed and saw the geometry of the room: the real corners and where the door opened. Maybe there was a way.

He moved the Chinese automatic far from the sphere, opened a link, and selected the quick-release option—then held that command. Jack pressed himself tighter into the corner and waited.

The door burst open.

The tent and the African savanna wavered as bubble circuitry compensated for the illegal interface.

Two NSO agents stepped into the room, guns drawn. One pointed his weapon into Jack's face—shouted, "DROP IT!"

They blocked Isabel's line of fire.

"No!" she screamed.

Jack quick-released the automatic. It uncoiled from his grip and fell to the floor.

He stabbed the mirror sphere's dimple and cast a shadow across the world.

The echo of gunfire followed him.

SECTION FOUR:

WORLD

16

JACK AND THE BEANSTALK

Jack stepped into the warehouse; the sound of gunshot ricocheted off the walls.

He tasted the copper-coated signals of the security system and felt the pinprick irritation of tripping pressure sensors. He squelched them, made the warehouse operating system think him a glitch.

He leaned on the thermite reactor where he had talked to Mr. White. Jack set the gateway down and examined his chest and arms and legs. No blood. He had gotten out in one piece.

Who fired the gun? He hadn't seen either NSO agent pull the trigger. That left Isabel. She had been his friend, before she became optimized, smarter, and lethal.

She would have killed him to keep the gateway.

Had the enzyme given Jack a killer instinct, too? No. He had set his gun on DEAD MAN'S REQUEST. He wouldn't have—couldn't have—shot first.

Maybe not every optimized person became ruthless. Like Zero had suggested, maybe it just made you more of whatever you were.

Had Isabel been that ruthless all along? Had she kept it hidden for fifteen years? Concealed behind a friendship that was paper-thin? She made him sick.

How could one person ever know, or trust, another?

A robotic stacker glided down the aisle toward him, sensing something not neatly placed on the lattice of shelves. Jack tapped into the machine and made it stop. He sat in the operator's chair, slumped over and trembled with fever and leftover adrenaline.

He had gotten away with the gateway. His crazy last-minute plan worked. There was still a chance to outmaneuver the NSO and Isabel.

A quick scroll through the inventory list on the stacker, then Jack instructed the robot to fetch a vacuum suit, portable bubble shell, workstation, and a six-pack of mineral water. The machine plucked items from the shelves with its nine arms and serpent-tongued fingers.

Jack settled in the center of the warehouse, next to an ESA self-launching satellite.

How was the enzyme changing him? Physically he was a mess; still shaking and flushed with fever. Cellular dialysis would have made it easier. He took a sip of water. The nausea was gone; that was something.

He was smarter, too. There was no hesitation in recall; no layers between memory and comprehension and inspiration. His brain was tighter and running faster. Good. He'd need all the intellect he could muster.

He had to hack Wheeler's gateway.

Jack set up the portable bubble, then sent a watchdog subroutine into the security net so he'd know if anyone paid a visit. He then established an optical link to his new microprocessor through the workstation, let it absorb the quaternary logic cells there.

ON-LINE, it wrote across the input pad. ADDITIONAL MEMORY INTEGRATED.

Wheeler's gateway had a lock on it, one that limited it to shifting between points on Earth. That didn't figure into Jack's plans. He was going to pick that lock.

He'd hack inside by connecting Wheeler's gateway to the translating power of the new microprocessor. Jack would be the link, the middleman.

He touched the black dimple of the gateway's mirror surface. The first red arrow appeared. He split his perceptions and activated the bubble.

"Help me understand," Jack asked the microprocessor.

WORKING . . . .

A cold stream of static entered his mind, surged through him, then swirled around the sphere, something else *thinking* its way though his implant and mind. It was so different Jack only understood parts of the network of alien microprocessors: abstract logic with illogical rules, a high-dimensional web of words and characters, curiosity, infinite patience . . . restlessly rearranging.

Cracks appeared in the gateway sphere, seams that Jack wedged his fingers into. He pried the metaphor open, peeled sections of mirror coating off like the rind of a metallic orange.

Inside was a core of code: icons of interlinked squares and sugar-crystal cubes, spirals of glass, and etched calligraphy that reverberated like tiny chimes and connected with wisps of spider silk that glowed copper and crimson. It pulsed and pumped light through the curls and lines and conduits like blood cells.

There had to be a position variable. Jack planned to find it, then discover how the alien program kept it on the Earth. . . . Assuming the gateway code was only disabled and this limitation wasn't hardwired into the program.

He pushed the dimple in the sphere's surface. The blue transition vector appeared.

A wave cascaded through the program—every symbol metamorphized: arcs and geometries inverted, pulled apart, then reformed; links boiled and recondensed.

It didn't look too stable. He'd have to be careful.

He nudged the blue arrow. The program reorganized again into a new, startling configuration.

In a normal program, even advanced parallel structures, there were fixed nodes and rules that were unalterable. In this code, however, every piece depended on the state of the whole webwork of symbols. Move one and they all changed. The variables, the links, the commands, and instructions—like programming in water.

A cluster of spikes and sine waves flashed.

Jack had seen that character in Wheeler's lexicon, one among billions of alien symbols burned into his new memory. He asked the microprocessors, "Can you translate?"

VIBRATION ENERGY OPERATOR.

Energy? That had been one of Isabel's questions: What powered the gateway?

He remembered something else about energy . . . something that might give him a way in after all.

Jack downloaded the alien math he had traded for. Parts of that theorem described how energy types interconverted. Quantum energies could be categorized into a variety of nuclear, electronic, vibrational, rotational, and translational types . . . and as Jack had conjectured, a positional quantum state as well.

With the alien math and his new awareness, Jack discerned how velocity and position and mass fit together, changed and flowed from one to another. It was a language. Jack wouldn't be writing any poems in it, but he might be able to muddle his way through Wheeler's gateway design.

He disentangled a few of the gateway's connections—there, another symbol, an oscillating bull's-eye of black and silver rings. He had seen that one, too, in Wheeler's lexicon.

"What's this?"

ROTATION ENERGY OPERATOR.

And another looked familiar: an explosion of arrows that zigzagged through space and circled back to its center. "And this?"

POSITION OPERATOR.

Position? Where did it connect to the part that calculated destination . . . and the lock he had to find?

"Stabilize the blue vector," Jack said. "Secure direction and length, then suspend the program."

He sensed the microprocessors reach into the code. The dynamic network slowed its transformations, wavered, and held.

Jack slipped his hand into the webwork of instructions and traced the links from that position operator.

One connection terminated in a rotating globe, the database of maps. He saw flashes of continents, cities, streets, details on every nook and cranny of the Earth.

Another link led deeper into a second, tighter core of instructions. Energy operators slithered through each other; the code compressed as he pulled on it. It was a mystery to delve into later. Maybe the gateway's power source?

He followed a third link from the position operator to a black dot. It attached the destination vector to the database of maps. A closer look revealed the dot was translucent, yet dark like obsidian, with tiny carved hands and python coils, vise clamps and chains and ropes—all rolled together.

Jack grabbed it.

"Translation?"

NO VALID TRANSLATION.

Was it the lockout? "Let's test a hypothesis, then. Release the code."

The gateway program seethed and flowed around Jack—except the black crystal dot he still held. It was the only thing that didn't change. It had to be the lock. All the other commands mutated.

Jack pinched the black ball between his index finger and thumb, squeezed and rubbed it, made it smaller and smaller, erased it from the code, until only the glass-fiber link remained.

He untangled himself from the program and made the blue arrow reappear, then opened the map database. He cast the vector across the Earth—out into the upper atmosphere, farther and farther, stretching into the void.

Jack smiled. He had outsmarted Wheeler. He wouldn't be isolated on the Earth anymore. Now maybe he could stay one step ahead of the alien.

But the sphere didn't contain any maps to the stars.

He connected to the Michelson Observatory on the dark side of the moon. The observatory had to know the relative positions of their interfometrically linked telescopes on the moon, in orbit, and on Earth within a fraction of a nanometer. To do that, they maintained X-ray lasers scattered across the face of the moon to triangulate position. Jack got the coordinates he needed from them.

A bark—the watchdog Jack set to guard the security net.

He checked. Nothing. The server reported an error. A false trip. No entry.

He didn't believe it.

Jack grabbed the clamshell backpack of the vacuum suit, slipped on the gloves and boots and suspension webs around his thighs and biceps, then sprayed himself with sealant. The navy blue polymer spread over his clothes, osmotically filled and stretched into a hard, yet flexible, membrane. His helmet went on last.

Five seconds later, the internal display gave him a green light on membrane integrity, the oxygen supply, and power.

Jack interfaced with the sphere again. The first red arrow appeared. There was no time to move one piece of equipment at a time. It would all have to go simultaneously.

Quickly, he rebooted the gateway program though a split screen, and a second red vector appeared. Jack rotated that arrow and attached it to a nearby stack of softweld I-beams. He made a third red vector appear, a dozen more, a hundred, and linked through the warehouse inventory, sticking red arrows to the walls, the lattice of shelves, the robotic stackers, crates, the thermite reactor—everything. The interior was a weave of crimson neon.

He heard voices, close. Footsteps.

If this didn't work, he could end up anywhere: inside the Earth, the sun, anywhere . . . or nowhere.

He made the blue destination vector bypass the normal maps and cast the arrow up and out, stretched across space to the moon.

Jack held his breath. Released the dimple—

—and static washed through his head. Explosion enveloped him. Whirlwinds and dust devils ripped at Jack and tossed him to the floor.

Crates fell off the shelves. Biolume balls shattered.

The warehouse doors ripped apart like tissue paper, bits hung and glittered in the air, slowly falling, corrugated tin confetti.

The rushing air stopped. It was absolutely silent.

Jack struggled to get up, unaccustomed to the low gravity and his new buoyancy. The containment monitor on his left thigh flickered between amber and green, but held.

He made it.

Amsterdam was going to have a hell of a mystery. Jack laughed and fogged his helmet. It wasn't going to be business as usual. Jack could take on Wheeler, Isabel, and the world.

He reached for his bottled water, then realized he wouldn't be drinking anything through his helmet. The water was boiling off. He tossed it, watched it fall in slow motion, drifting like a feather.

His stomach rolled around inside, internal fluids shifted, then settled.

Jack took a step toward the entrance. He had to scout the area and get the industrial tunnelers running; he hoped Mr. White got those foamed metal hydride tanks filled. Then he'd need power for the atmosphere regenerators. He'd have to work fast before anyone decided to pay him a visit.

He walked, half-bouncing, half-shuffling, to the blown metal doors, past a robotic stacker struggling to orient itself without a reference grid and frantically trying to get everything back on the twisted shelves.

Through a haze of dust, Jack saw the blazing sunlight, white and harsh, fill the world on his right, and on his left, long shadows stretched into pitch blackness.

He stepped out, left footprints in the powder, and mounted the thirty-meter rim of a crater. This world was without sound. Silver and black desert seas. Not a building or tree. A crescent Earth hovered on the edge of the sky. Jack thought it beautiful and horrifying.

His placement was good. Jack had landed a half-kilometer just past the moon's north pole.

He'd enjoy the view later.

Back into the warehouse he shuffled . . . then halted as he caught a glance of the expanded gateway code still linked to the portable bubble—an improbable jumble of shifting characters and commands and connections, polychromatic architecture, chaos, wonderful, and terribly alien.

The inner core of code glistened. He'd take a quick look, see if he could get to the center and discover what powered the thing.

He dug into the program. Deeper, it had acute angles and tighter curves and curls and got tangled. Many energy links terminated, connected to nothing, others radiated power as vibrational heat scattered among trillions of random atoms. It wasted a tremendous amount of energy. On purpose?

The code was too thick. Jack unscrambled bits and loosened their connections to see more.

The structure obeyed him; it expanded, a sphere of snarled string with mathematical ornaments strung upon it, larger and larger . . . then it wobbled and wavered and fell apart—silver lines and golden threads and crystalline symbols collapsed and clattered to the floor: a heap of jumbled sputtering lights and sparks. Hopelessly ruined.

"No!" Jack screamed.

He let out a strangled sound, then stomped around the mess, tried to push the knots back into the air . . . but the metaphor didn't work that way. By unraveling the program, he destroyed its underlying interdependent structure.

He had destroyed his only way back.

That fact sat in his stomach and turned sour, then froze, turned so cold that his hands and feet went numb. No. It was cold. Really cold. The helmet's display gave an external temperature of 207 Kelvin.

He cranked up the suit's heater; microthreads in the polymer skin warmed, but that took power and left only ten hours of energy to recycle oxygen.

Jack had wanted to come here . . . he had got his wish in spades. He'd stranded himself on the top of the moon.

Jack knew corporate history—the mythology of the Santa Sierra public school system—and he knew the industrial heroes like Rockefeller, Baklanov, and J. P. Morgan. The way an average corporation or CEO became a legend was by monopolization (although that term was always whispered because of American antitrust laws that had to be carefully and quietly broken).

The three routes to becoming a monopoly were: law, trade, and technology.

A corporation with law on its side had government approval to make a profit at the expense of others. It was the least desirable of the three. There were big kickbacks involved, and law had a bad habit of changing when it was least convenient.

A company with trade had exclusive use of a land, or a route to that land, and the resources therein. But it was only a matter of time before someone else muscled in.

Technology was the best method. Discover a better way to make a product like the Barlinque Corporation did when cigarettes were outlawed and you were set. They kept ahead of the pack of imitators with their tobaccoless, safe-smoke system, barely legal amphetamine additives, and breath-sweetening peppermint taste.

The legends of industry, the Dutch East India Company, De Beers Mining, and the PacRing Triad, always held more than one monopoly key.

DNAegis had all three. They had integrated the American government and European CCOs into their profit structure. They had a technology that would keep their competition baffled for a decade . . . and they had a secret trade route to the stars.

Jack monitored the news nets on Earth. Within two weeks of the public release, the enzyme reconstruction treatment exceeded projected profits eightfold.

Everyone wanted it. Cancer patients. The elderly. Young executives. Rumors circulated that it cured every disease, extended life span, made wrinkles vanish, and boosted intelligence. It was part truth, part marketing, and part biochemical snake oil.

The wealthy bought it. The working class indentured themselves for years to get it. Who wanted to age, to die, to be dumber than the guy in the next office?

There was a plague of illegal imitations, and millions of suckers got fleeced and exposed to dangerous side effects of bogus gene therapy.

The small war in Indo-Malaysia received no media coverage in the West, but from Jack's vantage on the moon, he tapped into Australian news reports. Enzyme technology leaked to mainland China. The United States threatened war, shouted the rhetoric of the Free Market Amendment, and demanded reparations.

Meanwhile, supplies dwindled, and the price of the enzyme rose. There were riots in Albuquerque and Chicago and a stock split for DNAegis.

But by then everyone who was anyone had had the treatment. They had a vested interest in restricting the wonder drug. They had to keep their edge. They had to be better than the rest of the pack.

Jack wondered if the genetic editing had made them better or if the enzyme had just cut out their souls.

Two weeks. Wheeler's deadline to locate another civilization to plunder had come and gone. Jack hadn't found them. He hadn't even tried. He wasn't going to be a party to genocide.

How long did he have before Wheeler came looking for him?

He inhaled his last drag on his last cigarette. Next time he'd pack more.

Jack sifted through the ashtray, hoping to find one that wasn't burned down to the filter. No luck. In the last two weeks, he'd puffed his way through twenty cartons while he got his base in the moon operational.

He fixed the gateway, too . . . sort of.

Sections of the inner gateway code had remained intact, clumped together and twitching in the bubble. It took him a week to reassembled those quivering parts. He'd been lucky—portions in the center realigned by themselves—and not-so-lucky because he hadn't gotten a look as it rearranged and snapped back into place. He still didn't know what powered the thing.

Jack had tested it twice—short jumps to the Apollo crater and back. The core of code looked wrong to him somehow. Had he introduced runtime errors? Would the system crash when he least expected it and needed the gateway the most?

If he was going to outmaneuver Wheeler, he'd have to use it. He'd have to trust that it worked. He didn't have a choice.

Jack leaned back onto the flexgel floor, made it soft, then sat up and made the surface as rigid as glass. No time for sleep.

His command center was a black circular room with no chairs. A dozen open windows spun in midair: Earth news nets and old movies, the images of galaxies tapped from the Michelson Observatory, and rumor mills in Hong Kong and Santa Sierra. The links illuminated the dark space and made the distant curved wall invisible.

He opened a view of the moon's surface and scanned the plains of black mare, pale seas of dust, and the De la Rue crater field. He could barely see his camouflaged solar arrays that collected and piped the sunlight underground through fiber optics.

A micromotion eye reported a tremble. He spotted a satellite overhead, a diamond pinpoint against the velvet black. Another scout from the observatory.

According to their reports, Jack's underground construction was hypothesized to be a seismic disturbance or possibly an untracked meteor. They were still curious, though. He'd have to be careful.

Jack opened a link to Wheeler's new collection of microprocessors. He had given them more memory, but in the rush to get the thermite reactor on-line and the oxygen cyclers up, he hadn't inspected the quaternary logic cells. That memory had been recycled; the quantum patterns in the solid-state cells contained fragments of games and literature and history lessons.

It gave the collective computer a few quirks. When Jack wasn't keeping it busy, it talked to itself in a variety of voices, favoring Theodore Roosevelt, Gandhi, Pope Sara II, and Jim Morrison.

How did that fit into the microprocessors' claim that it had rejected consciousness? Was it just studying human modes of communication? Or had it lied?

Whatever the case, Jack wasn't giving it free time to cause trouble. He had it create a virtual copy of the gateway program and set it the task of extrapolating the structure of the inner core. Learn what made the thing tick. What was the big secret in the center of that sphere that Wheeler didn't want him to find out? And why was it designed to waste so much energy?

"Any luck?" he asked.

LUCK NON SEQUITUR, it answered. TRILLIONS OF DYNAMIC COMBINATIONS TO BE TESTED. THERE HAVE BEEN SEVEN CLOSE MATCHES. ALL CONTAIN FATAL ERRORS.

They had one clue: what the surface of the inner core looked like before Jack had shattered it. Using that to figure out what was inside was like trying to count the number of seeds in a cantaloupe by feeling the texture of its skin.

"Continue, please."

Jack walked to dome two, through foamed metal tubes crowded with cannibalized warehouse walls, shrink-wrapped smelt, and crates of biolume spores. He had assembled an underwater habitat dome in a robot-fused tunnel, then filled in the spaces with softweld metal to make it airtight.

Sunlight was piped in from either side of the moon. Hybrid

watermelon-radishes had rooted and green shoots poked through the vermiculite soil. It was warm and humid and smelled fresh.

He crouched and touched synthetic earth. He'd have to get a variety of plants if he was going to be self-sufficient, lettuce, flash-grow legumes and tomatoes. Jack had only eaten rehydrated ice cream and chicken à la king these last weeks. Bad planning on his part, but he hadn't anticipated such an extended stay. Real food was on his list of priorities.

But highest on his list was Wheeler.

The clock was ticking. Should he contact Wheeler and make up some excuse? No. Wheeler was too good at lying; he'd see through Jack. If he kept quiet, maybe Wheeler would think Jack had died or been killed. That might buy him extra time. Acid burned through his stomach. Or maybe Wheeler wouldn't wait and just snuff the world.

Jack marched down the spiral of drilled rock, past striations of metal and compressed duststone, stepping aside the welders installing power conduits.

In a vaulted chamber, the thermite reactor stood three stories tall, covered with energy exchangers and displays. A link to its interior showed an ultraviolet fountain of plasma that blasted aluminum and iron oxide apart, rearranged them in exothermic brilliance into steel and synthetic rubies and sapphires.

He had to figure a way to outsmart Wheeler, trick him to leave Jack and the Earth alone, then Jack could deal with Isabel. She could mess everything up if she tried to bargain with Wheeler herself.

Jack was out of ideas. Who could he turn to?

His rendezvous with Panda in Tiananmen Square wasn't for another week.

Isabel? She wouldn't listen to his warnings about Wheeler. Even if she did, she likely wouldn't care. She was certain to have better security. And she'd kill him on sight this time.

Zero? He wasn't sure what the enzyme had turned him into. But Zero had always been smart and full of ideas. What about

Dr. Musa? Had Zero been part of that doublecross? Had he sent Dr. Musa to forge Jack's medical dossier for Isabel?

Something still nagged him. That message Dr. Musa had delivered: "The laboratory is still on fire." It was too vague for the scientifically precise Zero . . . unless that vagueness had meaning.

Zero had meant the lab in Amsterdam. That he would protect his research from the NSO. Or did the message refer to his original lab in Santa Sierra? The one he burned? Was there a hidden message in his message?

Jack walked up three levels to a storage dome and ordered a nine-armed stacker to pull a box off a high corner shelf.

Was there something Zero wanted him to see in Santa Sierra? Maybe a step down to the Earth was in order—grab some food and check out the ruins of his old apartment.

He rippled open the box, dug through foam grains, and removed a new Hautger SK semiautomatic. It wasn't Reno's Chinese special with smart ammunition and self-aiming options, but it was clean of gateway-interfering frequencies.

It would do—in case Zero turned out to be as good a friend as Isabel.

Retro heavy metal guitar riffs and jagged, razor static blew Jack's head apart. He dropped the mirror sphere and clutched his head. After the silence of Amsterdam and his shielded base on the moon, Jack had forgotten how bad the EM pollution was in Santa Sierra.

He got up and waved the Hautger SK down the alley at the curious watchers; an unemployment gang ran, while a stoned bum sat there and smiled. Jack scooped the gateway into his backpack, pocketed the gun, then stumbled out onto the street.

Workers pressed against him, dressed in suits and carrying slim briefcases and hurrying to work—more worried about timeslips than stepping on their neighbor's foot. Suckers all.

No. Just blind.

Jack had been the same way until he clawed his way out c

this pit—a miracle that he wasn't still marching to his Académe office every day, stumbling through life half-asleep, more robot than human, a contract slave bought by corporate grants.

If they could only see how trapped they were, they'd burn this city to the ground.

He shoved his way across the walkway, felt a tug at his pack, and wrenched it free from a feral kid who vanished back into the sea of bodies.

Jack elbowed and shouldered up to the corner of Fifteenth and Mosfet Avenue. He ducked into the alley and drew his gun.

The distant seawall filled the horizon. When it was high tide, the flexcrete barrier kept seventeen meters of ocean from flooding the city. Standing against that gray backdrop, a new structure had risen from the ashes of his apartment building—glass blocks and black heat collectors thirty stories tall, topped with the skeletal framework for ten more.

At the entrance terminal, a half-dozen nameplates clustered closer to him on the display. The one on the basement level was called OASIS INTERNATIONAL.

The lobby was vacant and locked; exposed optical conduits dangled from the ceiling. No one had moved in.

Jack pressed the access panel, ready to push his way through the protocol, but it recognized his palmprint and requested a scan. Something Zero had set up? Or an NSO trap? He let the door interface. It hissed open.

He clicked the safety off his gun, then stuck his left hand into the backpack and readied the gateway.

The new carpet smelled of vinyl glue. Fresh biolume colonies clung in perfect round clusters on the walls; they sensed his footsteps and glowed red and blue and green.

Jack took the stairs—pushed with the implant, swept the spiral stairwell with EM, but nothing bounced back except the hollow ping of steel handrails.

The basement was empty.

Not quite . . . in one corner was an old interface, plug inputs and outlets, antiques from the days when people still had sockets in their flesh. Left over from the original building? That didn't make sense.

He heard a whisper in his head, a faint access protocol. There was real bubble circuitry behind the old terminal and in the walls. Jack interfaced and Santa Sierra dissolved.

He blinked in the sudden sunlight Black and silver sand blew over his feet, and jagged rock walls rose in every direction. He stood in a volcanic cinder cone. A path led to an oasis and mirror-calm lake. The air shimmered and wavered over the water, a mirage?

Jack long-stepped it over there.

The shimmering air swarmed with butterflies and moths. On the edge of the lake was a tent of golden silk. Zero sat under the shade of the canopy and poured Jack a glass of iced tea.

"Sit, my friend." He gestured to the cushion next to him. "We have little time and much to discuss."

It looked like Zero. Jack pushed into the image, deeper into the person he thought he saw, was allowed to brush against the memory of an abacus given to Jack on his thirtieth birthday, the reverberation of morning prayers to Mecca, and a stray thought of how to coax a sequenced protein to fold into a spiderweb pattern—then bounced off an iron wall that shielded the gene witch's inner thoughts. Jack sat. It was Zero.

"I am glad you live," Zero said. "I had doubts."

"So did I." Jack took a sip of the iced tea. It quenched a thirst he hadn't noticed before.

"We must speak plainly. Isabel and the others will find this place. It is only a matter of time. I assume Dr. Musa delivered my message and that you have taken the series one enzyme?"

A chill crept down Jack's spine. Series one? There were others?

"Sure, I'm fine," Jack said. There was a question he had to ask, one that was festering inside him, something he suspected, but didn't wanted to believe. "Did you poison me, Zero?"

Zero lowered his black eyes. "To my eternal shame, yes." He offered Jack sugar for his drink, then said, "You would not have taken it otherwise, and you had to be made aware of our situation. When I saw what Isabel had become, or rather, what she had been all along, I realized what she might do to you. There was no other way."

Jack grabbed the sugar bowl from Zero and threw it on the sand. "You could have asked."

"You would not have believed Isabel could betray you. By the time the NSO arrived, it was too late to take chances."

"I thought we were friends."

"We are," Zero whispered, "but, Allah forgive me, this is more important than friendship. If I could kill you and me and Isabel to undo what has been done, I would not hesitate. The situation, however, has progressed past that."

How much did Zero know? Had he seen the logs Isabel had stolen from Jack?

"OK, so you got what you wanted—I'm optimized, smarter and ruthless."

"You, my friend, are not ruthless." Zero shook his head and poured Jack another glass of tea. "It is not in your soul. You will defend yourself, but you are not a destroyer. You create. You are the solver of puzzles. Half Prometheus and half trickster."

"Save the metaphysics for your prayers, Zero."

Jack reached out to the gene witch with his mind. There was no resistance, but there was nothing Jack could pin down—just fluttering images and thoughts—as if there were a million Zeros.

"What have *you* changed into?" Jack asked.

"I am my name. Do you know what it means?"

"Zero? Sure. Tack it onto a number and it gets multiplied by ten. It's nothing and everything."

"A very Zen answer." Zero smiled. "My clan name, al Qaseem, means 'to divide.' My ancestors were tax collectors and merchants who could squeeze the last dinar from any transaction. Added to my given name, it is a grand combination. You are a mathematician, Jack. Surely you understand."

"Divide a number by zero and the result is infinity."

"Exactly. But when a child has not yet learned to divide, do you know what such a name does? I was ever trying to prove I was more than my name. I had to be better. Always."

"I get the picture," Jack said. "I had to be smarter, too. Better than the rest to get out of Santa Sierra's public schools."

"It is what has driven me all my life." Zero looked to the horizon, focused his eyes upon the past. "I gave up wives and my family—to prove my intellect, and that is what the enzyme has enhanced, a burning, furious intelligence. Just as it has magnified Isabel's desire to rule by manipulation."

Jack opened his mouth to deny that, then closed it. Zero was right about Isabel. She had been so good at manipulating Jack that he was still trying to defend her actions.

A cloud of butterflies settled upon the sand, beating silk opals and quavering feathered petals that condensed into tiny x's, granular, looking more like bits of tightly coiled string than insects. They grouped into pairs, a grid eight by eight.

Zero brushed the tips of the trembling butterflies. "This is the eighth-generation enzyme sequence."

Jack recognized the pattern, or rather, a pattern, but it couldn't be . . . "Chromosomes? We only have twenty-three pairs, not sixty-four."

"All that will be changed." Zero cocked his head as if he heard something, then said, "You must take precautions. We have both started in the proper direction—but it is already too late for everyone else." He glanced over his shoulder. "We shall continue this later and perhaps trade. But now it is time to go."

"Trade what?" Jack asked.

"Run, Jack." Zero stood, tossed aside the table, smashing the pitcher of iced tea and scattering the butterfly chromosomes. "Run before you are buried here!"

Zero's robes rippled and fluttered apart, wings and antennae and pearlescent scales of cream and coral and sulfur-yellow, spots and stripes and waves of rainbows; he disintegrated into a million moths.

The interface terminated.

Jack blurred back to the empty basement, dizzy, and fell as the disorientation washed over him, then he got his bearings.

He didn't like this; something was wrong. Every nerve tingled with alarm, and it wasn't his implant or Zero's bubble. This was something organic—deep inside him, screaming to get out of the building.

Jack ran up the stairs and out into the street.

The feeling was worse out here—like being smothered, but the air was still. Too still.

He shook, trembled . . . it wasn't him.

The earth shuddered and rippled. An earthquake.

Jack knew the drill: get into a sheltered doorway, cover his head. The office building twisted and its windows burst into a hailstorm of green safety glass.

Seventeen blocks away, the gray seawall splintered and water fountained into the streets. Through the widening cracks, the ocean rushed.

Jack stood transfixed as a wall of water rushed down Fifteenth Street, swept aside cabs, and crushed people with white foam and thunder. He watched it as it rolled toward him.

He fumbled with his backpack, grabbed the gateway—

17

HIJACKED

Jack stumbled over garbage cans and ran into a brick wall.

This wasn't Santa Sierra. There was no thundering tsunami, no shaking earth. There was no neon-paint graffiti or old barnacles on the brick. It was quiet, clean, and the air was laced with the odors of simmering pork and hot peppers.

He interfaced with the gateway and traced his location to the coast of China . . . Shanghai.

Why jump here?

Jack remembered: this was near the address Reno had him memorize at Freud's Little Sister. He said it was the only place Jack would be safe. That must have stuck in his subconscious.

Maybe it was just as well. The old spy might know something useful.

Jack inhaled, savored the air, glad not to be buried under tons of ocean. He imagined he still heard it, though, the deep-bass rumble that shook him to the core; he tasted his lips—salty. He had been so close to the wall of water, it had sprayed his face.

Everyone else on Fifteenth Street had been swallowed by the sea—or was there still time to save them? He found Santa Sierra in the gateway's database. It showed a city intact on the coast. An old image, out of date.

He linked to the Michelson Observatory, bounced off a satellite, and reoriented on the city. It was all swirling water, backwashes, riptides, and foam; the entire continental shelf had tilted. There was nowhere to jump back to . . . and no survivors to be seen.

The city he had grown up in was gone—along with everyone in it.

He could have grabbed someone when he jumped, but he had operated on instinct, scared out of his mind. He was a rat—only thinking to save his own skin.

Preparation for disaster had been part of his childhood: the drills in school, memorizing evacuation routes, and the constant tests of the International Warning System.

But he'd forgotten everything when the seawall shattered. No one had taught him how to avoid a tidal wave.

Jack stuffed the gateway into his backpack. Why hadn't there been more warning? Why hadn't the geosensors predicted the quake? He couldn't recall a single time they had failed.

Wheeler was right. They were risk-takers all. Fools. Like Amsterdam, Santa Sierra had been built on reclaimed land, below sea level. They had to get to the valuable relics from the old San Francisco and the new pockets of oil and steam discovered there.

He hadn't seen the Académe, either. It had been designed to withstand tsunami and quakes. Without warning, maybe they'd been caught off guard, failed to release from the ocean floor, and got dragged to the bottom. Coit Tower was underwater again. What a waste.

And Jack had the feeling that somehow it was his fault.

His stomach growled. He ventured out of the alley.

A flash of short buildings and a sidewalk, then the Shanghai street became a bedlam carnival. People rode elephants and sea serpents and sat upon the backs of winged tortoises. They balanced on unicycles and carousel horses and swam through a river of musical notes that tinkled with Berlioz's *Symphonie fantastique* and a Dizzy Gillespie trumpet solo. They wore Kabuki makeup and terra-cotta burial masks; they bore aboriginal tattoos and jeweled Egyptian hieroglyphs. A man spat fire; another nibbled upon a girl covered with grapes. A group of five children rolled by, a ball of legs and whirling limbs.

Jack watched, not comprehending, stunned, and was caught in the kaleidoscopic tide, herded along by a laughing monkey in silver robes, swept up by a thunderhead with a thousand eyes——then stepped back into reality.

He walked upon a normal sidewalk with normal people, Asians in silk jackets and jeans, a few dark Russians, and golden Filipinos, and Australians with their wide-brimmed range hats. Bicycles were the only traffic in the street.

A glance over his shoulder and he saw the circus of chaos roiling behind him. Jack pushed and pierced the illusion. There were repeater stations in that portion of the street and in the connecting intersection. What did all this metaphor mean? Why was Shanghai part wonderland?

Reno said everyone had implants, that it was a virtually controlled democracy. Maybe he had told Jack the truth . . . about this one thing.

The Shanghai people maintained a small but respectable distance from Jack. They smiled at him or nodded. He smiled back.

There was no shoving to get to work. People loitered, waiting in line at a street vendor for deep-fried crabs or reading news boards that hovered in the air; they talked and smoked. The buildings had winged pagoda roofs, carved with koi and Buddhas and signs of morphing Mandarin calligraphy lacquered red and glistening emerald. Inside paper lanterns, fireflies flickered pink and gold and crimson.

Jack caught the scent of bread he had smelled in the alley. He followed the odor to an open-air bakery. The woman working there stopped kneading dough and raised an eyebrow at him. He pointed to a rack of golden loaves marked 100¥ and held up three fingers.

The woman wiped her hands on her apron. From her necklace of copper coins, icons sprang and flocked around Jack's open hand. There was the ivory Confucius of the Bank of Malaysia, the glimmering double-star sapphire of the Darwin Tidal Station Energy Exchange, and the crystal snowflake of the Antarctica Depository.

He touched a jade dragon, opened his Shanghai account, and paid. The woman handed him the buns. He bit through one of the fluffy loaves and into the rich sweet-and-sour pork filling, then devoured all three as he walked. After eating rehydrated food for the last three weeks, the warm bread was a treasure.

A group of seven old men strode past Jack. Their eyes stared straight ahead, and they walked a bit faster than everyone else.

Curious, Jack followed them over an arched bridge and muddy canal, past mah-jongg parlors full of smoke and hard currency and carved ivory tiles, and through open-air markets, past stalls selling watermelon and pickled squid and hanging smoked duck.

The old men marched into a park, crowded with people and rows of sycamore tress. The air was thick with dragons that clashed with one another and tore at an American flag, firecrackers igniting, and uncoiling DNA with razor-wire edges and attaching enzymes made of dollar and pound and yen signs.

Jack saw it with both eyes. A virtual community discussion?

The older men divided into two groups in the park. The images and sounds and smells faded.

Near one group, the ground turned into water, a pond that they waded across to a tiny North American-shaped island. They set up a vendor stall selling oversized gold tablets. Hard preconstructionist currency piled up behind them, overflowed into the water, and washed upon the distant shore.

The oldest man in the opposite group stepped forward.

The tiny ocean turned choppy, and wind knocked over their

stall. The North American continent broke free. A hurricane formed and drove it into the smaller crescent-shaped Indo-Malaysia.

The continent plowed under clusters of islands in its path, then the two landmasses collided. Indo-Malaysia split it into a hundred fragments that bobbed and sank.

The storm intensified and America steamed north, leaving in its wake blood that mingled with the seawater.

It crashed into the Chinese mainland, absorbed it, and grew larger, until the Asian coast sprouted a Maine isthmus and receded to form the Chesapeake inlet. Hong Kong in the south transformed into the Cuban-Florida archipelago.

The crowd booed and hissed; others shook their heads. Black-and-white tally marks appeared in the air. Were they voting? There was more discussion, shouting, metaphor clashing. Several people vanished, not really there at all.

The park had to be surrounded by repeater stations. Jack felt their presence, saw the ripples and bumps in reality. Like the Académe, Shanghai was part virtual and part real, only here, everyone knew about the illusion. They used it to illuminate instead of hide the truth.

This virtual democracy might have something going for it after all.

Jack spotted an information kiosk and wandered to it. He called up a map of the city, shifted the language to English, and located Reno's address: the Old Tea House Temple. A good place, nice and public. Only a kilometer away. He could use the walk to clear his head.

Before he left the kiosk, he pulled back and viewed the entire city. It stretched from the coast to meld with Hangzhou in the southeast and Nanjing in the northeast, covering fifty thousand square kilometers. It was a collection of tiny cities within cities, no one part urban or suburban or rural, but mixed, fields and factories and houses, and the architecture varied: Byzantine mosaic domes and sturdy Romanesque arches, Gothic vaults and spiral Islamic minarets, Baroque façades and piazzas, and Art Deco neon.

As Jack walked to the temple, he saw no cars or busses, just bicycles and pedal taxis and the occasional hydrogen-powered truck, and no EM pollution. There were biolume-tattoo parlors and karaoke bars and a farmer's market and an epitaxy laser manufacturer, residences with tiny courtyards with fountains and gardens—all clumped together. Like the map had indicated, no centralized zones. A community.

The Old Tea House Temple stood upon pilings in a wide canal. It was a five-story tower with upswept blue-tiled roofs, a half-moon arched gate, and connected to the shore with a zig-zag bridge.

Jack entered.

Inside were twin rows of spinning brass prayer wheels that chanted when he touched them. Sandlewood incense smoke made the air silky and set Jack's spirit at ease.

There was a hundred-handed Buddha statue, shrines to an elephant-headed deity and the graceful Xiwangmu. He lit three sticks of incense before the Buddha, even though he didn't believe in this stuff, and prayed for the lost souls in Santa Sierra.

A monk watched him. He wore blue-black robes, had a weathered face, and held a twin set of carved wooden rings in his hands.

Jack finished, then went to the monk and whispered, "Reno?"

The monk gave him a careful looking over, then nodded and led him to a back room. It had a window overlooking the water, pine floors, and a bamboo mat. Jack sat on the floor. The monk then slid the panel shut and left him alone with water reflections shimmering upon the ceiling.

Jack pushed. No bubble here.

He set his pack in his lap, made sure the gateway was accessible, but hidden . . . as well as the Hautger SK.

Five minutes later, the monk returned with two bowls: tea and rice.

Jack smiled, took them, and the monk left. It seemed rude not to eat what he had been offered, but Reno had drugged him, and Zero had poisoned him. He let the bowls sit and leaned against the wall, stared at the dancing waterlines of light.

What was he becoming? One of Nietzsche's supermen? Ruthless like Isabel? Intelligent like Zero? Or was he still just Jack? He didn't feel superior. He felt like a punching bag.

He ate the rice and took a sip of the tea. He was tired of being paranoid.

Jack closed his eyes—for a moment only. He had to rest, think; he dozed, then woke to the sound of the panel being slid open.

The old monk looked in on Jack, then whispered to someone in the hall.

Reno stepped into the room and closed the panel shut behind him. He wore a gray business suit, had a silver briefcase in his left hand, and looked more out of place in Shanghai than Jack.

"Hiya, Jack. You know why the bridge to this place is a zigzag?"

"Enlighten me."

"That old monk says evil spirits can only walk in a straight line. The bridge keeps them from getting into the temple. They fall off."

"Can't be true. You got across. I guess I'll follow your example, though, and take a few steps off the straight and narrow."

Reno reached out to shake his hand. Jack didn't move, so Reno set the briefcase down, lowered himself to the floor, and sat in a lotus position more graceful than a man twenty years older than Jack should be. "Glad you finally came to your senses and—"

Jack pulled the Hautger SK out of his pack and aimed it at Reno.

"You do your speaking with a gun these days?"

"What did you expect? After you blackmailed me. And after you sold me out to the NSO."

Reno removed a pack of cigarettes from his vest, lit one up, and didn't offer one to Jack. "OK, what do you want? Things are getting hot in the world and I'm a busy man."

"I bet." Jack raised his gun. "You can start by giving me those."

Reno laughed. "You'd kill me for a smoke? I don't think so."

Jack's glare didn't waver. "Let's not test that theory. I'm in a lousy mood."

Reno licked his lips. "OK." He leaned closer, reached forward with the pack.

"Just toss it."

Reno lobbed the pack.

Jack figured if Reno hadn't offered him one, they were clean. He tapped one out and let the thing self-ignite, savored the amphetamines and peppermint. "I saw your virtual democracy in action this morning. Lots of spirited discussion and metaphor. I like it. But there's still a hierarchy. Those old men ran the show."

"I'm impressed, Jack. You came all the way to China to talk politics?"

"It's my gun," Jack said. "My questions."

Reno glanced at the gun, then back up to Jack. "The longer you spend researching issues and making speeches, the more political prestige you get. These old guys make it their job. Government gives them a stipend to live on. They're what you might call career politicians or maybe public performers. It's a lot better than all that 'Everyone's created equal' crap in the American Constitution."

"So where do you fit in the system?"

"Nowhere. I don't have the time to do my homework and be a good little citizen. Too busy with important meetings like this."

"I know the kind of double crosses that keep you busy," Jack said. "You know something about everyone, don't you? The NSO, DNAegis, Isabel, Panda, Zero—"

"Not the gene witch," Reno said. "Funny how all of a sudden everyone's been asking me what happened to your buddy." He leaned back against the wall. "Even his oil clans. Nice trick to get beyond their influence. If you had any clues, I'd be willing to trade you some dirt on your old girlfriend, Isabel."

"Forget it, Reno. No trades. I've got the gun, remember?"

"You're forgetting all the favors I've done for you, Jack-O. The money to start up that company of yours, the helpful illegal weapons, and don't forget what's in your head. You would have never got out of the Académe without my help. It's payback time."

"I'm glad you brought that up, Reno. *You* were in Santa Sierra when my office got ransacked. You said it was to square any favors you owed my parents . . . but you're a busy spy. How'd you get there so fast?" Jack clicked the gun's safety off. "How dumb do you think I am?"

Reno smiled, and that worried Jack. "Not at all," he said. "That's why I was sent there in the first place. Shanghai knew about Beijing's connection with Dr. Bruner and their new interest in you. What we didn't know was what was so important that Beijing sent Panda, their best agent."

"My research? They sent you to steal it, too?"

"We're not amateurs. If that's what we wanted, I woulda cracked your memories when I had your brain open."

Jack puffed on the cigarette, then suddenly didn't want anything that Reno had touched and crushed it out. "That blood in my office. Panda wouldn't have been wounded. She could have easily slipped away. You planted it?"

"Give the man a cigar. Stole a sample of her type-O from Beijing." Reno leaned forward and asked, "Now, can you figure out why?"

Jack's dead left eye itched, but he didn't let it distract him or his aim. "If you were running an operation under the NSO's nose, it would have been better for you if they were looking for Panda and not you. You used her as a decoy?"

"That's pretty close. I also had a score to settle with her. Too bad she wasn't caught in Santa Sierra or Amsterdam."

"Wait. You never explained why you put this hardware in

302

my head. It's a big investment for someone who isn't even on your side."

"Finally we get to that," Reno said and sighed. "Let me show you?" He nodded to his briefcase.

"OK, but slow."

He turned the puzzle lock, then flipped open the right-hand catch. A pink LED blinked.

A spike of pain flashed through Jack's skull; he lost focus in his good eye, then it returned, but filmed over.

"There," Reno whispered. "You were right, Jack. *We* were never on your side . . . but you've always been on ours." He reached over and took Jack's Hautger SK.

Jack let him. "I don't . . ."

"Just relax. I'll ask the questions." Reno winked his blue eye.

Jack stared at the pink light on the briefcase, found it hypnotic.

"We needed more than what you already knew. What we wanted was everything you *would* know." Reno took the cup of tea the monk had left Jack. He stroked the ceramic warming strip, set it heat to steaming, then sipped.

"Why don't you tell me what happened since the first NSO interview," Reno suggested. "Concentrate on the technical details."

Jack opened his mouth to tell Reno to go to hell—but started to speak instead. He had no control.

Jack spilled his guts.

He told Reno about the physics of noise, the reconstituted signal from cosmic sources, and how he had escaped DeMitri and set up his own business. Both Reno's blue and brown eyes widened when he spoke of his contact with Wheeler, the new microprocessors, and the gateway.

This was the right thing to do, wasn't it? It seemed like a good idea to tell Reno everything. Jack tried to stop. Couldn't. He could only watch as he talked too much.

He mustered his concentration, but that didn't pierce the fog that shrouded his conscious. Part of his thinking started to rearrange, though, shifted into a fluid configuration, compact and faster, as if the enzyme was reoptimizing his mind.

Jack managed to whisper, "What are you doing to me?"

Reno arched an eyebrow in surprise. "You've got a thicker head than I thought." He grabbed his cigarettes back from Jack, then lit one up. "Your implant has a few tricks, but it's primarily designed to download memory, bypassing all those awkward conscious-level inhibitions." He smiled his crooked-toothed grin. "You were our mole."

Reno blew smoke into Jack's face. "Don't take it so hard. It wasn't such a bad deal. If you didn't have the implant, you would have ended up on an NSO dissection table."

Jack's mind continued to move—emotions rearranged and swapped with pieces of memory and ego. He felt as if he were swimming through thick liquid, struggling to find air. Struggling to regain control.

"Tell me more about this gateway."

Jack told him what he knew about its programming structure and how he had bypassed the lockout.

Reno held up his hand. "Wait a second." He opened the briefcase, slipped his hand into the interface. "I have to encrypt and transmit that part. That's the information I'm getting paid for."

"Paid? By who?" Jack asked.

Reno laughed. "Even brainwashed, you're full of questions. I'm half-surprised this hardware works at all on your stubborn brain. With the information you just gave me, I'll swap DNAegis for the data we need to make our own microprocessor . . . and our own gateway . . . and maybe make our own contact with Wheeler."

"You can't!"

Reno shrugged. "Sure we can. We've already got people working with DeMitri and your old girlfriend. We'll have all the pieces soon enough. That's how this corporate geopolitics stuff works, Jack. You steal from everyone. You sell to everyone. An you make sure you always got a deal to offer. There are no sides. Just losses and profits. Get it?"

Reno reached into his briefcase and Jack felt the frequency and power of the signal boost, more pain in his head, and more fog in his mind—that cleared as fast as it formed.

Jack was getting control back.

He played dumb and sat there with his eyes staring straight ahead.

"What else about the gateway?"

"It's how I got here," Jack whispered. He reached into his pack and withdrew the sphere, set it in his lap . . . and nonchalantly placed his hand on the interface dimple.

Reno grinned ear to ear. "That's perfect, Jack. I knew I could count on you. Now, hand it over."

"I'd like to, Reno. I would." A blue line of spider silk stretched from the Earth to the moon; for an instant, Jack was a split-quantum ghost, a wavering bifurcated wavefunction, in Old Tea House Temple and over three hundred thousand kilometers distant. "But I don't think you can reach that far."

Reno's smile disappeared. "Wait." He raised the gun.

Jack blurred—and vanished.

It had been seven hours since Jack left Reno, but he still felt lousy. He sat in the shadow of a crater and watched the Earth rise. The sky was black, a mirror for Jack's feelings. The West Coast of America lay under clouds and mist, under that the Pacific Ocean, and under that, Santa Sierra and its twelve million people.

They had struggled through school, worked sixty-hour weeks, and had precious left over to call a life. Jack wanted to raise the city and bring them all back. He'd show them how the Shanghai political system worked. Make a change.

If Jack had more technology from Wheeler, he might be able to shift tectonic plates and raise the dead—but he'd never be able to fix their lives. They'd be back at work the next day. Nothing would change.

What was the use with politicians and corporations controlling the world? And spies like Reno lurking in the shadows?

Had he given Reno enough information to reverse-engineer the gateway? If he was working with Isabel, they might be able to do it.

Jack had been lucky Reno focused on the details of the gateway; they never got around to discussing the location of his moon hideout.

He should never have trusted the spy. Next time Jack saw him, he'd shoot first. No more questions.

A wave of his hand cleared the access plate of dust. Jack punched in the code that released the air lock and a portion of the shadow opened. He entered, repressurized, then dissolved his vacuum suit off. An elevator dropped him down to the command center.

The microprocessors had two dozen windows open, in each a section of code ran, part of the inner core of the gateway. Symbols and links disconnected and shattered and tangled into fatal runtime errors.

"Report," Jack said.

Its answer scrolled across the nearest display:

> THREE BILLION COMBINATIONS I HAVE TRIED;
> EACH ONE FAILED, EVERY ONE DIED.
> A BEHAVIOR THAT SEEMS TO COINCIDE
> WITH COMPUTER CODE SUICIDE?

Nursery rhymes? What next, sonnets? Still, it was right. If Wheeler didn't want anyone hacking into the secrets of his gateway, then Jack and his twenty-first-century technology weren't getting inside.

Jack watched as the microprocessors returned to the hopeless task of unraveling the code. The synthetic intelligence had stopped requesting more memory and data. That worried Jack. When he looked at the nano-structure, he found it had altered the pseudo-dynamic memory cells he had already given it. They had changed into something Jack didn't understand.

If the microprocessors were a booby trap set by Wheeler, waiting to cause trouble—there were still the robotic assemblers embedded in the center. Jack had abandoned them when he manufactured the electronics. If he had to, he could reactivate them and destroy the semiconductive substrate from within.

But he didn't want to do that. He needed its alien logic. He needed the synergy of two minds working on the same project. Like when he had worked with Isabel.

Could Jack sink into the microprocessor, let it fill the deepest parts of his personality? He had already linked with it, but this would be different. He'd need a more intimate contact than he had had with Panda. The kind of contact he had thought he had with Isabel. His mind might be plastic enough. It had squirmed out of Reno's implanted control.

They would be two minds acting as one. Electronic and biochemical. The synergistic effect might give them the cognitive leap needed to solve the puzzle.

Or it could destroy his mind.

Was Wheeler's gateway secret worth the risk? Jack was willing to gamble that it was.

"Open window," he said, "and prepare an interface."

LINKING TO?

"Me."

The collection of microprocessors paused for a full three seconds, then . . . PURPOSE?

It had never asked why before. Jack guessed it deserved an answer; this could fry its circuits, too. "Neither of us sees a solution. We are restricted to our particular problem-solving algorithms. A shared viewpoint might circumvent our blindspots."

A window popped open; it held a reflection of himself.

Jack guessed that meant OK.

He touched it, sank through the reflective pane, through layers of protocols, felt cold surges flow through his mind as he had before, but they sank in deeper, through his memory and perceptions and personality.

And Jack felt the jagged edges of its collective mind. A thousand voices that spoke simultaneously. They whispered to one another, laughed, cried, like a community, a city of computers rather than one thinking machine.

The collective copied portions of Jack, integrated them, then reorganized itself in a flash. New connections and new voices appeared . . . and one of them was Jack.

Together they watched the virtual mock-up of the gateway code. And unlike before, Jack was able to focus his attention on hundreds of sites at the same time. And unlike before, the collection of microprocessors had a sense of desperation and a sense of wonder.

They tugged at the code; it unraveled.

Jack tried a thousand approaches, but he could never get to the center of that inner code of core. It was tamperproof.

There was a pattern, though. Not in the programming, but in the way it collapsed. It broke in a cascade of waves throughout the sphere.

Jack made it fall apart on purpose, by tugging certain links and variables, and could see through fissures, deep into the code before the entire thing self-destructed.

The inner core had a coating of the oscillating black and silver rings, rotational energy operators, and a million links that radiated that energy into the void.

A thousand more simulations and Jack and the collective discovered a connection to the flitting zigzagging position operator.

Jack found the link that pulled them together: a connection to the center of the database of maps. It was a site he hadn't seen before, with geological blueprints of the interior of the Earth, the crust and mantle, irregularities in the Gutenberg discontinuity between outer core and mantle, and the spinning solid center of nickel-iron. The link connected to the heart of the Earth.

Why underground? Why so much wasted energy? The code even separated the rotational components, didn't access the orbit of the Earth around the sun, only used the revolving motion around its axis. And why only that rotation when it could be tapping nuclear motions or the heat from molecular vibrations?

Jack opened a window and watched the Earth floating across the moon's horizon.

It was designed by Wheeler . . . who had something hidden up his sleeve. That fact didn't comfort him.

The collective searched for clues and associations through their memories: Panda and Isabel; Santa Sierra and Shanghai; position and rotation; the enzyme and Zero, his butterflies and earthquakes.

Butterflies and earthquakes? One was an insect, nothing gentler than the beating of its wings, the other, millions of tons of earth sliding and crushing over one another. The inobvious and the titanic. Gentle calm and destruction released from within the Earth.

The microprocessors halted—for the first time, they knew fear.

Jack went cold inside, too. He felt everything within him pause, suspecting, comprehending . . . dreading what that meant.

With a snap of his fingers, he opened his back door to the Michelson Observatory and drifted into the interface. Celestial metaphor filled the command center with oversized, chromacolored planets and moons and stars that winked tiny coordinates at him. Something was out of place.

The near-Earth asteroid database was missing. Where there should have been a gossamer comet orbiting him, there was only darkness. He looked deeper and saw that the database was obscured by veils of interstellar dust . . . and lurking in the interface, in jet-propelled pressure suits, floating and waiting for intruders, were NSO counterhackers.

Whatever they were up to, it couldn't be any good.

Jack pulled back. He more important things to do, however, than play tag with those goons.

He turned toward the satellite relay icon, a spinning silver dodecahedron between the moon and Earth, and linked. He called up the American images. Chicago.

A line of shadow crossed the world, retreating before the sun. It divided the continent and made the Mississippian Sea shimmer.

While he waited, Jack called the astronomical almanac and looked up the time of dawn in Chicago on June 3: 5:47:37.

The line of light, the demarcation between day and night, touched the edge of the city, warmed the suburbs. The observatory recorded the official time of dawn as 5:48:09.

. . . A full half-minute later than it should have been.

Jack let the interface dissolve. He slumped to the padded floor.

That was the connection. Why the gateway wasted power. Why it used rotational energy to fuel the conversion of quantum mechanical position state. By robbing the Earth's inner spinning motion, the gateway was a ticking time bomb.

Horror crystallized inside Jack. He had caused the earthquake in Santa Sierra.

With every jump, the Earth's core slowed . . . and as it slowed, the Earth's crust was skidding to a halt.

18

JACKSTRAW

Pinwheel flowers sputtered; firecrackers exploded. Twenty thousand people crowded into Tiananmen Square for the Democracy Day celebration.

Jack was jostled by children in red school uniforms. He had to duck under yellow parasols and rippling flags of crimson and wade through a swarm of gold stars. Musicians played seven-stringed zithers, panpipes, drums, and gongs under the sweltering noon sun. Jugs of plum wine and slabs of watermelon passed from person to person.

Everyone was having a great time . . . except Jack.

In the center of the square towered the forty-meter Goddess of Democracy, cut from silver-flecked alabaster, a younger sister to America's submerged and lost Statue of Liberty. This statue, however, wasn't static; her robes and hair flowed. Carved in midstride, she was part stone, part wind, and all glory. She seemed to smile at everyone.

There was another explosion, and a rainbow of virtual sparks showered over the square, cooled and solidified into crystals: gold nuggets and garnets, tiger's-eye and turquoise that scattered over the flagstones.

Jack picked up a pearl. He ran his finger over the Mandarin pictograph carved upon it and translated: hope.

He had no hope today. And no desire to celebrate. Still, he polished the silky illusion on his shirt as if some of its optimism might rub off.

Jack had abandoned the moon.

The gateway was in his pack, and he would have smashed the thing if he didn't need it to solve the mess he had caused.

Jumping from Amsterdam to the moon and back had slowed the Earth's spinning core by two-tenths of a millisecond, used the rotational energy to fuel a positional shift. As the crust decelerated, tremors and cracks appeared. Other cities like Santa Sierra would drown.

It would be his fault. Wheeler's fault, really. But he couldn't loosen the shroud of guilt smothering him. He made his way to the edge of the celebration.

A fountain of fire, real as far as Jack could perceive, dominated the entrance to the square. It spouted fuel that cascaded over five tiers. A path spiraled about its base, and inscribed along the walls of that path were names: most Mandarin pictographs, but some in English, French, and German.

People lit incense from the fire. The place reeked with the smoke of musk and pine, jasmine and sandalwood.

"Need a taxi, Jack?"

He turned; it was Panda. She wore a blue silk jacket and jeans. She tucked her hair behind her ears, then said, "I'm glad you understood the message I left in Amsterdam."

"I'm glad you're here." He tried to touch her with his mind—forgot this wasn't virtual, that he'd have to show his joy some other way. Jack reach down and stroked her cheek. "It's been a long three weeks."

Then he remembered that this visit wasn't just for Panda or for him. "I have something that I need to—"

"Before questions, let me show you something." She grabbed his hand and led him up the spiral to the volcanic fountain. "Here." She handed him a cone of alderwood incense and carefully held his fingers along the edge of flames until the incense ignited, then set it smoldering upon the rim.

"What was that for?"

She faced him. "For those who died in the massacres. For those who died for freedom."

Panda knelt. Jack thought she was going to pray, but she pulled him down with her and pointed to a pair of the names carved on the wall.

He squinted and saw a tiny raised red star and the names: JOHN AND ROSE POTTER.

"It's true, then?" Jack asked himself. "They defected?" He looked to Panda. "They were Chinese operatives?"

"That is part of the truth."

"Tell me all of it."

She pushed her bangs away from her face and whispered, "After the quakes, mainland China was in chaos, and Taiwan, with the help of the United States, attempted a coup. Your parents were part of an NSO counterespionage operation. They infiltrated China's fledgling network connections, promoted subversive democratic messages, and organized students into secret societies.

"The land was ripe for a revolution. Beijing had refused external world aid and suffered for it. Many died. There was a civil war and eighty million perished so we might be free." She stared at the flames, then said, "John and Rose Potter were part of that revolution. They helped construct a real democracy instead of the Taiwan-controlled farce the NSO had planned."

Jack touched their names and the tiny raised star. Was it true? How could they be traitors if they had helped China become a free nation? The same way information in America had been filtered and censored and edited into lies. The NSO.

When he had hacked into the Santa Sierra CCO and found

the NSO files on his parents, there had been references to electronics smuggled into Beijing, a list of student contacts, and details of underground movements. That confirmed Panda's history lesson.

The Great Wall rose because China had linked trade deals to human rights and protested American brutalities. China had been a young democracy, idealistic and just, while the United States had been, and was, not so free.

"Thanks," he whispered to her. "Thanks for the truth."

Jack looked at the Goddess of Democracy and the people dancing around her. She smiled at him. An optical illusion? Or maybe it was something inside Jack. For the first time in his life, he was proud to be his parents' son. That was a gift the NSO couldn't take away.

And maybe he could do something that would have made John and Rose Potter just as proud.

Panda stood and they left the fountain memorial.

"This is a democracy like Shanghai?" Jack asked.

"Similar." She pointed east, past the gilt-domed Hall of the People to the cluster of white marble buildings with Ionic columns and ivy-covered terraces and slender towers. "There is where our democracy begins. With the twenty-three million students of the Beijing Institute."

"Millions? How can you afford to teach so many?"

"How can we afford not to? We educate all our people. Only after they graduate do they earn the privilege of voting."

It was a democracy like Shanghai, but balanced. As a bonus, Beijing's citizens were educated. It made sense to Jack.

"I came to give you something," he said. "Your government will need it."

Panda put a finger over his mouth and glanced over her shoulder. "Let us go where we can watch the celebration, but private, so we can talk as well." She took Jack by the hand and led him away from the square, across the street to the Ambassador Hotel.

They rode a glass elevator to the top. Panda excused herself to the head of a long line leading into the rooftop restaurant and whispered to the headwaiter. They were immediately shown to a table in the corner. Three silk screens materialized, shielded them from the other patrons, but did not obstruct their view of Tiananmen Square and the upswept roofs of the Forbidden City, and to the south, the Temple of Heaven with its red- and blue- and gold-lacquered tower.

Panda ordered two drinks called *panax black*. "We may speak here," she told Jack. "It is safe."

Jack pushed and found a menu interface, a slight presence from Panda's hardware—the scent of licorice—but nothing else.

Panda scooted her chair closer to Jack to watch the fireworks and fluttering flag dancers and fire-eaters across the street. She whispered, "You were saying that you had something for me?"

"For your government."

She leaned closer.

Jack gazed into her wide brown eyes; butterfly colors fluttered upon her lids and brow . . . how easily could he fall into them? There were more pressing matters, however. It was bad timing all the way around.

He set two data cubes on the white linen tablecloth. "Remember I told you about those signals I found? And the new technologies? You can have them."

Panda touched the cubes with her index finger, rocked them back and forth, then asked, "For what price?"

"None. I'll explain the data, too. Help you build the new microprocessor."

Panda sat back and crossed her arms. "There is more to this than you are telling."

"There is another technology we haven't discussed, one that shifts quantum positional states and allows instantaneous transport."

Panda uncrossed her arms. "We know of this technology."

They did? Jack hid his surprise. "Then you know what will happen if the NSO gets their hands on it. They don't have all the pieces . . . yet." He scooped up the data cubes and placed them in her hand. "One side will eventually, though, either as a gift, or purchased, or taken. I want it to be yours."

Panda nodded. An itchy sensation emanated from her. She waved to the waiter, who brought them frosted mugs filled with cream and dense, dark chocolate swirling at the bottom. It smelled of cloves and ginseng.

She set Jack's data cubes upon the waiter's tray, then covered them with a napkin.

The waiter whisked them away.

"I am authorized to accept your defection," she said. "That is what you are doing, isn't it?"

"Switch sides like my parents?" Jack took a sip of the iced, spiced cream and chocolate. The cloves and ginseng burned on their way down. Not half-bad. "I guess so. I've seen how the NSO operates. I'd be happier on the other side from them."

"There is more, isn't there?"

"The most important piece of information. But first tell me how you knew about the gateway. Reno?"

Her eyes dropped to her fidgeting fingers. "We could not afford to ignore such data if it were true. As you have indicated, the tactical advantages of possessing such a device were too great."

"He sold you the data he stole from DNAegis? And the material he pried out of my mind?"

"I was not aware that he obtained it from you." Panda looked up. "I am sorry. Had I known . . . No. We still would have bought his information. I will not lie to you."

Jack took another sip of his drink. "I appreciate that. More than you know."

In Tiananmen Square, a thousand parasols twirled and children sang and chanted and laughed.

"The data I just gave you," he said, "should put you far ahead of the NSO, but there's one more thing you have to know. Something no one knows yet."

Panda set a slim black fountain pen on the table. "Do you mind if I document this?"

"Please."

She clicked the pen and a red light blinked on its cap.

Jack braced himself, but sensed no invasive probe like the one he had from Reno's briefcase.

"The gateway is a time bomb," he whispered. "It converts the rotational energy of the Earth's core to power its positional shifts. It's making the Earth spin slower. Check your satellite observations. Day and night are longer by more than half a minute."

Panda sat there a moment, blinked, then asked, "Is there a connection to the recent earthquakes?"

"Yes. The stress in the crust triggered it."

That sounded so scientific—like it wasn't his fault that Santa Sierra was underwater along with the Académe.

He clicked the pen off. "That's what I had to tell you before I showed you something that's going to solve all your problems." He pulled his pack out, opened it, and removed the mirror sphere. "This is the only working gateway."

Panda's brows arched. She stared at it a few seconds, then reached out with her hands and mind, interfaced, and a red arrow appeared.

Jack saw a flicker of maps through his dead eye. "I wouldn't do that." He gently pulled her hand away. "I've made a few modifications to the interface. Dangerous modifications."

"Amazing."

Wheeler's database of maps was window dressing. Jack had linked the gateway's coordinates to the Michelson Observatory and their triangulating laser array. Without the proper interface, someone might think they were jumping to Chicago and end up in Antarctica.

"I can't offer this to your government unless you can persuade them *not* to use it."

Panda shook her head. "Then why offer it at all?"

"To balance the West's attempts to reverse-engineer the hard-ware and copy the software. I'm not sure they'll ever figure out the alien technology. But they might be able to kill me and steal this prototype. They'd use it for terrorism and murder."

Panda was silent a moment, then whispered, "What makes you think our side will not?"

"You know now that every time it's used, the Earth slows. There could be more earthquakes—worse than the big shake-up seventy years ago. Sitting on the ring of fire, China has a lot to lose. I'm trusting you to not let that happen."

Her lips pressed into a single white line. "I do not know if I can convince my superiors. Not with the conflict in Indo-Malaysia. Not with the West researching their own prototype."

"I see."

"I will have to take it and you in . . . regardless of the consequences."

"I figured there wouldn't be much of a choice." Jack rolled the gateway into the center of the table. "I just wanted to get all the facts straight first."

"There is one thing I do not understand," Panda said, staring at her inverted reflection on the gateway's mirrored surface. "This device uses the energy from the spinning Earth? Can it be altered to use another power source? Or were you traded a defective piece of technology on purpose?"

"I've been thinking a lot about that. The West isn't your only worry. The source of the gateway—"

The festival music ceased. Jack turned toward Tiananmen Square.

The people dancing around the Goddess of Democracy screamed and fled, pushing over one another, stepping on those that had fallen, a wave of human bodies, struggling to get away . . . like their lives depended on it.

Panda drew a window in the air, interfaced with the sightseeing magnifier of the restaurant.

Seven men in black hoods stood at the foot of the Goddess. Each carried automatic weapons. One of them held a mirror sphere. And next to each man lay a metal canister.

The hooded figures fired into the crowd.

Hundreds of celebrants fell; tens of thousands screamed.

"No!" Jack got to his feet. They had a working gateway? Impossible. They might have broken the software puzzle, but the hardware was a millennium ahead of any science humans had.

Everyone else in the restaurant ran for the exit. Jack couldn't leave. He had to see what would happen.

The one with the mirrored sphere waved to his partners, and they ceased firing.

The seven murderers vanished.

The canisters remained . . . and exploded.

White fog billowed from the base of the Goddess and spread over Tiananmen Square. The crowds fell in midstride. Their screams twisted into shrieks. They writhed and choked, then stopped moving.

"Nerve gas!" Panda cried. "Nothing kills so quickly. We have underestimated the other side. Your gift may be too late."

The cloud diffused; translucent vapors blew into the street where hundreds collapsed and died.

Another explosion in the distance, then a second, and a third. The Beijing Institute and the Temple of Heaven were obscured in fog.

The wind shifted. Smoke drifted toward the Ambassador Hotel.

Panda grabbed the gateway. "We must go."

"We can't. The Earth will slow down. More deaths—"

Jack's skin itched. The gas?

"Death by earthquake," Panda said, "is the least of our worries." She made the first red vector appear. Maps fluttered as she scrolled through the database of maps—bits of the meandering Yangtze River, the convoluted coast of Cambodia, and steep topological lines of the Himalayas.

"That's the wrong link."

Jack's right eye watered and blurred. He could still see the gateway interface, however, through his dead eye. He set his hand over hers, forced a new link, shifting from Wheeler's database to the Michelson Observatory. Their blue destination vector had been pointing into the troposphere.

Jack smelled a whisper of chlorine mixed with the licorice scent of Panda. They vanished.

Panda screamed, clutched her head, and fell to the floor.

Jack felt the pain, too; needles twisting into his skull, but he was used to it, maybe because his brain was half-burned-out already.

A hundred windows spun around him, filled the air with simulations of the enzyme and gateway code, data on cosmic background radiation, a Barlinque commercial, and black-and-white movies. They collapsed in the blink of an eye.

Jack and Panda had made it to his command center in the moon. He sat next to her on the textured flexgel floor.

A link winked open to the microprocessors, and they asked: HOW MAY I HELP YOU, JACK?

What was it doing with all those active windows?

He still smelled the gas—an unnatural scent, something you were only supposed to smell once, then die.

Why had Beijing been attacked? Because it was Democracy Day and there would be hundreds of thousands of people? Or was it because he was there? Had Isabel or the NSO or Reno somehow found him?

Jack left a bloody trail every time he used the gateway. It had to stop.

Panda stood, unclenched her fists and opened her eyes. "What was that?"

"A change in the magnetic field. The flux induced current in your neuralware."

She shook her head. "A side effect of the gateway?"

"No. We jumped to the moon." Jack opened a link and showed the Earth in the black sky. "And the moon has no magnetic field."

She stared at the stars, then said, "I thought our destination was Tibet. We have to get that gateway to my people. It doe no good here." She looked around; Jack felt static brush along his arm. "This is a bubble. How do I know that we are on the moon?"

"Suit up and go outside, if you want." Jack squinted at her with his one good eye. "I thought you trusted me."

How had the NSO understood Wheeler's gateway, the software and the hardware, so quickly? They couldn't have built one . . . not by themselves.

She picked up the gateway. "Tibet. We must go. Thousands have been killed. And if our Institute—"

"Let's see what's happened before we jump anywhere." He spread his hands and opened windows to the Australian news nets and Asia World Press. The International Warning System chime blared through the channels. That wavering tone was the signal for impending earthquake and tsunami; it made Jack's insides freeze.

He told the microprocessors, "Scan for terrorist attacks, war, or natural disasters." He then whispered to Panda, "It may be too late for us to do any good."

"Let me take it to my people. It is not too late. It cannot be." She pressed the dimple, made the red vector appear.

"I wouldn't do that. You got the wrong coordinates last time. Use it again and you could end up floating in vacuum."

She shot a glare at Jack. Rage, waves of heat, filtered through the bubble interface and made his skin turn into gooseflesh. Then her shoulders slumped, and she set the gateway down.

Reports spilled through the open displays. Aerial shots of Tiananmen Square from satellite relays, tens of thousands lay in the streets, piles of bodies, dead children's hands still clutching celebration parasols.

Jack touched the image. It was flat, no sensations piped into the connection. But he felt them nonetheless. He grieved for them: mothers and fathers, brothers and sisters. They had been dancing one moment, then a split second of terror and they were gone.

Why had he been spared?

Panda watched with him as emergency teams in yellow chemical suits lumbered into the disaster. She didn't cry. She didn't say a word.

Was this Jack's fault? He wasn't the one who shot men and women and kids. He wasn't the one who detonated chemical warheads in the middle of a city. He denied this guilt. He had been there to try and stop it. This was Wheeler's doing. De-Mitri's. Or Isabel's.

Panda set a hand on his shoulder, embraced him, and Jack relaxed. She brushed away the tears from his lips.

He hadn't realized he was crying.

"We must do something," she said. "Anything."

"Doing 'anything' is what got me into this mess."

Panda took a step back. "I have a duty to my country— whatever personal admiration I have for you and your family, I will not allow that to interfere with what is best for my people."

"You're the only person I know who puts something other than herself first." He removed a pack of Chinese cigarettes, real tobacco, tapped two out, and offered her one. The tip ignited and Jack inhaled the harsh, unfiltered smoke. "There's another person involved, though, the alien I've been trading with, Wheeler. He's tangled up in what's been happening somehow. The slowing of the Earth. The killing. He *wants* this to happen."

Panda lit her cigarette, didn't inhale, just watched the smoldering tip. "Why?"

"I'm not sure." Jack chewed his cigarette. This wasn't the time for keeping secrets, not with the world falling apart, literally.

"Wheeler used me to gain the trust of others." Jack gestured to the open window, past the Earth to the stars. "There was a world . . . out there, that had been nicely hidden before I came along and found it for him. He stole their technology, then destroyed them. Somehow that connects to what's going on here. I can feel it."

"Then we need more information about this Wheeler. Where is he from? How does he—"

A world map materialized and filled the command center. The microprocessors said: DETONATION DETECTED.

The world map rotated over the hundred lakes of the Ural steppes and centered upon the crescent-shaped continent of Indo-Malaysia. Fifty kilometers off the coast, a tiny island turned into a pinpoint of light. White-hot, it faded to yellow and smeared, then turned red and wavered—the satellite net enhanced the image, zoomed closer—until boiling clouds of dust resolved, sucked into the center of a rising mushroom cloud.

FIFTEEN-MEGATON YIELD. CLEAN NEUTRON-RICH BURST. ORIGIN OF DEVICE UNKNOWN.

"Reno's Indo-Malaysian lab."

"And the city of Singapore," Panda said. "The electromagnetic pulse from that nuclear detonation will kill every implanted citizen within a hundred kilometers . . . eleven million people." She grabbed Jack and dug her nails into his arm. "Are we are going to stand and watch while America bombs the world?"

An impenetrable cloud covered the island; ocean waves rolled out, a hundred meters tall, and crashed against the coast of Indo-Malaysia. Drowned like Santa Sierra.

Jack may have accidentally caused that earthquake, but Isabel and DeMitri had deliberately wiped out their competition—a quick, clean gatewayed-in bomb that circumvented any antimissile defense . . . and murdered too many people to comprehend.

"They've won," Jack whispered. "Giving your government the gateway now will only incite retaliation."

"We must! They have to be made to stop. You said if one side had to have the technology, it should be ours. If you let me take your gateway, it will balance the power."

"There is no balance of power with the gateway. I never wanted neutron bombs materializing in the middle of cities. You want strikes and counterstrikes? The kind of balanced power that gets the world destroyed?"

It was too late to give China the technology. If they used it to retaliate, the Earth would slow; there'd be more earthquakes. It was too late to do anything.

Maybe Isabel and the NSO had won.

He couldn't let the violence escalate. He couldn't stop it, either.

It was like Wheeler's setup; Jack wasn't going to help him find other civilizations . . . but he couldn't stop him. Jack was caught in the center—where middlemen usually got stuck.

"Then what do you suggest we do?" Panda asked.

Jack tapped into a robotic stacker in storage and had it fetch an item.

He wished Zero was with him. With his boosted intelligence, he'd have a clue what to do. Jack had no answers to solve this problem, but there was another mystery that he might be able to solve. A mystery that connected.

"How good are you and your implant at cracking computer codes?" he asked.

"I bypassed your Académe's security and the NSO counterhackers there. Why?"

"That's a start." The elevator opened and the stacker delivered a foil packet to Jack. He tossed it to Panda. "You'll need more, though. That is the enzyme. You don't have to take it, but I could use another optimized mind to help."

"Doing what?"

Jack opened a window and let Wheeler's tangle of gateway code spill onto the floor. "We're going to figure exactly what makes this thing work."

Panda found weak spots in the gateway's code. She compared sifting through the falling-apart program to the short, sharp blocks and thrusts of her kung fu. The virtual model still self-destructed—that appeared to be hardwired into the gateway's structure—but together they learned that the energy used was proportional to the mass moved, and was nonlinear with respect to distance.

Smaller jumps were less efficient. Longer jumps always consumed more energy, but there was an exponential drop-off after ten thousand kilometers.

Jack did a quick calculation, factored in his first jumps and the gigantic shift of the warehouse to the moon. That only accounted for a tenth of the half-minute deceleration he initially detected in the Earth's rotation.

So who was doing the rest of the jumping?

Had Isabel used the gateway before Jack stole it back? She couldn't have cracked the lockout before he had. So what was causing the slowdown? And who had been smart enough to reverse-engineer the alien hardware?

A newscast caught his eye; he focused upon it and brought up the sound: riots at Darwin Tidal Station. The Cult of the Comet clashed with police in the streets. They claimed that swarms of comets orbited Mars. That it was a signal for the end of the world. They projected slogans into the air: GOD IS COMING. ARE YOU READY?

Jack unwrapped a bottle of mineral water and passed it to Panda. "How are you feeling?"

She was huddled in a blanket next to the wall, bedpan in hand, pale and feverish. "You did not say it would be like this." Panda closed her eyes and squeezed the bridge of her nose. Her rainbow eyelids had muted gray. "The first hour was wonderful. I was smarter. My central nervous system ran faster and tighter. But I am fuzzy now. Cannot think. Everything is filled with pain. I want to die."

"It's like that for a day or two. My ex-business partner, Zero, said the enzyme is supposed to make you more of whatever you are. I don't know if I believe that."

"You took the enzyme. What are you more of now, Jack?"

What was in his center? A middleman? No. If that's all he was, he wouldn't have felt anything when Santa Sierra drowned, or Beijing got gassed, or Singapore died. "I'm just a normal guy," he told her.

"I don't believe that. You escaped your totalitarian society. You contacted another civilization. You are anything but normal."

"What good has that done me? Or the world? I started this."

He waved to the map of the world that filled the curve of the opposite wall. "It would have been better if I was normal."

THREAT ALERT scrolled across the microprocessors' window.

On the coast of the great inland Mississippian Sea, two points of light flashed: in the center of Chicago and along the shore of Austin, Texas. The light boiled and wavered, shock waves rippled along the earth, then the centers of the fireballs cooled to red, and cyclones of dust were sucked into the middle, rose, and obscured the view.

TWENTY-TWO-MEGATON YIELD. EIGHTEEN-MEGATON YIELD. CLEAN NEUTRON-RICH DEVICES. ORIGIN OF DEVICES UNKNOWN.

"A second strike?" Panda asked. "On American soil? Why?"

"It's not a second strike. It's return fire." Jack watched the black smears of destruction. Millions of screams tore through him. Lost souls.

"Apparently your people solved their code and hardware problems . . . with my data. I gave them the key to slip though world antimissile nets. I gave them a way to bomb the hell out of each other."

"Perhaps they will cease fire."

"No. This is the end of the world. Millions drowned in Santa Sierra, and gassed in Beijing, electrified in Singapore, fifteen million more in Chicago, and twenty million flash-vaporized in Austin."

Maybe his soul had been edited, too, because Jack didn't feel the urge to swallow his Hautger SK. He should have. That would have been better than watching the world die because of his mistakes.

All he knew, deep down inside, was that he was glad he had gotten away. Glad to still be alive. Was that indifference or innocence? Selfishness or self-preservation?

Panda was silent. They watched the world.

There were tremors in the Indian Ocean; tidal waves submerged the coast of Sri Lanka; volcanic eruptions along the Cuban-Florida archipelago spouted poisonous gases and ash into the atmosphere.

From the global satellite network, the microprocessors spotted nonnatural anomalies: a fleet of missile-frigates and destroyers materialized in the Arabian Ocean; a thousand Chinese shock infantry and mobile artillery winked into the Mojave Desert coast; Russian tanks popped into Banker's Square in Geneva; and armored personnel carriers appeared in Amsterdam.

"You may have been correct," Panda said. "It appears there is nothing more for us to do. Except wait and observe."

Jack exhaled. "And survive." He had been holding his breath without realizing it.

During the next three hours, he smoked a pack of the Chinese cigarettes, watched the heat signature shadows of submarines flicker underwater in Pacific trenches, the Salton Sea, and the Yangtze River. Fault lines buckled and bridges toppled; steam erupted from the Hudson Bay.

A quick calculation showed that the Earth continued to slow, day and night had grown by seventeen minutes. How much stress could the crust take before there was a major split?

"It's been hours since Chicago and Austin," Panda said. "No further tactical strikes. Why don't you get some sleep?"

"Because something is happening," Jack answered without looking away from the open windows.

Chinese infantry in the American Southwest vanished. Submarines in the Yangtze River faded. Tanks and destroyers and missile frigates dissolved.

"They're standing down," he whispered—afraid that if he said it too loud, someone might hear and start the bombing again.

It was the end of the Information Age.

Wholesale manipulation and generation, creation and suppression of data was about to stop. No one would be able to control data with gateway technology present.

The Great Wall was down. They had to be talking down there, maybe negotiating a cease-fire. Or maybe the CCOs of the world's city-states were forcing a peace. After all, mass destruction was bad for business.

Jack focused on the Australian news nets: rescue operations on the Indo-Malaysian coast, hundreds of thousands dead in the capital, and riots continued at Darwin. The Cult of the Comet had burned city hall. He stared at their signs that projected flaming comets and asteroids into the air.

Comets and asteroids? He had seen NSO counterhackers guarding that database at the Michelson Observatory. Was there a connection?

He opened a link to the observatory. Space compressed into metaphor, shrank to the size of the command center, filled with chromacolor planets and stars that left trails of celestial data as they wheeled overhead.

In the virtual information void between Earth and the moon, thousands of spider silk links twinkled. NSO in space cruisers and straddling satellites severed them as quickly as they formed. Counterhackers swarmed through the vacuum in jet-propelled suits, waving improbable-looking ray guns, zapping shadow-intruders crouching in the darkness. Everyone suddenly wanted access to the observatory's imager and communication networks.

Jack switched to his hard connection kilometers to the south under the Avagadro crater. He tried to link to the near-Earth asteroid database, but it was obscured by interstellar dust and thick with floating eyes and ears and fingertips waiting to detect intruders like him.

What was so important?

Jack scanned the metaphorical night sky, looking for a clue, something amiss. There were links to sulfurous Io, the glittering silver sparks of the asteroid belt, Venus, sterile Mercury, and the solar flare database.

. . . Mars was gone. Or rather, the connection to its image.

He tapped the observatory's telescopes and discovered that half of them were pointed toward the Red Planet.

Jack intercepted and unscrambled the incoming data. Images of Mars resolved: amber rocks, orange dust drifts, dark jagged canyons filled with morning ice-crystal mist. A halo of asteroids orbited the planet. Thousands of them.

And where the underground Armstrong Colonies, man's first foothold on the planet, should have been, there was only a smoldering crater.

Lightning flashed from an asteroid; it fell upon the surface, splintered Arias Mons, turned the ridges of the mountain molten, and cracked the surface deep enough so fountains of magma sputtered and showered from the rupture.

Jack's heart skipped a beat.

The rock was three kilometers long, sleek in parts, clusters of oval bumps in parts, a rounded tapered nose, and scattered along its side like the lateral line of a fish were a rainbow of blinking lights . . . with dozens of smaller stones swarming about it. They veered and stopped and shifted direction at right angles.

Those weren't asteroids. They were ships. An alien fleet.

He selected a different data set, pulled back to a wider image, and watched as they broke away from the Martian gravity well.

"What are they?" Panda whispered.

"Business associates," Jack muttered. "I had it right the first time. This is the end of the world."

19

JUMPING JACK

The smaller ships filled the void between Mars and Earth—multiplying across the distance in million-kilometer arcs—cobalt dotted lines of ten-meter-long needles. They vanished one by one from the tail end of those trajectories, then started the process over, playing hopscotch through space.

Were they making copies of themselves? Or was it an illusion from the gateway technology? Copies of their wavefunctions appearing and collapsing, smeared through space?

Whatever it was, Jack didn't like it.

Hundreds appeared over Earth, splinters and shards that looked like the sky shattered. They docked together, fit snug like the pieces of jigsaw puzzle, made a pyramid, a cube, an isohedron, then broke apart and flitted into elliptical orbits.

Each left radar shadows; positional blurs that made pinpointing exactly where they were, or how many, impossible.

Panda said, "Look." Before her hovered an open window with an image of Mars.

The battleships blinked once along their lateral lines of light. Rainbows stretched through the infrared into soft X rays, curved and dissipated into ethereal smoke. The ships dimmed, and a halo of gamma radiation became visible around their shell.

They moved away from Mars.

She stared deeper into the link, then whispered, "Twenty-eight minutes until they rendezvous with Earth. What do they want?"

Jack's first impulse was to grab the gateway and leave; go someplace that no one could find him.

He took a deep breath. "Remember I told you about Wheeler?"

She faced him.

"It must be him. I was supposed to find him another civilization . . . a week ago. He could be here to find out why I haven't."

Jack opened a link to the isotope circuit; broad bands of silver static resolved, flashes of light that combined into Wheeler's electronic handshake signal:

HELLOJACKHELLOJACKHELLOJACKHELLOJACKHELLOJACK

He set up a bubble interface—stopped.

It had to be Wheeler out there. He had stolen the other aliens' technology, then butchered them to keep word from spreading about his operation. "It's not the A-Colonies or just the Earth he's after," Jack said to himself. "He has to kill me as well to make sure his secrets stay secret."

"What do you mean?" Panda's mind pushed softly against Jack's, reached into him with whispers and the brush of velvet and the faint scent of licorice.

He wanted to throw a wall of prime numbers between them—blur the connection with unbounded summations—but now wasn't the time for secrets. Not from Panda. And not with so much at stake.

Jack showed her Wheeler's solid black eyes and the obsidian

gears and cold iron sprockets turning inside, and how terrified he was at getting caught in the middle of the alien's schemes.

"Wheeler was thrilled when I found him," he told her. "Especially when he learned I was working alone. No governments. No news leaks. I'm the only one who knows about him, the only one who needs to be silenced."

"Why all the ships, then?" Panda asked.

"Life means nothing to Wheeler. Even if I gave myself up to him, he'd destroy the planet. He won't take the chance of anyone on Earth advertising how his operation works. It would be bad for business."

How many other worlds had Wheeler obliterated? Jack had to stop him. Do something.

"What can we do?" Panda asked. His fears echoed inside her; in the reflections of her eyes, Wheeler's gears turned. He shouldn't have shown her that.

How far could the two of them jump? Not far enough. And Jack had a hunch it would take more than "distance" to outrun Wheeler.

He gazed through the open window to Earth. "I've got to help," he whispered. "I was responsible for Santa Sierra and I'm responsible for this. I can't just stand by and watch."

"Can we use their technology against them?" Panda bit her lower lip. "Gateway a bomb into one of their ships?"

"No luck. The heaviest artillery I have is a Hautger SK."

He tapped into the microprocessors and together they watched as dawn broke over London. Wind whipped the North Atlantic into a hurricane spiral.

The microprocessors estimated the deceleration of the planet's rotation; seconds adding into minutes and minutes into hours. A day was now twenty-nine hours and forty-seven minutes long.

"What I had in mind was stepping down to Earth, grabbing a few people, and bringing them back here before Wheeler arrives . . . just in case he pulls a repeat performance of the A-Colonies."

"Won't this slow the Earth even more?"

He tapped into a robotic stacker and had it fetch a few items from storage.

"Not enough to matter. It's the rest of the world, shifting tanks, fleets of destroyers, and squads of infantry that are doing the real damage."

Jack did a quick estimation of the energy robbed from the Earth. Even if there had been thousands of jumps with hundreds of millions of tons of equipment . . . that still didn't account for this magnitude of deceleration.

Math didn't lie—something else must be happening.

Panda linked to the base's reactor. "I'm shutting down power, bringing the batteries on-line." The open windows flickered, dimmed, then stabilized. "Those ships might be able to sense the reactor's thermal signature." She reached into the interface. "I'm sealing all interior doors and depressurizing unnecessary compartments—just in case."

In case they found him? If that happened, sealing compartments wouldn't help; they vaporized the Armstrong Colonies—a site professionally planned and fortified against disaster. In comparison, Jack's hole in the moon was a buried tin can.

"Good idea," he said and repressed any emotional leak.

Jack secured his connection to the Michelson Observatory, constructed dead-code walls and rat mazes to keep the NSO from stumbling across it. He'd need the observatory's laser coordinate system to triangulate his jump to Earth.

He told the microprocessors, "I'll give you notice of where I'll be going. Warn me of impending disasters."

GOOD LUCK, JACK, it replied.

The elevator opened and the robotic stacker delivered the four packages he had ordered. In a lotus-folded container was a portable bubble. Jack unwrapped a relay node, a half-sphere the size of a grapefruit; its edges undulated, trying to capture signals that weren't there.

He linked the bubble relay to the gateway code—crystalline commands and math-code endlessly seething—and encrypted the input. He then set the relay and gateway into his pack.

Jack could now activate it without his hands. No more fumbling with the slippery mirror sphere like he had in Santa Sierra.

In the next box was a new matte-black Hautger SK. He unzipped three clips of ammunition: one armor-piercing and two anatoxic plastocene.

The third package was a shrink-wrapped pouch with a cell phone patch and booster card. He gave Panda the secured number, then tossed it into his pack.

She said, "Communication will be delayed a few seconds because of the distance. If something is coming at you, there may not be much warning."

"Understood."

In the last softgel wrapper was a vacuum suit. The clamshell portion with the oxygen recyclers and power unit he ditched. Too bulky. Jack grabbed the helmet, though; its reactive circuits would shield him from electromagnetic flux. He also tossed the spray-on membrane sealant into his pack. The teflon polymer could seal wounds or splint broken bones.

Panda grabbed him by the arm and made him look at her. "How many can you save? Is it worth the risk?"

"There's time. I've got twenty-three minutes before those big ships get to Earth. This place is self-sufficient for maybe half a dozen people . . . for a while. I won't get more than that."

"I should go," she said. "I weigh less and therefore require less energy to jump. And I am the better fighter."

"No. It's my fault. I'll be the one who risks his neck."

Panda narrowed her eyes.

Through the bubble circuitry, Jack felt himself pulled toward her, a gravitational attraction; Panda wanted him to stay; he tasted cold brine: her fear that if he left, he wouldn't come back.

But Jack had loose ends dangling back on Earth. Zero and Isabel. He wanted to rescue the gene witch because he was brilliant, the closest thing Jack had to a friend.

And he had to see Isabel again. Jack wanted to hear her say that she needed his help. That she had been wrong. Then he might leave her behind anyway for taking a shot at him and teaming up with DeMitri. He'd decide when he saw her.

The people he saved might be the only ones to survive. He had to hand-pick them. He wanted no dead wood.

SUDDEN SHIFT IN EARTH'S CORE STRUCTURE scrolled across the microprocessors' display. ROTATIONAL PERIOD INCREASED AN ADDITIONAL SEVEN HOURS FOUR MINUTES. TECTONIC SHIFTS IMMINENT.

"I have to go," Jack said and grabbed his pack. He interfaced with the gateway and made the red origin vector materialize.

Panda stood on her toes and kissed him. "You are a fool," she whispered.

"I know."

He split-screen-interfaced and gazed out his dead eye through weather satellites—he was a shadow hovering over the world. He spotted the al Qaseem oil fields on the Arabian peninsula . . . or rather, where they had been. Millions of hectares burned. An ocean of flaming oil. Thunderheads of black-pitch smoke veiled the desert. Hell on Earth.

Jack leapt down.

He landed on a catwalk strung between two towers, a hundred meters off the ground. He grabbed the railing—resisting the urge to clutch his head. Static and flashes of green light strobed through his mind. He'd forgotten to put on the helmet.

He shook his head clear, stood, and surveyed the fields of steel pipes and distillation columns and skeletal supports, kilometers of unnatural landscape. Zero's family business.

An explosion—close—made the catwalk sway. Jack turned and saw a ruptured tank, a ball of flame, expanding, blossoming under the tower on his right. He felt a blast of heat on his face. The air was full of fumes and the smell of hot metal. It was hard to breathe.

This jump was a long shot.

But it was the only place Jack might find a clue to Zero's whereabouts. Reno had said the al Qaseem family didn't know where Zero was. Jack was betting that if they had known, they wouldn't tell a spy like Reno. He was betting that one of the al Qaseem clan would be here in charge.

No one could be in this inferno, though.

Jack made the red origin vector appear, prepared to jump away, then a motion in the corner of his eye made him halt.

Two hundred meters to the south, an exoskeleton marched through a wall of fire. The machine had three heavyset legs, one along each side, nine arms, and dozens of hydraulic tentacles. It looked to Jack like three Medusas welded together at the waist as it stepped and slithered and pulled its way through the tangles of pipes and twisted metal. It was as large and as heavy as an armored tank.

It had an egg-shaped heart, a semireflective operator's capsule. Jack saw a person inside.

The exoskeleton advanced to a broken pipe spewing petroleum, walked through the high-pressure flames, then wrapped three clamping arms around it and squeezed shut. A tentacle snaked forward. There was a burst of violet light and the end of the pipe turned into solid lump.

The machine backed away, swiveled, then headed toward another fire.

It was foolish. Heroic.

Jack linked though an Egyptian weather satellite and saw a thousand fires throughout the refinery. More explosive blossoms in infrared. It was turning into a firestorm . . . and spreading.

Ten kilometers south of the fire-fighting exoskeleton, a string of railroad cars detonated. Jack zoomed in and read the sides of the tanks: LIQUEFIED NATURAL GAS. He followed the tracks, saw tanks of gasoline and kerosene—all waiting to explode like a string of firecrackers.

This place was going to go up in smoke. Soon. And the operator didn't know.

Jack had to save him.

An incoming message filtered through the cell phone and

scrolled across Jack's field of vision: THREAT WARNING. TREMOR IN AFRICAN RIFT VALLEY. 7.1 MAGNITUDE.

The catwalk vibrated. The two towers it joined rocked back and forth; Jack gripped the railing tighter and watched the land ripple.

How to get the operator out? The red origin vector wouldn't stretch that far. He couldn't jump on the machine, then jump out. The external temperature would fry him.

There, twenty meters west of the fire-fighting exoskeleton, was a blasted, blackened open space. An island in the fiery sea.

Jack stretched a blue arrow there and stepped across—

—it was hotter than he anticipated. There was nothing to inhale but scalding vapors and caustic gases. Jack choked and coughed and tried to wave frantically at the machine.

Its midsection pivoted; the thing lumbered toward him, running and pushing through oil sludge and flame and smoke.

One arm sprayed jets of cold water ahead and doused Jack. An external loudspeaker blasted at him, something in Arabic.

He shook his head, couldn't reply as he gagged on the fumes.

The machine bent lower on two knees, and the canopy unsheathed, layers of reflective silver retracted. The operator pulled off an oxygen mask, and stuffed it over Jack's mouth.

It could have been a younger Zero, with a slimmer nose and chin, softer skin, and blue eyes . . . and a woman. She wore a military uniform, rampant lion insignia, and black beret.

"American?" she whispered.

Jack took off the mask. "I was looking for Zero al Qaseem. But there're gas tanks"—he coughed—"about to go."

"You are Dr. Jack Potter of DNAeagis." Black circles of fatigue ringed her eyes, and her left arm trembled. "My cousin, Zero, spoke highly of you. I cannot believe you survived this inferno. The hand of God has truly touched you."

"The hand of God is about to touch both of us," Jack rasped. "There's a line of natural gas railcars—" He pointed.

She mouthed something that Jack didn't catch, then pulled

him into the canopy. It sheathed closed. She interfaced with the inductive webwork, and the machine lurched forward.

Zero's cousin? That made her a princess of Arabia. It explained the foolish heroics, but not why she was out here getting her hands dirty.

"I was looking for Zero," Jack said.

"He is in heaven." She glanced over her shoulder. "Where we shall be soon if we do not leave this place."

Jack made a red arrow appear, pushed through her machine's interface, and connected a blue line to the moon.

"Not quite heaven," he said.

They blinked into a cave on the moon, and magnetic flux tore through Jack's head.

Dull red light from the cooling thermite reactor made the skin of Zero's cousin flush and her blue eyes darken to violet.

Jack had taken the exoskeleton as well; she'd been too integrated into feedback webs for the gateway software to extract her. The machine must have weighed twenty tons and stood as tall as the reactor in the three-story chamber. It had burned up a lot of rotational energy to get here.

Jack untangled himself from her, climbed out of the operator's capsule, and dropped to the floor.

She extracted herself from the exoskeleton, every motion exaggerated in the reduced gravity, then jumped beside him, bounced on the landing. She stood a half-head taller than him. A confused look crossed her face.

Jack was about to explain—when she drew her sidearm.

A fast recovery; it would have taken him a few minutes before he regained his senses. Then again, she was part of the al Qaseem clan—trained from birth to protect herself from clan assassins.

"You passed out," he said. "Must have been the heat and fumes. We're safe. Relax."

"I feel . . . strange. Light-headed." She frowned, but lowered the muzzle, then holstered her gun. His lie was infinitely easier to accept than the truth.

"My name is Safa." She removed her beret and scratched her close-cropped hair "You mentioned Zero. Is my cousin here?"

"Didn't you say that Zero was in heaven?"

"His version of heaven, I assure you."

"Then he's alive?"

"Perhaps," she whispered. "Our best agents could not locate him, yet I suspect he lives." Her eyes hardened. "But this is family business. So now, if you do not mind, I shall ask you questions."

Jack only had minutes until the Mars party arrived at Earth.

He had to give up on Zero. Wherever he was, Jack was out of guesses and out of time. He had a feeling the gene witch could take care of himself . . . somehow.

"We'll talk later." He pointed to the elevator. "Take that to the command center on level three. There's a woman there who will explain everything."

Safa stood straighter, opened her mouth, but before she could say anything, Jack linked through the cell phone and said to Panda, "You've got a visitor."

He stretched a blue line across space and through veils of atmosphere, then whispered, "I'll be in—"

"—Shanghai."

He stood in a meter of water. Hot water. The street shifted under his feet, and the city smelled of brimstone.

Through the phone, Panda spoke: "Volcanic eruption. Ring of fire is unstable. Explosive wave of steam headed your way. Fifty seconds. Hurry."

The western sky was a wall of boiling clouds, steel gray—moving fast toward him.

The water was so high in the canal, Old Tea House Temple seemed to float. Jack crossed the zigzag bridge; water lapped under its wooden slats.

He was careful to walk crooked. A straight step and he'd flounder in the water. No time for that. No time at all.

Jack stopped, called Wheeler's old database of maps from the gateway, got Shanghai, the canal district, then the blueprints for Old Tea House Temple.

Thirty-three chambers. Too many. He couldn't move that fast. Unless . . .

He programmed a sequence of automated jumps, gave himself a half-second in each room—

—a quick look; he saw hanging calligraphy scrolls, and spinning brass prayer wheels, and statues of Buddha, and an overflowing toilet as he flickered through the temple.

In the top room was the old monk in his blue-black robes. He held a string of prayer beads and chanted before a disk of gold suspended by wires from the roof.

Jack halted the program.

He glanced over his shoulder, half-expecting to see Reno. No dice. The rat was probably hiding in a hole. Jack wouldn't have taken him anyway. He'd come for the monk.

Jack had known dozens of scientists that he would have liked to take back to the moon—all drowned along with the Académe.

Friends other than Isabel or Zero? He'd never been the type to make friends easily. You never knew who'd turn out to be competition. Jack hadn't been given a gift without strings attached . . . since this monk had given him a bowl of rice and tea.

"I wanted to thank you for your hospitality," Jack said.

The old monk didn't look startled. He bowed to Jack. In perfect English, he said, "I had hoped you would return, traveler. I sensed you require spiritual guidance." He turned to the hanging disk of gold; eight spokes radiated from a mandala in the center. It was a meter across and looked solid. "We must not leave the Wheel of Law."

Had Reno told the old guy about Jack and the gateway? Were they working together?

No time for second guesses. He'd made up his mind to take the old monk, but that gold wheel had to weigh a ton.

He spoke into the cell phone, "One more coming up . . ."

The old monk stared straight through Jack, a gaze that needed no bubble circuitry to let him know that he would rather die than leave his damn wheel.

Jack sighed. ". . . with baggage."

The old monk clasped Jack's arm and said, "Our journey begins."

Denver was a mess.

The air was veiled with ash. Rising mountains had crushed the outskirts of the city, covered them so only a pocket valley remained, surrounded by unstable walls of rock.

In the time it took for Jack to travel to the moon and back, the Earth's rotational period had increased by ninety-six hours. Impossible. At least, it was impossible as Jack understood the gateway. Could the alien ships be causing it? At this rate of deceleration, the world might come to a standstill.

From his vantage atop a granite peak, Jack saw distant cinder cones. They weren't on Wheeler's map. They rumbled and smoldered and glared up into the black sky, illuminating the thick atmosphere from below.

Three helicopters buzzed over the city, and a jet followed, but Jack didn't see any motion in the street. Where had everyone gone? Underground bomb shelters? To a higher elevation? Or were they all dead?

The Denver Institute of Technology was a square of green lawn and gray stone buildings upon the foothills. A few towers had toppled, but it was otherwise intact. For the moment.

There was one more loose end there to tie up: Bruner.

A red arrow, a blue, and Jack stepped—down a thousand meters, onto broken flagstones, among long shadows and yawning arched hallways and scattered maple leaves on the lawn.

Bruner had told Jack he had a lecture series lined up here for the summer.

He summoned Wheeler's map, found the mathematics building, took another step—and stood in front of a Greek temple with columns and cornices and covered with carved geometrical theorems.

Jack tapped the information kiosk and located Bruner's office. He ran upstairs to the third floor. The room was empty: a padded chair, but no metaphor or illusion within the office. A push with the implant yielded no echoes or active circuits.

Bruner and Jack would have killed each other for that tenured position at the Académe. Bruner had framed him, but Jack had started the fight by trying to discredit Bruner's research.

Too bad he wasn't here. Maybe if he had saved his old enemy's life, he'd have felt better about himself. Too little. Too late.

He spied a note taped to the chair:

Gone to the Alexander Brandy to get drunk. Anyone who wants to join me can.

—B.

Flipping through the gateway's maps, Jack located the watering hole downtown, then linked through the Northwest Bell satellite and found it had shifted a half-block north.

He took a sideways leap—

—landed in a room of broken glass and an atmosphere thick with the fumes of beer and brandy, wine and whiskey. Every bottle and mirror and highball glass and table in the place had shattered.

. . . Almost.

Next to the fireplace in the back sat a dozen unbroken bottles and a drunk. Bruner.

Jack recognized his wild beard that shot out straight from his chin. His glazed eyes reflected the flames in the fireplace. He hadn't seen Jack arrive.

A message from the microprocessors: EARTHQUATE 9.8 MAGNITUDE. COLLAPSE OF INDO-AUSTRALIAN PLATE. EARTH ROTATION PERIOD INCREASED BY SEVENTEEN DAYS. RAPID INTERNAL GEOLOGICAL SHIFTS. EXERCISE EXTREME CAUTION.

Seventeen days? No jump could cause that sudden deceleration. Even if every person on Earth jumped from one pole to the other. It had to be Wheeler engineering it.

342

Jack removed his helmet.

"As I live and breathe," Bruner declared, "which may not be for long, it is Dr. Potter." He stood, a thin figure silhouetted by the fire, then fell back into his chair. "Come here, Jack. Have one last drink with a fellow alumni."

Jack picked through the glass on the floor. "Bruner. I figured you might be one of the survivors."

"Survivors?" He laughed and sprayed flecks of spit across the table. "That's funny. This is the end. No one's going to live through this. It could only be worse"—he filled his tumbler with Jamaican rum and tossed it back—"only be worse if there was nothing to drink."

"We have to go," Jack said.

Bruner ignored him. "I got that tenured position, you know?" He turned to Jack, so his flared black-and-white beard pointed straight at him. "The NSO revoked that, though, when I refused to be their boy. Bastards. Guess I had it coming. What comes around goes around, huh?" He laughed again and half-poured, half-spilled a shotglass of whiskey for Jack.

Jack took it, but didn't drink. "I'm sorry. I tried to—"

"Don't!" Bruner threw his drink into the fireplace and the flames flared. "Don't piss all over yourself. We both did what we had to do. Now it doesn't matter." He grinned. "So have a drink with me. The world is going to shit."

"It's worse than that," Jack whispered. "Far worse than just the end of *this* world."

Bruner glared at him with his beady eyes. "What's that mean?"

"You want to see?"

Jack took Bruner by the shoulder, anchored a red arrow to him . . . then gave him the view of his life.

One last person to save.

Jack watched the world with blurry satellite-vision. Half the communication net had failed, jammed with requests for information or burned up in decaying orbits.

Tidal waves battered the coast of Spain, plunging Madrid underwater. Explosive auroras borealis and australis made flickering curtains and spirals of ghostly green and red and blue excitation that stretched to the tropics of Cancer and Capricorn.

The Earth was covered with clouds: typhoons and hurricanes and waterspouts. Volcanic plumes of ash smeared the sky. Lightning storms raged—high-voltage cascades that danced from troposphere to mesosphere in sheets and bolts and amber jets of positive charge.

The electricity blinded and terrified Jack. Even with a reactive helmet, the high-voltage charge would fry his implant. He'd keep his head far away.

Radar pierced the blankets of mist and revealed wrinkled landmasses. The China coast was dotted with infrared flares from erupting calderas. New Zealand was missing.

An isthmus stretched from England to Norway to the Netherlands.

Jack made sure his helmet was on snug, stepped down—

—to the *Zouwtmarkt*.

Amsterdam was a series of hills from which Jack could see for kilometers over the muddy flats that had once been submerged. No gardens obstructed that view. Everything had burned. The poplars that had lined the pathways were charred sticks; melted metal spires, fountains bent into unnatural shapes that would have made Dali pause.

The crystal dome, the front for the DNAegis underground industrial complex, was cracked, shattered in the center. It looked like a great bloodshot eye staring up into heaven.

The inside of his skull itched. There were no electrical storms overhead. What could cause a big enough flux to induce current through his vacuum suit helmet?

A slight shaking of the earth made Jack step crookedly. Another quake.

He knelt and braced himself. He was out in the open; he should be safe. The vibrations magnified; he saw waves ripple through the ground, faster and higher. Jack lay flat, hugged the earth.

The world rolled and pitched. Jack grabbed fistfuls of blackened grass and baked soil.

It was like being on a small boat in a hurricane: up and down and no stopping it.

The ground undulated, picked him up, and threw him into the air, tossed him, bounced him upside-down; he landed on his ankle, his head, and up again, and down; he landed on his back—got the wind knocked out of him.

The shaking slowed and subsided, but didn't stop. Shuddering aftershocks reminded him that the earth beneath him was dangerous and unpredictable.

Jack was still shaking, too.

What kind of earthquake had that been? More than shifting tectonic plates . . .

He could jump back. No. He had to save Isabel.

Panda's voice crackled through the cell phone: "—attacking the Michelson Observatory, Jack. The satellite nets. We're switching channels as fast as we can. You have to come back. They're headed for—"

A pulse-compressed message cut her off and streamed into Jack's head: EARTH DECELERATION FASTER THAN ANTICIPATED. MAGNETIC FIELD COLLAPSE. INDUCTION DANGER. INSUFFICIENT TERRESTRIAL ROTATIONAL ENERGY. MOONQUAKES—

The message ended.

Jack tried the cell phone, but every channel was dead.

He got up and ran to the dome, got out his Hautger SK.

He should jump back. Now. Save himself and forget Isabel. Would she even let him save her?

The doors to the DNAegis crystal dome were shut and locked. Jack fired compression burrowing rounds, shot the fiber-reinforced glass apart, and stepped through.

There was no automated receptionist and no electricity in the lobby. He crossed a fractured marble floor, pushed open the doors to the stairwell, ready to fight his way down past NSO agents—then halted.

There were no stairs.

The skeletal remains of the handrail twisted into a hole and vanished. Just darkness beyond. The massive industrial complex was missing, twenty levels that sprawled under the *Zouwtmarkt* . . . gone. No enzyme bioreactors, no corporate offices, only a gaping hole.

Jack pushed with the implant and no echoes returned. Nothing.

He backed away from the cavern—the floor might go and take him with it. Jack ran out of the dome, into the blackened gardens of the *Zouwtmarkt*.

Isabel had moved the entire complex with a copy of the gateway. What good would that do? Had she feared a direct nuclear strike? Where had she gone?

Wherever she was, Jack couldn't save her.

The last person he would have to rescue was himself.

He looked into the overcast sky. Without satellite links and the observatory's laser triangulation arrays, he could only estimate the position of the moon. If he got close, though, he could make a series of smaller jumps by eye.

Jack's stomach froze . . . he remembered that he had only taken the vacuum suit helmet and spray-on membrane. No webbing supports. No clamshell power pack to provide heat and recycle the oxygen.

If the suit didn't immediately blow, he might be able survive without air for a few minutes. Provided he didn't freeze first.

Not much of a choice.

He secured the helmet, then sprayed on the navy blue polymer. It flowed over his body and hardened. The membrane integrity display inside the helmet flickered between orange and red—it wouldn't withstand micropressures for long. If at all.

There had to be a better way. Someplace on Earth to run o hide. No. No place. Jack was out of options.

He hyperventilated, increasing the oxygen supply in his blood then exhaled—remembering that holding your breath was the last thing you wanted to do in a vacuum.

He interfaced with the gateway and stretched a line out into the atmosphere.

The blue destination vector extended two hundred forty thousand kilometers, then it faltered and faded. Less than two-thirds the distance.

There wasn't enough energy.

No. That couldn't be right.

Jack made the red arrow appear, then the blue, and cast it up and out—two hundred twenty-eight thousand kilometers.

It didn't reach to the moon.

That's what the microprocessors had tried to tell him. Insufficient rotational energy to return.

Jack was stuck.

Stuck on the Earth meant death, swallowed by the ground, blown apart by volcanic eruption, or whatever pyrotechnics his alien friends had planned.

But the microprocessors had mentioned something else . . . moonquakes?

A flicker of hope kindled within him. Maybe there was a chance.

There was enough energy for *a* jump. Just not all the way to the moon. He was a hundred thousand kilometers short.

He had to make the leap. It was better than being a sitting duck on the ground. And if he was wrong, it would be a quicker death, at least.

Jack cast a blue line into space, into blackness and emptiness. He jumped.

20

JACK-OF-ALL-TRADES

Jack tumbled in space.

His field of vision was limited to what flashed across his faceplate: the Earth spun past, the moon half-full, velvet darkness, the blinding sun, then the Earth again.

It made him dizzy . . . nauseated. His internal organs rearranged.

There was nothing to hold on to. No up and no down. He couldn't think while he gyrated out of control.

His pulse pounded in his temples. Had to calm down—useless oxygen.

The helmet's internal display reflected upon the faceplate. A line of growing red diodes indicated the suit's rapidly deteriorating membrane integrity.

Jack closed his eyes, extended his arms and legs to decrease his angular velocity, then looked. His spinning had slowed, and the Earth floated before him.

Thousands of scout ships, needles of midnight blue, swarmed in orbit. Dozens of larger ships appeared, scintillating green-and-gold, then one of the big ships arrived, three kilometers long; bumps bubbled along its side, and flashed surrealistic rainbows.

Jack's heart beat faster and the faceplate fogged. That ship had turned the Armstrong Colonies into a molten crater.

He continued to spin; across his field of vision, the Earth set and the moon rose.

Jack hoped this worked, that there was another power source available to the gateway, one that he had used before and not realized: the moon. He had forgotten that the moon rotated. It was phase-locked with the Earth, so every orbit the moon turned once on its axis and kept the same face toward Earth.

That's what he hoped the microprocessors had tried to tell him. Moonquakes. Shifts in its structure from its lost rotational energy. Deceleration caused by Jack's previous jumps down to the Earth.

He interfaced with the gateway—had to get out of here before the suit ruptured or he suffocated. The red origin vector appeared, then the blue destination vector, a handsbreadth wide and thousands of kilometers long. Jack moved it to the lunar north pole.

The arrow faded and vanished.

Adrenaline flooded his body, but he didn't dare move. He couldn't even scream because that would waste air. Why hadn't it worked?

He rotated away from the moon, faced the stars, and between them, infinitely deep shadows.

His arms went numb and frost spread across the helmet's faceplate.

What caused the failure of the destination vector? He was closer to the moon than the Earth. Was the gateway confused which planet to lock on to as a power source?

Another revolution; he faced the Earth.

Jack accessed the magnification in his faceplate and zoomed in on the alien battleship as it descended into the Indian Ocean.

The cloud-covered atmosphere parted, and beneath, water boiled away; cracks splintered along the crust, and red rifts of magma glowed.

The Pacific plate was weakened by the collapse of the Indo-Australian plate. If it went, the entire surface could rearrange, plunge into a molten sea, or drift into new configurations, shuffling continents like mah-jongg tiles.

Water rushed into the volcanic rifts; jets of steam detonated into the air; lightning tore at the new clouds, and they turned silver gray, black, then mottled with poisonous ocher and yellow.

He rotated away from the dying world, gazed into the same blackness that filled his soul.

What had Zero said? He would have killed Jack and Isabel and himself if that would have stopped Wheeler. Jack understood what he had meant now: the guilt of surviving.

Purple splotches danced in his peripheral vision. . . . Almost out of oxygen.

He turned toward the moon, half-silver orb; red arrow, blue, and Jack sensed the gateway lock on to a destination, over the lunar pole. He slipped through a hole in space—

—and floated a hundred kilometers over the gray powder and black pockmarked surface. The moon had never looked so good to him.

On the far side, near the Mach crater, the radio and optical telescopes of the Michelson Observatory were gone. The shield dome of the science center was a blackened hole.

Jack turned his head—made himself precess out of control—spotted the pattern of craters close to his hidden airlock. It was still there. Wheeler hadn't found his base . . . yet. He thanked the lucky stars that surrounded him.

Another jump down—

—two meters above the surface. He let gravity pull him and settled upon the sterile soil. Too weak to stand, he crawled into the shadow of a crater, opened the airlock, and cycled through.

Jack ripped off his helmet and inhaled the cold, crisp air in gulps. He made it. Did Wheeler know where he was? Would he destroy the moon as well? Jack couldn't stop shivering.

He took the elevator to the control center.

Panda waved a gun at Jack when he entered, then lowered it. She stepped closer to him.

All the virtual interfaces in the command center were dampened. He wasn't sure if she'd embrace or shoot him.

A single window was open—a view of Earth, partially occluded by shadow; the poles were clear and crystalline white, but the Pacific was thick with clouds. Hawaii sat in the eye of a volcanic hurricane the color of rust.

The monk sat cross-legged staring out the window, holding his prayer beads and chanting softly.

Bruner watched, too. He held a paper cup of steaming black coffee. He didn't look drunk anymore. He looked like he wished he was, though.

Zero's cousin, Safa, leaned against the far wall. She strangled her black military beret inside her fist and glowered at Panda.

"I am pleased to see you," Panda whispered. She smiled, but the affectation vanished as quickly as it appeared, like it might have been painful. She kissed him, then pulled away.

The gun she held had belonged to Safa.

"What happened in Amsterdam?" Panda asked.

"That's what I'd like to know."

"We must discuss your selection of people to rescue," Panda said and glanced at Safa.

"Later," Jack said. "I have to talk"—he nodded to the screen and the ships in orbit—"to them."

"Talk?" Bruner jerked and spilled coffee over his fingers. "Send a signal and they'll pinpoint this location. You want to die?"

Jack opened a link to the isotope circuit. "This signal originates inside the space of a superheavy element. There's no location, as we think of it, to pinpoint."

"Can you stop what is happening?" Safa asked and took a step toward him.

"I don't know."

"I shall pray for Allah to guide you." She sat next to the monk, who offered her his beads. She shook her head, then bowed toward Mecca on Earth and quietly chanted alongside him.

"This will require more than prayer," Panda whispered.

Jack reached into the interface and pulled out one-way mirror shards, reflective from his side, jagged and dangerous along the edges. It would let the others see in, but not interfere—part of Jack's new policy of no secrets. They had a stake in this conversation with Wheeler. Everyone did.

He piped in the light from the decaying isotope, ultramarine and amethyst and turquoise frequencies that filled the air with vibrating lines and shimmering static.

Jack separated strands, braided them into a mathematical series, then connected that fiber to an open link. Through the window scrolled the electronic handshake:

HELLOJACKHELLOJACKHELLOJACKHELLOJACKHELLOJACK

"Hello, Wheeler," he whispered, then submerged, expanded the bandwidth, and wriggled into another bubble.

The place gave Jack déjà vu. It was Earth; he recognized the color of the sky and setting sun. The hills and the ocean at his back were maddeningly familiar.

Jack pushed, but he sensed no directories or command interfaces.

He walked through tea gardens, past fountains, and onto a concourse where vendors sold ripe oranges and white wine and souvenir paper fans.

In the center of this park was a lavish tower decorated with jewels. There was a Greek palace across a distant lagoon, a Turkish mosque surrounded by palm trees, a four-story Buddhist temple, and a gilt-trimmed dome under which an orchestra played *The Stars and Stripes Forever*. Flags fluttered atop poles, colors from every nation. It was as if the Earth had been compressed and transported here.

Men appeared in swallow-tailed tuxedoes and women wearing long gowns and fur coats wrapped tightly around them to ward off the chilled fog that rolled in from the harbor.

Wheeler stepped from the encroaching mist and strolled up to Jack. He wore a black suit with white scarf and a chesterfield overcoat the color of empty space. He clapped Jack on the shoulder. "My boy, I thought you would never arrive."

Jack closed his fist, collected his hate, all the loathing he had for the alien who was burning his world . . . then he took a deep breath, let it go, and relaxed. He couldn't outmuscle Wheeler. He had to outthink him.

"How glad can you be to see me alive?" Jack asked and squinted with his dead eye. "You're trying to kill me. It's you in orbit, isn't it?"

"Of course we are in orbit, but certainly not to kill you." Wheeler waved his hand extravagantly. "Look about. Would I go to this trouble for a man I wanted dead? Do you not recognize it?"

"Should I?" What kind of game was Wheeler playing this time?

"This is your beloved San Francisco. The Panama-Pacific Exposition of 1915."

Jack shook his head.

"It celebrates the opening of the Panama Canal and the rebuilding of the city after the great quake and fire."

"Rebuild?" Jack snorted a laugh. "Are you suggesting that the Earth can be rebuilt after you're done with it?"

"Oh no," Wheeler said and smiled with teeth too white to be real. "Nothing of this glamour will survive. The Greek Rotunda lasted for decades as a museum, then went underwater with the rest of the city. All this beauty, in the past and in the present, all so hideously temporary. Is that why you treasure it so?"

Wheeler didn't wait for his answer; he walked down the concourse, past displays of electric lights and merchants selling stuffed figs from Baghdad, fried bat from the Spice Islands, and white Syrian cherries.

Jack followed. He paused by a booth that proclaimed: NUMER- OLOGY—WHAT DOES YOUR NAME MEAN? DISCOVER THE SECRETS OF THE NUMBER ZERO! Upon a table lay pamphlets that had so- phisticated mathematical expansions and theorems.

"Come," Wheeler said. "I did not mean for you to become distracted, only amazed at our creation."

Jack took a flier and shoved it into his pocket. "You're de- stroying my world. You bet your ass I'm amazed."

"That is what I like about you, Jack. Attitude and bravado. You never allow yourself to be backed into a corner. Always ready to bargain." Wheeler strolled to a wooden bench. It faced a golden-globe fountain lit from beneath with red spotlights. "This will do."

Jack sat next to him. "I've got a lot of questions."

"I have time for questions," Wheeler said. He took out two cigars, offered one to Jack, and when he declined, lit one for himself.

"What can I trade you to leave the Earth alone?"

Wheeler examined the ember at the tip of his cigar, then re- plied, "As much as I would enjoy bartering with you, there will be no trades today. My purpose, to use the colloquial expression, is a hostile takeover."

"Of Earth?"

Wheeler laughed and slapped his knee. "Your world had little to offer. The few sciences and arts of interest, we have already taken." He turned to Jack. "You misunderstand. We want you."

Jack opened his mouth—stopped himself. If he kept quiet, he might be able to figure how all the pieces fit together. "I'll take that cigar now, if you don't mind."

"Excellent." Wheeler removed the Mariposa cigar from his vest pocket. It was already lit and smoldering.

Jack puffed. "You gave others the gateway." That was a guess, but how else had Isabel and China built theirs?

"Yes," Wheeler replied. Smoke lingered around his mouth.

"To slow the world. To make us destroy ourselves."

"You comprehend, then, Jack. You are practically one of us."

Us. The word sent a chill down his spine. How many of "us" were there? Maybe Wheeler didn't represent a single race of aliens. Maybe they were a collection of hustlers and con artists. Businessmen.

"One person," Wheeler said, "with one gateway might take decades to appreciably slow the rotation of your world."

"Especially when the gateway you gave me only works on Earth."

"Naturally we couldn't allow you access to the universe, nor could we allow your species to continue their unrestricted use of isotope communication." Wheeler's eyebrows cocked asymmetrically. "Rumors could be spread of us, and valuable information might be given away for free."

Then he didn't know . . . ? Jack squelched that thought, enveloped it with exponential walls. Wheeler believed Jack was trapped on Earth. He was too confident that no one could have circumvented his lockout in the gateway.

"But the world didn't slow fast enough for you," Jack said.

"Not after you reneged on our deal." Wheeler's eyes darkened from sparkling blue to indigo to jet.

"That was no deal. It was extortion."

Wheeler ignored him. "Your poor ethics are no surprise to us. Many of our agents initially display such hesitation." He set his hand on Jack's shoulder. "Eventually, though, you shall come to appreciate the beauty of our business."

He stared into Jack; Wheeler's eyes filled with formulas and diagrams and sciences that were part wonder, part terror, and part madness. In his fathomless orbs floated a hundred thousand dead worlds.

Jack blew smoke into his face. "So what about those free gateways?"

"Yes." Wheeler blinked and the worlds vanished. "We were contacted by others of your world, Ms. Isabel and Mr. Reno. They wanted so desperately to trade for gateways. So we did."

"Knowing they'd kill one another and take the rest of the Earth along with them."

"That was what we had hoped." Wheeler leaned back and crossed his legs. "Regrettably, not fast enough, so we helped them. Thrice."

Jack was about to guess Wheeler's "help" were those ships in orbit, robbing Earth's rotational energy, but there were hundreds of them. Not three . . .

"Three," Jack whispered. "Shanghai, Chicago, and Austin. The three neutron bombs?"

"Alas, even that did not provoke them to annihilate one another. Your race, I'm afraid, has too much patience and want for peace." Wheeler blew three smoke rings. "As long as it was just you, Jack, we might have continued to trade. But too many people know of us. Surely you can appreciate the dangers of having too many business partners? There are potential data leaks and loose ends that must be seen to."

"Loose ends? Billions of people killed?" Jack wanted to crush his cigar into Wheeler's virtual face.

Wheeler shrugged. "You make it sound like such a bad thing. Your economy is a mirror for what we do: corporations with their takeovers and mergers. It makes the survivors better. It's evolution. Progress. It is only good business."

"Your business. Not mine."

"Do not be difficult, Jack. There is no choice. Tell us where you are hiding before the remainder of your world is extinguished."

He couldn't let the world be killed. There had to be another way. A way to fight back.

There must have been a subliminal leak from Jack; Wheeler answered him: "Do you think there was ever a chance of escaping? Had we desired, the Earth could be moved into the sun in the blink of an eye. The Armstrong Colonies and the ships in orbit—they were for your benefit."

"How's jeopardizing my life benefiting me?"

Wheeler waved his cigar dismissively. "You had a gateway;

we assumed you would have the sense to move out of harm's way. We wanted to give you an opportunity to consider the ramifications."

"All for me? To give me a chance to think it over? To get off the sinking ship like the rat that I am?" Jack felt like he had stepped onto an elevator, accelerated down, while his gut stayed on the ground floor. "It's not economics you're asking me to be a part of, it's genocide. The answer's no."

Wheeler sighed. "We acquire technology not merely as a matter of economics, Jack, but for survival. I do not expect you to fully appreciate how addicted one can become to new discoveries and the hyperacceleration it induces in our culture. But without it, we would die."

"You ever hear of trade or diplomacy? Ever try doing the scientific research yourselves?"

"It has been attempted and failed." Wheeler looked down, almost sad, then he met Jack's gaze again. "I am afraid our aggressive business practices are the only ones that meet our appetites. As I said, I did not expect you to fully understand . . . yet."

But Jack did. Humans did the same thing on a smaller scale. It was easier to steal or built on another's discovery than invent something new. Was that laziness or greed or maybe just the most effective survival strategy? Jack couldn't believe that.

"Why invite me to join your little club?"

"By our estimates, you contacted us three hundred years before you should have, traded with me, and with others whose caution was legend. You were born to communicate."

It was Jack's turn to laugh. It had taken the enzyme—having his DNA removed and modified—just so he could communicate with himself and realize that he was more than a middleman.

"You are the best agent we have found in millennia." Wheeler stood and held out his hand. "Do not waste this opportunity. There are technologies waiting to be taken. Wonders you cannot even imagine. Come with me."

Jack stared at the alien's hand; it was a mirror-image copy of his own.

When he had been at the Académe, all he had wanted was tenure, to escape the money-grabbing and power-positioning. Then he embraced the system he hated, became part of a multinational corporation, surpassed his wildest dreams of wealth and power . . . and never thought twice of what he was doing to the rest of the world.

And now? Wheeler had offered him a deal that made DNAegis look like small change.

He slapped Wheeler's hand out of his way, stood, and said, "No thanks."

"The universe is filled with others willing to serve. Yet, none are as good a middleman as you. I ask you to reconsider."

" 'Good' men don't murder for a profit. My answer's still no."

"It would have been a glorious transaction . . . but I sense your resolve." Wheeler shook his head. "Such a waste of talent." He turned and walked slowly down the concourse.

Jack pushed. There was the barest hint of an interface. Wheeler was leaving. Twentieth-century San Francisco faded. The focus in Jack's dead, left eye blurred.

"Goodbye," Wheeler whispered, then vanished into the fog.

Jack stood alone in the dissolving bubble world.

"Goodbye?" He uncrumpled the pamphlet he had taken from the numerology booth and downloaded the information. "That's what you think."

This is the way the world ended.

Jack watched from the moon: the Earth was an abstract portrait of weather driven to unnatural ferocity: swirling cyclones and lightning that flashed from pole to pole, silver and charcoal and soot-colored clouds, plumes and eddies and whirlpools of chlorine green and sulfur yellow.

The atmosphere disappeared; triangular sections vanished one by one. Condensed or blasted or gatewayed away. Oceans and rivers boiled off—leaving the ground bare.

Tectonic plates cracked into a thousand eggshell fragments;

the Pacific plate first, then North America. Ruptures spread across the world.

Through those fissures, magma swelled and welled and covered the land with molten stone. The platelets submerged, dissolved, until the face of the Earth glowed with the red gold of liquid iron and silicon, like it had when it had first condensed from stardust.

Nothing survived.

No trace of human civilization. No city. Every country and continent pushed under flowing rock. Buried and forever gone.

Jack disconnected and let the command center settle back into his perceptions. The end of the world. Billions dead. He wished for a real window—to fix the reality of what had happened—to make certain it wasn't just one more fantastic image in a lifetime of bubble-induced illusions.

He regretted everything he had ever done . . . felt a noose of guilt tighten around him. Not guilt over the lost lives, but guilt because he was happy to have made it out in one piece.

And deep within his center: a fragment of hope.

The old monk stared at the angry molten Earth. He set his prayer beads down, then said, "Suffering has ever been present in the world. Now . . . a bitter end." He got up, stretched his creaking bones, then whispered, "So it goes."

Safa continued her prayers, faster and louder.

Panda went to her, then set a hand on Safa's shoulder. "Stop," she whispered with surprising compassion. "There is no more Mecca to pray toward."

Safa ceased and replied, "This cannot be God's will."

"God had nothing to do with this," Jack answered.

Bruner drained his coffee, crushed the paper cup, and threw it at the image of Earth. "Let's save the religious talk for Sunday. Did you really contact those aliens? Holy shit, Jack. Will they come after us next?"

Safa rose, moved to Bruner in two steps, and struck him so

hard his head whipped back and he fell over. "Silence. I shall not tolerate your blasphemy."

"Let's not kill each other," Jack said to her, then looked at Bruner. "We have more important things to take care of."

"Things?" Bruner said. He moved his jaw, checking if it was broken. He stayed on the flexgel floor. "Things? You must be kidding. Look at what's left of the world! There's nothing left to take care of."

"Power," Panda said, "then air, water, and food, in that order. I'll organize a search of the Michelson Observatory. There may be survivors." She told Bruner, "You will monitor the Earth and lunar orbits for any alien ships."

"A good idea," Jack said, "but not exactly what I had in mind." He opened a window and let mathematics scroll across the display.

"What's that?" Bruner asked, sitting up, but keeping one eye on Safa.

"You saw the booth in the park? And the pamphlet I took? This"—he gestured to the window—"is the secret meaning of zero."

Bruner squinted at it. "Two series expansions of functions that cancel one another exactly. It's nothing. Zero."

"Unless," Jack replied, "the terms in those series are tampered with and a signal is piggybacked onto them. Someone eavesdropped on my conversation with Wheeler. It's not meaningless. But it is Zero."

Jack linked to the isotope. "Get ready for anything," he whispered to Panda, then set up the one-way mirrors as he had done before.

He let bands of blue radiation filter into the command center, caught them, thickened the lines of light, and wove a web whose center stretched into an infinite tunnel.

There was a connection.

Jack stood under a canopy of aspen and pine that dappled the ground with shadow. Prism pine needles fractured the light into rainbows; leaves glowed translucent gold and vermilion and jade. The patterns of illumination appeared as mounted knights that chased serpentine dragons, saints that marched in procession, and the hand of God reaching out toward an outstretched Adam. Stained glass in a cathedral bioengineered by Zero.

He touched the trunk of a sugar maple. The bark flaked away under his fingers, revealing amber tubes that gurgled and pulsed with sap.

Vines twisted across the canopy; metallic morning glory opened and closed; mouthlike petals hissed perfumes and copper pollen that attracted glistening silver bees. Spiders wove silk masterpieces of geometric precision: star charts and the double helix strands of DNA.

Jack knew Zero had a predisposition for twisting nature into whatever struck his fancy. That's what gene witches did. But why this heavy-handed metaphor?

He walked for a while. The forest opened into a meadow: strands of blond grass and flowers that shuddered in the breeze. Jack crouched and touched the earth. It was too level, and there wasn't a stone or twig or animal dropping. He gathered a handful of the stuff. Granulated plastic.

Upon a distant hill was an illusion of the Academé. Coit Tower gleamed golden, absorbing the rays of the rising sun. It looked like Camelot. He wished it was real.

"Jack."

He turned to the familiar voice.

"Zero."

The gene witch wore a simple blue shirt and cotton trousers with grass-stained knees. He embraced Jack. "My friend, it is good to see you."

Jack could have hugged him forever. Someone else had survived.

But suspicion blended with that relief. How had Zero escaped? Could this be another of Wheeler's tricks? Jack pulled away and asked, "You're not surprised to see me?"

"Never surprised. Never with you." Zero's brown eyes sparkled and Jack heard distant laughter as the gene witch's joy leaked through the interface. "I was confident you would get my message. I was uncertain, however, that you would use it after our last conversation. So much was left unsaid in Santa Sierra. I am relieved that you still count me a friend."

"Are you?" Jack crossed his arms. "Where the hell are you? Not on Earth."

"That," Zero whispered, "is the one thing you must not ask."

"Of course." Distance was meaningless because of gateway technology and isotope communication. Location was everything; it had to be kept a secret at all costs.

Jack glanced about, quick, stretched his senses over the engineered landscape, through glen and forest, soared over streams and mirror-calm lakes, valleys and granite pinnacles, searching for another presence.

"What is it?" Zero asked.

Jack snapped back to the meadow. "If Wheeler eavesdrops on us like you did to him, he'll know I've unlocked his gateway. He'll know I'm still alive. A loose end that needs to be taken care of."

"Worry not." Zero set his warm hand on Jack's shoulder. "I had the exact set of frequencies to access his signal. There are infinite combinations. He will not find this transmission."

"Unless he found your clue, too. Let's keep this short until I can devise a secure encryption scheme."

"As you wish." Zero lowered his eyes, then asked, "Has the Earth perished?"

Where was Zero that he hadn't seen the end? Jack knew he didn't want to answer, but he asked anyway: "Are you outside the solar system?"

Zero frowned. "Yes. Your Uncle Reno sold me the technique to unlock the gateway's destination vector."

Jack kicked the synthetic soil. "He's not my uncle, and there wouldn't be enough energy left in the Earth for that magnitude of jump."

"Our world is not the only spinning body."

Other spinning bodies? Like other planets? Clever. Zero could have jumped to Mars, then used all of its rotation. The gateway was more efficient the longer the jump. And if Zero plugged the leaks wired into the gateway—he could have made a series of jumps, using different planets along the way. He could be anywhere.

Maybe that was a trick Jack could use.

"So why pick this place to meet? It feels like your work."

"These are my most recent creations, all renditions of working products."

"Not all." Jack nodded to the hill and the phantom Académe.

"That as well. I took it during the earthquake. When Santa Sierra collapsed, no one noticed what happened to the tiny island."

Jack calculated the energy needed. Those last decelerations of the world began to make sense. "Congratulations. By moving the Académe, you caused floods and earthquakes and volcanic eruptions."

"I do not deny it."

Jack glanced at Coit Tower. He was happy it had made it unscathed, but it wasn't worth the cost. "What about all the people you killed?"

"They were dead already, Jack." Zero's eyes clouded over, and the temperature dropped. "I told you the end was coming. Wheeler had to kill us. It was clear."

He scrutinized the gene witch. What was he? Human? Jack doubted it. Had he altered himself beyond Wheeler's enzyme? Those sixty-four chromosome pairs he had shown Jack, was that Zero's vision of perfection?

Jack reached out with his mind—the air thickened and Jack slowed; it was full of butterflies, flashes of pearlescent silver and powder blue and feather antennae and curled proboscises and cerulean dots—all in a whirlpool. There was nothing in the center. Maybe the entire collective cloud of fluttering bewitchment was Zero.

Whatever it was, Jack didn't recognize anything human about it. He pulled back.

"What have you done to yourself, Zero?"

"Something rich and strange." He smiled. "One day you may discover for yourself."

"No thanks."

Zero raised his arms, turned to his forest, then said, "I have saved seventeen thousand plant and four thousand animal species from the Earth."

"Big of you." Was he playing Noah? Or did he just want raw genetic stock for his experiments? Jack no longer knew, or trusted, Zero. He felt like he was dealing with Wheeler . . . or Isabel.

"Wait a second, Zero. You inserted a message into Wheeler's transmission, so you had to access the frequencies that flash through the isotope."

"Yes. Of course."

Zero might have duplicated his own isotope. But where did he get the mathematical keys to decrypt that signal? Jack was the only one who knew how. The only one, that is, before his files got hacked into at DNAegis.

He smelled apricot and champagne perfume. "You weren't the only one to escape."

"Naturally." Zero pointed across the field.

Isabel trod through the grass in her khaki shorts, white silk blouse, and pith helmet. She had an elephant rifle slung over her shoulder. Her hair was braided with fiber optics that winked on and off. With skin so white, she reminded Jack of the alabaster Goddess of Democracy . . . or her evil cousin.

If she was here, was this a trap? They couldn't trace his location through the isotope circuit, but they might be able to lock him in silent Möbius loops or kill him with his own fear like Panda could.

He relaxed. Panda and the others were watching. They'd pull the plug if anything happened. Still, Jack moved to the other side of Zero when Isabel got close.

She gave Zero a kiss on his cheek. "I am pleased to see you

gene witch." She leveled her cool emerald eyes upon Jack. "And I am pleased to see you."

"I doubt that." Jack's emotional walls slid unconsciously into place, slid over barriers that Isabel had already erected.

"We have all made mistakes." She ran a ruby fingernail down Zero's arm, then gave his hand a squeeze. "I have forgiven Zero for his defection. And I have forgiven your sabotage."

Jack doubted that, too, but he kept his mouth shut and sucked in his emotions. "OK. So we're one big happy family." He did not try to mask the sarcasm that seeped into his voice. "What's the deal?"

Zero said, "Jack has expressed concerns about eavesdropping parties. Perhaps we should get to the heart of the matter and reconvene when a secure channel has been constructed."

"Agreed," Isabel said.

In the field, a round table and three chairs sprouted; their roots reached into the plastic soil. The three of them sat.

Isabel held out her hand, palm up. Upon it appeared motes of lazulite light that cavorted and blurred, vanished and reappeared in arcs and spiral trajectories.

"I've cobbled together a blend of the single-electron microprocessor and the isotope circuitry," she said. "This is a subquantum data processor. Quadrillions of connected units that hover on the edge of existence within a single top quark."

Jack stared into the sparkles and saw the data behind it: the mathematical theorem he had traded for—and Isabel had stolen—a new superheavy isotope, and electronics that used scattering to pierce the realm of the subquantum.

It was magic. Jack could have never cooked that up. Even for Isabel, it was a wonder.

She closed her hand and severed the link before he could see more.

Zero waved his hand over the table and butterflies landed here—not the sixty-four pairs he had shown Jack in Santa Sierra, but forty-eight pairs. "I offer my series four enzyme. It selectively provides beneficial mutations in offspring, while suppressing congenital disorders. This will allow us to propagate within our limited gene pools."

How many people had Zero and Isabel spirited away . . . just how many humans were left in the universe?

Isabel nodded, then she turned to Jack and said, "Well, what can you offer?"

Jack's insides curdled.

Zero's message wasn't for friendship or help; it had been an invitation to do business.

"Everything I had in my head you got from Reno."

Isabel and Zero exchanged a glance, then she said, "Not true. When I last spoke with Wheeler, he was annoyed that you had not found him another client. A client whose frequency set he had entrusted to you."

Those were the frequencies Wheeler had shoved into Jack's hand. They were the calling card to another race, one that Wheeler had wanted Jack to locate. Wheeler had, unknowingly, given him something of value for free.

Zero and Isabel wanted those frequencies because there were infinite combinations in the noise. And unlike Wheeler's original message—those signals were extremely well hidden.

Had they embraced Wheeler's corporate-raiding philosophy? Were they going to play the same game he did: plundering worlds? Hadn't they learned anything?

Jack scratched his two day's worth of stubble, then shook his head. "Forget it."

Isabel let out an explosive breath. "Let's be civil about this Jack. If we're going to survive, we need to share resources One day Wheeler—or others like him—will find us. We have to be prepared. . . . And we may have to take advantage o others."

"You want me to talk to these aliens and get them to trade Maybe extract their location? I won't be your middleman again.

"Please reconsider," Zero said. "We need you."

Isabel had a point about Wheeler still being out there, bu dealing with her was like dealing with the devil. "I'll thin about it," he said. "Doesn't mean I'm agreeing to anything, though."

"Excellent." Zero clapped his hands over the buttlerflies and they scattered upon the breeze. "I must go." He nodded to Isabel, then said to Jack, "Do not linger. As you pointed out, we must secure this line." He gave Jack's shoulder a squeeze, then stood and walked into his forest of illusions.

"Goodbye, Zero." Jack wondered if he'd ever see him again.

Isabel traced the grain of the wood with her fingernail. "I suppose you want to ask a few questions?"

"Like why you betrayed me to the NSO? Like why you installed a back door into my office? No. I don't care anymore."

"Well, I've got a question for you." She set her hand flat on the table. "Why didn't you try to work with me?"

Jack corrected her: "You mean you and DeMitri."

She ignored that. "We accomplished so much, but we could have worked miracles if we had you. If you hadn't kept secrets from us. If you hadn't gone off playing Robin Hood."

"Like what exactly?"

"Like perhaps none of this would have happened."

Jack laughed and Isabel clenched her jaw.

"You have a lot to make up for," she whispered. "After Reno sold us your gateway information, it took every engineer at DNAegis working around the clock to build one. If you had been with us—if you hadn't stolen the damn thing in the first place— we could have gotten out of there faster. More lives could have been saved."

She was trying to manipulate him. Isabel got her gateway from Wheeler. The alien said he'd given it to her so she'd use it and destroy the world. Between Wheeler and her, he trusted the alien more.

"Save your breath," he said and stood.

"Wait, Jack." She got to her feet, too. "At least consider our offer. You stand to profit enormously by it, and despite our past, we have to work together. How long will it take Wheeler to find us? We have to do business."

He gazed at Isabel: perfect bone-white skin and copper hair. Beautiful Isabel. His friend, Isabel. Isabel, who helped him pass complex analysis. Isabel the betrayer. He had loved her . . . once. He was through with her.

"If I do business with you, it's going to be on my own terms. People will come first, not profits or power. It won't be business as usual."

Jack turned his back. "Like I said, I'll think about it. But for now, leave me the hell alone."

Zero and Isabel were probably light-years distant—not far enough, as far as he was concerned.

Jack slipped through the bubble and stepped back to the moon.

The dark circular room of the command center was full of active links. Panda connected with three simultaneously: directing welders to spot-fuse leaks, coaxing the backup oxygen recycler to function, and rerouting power conduits.

"We have experienced two moonquakes," she said without looking at Jack. "There is damage to the thermite reactor and three tunnels have collapsed."

"Are we safe?" he asked.

Panda worked a moment, then brushed her bangs from her eyes and answered, "Perhaps, but without the reactor, we cannot last more than three days."

Her eyelids were vivid with color again, soft swirls of steel and pink and tangerine. She was recovering from the enzyme. What would it turn her into? Another Isabel?

Jack reached out with his mind, and Panda paused in her thoughts; they sank into one another; his mind churned with the memories of the Santa Sierra tidal wave, Denver crushed, and the blackened *Zouwtmarkt;* Panda grieved for a sister lost, friends that she would never see again, and her miraculous country . . . gone. Their sorrow mingled; Jack tasted the salt of their tears, their guilt and anguish, combined. Whatever she was becoming, Jack trusted her.

"Snap out of it," Bruner said. He grabbed Jack's arm.

Safa wrenched Bruner's hand off Jack, then pushed the ex-professor against the curved wall.

She turned to Jack. "My cousin lives," she whispered. Safa's emotions were shielded behind barriers of cursive Arabic script, but Jack saw relief in her eyes nonetheless, and worry, too.

"It appears he is alive, but whether he's your cousin anymore . . . or if he's even human, I don't know."

The old monk sat on the flexgel floor and spooned rehydrated chicken à la king into his nearly toothless mouth.

These people he had saved, the people he was stuck with, they were an odd mix of religions and races and values. Not like the teams of professionals Zero and Isabel had undoubtedly taken. That suited Jack. His group was as normal as he was—which wasn't saying much. He had to get them to work together or, at least, get them not to murder each other.

"Are you going to do what they want?" Bruner asked. "Are you going to talk to those other aliens?"

Jack connected to the isotope circuit and static filled the room. The information was a shower of blue-silver sparks from deep inside the subquantum domain of the crystal. He let his mind wander. It was glistening wavelets upon a lake. It was a swarm of dragonflies iridescent in the summer sun and fireworks blossoming in the Fourth of July sky. It was snow falling in the moonlight.

He didn't know what to do.

Every aspect of business, every backstab and double cross . . . and the occasional fair deal—those were the essence of humanity. He couldn't escape it. He couldn't pretend they were only tools that he used. It was what Jack was.

Bruner whispered conspiratorially to the old monk, "I think he's lost it."

The old monk licked the plastic self-heating bowl clean, wiped his hands on his robe, then stood. "No," he replied. "It is only now being found."

Jack watched the static that looked like embers streaming skyward above a campfire. He waved his hand through it, scattering the bits.

If humans were destined to trade and make deals—he transformed the data so they appeared as constellations and galaxies—then humans belonged out there, among the stars. Where the action was.

He smelled licorice; Panda had left her emergencies and stood close to him.

"We might be able to survive." She let her whispering uncertainties spill into his mind. "But survive to do what?"

The monk came to Jack and said, "You have the key. Think. Look!"

Jack stared into the stars, rearranged them into spectral bands, and grasped the jagged frequencies in his right hand—Zeus with his bolts of lightning.

The universe was a place where the successful eluded detection or could move at a moment's notice. There were huge technological jumps and societies that integrated that science with astonishing speed. Wild, chaotic civilizations that rose and fell in a heartbeat. Darwinian competition, survival of the fittest, and natural selection exponentially magnified.

But natural selection also favored cooperation: primitive cells clustered together for protection and to specialize; honeybees gathered nectar and built hives; so perhaps humans could relearn how to work with one another as well.

Communication was the key.

Jack had cracked codes, solved mathematical riddles, and unraveled topological knots, but words were a puzzle that he barely understood. It was the greatest mystery he ever had to answer. What did people mean when they said hello to you? Maybe he'd never know.

"There are other civilizations out there," he told Panda. "Zero, and Isabel, and maybe even Reno, too. We're going to rebuild; that's what we're going to do. We're going to exchange technologies and cultures and ideas. We're going to work together for mutual profit. We're going to grow. Prosper. . . . And one day even take on Wheeler."

Jack listened to the static hissing between the stars. He scanned the countless voices for new signals in the noise.

"What will we do?" He turned to her. "We've just gone into business."

We hope you've enjoyed this Avon Eos book. As part of our mission to give readers the best science fiction and fantasy being written today, the following pages contain a glimpse into the fascinating worlds of a select group of Avon Eos authors.

In the following pages experience the latest in cutting-edge sf from Eric S. Nylund, Maureen F. McHugh, and Susan R. Matthews, and experience the wondrous fantasy realms of Martha Wells, Andre Norton, Dave Duncan, and Raymond E. Feist.

SIGNAL TO NOISE

Eric S. Nylund

Jack watched his office walls sputter malfunctioning mathematical symbols and release a flock of passenger pigeons; his nose was tickled with the odor of eucalyptus. Inside, the air rippled with synthetic pleasure and the taste of vanilla.

"I need to get in there," he told the government agent who blocked the doorway.

"No admittance," the agent said, "until we've completed our investigation on the break-in."

Puzzles, illegalities, and dilemmas stuck to Jack—from which he then, usually, extracted himself. That gave him the dual reputation of a troubleshooter and a troublemaker. But the only thing he was dead sure about today was the "troublemaking and sticking" part of that assessment.

The agent stepped in front of Jack, obscuring what the others were doing in there. National Security Office agents: goons with big guns bulging under their bulletproof suits. And no arguing with them.

Today's trouble was the stuff you saw coming, but couldn't do a thing about. Like standing in front of a tidal wave.

Jack hoped his office *had* been broken into, that this wasn't an NSO fishing trip. There were secrets in the bubble circuitry of his office that had to stay hidden. Things that could make his troubles multiply.

"I'll wait until you're done then."

The agent glanced at his notepad and a face materialized: Jack's with his sandy hair pulled into a ponytail and his hazel eyes bloodshot. You have an immediate interview with Mr. De-Mitri. Bell Communications Center, sublevel three."

Jack's stomach curdled. "Interview" was a polite word that meant they'd use invasive probes and mnemonic shadows to pry open his mind. Jack had worked with DeMitri and the NSO before. He knew all their nasty tricks.

"Thanks," Jack lied, turned from the illusions in his office, and walked down the hallway.

From the fourth floor of the mathematics building, he took the arched bridge path that linked to the island's outer seawall. Not the most direct route, but he needed time to figure a way out of this jam.

Cold night air and salt spray whipped around him. Electromagnetic pollution filtered through the hardware in his skull: a hundred conversations on the cell networks, and a patchwork of thermal images from the West-AgCo satellite overhead.

Past the surf and across the San Joaquin Sea, the horizon glowed with fluorescent light. Jack regretted that he'd stepped on other people to get where he was. Maybe that's why trouble always came looking for him. Because he had it coming. Or because he was soft enough to let little things get to him. Like guilt.

Not that there was any other way to escape the mainland. Everyone there competed for lousy jobs and stabbed each other in the back, sometimes literally, to get ahead. He had clawed his way out with an education—then cheated his way into Santa Sierra's Académe of Pure and Applied Sciences.

But it wasn't perfect here, either. There were cutthroat maneuvers for grants, and Jack had bent the law working both for corporations *and* the government. All of which had helped his financial position, but hadn't improved his conscience.

He had to get tenure so he could relax and pursue his own projects. There had to be more to life than chasing money and grabbing power.

Now those dreams were on hold.

His office had been ransacked, and the NSO had got too curious, too fast, for his liking. Had they been keeping an eye on him all along?

He took the stairs off the seawall and descended into a red-tiled courtyard.

In the center of the square stood Coit Tower. The structure was sixty meters of fluted concrete that had been hoisted off the ocean floor. It had survived the San Francisco quake in the early twenty-first century, then lay underwater for fifty years—yet was still in one piece.

Jack hoped he was as tough.

The whitewashed turret was lit from beneath with halogen light, harsh and brilliant against the night sky. Undeniably real.

Jack preferred the illusions of his office; sometimes reality was too much for him to stomach.

No way out of this interview sprang to mind, and he had stalled as long as he could. The crystal-and-steel geodesic dome of the Bell Communications Center was across the courtyard. Jack marched into the building, took the elevator to sublevel three, and entered the concert amphitheater.

On the stage between gathered velvet curtains, the NSO had set up their bubble.

Normal bubbles simulated reality. Inside, a web of inductive signals and asynchronous quantum imagers tapped the operator's neuralware. It allowed access to a world of data, it teased hunches from your subconscious, and solidified your guesses into theories. They made you think faster. Maybe think better.

But this wasn't a normal bubble. And it was never meant to help Jack think. It was designed for tricks.

THE DEATH OF THE NECROMANCER

Martha Wells

She was in the old wing of the house now. The long hall became a bridge over cold silent rooms thirty feet down and the heavy stone walls were covered by tapestry or thin veneers of exotic wood instead of lathe and plaster. There were banners and weapons from long-ago wars, still stained with rust and blood, and ancient family portraits dark with the accumulation of years of smoke and dust. Other halls branched off, some leading to even older sections of the house, others to odd little cul-de-sacs lit by windows with an unexpected view of the street or the surrounding buildings. Music and voices from the ballroom grew further and further away, as if she was at the bottom of a great cavern, hearing echoes from the living surface.

She chose the third staircase she passed, knowing the servants would still be busy toward the front of the house. She caught up her skirts—black gauze with dull gold striped over black satin and ideal for melding into shadows—and quietly ascended. She gained the third floor without trouble but going up to the fourth passed a footman on his way down. He stepped to the wall to let her have the railing, his head bowed in respect and an effort not to see who she was, ghosting about Mondollot House and obviously on her way to an indiscreet meeting. He would remember her later, but there was no help for it.

The hall at the landing was high and narrower than the others, barely ten feet across. There were more twists and turns to find her way through, stairways that only went up half a floor, and dead ends, but she had committed a map of the house to memory in preparation for this and so far it seemed accurate.

Madeline found the door she wanted and carefully tested the handle. It was unlocked. She frowned. One of Nicholas Valiarde's rules was that if one was handed good fortune one should first stop to ask the price, because there usually was a price. She eased the door open, saw the room beyond lit only by reflected moonlight from undraped windows. With a cautious glance up and down the corridor, she pushed it open enough to see the whole room. Book-filled cases, chimney piece of carved marble with a caryatid-supported mantle, tapestry-back chairs, pier glasses, and old sideboard heavy with family plate. A deal table supporting a metal strongbox. *Now we'll see,* she thought. She took a candle from the holder on the nearest table, lit it from the gas sconce in the hall, then slipped inside and closed the door behind her.

The undraped windows worried her. This side of the house faced Ducal Court Street and anyone below could see the room was occupied. Madeline hoped none of the Duchess's more alert servants stepped outside for a pipe or a breath of air and happened to look up. She went to the table and upended her reticule next to the solid square shape of the strongbox. Selecting the items she needed out of the litter of scent vials, jewelry she had decided not to wear, and a faded string of Aderassi luck-beads, she set aside snippers of chicory and thistle, a toadstone, and a paper screw containing salt.

Their sorcerer-advisor had said that the ward that protected Mondollot House from intrusion was an old and powerful one. Destroying it would take much effort and be a waste of a good spell. Circumventing it temporarily would be easier and far less likely to attract notice, since wards were invisible to anyone except a sorcerer using gascoign powder in his eyes or the new Aether-Glasses invented by the Parscian wizard Negretti. The toadstone itself held the necessary spell, dormant and harmless, and in its current state invisible to the familiar who guarded the main doors. The salt sprinkled on it would act as a catalyst and the special properties of the herbs would fuel it. Once all were placed in the influence of the ward's key object, the ward would withdraw to the very top of the house. When the potency of the salt wore off, it would simply slip back into place, probably before their night's work had been discovered. Madeline took her lock picks out of their silken case and turned to the strongbox.

There was no lock. She felt the scratches on the hasp and knew there had been a lock here recently, a heavy one, but it was nowhere to be seen. *Damn. I have a not-so-good feeling about this.* She lifted the flat metal lid.

Inside should be the object that tied the incorporeal ward to the corporeal bulk of Mondollot House. Careful spying and a few bribes had led them to expect not a stone as was more common, but a ceramic object, perhaps a ball, of great delicacy and age.

On a velvet cushion in the bottom of the strongbox were the crushed remnants of something once delicate and beautiful as well as powerful, nothing left now but fine white powder and fragments of cerulean blue. Madeline gave vent to an unlady-like curse and slammed the lid down. *Some bastard's been here before us.*

SCENT OF MAGIC

Andre Norton

That scent which made Willadene's flesh prickle was strong. But for a moment she had to blink to adjust her sight to the very dim light within the shop. The lamp which always burned all night at the other end of the room was the only glimmer here now, except for the sliver of daylight stretching out from the half-open door.

Willadene's sandaled foot nearly nudged a huddled shape on the floor—Halwice? Her hands flew to her lips, but she did not utter that scream which filled her throat. Why, she could not tell but that it was necessary to be quiet now was like an order laid upon her.

Her eyes were drawn beyond that huddled body to a chair which did not belong in the shop at all but had been pulled from the inner room. In that sat the Herbmistress, unmoving and silent. Dead—?

Willadene's hands were shaking, but somehow she pulled herself around that other body on the floor toward where one of the strong lamps, used when one was mixing powders, sat. Luckily the strike light was also there, and after two attempts she managed to set spark to the wick.

With the lamp still in hands which quivered, the girl swung around to face that silent presence in the chair. Eyes stared back at her, demanding eyes. No, Halwice lived but something held her in thrall and helpless. There were herbs which could do that in forbidden mixture, but Halwice never dealt with such.

Those eyes— Willadene somehow found a voice which was only a whisper.

"What—?" she began.

The eyes were urgent as if sight could write a message on the very air between them. They moved—from the girl to the half-open door and then back with an urgency Willadene knew she must answer. But how— Did Halwice want her to summon help?

"Can you"—she was reaching now for the only solution she could think of—"answer? Close your eyes once—"

Instantly the lids dropped and then rose again. Willadene drew a deep breath, almost of relief. By so much, then, she knew they could still communicate.

"Do I go for Doctor Raymonda?" He was the nearest of the medical practitioners who depended upon Halwice for their drugs.

The eyelids snapped down, arose, and fell again.

"No?" Willadene tried to hold the lamps steady. She had near forgotten the body on the floor.

She stared so intensely as if she could force the answer she needed out of the Herbmistress. Now she noted that the other's gaze had swept beyond her and was on the floor. Once more the silent woman blinked twice with almost the authority of an order. Willadene made a guess.

"Close the door?" That quick, single affirmative blink was her answer. She carefully edged about the body to do just that. Halwice did not want help from outside—but what evil had happened here? And was the silent form on the floor responsible for the Herbmistress's present plight?

With the door shut some instinct made the girl also, one-handedly as she held the lamp high, slide the bolt bar across it, turning again to find Halwice's gaze fierce and intent on her. The Herbmistress blinked. Yes, she had been right—Halwice wanted no one else here.

Then that gaze turned floorward, as far as nature would let the eyes move, to fasten on the body. Willadene carefully set the lamp down beside the inert stranger and then knelt.

It was a man lying facedown. His clothing was traveler's leather and wool as if he were just in from some traders' caravan. Halwice dealt often with traders, spices, and strange roots; even crushed clays of one sort or another arrived regularly here. But what had happened—?

Willadene's years of shifting iron pots and pans and dealing with Jacoba's oversize aids to cooking had made her stronger than her small, thin body looked. She was able to roll the stranger over.

Under his hand his flesh was cool, and she could see no wound or hurt. It was as if he had been struck down instantly by one of those weird powers which were a part of stories told to children.

THE GILDED CHAIN
A Tale of the King's Blades

Dave Duncan

Durendal closed the heavy door silently and went to stand beside Prime, carefully not looking at the other chair.

"You sent for us, Grand Master?" Harvest's voice warbled slightly, although he was rigid as a pike, staring straight at the bookshelves.

"I did, Prime. His Majesty has need of a Blade. Are you ready to serve?"

Harvest spoke at last, almost inaudibly. "I am ready, Grand Master."

Soon Durendal would be saying those words. And who would be sitting in the second chair?

Who was there now? He had not looked. The edge of his eye hinted it was seeing a youngish man, too young to be the King himself.

"My lord," Grand Master said, "I have the honor to present Prime Candidate Harvest, who will serve you as your Blade."

As the two young men turned to him, the anonymous noble drawled, "The other one looks much more impressive. Do I have a choice?"

"You do not!" barked Grand Master, color pouring into his craggy face. "The King himself takes whoever is Prime."

"Oh, so sorry! Didn't mean to twist your dewlaps, Grand Master." He smiled vacuously. He was a weedy, soft-faced man in his early twenties, a courtier to the core, resplendent in crimson and vermilion silks trimmed with fur and gold chain. If the white cloak was truly ermine, it must be worth a fortune. His fairish beard came to a needle point and his mustache was a work of art. A fop. Who?

"Prime, this is the Marquis of Nutting, your future ward."

"Ward?" The Marquis sniggered. "You make me sound like a debutante, Grand Master. *Ward* indeed!"

Harvest bowed, his face ashen as he contemplated a lifetime guarding . . . whom? Not the King himself, not his heir, not a prince of the blood, not an ambassador traveling in exotic lands, not an important landowner out on the marches, not a senior minister, nor even—at worst—the head of one of the great conjuring orders. Here was no ward worth dying for, just a court dandy, a parasite. Trash.

Seniors spent more time studying politics than anything else except fencing. Wasn't the Marquis of Nutting the brother of the Countess Mornicade, the King's latest mistress? If so, then six months ago he had been the Honorable Tab Nillway, a younger son of a penniless baronet, and his only claim to importance was that he had been expelled from the same womb as one of the greatest beauties of the age. No report reaching Ironhall had ever hinted that he might have talent or ability.

"I am deeply honored to be assigned to your lordship," Harvest said hoarsely, but the spirits did not strike him dead for perjury.

Grand Master's displeasure was now explained. One of his precious charges was being thrown away to no purpose. Nutting was not important enough to have enemies, even at court. No man of honor would lower his standards enough to call out an upstart pimp—certainly not one who had a Blade prepared to die for him. But Grand Master had no choice. The King's will was paramount.

"We shall hold the binding tomorrow midnight, Prime," the old man snapped. "Make the arrangements, Second."

"Yes, Grand Master."

"Tomorrow?" protested the Marquis querulously. "There's ball at court tomorrow. Can't we just run through the rigmarol quickly now and be done with it?"

Grand Master's face was already dangerously inflamed, and that remark made the veins swell even more. "Not unless you wish to kill a man, my lord. You have to learn your part in the ritual. Both you and Prime must be purified by ritual and fasting."

Nutting curled his lip. "Fasting? How barbaric!"

"Binding is a major conjuration. You will be in some danger yourself."

If the plan was to frighten the court parasite into withdrawing, it failed miserably. He merely muttered, "Oh, I'm sure you exaggerate."

Grand Master gave the two candidates a curt nod of dismissal. They bowed in unison and left.

KRONDOR
The Betrayal

Raymond E. Feist

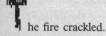he fire crackled.

Owyn Belefote sat alone in the night before the flames, wallowing in his personal misery. The youngest son of the Baron of Timons, he was a long way from home and wishing he was even farther away. His youthful features were set in a portrait of dejection.

The night was cold and the food scant, especially after having just left the abundance of his aunt's home in Yabon City. He had been hosted by relatives ignorant of his falling-out with his father, people who had reacquainted him over a week's visit with what he had forgotten about his home life: the companionship of brothers and sisters, the warmth of a night spent before the fire, conversation with his mother, and even the arguments with his father.

"Father," Owyn muttered. It had been less than two years since the young man had defied his father and made his way to Stardock, the island of mgicians located in the southern reaches of the Kingdom. His father had forbidden him his choice, to study magic, demanding Owyn should at least become a cleric of one of the more socially acceptable orders of priests. After all, they did magic as well, his father had insisted.

Owyn sighed and gathered his cloak around him. He had been so certain he would someday return home to visit his family, revealing himself as a great magician, perhaps a confidant of the legendary Pug, who had created the Academy at Stardock. Instead he found himself ill suited for the study required. He also had no love for the burgeoning politics of the place, with factions of students rallying around this teacher or that, attempting to turn the study of magic into another religion. He now knew he was, at best, a mediocre magician and would never amount to more, and no matter how much he wished to study magic, he lacked sufficient talent.

After slightly more than one year of study, Owyn had left Stardock, conceding to himself that he had made a mistake. Admitting such to his father would prove a far more daunting task— which was why he had decided to visit family in the distant province of Yabon before mustering the courage to return to the East and confront his sire.

A rustle in the bushes caused Owyn to clutch a heavy wooden staff and jump to his feet. He had little skill with weapons, having neglected that portion of his education as a child, but had developed enough skill with his quarterstaff to defend himself.

"Who's there?" he demanded.

From out of the gloom came a voice, saying, "Hello, the camp. We're coming in."

Owyn relaxed slightly, as bandits would be unlikely to warn him they were coming. Also, he was obviously not worth attacking, as he looked little more than a ragged beggar these days. Still, it never hurt to be wary.

Two figures appeared out of the gloom, one roughly Owyn's height, the other a head taller. Both were covered in heavy cloaks, the smaller of the two limping obviously.

The limping man looked over his shoulder, as if being followed, then asked, "Who are you?"

Owyn said, "Me? Who are you?"

The smaller man pulled back his hood, and said, "Locklear, I'm a squire to Prince Arutha."

Owyn nodded, "Sir, I'm Owyn, son of Baron Belefote."

"From Timons, yes, I know who your father is," said Locklear, squatting before the fire, opening his hands to warm them. He glanced up at Owyn. "You're a long way from home, aren't you?"

"I was visiting my aunt in Yabon," said the blond youth. "I'm now on my way home."

"Long journey," said the muffled figure.

"I'll work my way down to Krondor, then see if I can travel with a caravan or someone else to Salador. From there I'll catch a boat to Timons."

"Well, we could do worse than stick together until we reach LaMut," said Locklear, sitting down heavily on the ground. His cloak fell open, and Owyn saw blood on the young man's clothing.

"You're hurt," he said.

"Just a bit," admitted Locklear.

"What happened?"

"We were jumped a few miles north of here," said Locklear.

Owyn started rummaging through his travel bag. "I have something in here for wounds," he said. "Strip off your tunic."

Locklear removed his cloak and tunic, while Owyn took bandages and powder from his bag. "My aunt insisted I take this just in case. I thought it an old lady's foolishness, but apparently it wasn't."

Locklear endured the boy's ministrations as he washed the

wound, obviously a sword cut to the ribs, and winced when the powder was sprinkled upon it. Then as he bandaged the squire's ribs, Owyn said, "Your friend doesn't talk much, does he?"

"I am not his friend," answered Gorath. He held out his manacles for inspection. "I am his prisoner."

MISSION CHILD

Maureen F. McHugh

Listen," Aslak said, touching my arm.

I didn't hear it at first, then I did. It was a skimmer.

It was far away. Skimmers didn't land at night. They didn't even come at night. It had come to my message, I guessed.

Aslak got up and we ran out to the edge of the field behind the schoolhouse. Dogs started barking.

Finally we saw lights from the skimmer, strange green and red stars. They moved against the sky as if they had been shaken loose.

The lights came toward us for a long time. They got bigger and brighter, more than any star. It seemed as if they stopped, but the lights kept getting brighter. I finally decided that they were coming straight toward us.

Then we could see the skimmer in its own lights.

I shouted, and Aslak shouted, too, but the skimmer didn't seem to hear us. But then it turned and slowly curved around, the sound of it going farther away and then just hanging in the air. It got to where it had been before and came back. This time it came even lower and it dropped red lights. One. Two. Three.

Then a third time it came around and I wondered what it would do now. But this time it landed, the sound of it so loud that I could feel as well as hear it. It was a different skimmer than the one we always saw. It was bigger, with a belly like it was pregnant. It was white and red. It settled easily on the snow. Its engines, pointed down, melted snow underneath them.

And then it sat. Lights blinked. The red lights on the ground flickered. The dogs barked.

The door opened and a man called out to watch something but I didn't understand. My English is pretty good, one of the best in school, but I couldn't understand him.

Finally a man jumped down, and then two more men and two women.

I couldn't understand what anyone was saying in English. They asked me questions, but I just kept shaking my head. I was tired and now, finally, I wanted to cry.

"You called us. Did you call us?" one man said over and over until I understood.

I nodded.

"How?"

"Wanji give me . . . in my head . . ." I had no idea how to explain. I pointed to my ear. "Ayudesh is, is bad."

"Ask if he will die," Aslak said.

"Um, the teacher," I said, "um, it is bad?"

The woman nodded. She said something, but I didn't understand. "Smoke," she said. "Do you understand? Smoke?"

"Smoke," I said. "Yes." To Aslak I said, "He had a lot of smoke in him."

Aslak shook his head.

The men went to the skimmer and came back with a litter. They put it next to Ayudesh and lifted him on, but then they stood up and nearly fell, trying to carry him. They tried to walk, but I couldn't stand watching, so I took the handles from the man by Ayudesh's feet, and Aslak, nodding, took the ones at the head. We carried Ayudesh to the skimmer.

We walked right up to the door of the skimmer, and I could look in. It was big inside. Hollow. It was dark in the back. I had thought it would be all lights inside and I was disappointed. There were things hanging on the walls, but mostly it was empty. One of the offworld men jumped up into the skimmer, and then he was not clumsy at all. He pulled the teacher and the litter into the back of the skimmer.

One of the men brought us something hot and bitter and sweet to drink. The drink was in blue plastic cups, the same color as the jackets that they all wore except for one man whose jacket was red with blue writing. Pretty things. I made myself drink mine. Anything this black and bitter must have been medicine. Aslak just held his.

"Where is everyone else?" the red-jacket man asked slowly.

"Dead," I said.

"Everyone?" he said.

"Yes," I said.

AVALANCHE SOLDIER

Susan R. Matthews

It lacked several minutes yet before actual sunbreak, early as the sun rose in the summer. Salli eased her shoulder into a braced position against the papery bark of the highpalm tree that sheltered her and tapped the focus on the field glasses that she wore, frowning down in concentration at the small Wayfarer's camp below. They would have to come out of the dormitory to reach the washhouse, and they'd have to do it soon. Morning prayers was one of the things that heterodox and orthodox—Wayfarer and Pilgrims—had in common, and no faithful child of Revelation would think of opening his mouth to praise the Awakening with the taint of sleep still upon him.

The door to the long low sleeping house swung open. Salli

tensed. *Come on, Meeka,* she whispered to herself, her breath so still it didn't so much as stir the layered mat of fallen palm fronds on which she lay. *I know you're in there. Come out. I have things I want to say to you.*

The camp below was an artifact from olden days, two hundred years old by the thatching of the steeply sloped roofs with their overhanging eaves. Not a Pilgrim camp by any means. No, this was a Shadene camp built by the interlopers that had occupied the holy land in the years after the Pilgrims had fled—centuries ago. A leftover, an anachronism, part of the heritage of Shadene and its long history of welcoming Pilgrims from all over the world to the Revelation Mountains, where the Awakening had begun. Where heterodoxy flourished, and had stolen Meeka away from her. And before the Awakened One she had a thing or two to tell him about that—just as soon as she could find him by himself, and get him away from these people . . .

Older people first. Three men and two women, heading off in different directions. The men's wash house was little more than an open shed, though there wasn't anything for her to see from her vantage point halfway up the slope to the hillcrest. The women's wash house was more fully enclosed. That was where the hotsprings would be, then.

Where was Meeka?

The sun would clear the east ridge within moments, and yet no man of Meeka's size or shape had left the sleeping house. In fact the younger people were hurrying out to wash, now, and there were no adults whatever between old folks and the young, so what was going on here?

Then even as Salli realized that she knew the answer, she heard the little friction of fabric moving against fabric behind her. Felt rather than heard the footfall in the heavy mat of fallen palm fronds that cushioned her prone body like a feather-bed. Well, of course there weren't any of the camp's men there below. They were out here already, on the hillside.

Looking for her.

"Good morning Pilgrim, and it's a beautiful morning. Even if it is only a Dream."

She heard the voice behind her: careful and wary. But a little amused. Yes, they had her, no question about it. She could have kicked the cushioning greenfall into a flurry in frustration. But she was at the disadvantage; she had to be circumspect.

"How much more beautiful the Day we Wake." And what did she have to worry about, really? Nothing. These were Wayfarers, true, or if they weren't she was very much mistaken. But there were rules of civility. She had meant to get Meeka by himself, without betraying her presence; but she had every right to come here on the errand that had brought her. "Say, I imagine you're wondering what this is all about."

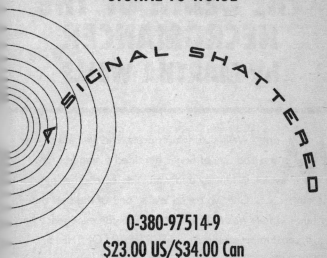